P9-DMR-158

ACCLAIM FOR
THE LORDS OF SALEM

"Between Rob Zombie and B.K. Evenson, we've got a gem on our hands...The novel kicks serious satanic ass...THE LORDS OF SALEM bowls over the imagination with in-your-face brutality, graphic imagery, unforgiving menace, and, believe it or not, some touching humanity...a scintillating story that grabs readers by the balls and refuses to relinquish a death grip that keeps the eyes bulging."

—HorrorNovelReviews.com

"A fun, lofty read...a lot of beautiful, dark imagery...a quick, exciting read."　　　　　　　　　　—FascinationwithFear.blogspot.com

"A rollicking good time for die-hard horror buffs."

—TheDarkeva.com

"Solidly written."　　　　　　　　　　　　　　　—HellNotes.com

"The book moves along at a brisk pace juxtaposing between mystery and ultra-violence...Fans of Rob Zombie do well to pick this one up."　　　　　　　　　　　　　　　—HorrorTalk.com

ROB ZOMBIE
THE LORDS OF SALEM

WITH B.K. EVENSON

GRAND CENTRAL
PUBLISHING

NEW YORK   BOSTON

This book is a work of fiction. Names, characters, places, and incidents are the product of the authors' imagination or are used fictitiously. Any resemblance to actual events, locales, or persons, living or dead, is coincidental.

Copyright © 2013 by Spookshow Deluxe, Ltd.

All rights reserved. In accordance with the U.S. Copyright Act of 1976, the scanning, uploading, and electronic sharing of any part of this book without the permission of the publisher is unlawful piracy and theft of the author's intellectual property. If you would like to use material from the book (other than for review purposes), prior written permission must be obtained by contacting the publisher at permissions@hbgusa.com. Thank you for your support of the author's rights.

Grand Central Publishing
Hachette Book Group
237 Park Avenue
New York, NY 10017

www.HachetteBookGroup.com

Printed in the United States of America

RRD-C

First trade edition: October 2013

10 9 8 7 6 5 4 3 2 1

Grand Central Publishing is a division of Hachette Book Group, Inc.
The Grand Central Publishing name and logo is a trademark of Hachette Book Group, Inc.

The Hachette Speakers Bureau provides a wide range of authors for speaking events. To find out more, go to www.hachettespeakersbureau.com or call (866) 376-6591.

The publisher is not responsible for websites (or their content) that are not owned by the publisher.

The Library of Congress has cataloged the hardcover edition as follows:
Zombie, Rob, 1966—
  The Lords of Salem / Rob Zombie with B.K. Evenson.
    pages cm
  Summary: "The chilling first novel from mind-bending horror auteur Rob Zombie, THE LORDS OF SALEM is a terrifying plunge into a nightmarish world where evil runs in the blood."—Provided by publisher.
  ISBN 978-1-4555-1917-0 (hardback)—ISBN 978-1-4555-1918-7 (ebook)—ISBN 978-1-61969-022-6 (audiobook)   1. Disc jockeys—Fiction.   2. Rock groups—Fiction.   I. Evenson, Brian, 1966—   II. Title.
  PS3626.O58L67 2013
  813'.6—dc23
                                                                    2012045478

ISBN 978-1-4555-1919-4 (pbk.)

THE LORDS OF SALEM

PART ONE

SALEM, MASSACHUSETTS

SEPTEMBER 16, 1692

Chapter One

S he awoke. There was pressure on her arms as if they were pinned under something, and then her hands were tugged farther over her head and she realized that they were being held. She opened her eyes, but something was wrong with her vision, everything blurry, everything distorted, everything just wrong. What was happening to her? Was she sick? Had she been poisoned?

She cast her eyes around desperately. She could make out, just behind her, a line of bedposts that slowly resolved into a single bedpost before spreading out again. Had she been drinking? No, she didn't think so, couldn't remember having done so. She knew she shouldn't, because of the danger it would be to the child. But something was wrong. Her heart was beating wrong, fluttering too fast in her chest, and her tongue sat thick in her throat. She tried to speak, but what came out weren't words and didn't make much sense at all.

Someone held something sharp and bitter beneath her nose and she drew away in disgust. She shook her head and for a moment things became clear. She was in a room, but it was not her room. It had a strange, earthy smell to it. The walls were rough-hewn, a kind of shack or hovel, nowhere in the town proper—the kind of place you would stumble across deep in the woods, out in the middle of nowhere. It was no place she had ever been before.

Above her, clear for a moment before smearing into several versions of itself, was a wooden birdcage. But instead of holding a finch

or a canary or some other lovely songbird it was stuffed nearly full
with a large chicken. It was hard to imagine how it had gotten in
there. The creature could hardly move or turn, and she could tell it
was alive only because of the way its head kept jerking against the
bars. Below the cage, hanging from its base, was something spinning
back and forth, twirling, twirling. What was it? It seemed like pieces
of bone, bits and gobbets of gore, too, but no, why would it be that?
She must be seeing it wrong, must be imagining things.

She tried to will the cage back into focus, until something came
between it and her, a distorted, broken face. Again, something was
held beneath her nose and the smell thrust like a knife deep into her
brain and some things grew clearer and others less so.

The room around her became less clear, seemed now to be shim-
mering with an odd, uncanny heat. The distorted face grew more
distinct, though: a woman's face, the face itself severe and extreme
and frowning slightly. The face was framed by a dark hood, a black
expansive cloak that fell long to hide the body below it. From the
collar, she could see protruding the fur of an animal, fox perhaps or
even wolf, but poorly cured and still bloody.

She shook her head again. She was waking up now, starting to see
things clearly. But what she was seeing was incredible.

And then the cloaked woman took a step to the side and raised one
hand, something glinting brightly in it. A knife.

Her panic began to grow. She tried to lower her arms, but something held them still. She writhed and looked behind her, saw a pair
of grimy hands with broken nails roughly grasping her wrists, as
another hand bound those wrists tightly with rope. She felt the nails
sink in, drawing blood. She tried to get her legs off the bed so as to
stand, but they would hardly move either. She managed to raise her
head enough to see there, past her swollen belly, her ankles bound
tightly with rope and tied off to the post at the bed's foot. Then her
arms were pulled back hard enough to make them ache painfully in
the sockets. She flailed her head back and saw they had been tied to

one of the posts at the top of the bed. She was trussed now, spread taut on the bed, unable to move.

"Why are you doing this to me?" she asked the cloaked figure. Her voice sounded odd and foreign to her own ears, the words muddy and slow, and fear made her voice crack. But the cloaked woman did not answer her. She did not even seem to have heard. She just passed the winking blade back and forth in a sinuous pattern above her body, mumbling a strange sibilant chant.

"Who are you?" she asked.

The cloaked woman still did not answer, but she felt another's warm and corrupt breath in her ear and heard a low whisper say, *The Devil's children.* She turned and there was a face there, too close. A woman in a ragged cloak, missing many of her teeth and with a smile of idiocy or ecstasy fixed to her face. Her breath smelled of rotted meat.

She turned away and to the other side, but found a face looming there, too—a rail-thin woman with matted and coarse white hair, her eyes like two burning embers, her body dressed in rags and skins. And indeed, faces now were gathering in a semicircle around the bed, all of them watching her, all of them eager. Mouths were open, some of them mumbling, some slobbering. The woman with the knife was speaking now in a guttural language she couldn't recognize, the other women beginning to rock and sway, their voices rising and falling.

"Help me!" she shouted.

She struggled against the ropes and screamed once, then again. The knife rose and fell and she felt a line of fire slicing into her side and through it and there was a dull, wet sound that it took her a moment to realize was the sound of her own flesh being cut. She lifted her head and watched the bony hand pull the knife farther through her belly, sawing the blade up and down. The flesh tore painfully and slowly, the blood spraying the arm holding the knife and then welling up slowly and inexorably. The knife kept sawing, and the flesh pulled along with it. She screamed again, much louder this time, but a withered hand clamped down hard over her mouth, muffling her screams, cutting off her breath.

She felt hands pushing their way into her, fingers forcing the lips of the wound wider, the flesh tearing, and then the knife pierced something deeper inside her. There was a slick torrent of fluid and blood, and then it was as if she had been turned inside out. She tasted blood in her mouth and felt a chunk of slick flesh. It took her a moment to realize she'd bitten through her tongue. She struggled again to free her head and managed to lift it just long enough to see her own torso cut open and spread out, hands gripping the edges of the wound and holding them open as the leader of the women, her hands up to the elbows in blood and gore, felt around inside her. A loop of intestine jiggled its way out, smeared with blood flux, then something smaller, a veined and ridged tube, and then, among it all, a tiny and flexing hand.

She tried to move her arms, her feet, but she was weaker now and her limbs seemed so distant, hardly subject to her control. She struggled weakly against the hand clamped over her face. When the hand was removed she found she had no energy to scream.

She lay there on the bed, the life leaking out of her.

The last sounds she heard were the cries of a child. *Her* child, she dimly realized. *What would they do to him?* she wondered. And then she died.

Chapter Two

The newborn child struggled, yowling still, uncomfortable in the twisted hands that awkwardly clutched it. The woman in the hooded, dark cloak had turned away from the bed now and moved toward the center of the room. She drew back her hood and crouched there now, bent over a fire pit in the floor, where over a surface of dying embers she was creating a figure out of woven branches and sticks, making an effigy of a man with her still-bloody hands. The other members of the coven watched her, slowly drifting away from the bed and the bloody, dead woman lying there with her insides, and turned out to gather around the fire pit. The rail-thin woman holding the child approached the cloaked one deferentially from behind, leaned toward her ear.

"We have it, Mistress Morgan," she said in a loud whisper. "Still slick and bloody from its birth from death into life. Shall we make it bloody with its own blood and let the life ooze back out of it and make our summoning?"

"All in good time, Clovis," said Margaret Morgan, not looking away from the figure she had arranged. She had steady, brown eyes so dark that in the low light they seemed nearly black. They were set in an austere face with high, almost aristocratic cheekbones. Her mouth was cruel, her lips bloodless, and her face, too, was pale, as if drained of blood. She blew steadily before speaking again, the gray embers beginning to glow red. "All in good time."

Clovis bowed and stepped back, the baby still wailing. Morgan blew steadily again and the embers grew redder and in a sudden rush the legs of the wooden man came aflame.

Once she was satisfied the fire had caught, she stood and stepped back. She inscribed an unholy figure in the air with the bloody tip of her knife, her dark eyes steady but shining with zeal.

"In the name of Satan, Ruler of the Earth, the King of the World, the Lord of the Oppressed," she intoned, gesturing to the motley collection of witches gathered around her, dressed in cloaks of skins and rags, "I command the forces of darkness to bestow their infernal power upon the wretched vessels I have set before you."

Behind her, Clovis held the baby like a chicken, dangling it now head down by its feet, both ankles gripped in her fist. It continued to squeal, its face deep red, its body tensed and its arms spread. Slowly, Clovis stepped forward, moving nearer to the fire. She bowed slightly and swung the child out before her, presenting it to Margaret Morgan, the leader of the coven.

"I beg of thee," Clovis said, her head still bowed as she recited the memorized words, "take this gift and heal me of these mortal wounds inflicted by the Christian faith."

Morgan slid the knife into her belt and accepted the child. She held it coldly in front of her, frowning slightly, her gaze hard and stony. When she began to speak, her voice had a deep crooning quality, almost hypnotic.

"O Lord Satan, Spirit of the Earth," she said, "open wide the gates of Hell and issue forth from your blessed abyss."

She raised the child high above her head, her eyes glittering. Before her the flames surged up and seemed to become a living thing. The flaming effigy within the fire seemed to give utterance to moans and wails, as if the wall between this world and Hell had begun to collapse, allowing Hell to ooze its sickly way through.

"Sisters!" said Morgan, casting her gaze on the coven gathered around her. "Reveal yourself to the master of our Lords! I am but your humble servant in this land of misery."

The coven answered her in one voice, the fire casting their distorted shadows in a dark dance along the walls of the hut. "All hail!" they proclaimed. "Unholy Father, make your presence known this night!"

Morgan turned back to the flames and tilted the now-screaming baby toward the fire. "Help me breed this new world with your blessed spawn of glory," she said.

A pale-faced woman with long and tangled dark hair stepped forward, swooning as if in a trance. "I am ready!" she said.

"And for what is it that you are ready?" asked Morgan of her. "Shall you commend yourself to our Dark Lord and Master, Mary?"

Mary nodded, her eyes sliding back and forth independently in the sockets, unfocused. "I am ready to abandon this mortal existence and deny Christ Jesus, the deceiver of all mankind!"

The fire climbed higher, the burning figure seemingly larger than before. Morgan nodded at Mary in approval. "What others among us are ready?" she asked. "Who among you shall abandon the deceiver of all mankind and embrace the one true Lord of Darkness?"

A plump woman, her face spread with large, seeping boils, stepped forward, swaying. "I, too, am ready," she said.

"Speak, Abigail," said Morgan. "He presses his ear against the wall of Hell and listens to you."

Abigail took a deep breath. When she spoke, it was all in a single burst, the words tripping over one another. "I hold in contempt all of the symbols of the Creator. I swear on this day to be a faithful servant to the prince Lucifer."

The fire rose again with a deep hissing sound. Impossibly, the flaming figure made of wood seemed to *move* as if it were coming to life. Again Morgan nodded. She began to reiterate the invitation to join, but one of the other women had already stepped forward. She was a hunched woman who looked closer to a beast than a human. Her dirty mane of hair was twisted with leaves and ribbons and seemed as if it had never been washed. She threw her arms upward.

"Speak, Sarah," said Morgan. "The Dark Lord has thrust his head through the breach we have created in the walls of Hell and waits for you to beckon him forth and birth him into this world of pain."

Sarah let out a burst of raucous laughter. "I pledge myself mind, body, and soul to fulfill the designs of our Lord Satan and his disciples!"

The fire rose again, and the figure, wreathed in flames, now seemed to writhe. "He comes," hissed Morgan. "He comes!"

Two others stepped forward, hand in hand. At first, in the flickering flames, they looked like a mother and her child, but when they entered fully into the light it was apparent that one was a crusty old hag and the other a tiny dwarven woman. "Speak, Martha. Speak, Elizabeth," Morgan said.

The dwarf spoke in a high, quavering voice. "We trample on the cross!" she screeched.

The crone's voice was deeper but broken, as if half her vocal cords had been torn out. "We spit upon the book of lies!" she said.

For a moment the fire guttered. And then it rose higher than before, the whole hovel in danger of igniting. The wooden figure was suddenly, as if instantly, consumed and the flames took on a ruddy hue. And though the wooden figure was gone, the flames now seemed to flex and turn like limbs, a strange, flitting humanlike shape flashing here and there over coals that were long expired and yet continued to burn.

Morgan slowly lowered the baby until it rode in her hands just beside the flames. The flames themselves seemed to sense it there, the fire bending toward the child, licking out at it, as if preparing to consume it.

Morgan had to shout now to be heard over the roaring of the

flames. "In our allegiance to our Master Satan we promise contempt to the faiths of all others. Stand ready to desecrate these false bodies! Show yourselves!"

Around her the coven began to cast aside their filthy clothing and rags and furs, stripping rapidly and quickly down until they stood stark naked before the roaring flames. Their bodies had been daubed with blood and painted with uncanny symbols. They had the appearance of letters, but not of any human alphabet, and they seemed almost alive, winding and wriggling on the skin as the coven swayed and moved. They were runes, but again of no recognizable system, and when one of the women came too close to the fire the flames licked out and imbued them for a moment with an unearthly glow. They were all varied except that they all had the same symbol between their breasts: a circle holding an inverted cross, mounted by an upturned semicircle with a downturned semicircle. The mark of their coven.

Morgan gave a curt nod and abruptly they began to speak in unison, the flames leaping and dancing as if in time to the words.

"Together we desecrate the virgin whore! Together we blaspheme the Holy Spirit. Together we laugh at the false redeemer's suffering!"

"Sisters!" yelled Morgan. "Gather your tools and release the master!"

The naked women turned briefly away, groping along the dirt floor behind them to come up with half-broken and makeshift musical instruments. One had a sort of violin missing half its strings, which she played with a knobbed stick that made it utter an unearthly screeching, like a cat being tortured. Another had a flute carved from a bone that let out a high piercing sound. Another still had a basin whose top had been covered with an animal skin, which she beat in time to the baby's screams. Each of them played to a different tune, the resulting cacophony swirling about the fire and melding with the newborn's cries like the utterance of chaos itself.

Morgan moved the infant yet closer to the fire and now the flames leaped out and licked at its body, touching it for only the merest moment but leaving always in its wake a glowing, faded symbol not unlike those on the witches' bodies.

Soon, the infant's whole body was blistered and colored by these symbols and the screams and music had risen to a fever pitch. The fire contracted and seemed to gather itself, and suddenly an acrid red smoke began to billow from the coals. The shape that had been flitting through the flames suddenly resolved into a hideous creature, a demonic presence. Its body of flame shifted, becoming something made out of coils of the reddish smoke, and then that suddenly stiffened, hardened into leathery red flesh. Its face was uneven, its jaw drooping and slavering. It had horns, one of which had turned back on itself to penetrate its temple, and its eyes, one of them much larger than the other, were glowing red like a pair of coals.

It snarled, blood dripping from its mouth, and quickly reached out, taking hold of the infant. Morgan released it, and the creature dragged it back into the fire.

The child immediately caught flame but continued shrieking. The creature toyed with it, dangling it by one foot and regarding it with its smaller eye with curiosity and hunger. And then with a single sharp movement it snapped the child like a whip. The newborn suddenly fell silent, its neck broken. The creature dashed its head against the floor once, hard, and when it came up again, the flaming head was loose and pulpy and dripping blood. The creature held the baby up again, looking at it now with its larger eye, and gave a hideous smile. With the dirty red nails of its other hand, it began to scrape away the child's skin.

All around the fire the coven swayed, now lost in a trance. Some mumbled and babbled; others raised their hands high above their heads with their hands flopping on the ends of their wrists like birds with broken wings; others frothed at the mouth, their eyes rolled far back into their heads. First one and then slowly all the others began to drool, long strings of spittle slipping from their mouths, as if they were having a fit. And then the spittle grew dark, became a sticky black substance that descended in thick cords down their chins to drip along their naked flesh.

Chapter Three

Justice Samuel Mather strode quickly down the rutted wagon path and toward the town, his stick-thin body moving jerkily. He was waving his walking stick about, gesticulating with it rather than using it for walking. It had finally happened. Before, there had been rumors, a sense that evil was afoot, but he had never managed to catch the women in the act of pledging themselves to Satan. But all the nights of waiting and watching, sitting hidden in the woods outside of Margaret Morgan's hovel until the midnight hour and even long past, hidden and shivering in his dark cloak, his thin hands clenched tight against the cold, had finally paid off. Or would, if he managed to gather the others in time.

He had watched the other women enter, one by one, each of them cloaked or dressed strangely, often in furs or rags. And then he had waited until the smoke began to rise from a chimney placed, oddly enough, in the center of the hovel, not near a wall like a chimney should be. Even still he had waited, not wanting to believe that what he and Hawthorne had feared to be the case was finally to be proven real. But when the smoke rising from the chimney had taken on a reddish tinge, he knew there was no denying what was happening.

He had reached the bridge, Salem lying just on the other side of it. The fog was rising off the river and obscuring the bridge itself, making it seem as if it dissolved halfway across the water. He hesitated for a moment before crossing over it, his footsteps echoing against the planks. The bridge slowly appeared out of the mist in front of him, becoming firmer, becoming real. But when he turned and looked back behind him it had begun to vanish. He hurried his steps, breathed a sigh of relief when he was finally on solid ground again.

He hurried through the muddy streets of town, past some of the newer and smaller dwellings, many of them still unfinished, until he came to a saltbox house with a long sloping roof. Well-made and painted a dark red, it was the largest house on the street and perhaps in the town. He pounded on its door with the knob of his walking stick. He waited impatiently, and when there was no answer, he knocked again.

After a moment the door swung open. Behind it was a man in his early fifties, nearly large enough to fill the doorway. John Hawthorne. He held a candle. He had shoulder-length hair and his feet were bare. He was dressed in a nightshirt made of rough linen, held gathered by strings at the neck and the wrists, and though he appeared to have been awoken from sleep, his appearance was not befuddled but focused and sharp.

"Brother Mather," he said. "What cheer?"

Justice Mather shook his head. "None," he said. "I have seen the smoke. I was right to suspect Margaret Morgan. It is happening. It is happening even now."

Hawthorne's lips thinned, his brow furrowed. "The red smoke of death," he said, his voice heavy. "Then it is as we feared."

"Aye, brother. I can only pray the angels protect us in our quest to drive this vile serpent from this township."

Hawthorne took a deep breath, nodded. "I fear the Devil himself walks among us. I fear the Lord has turned a deaf ear to our most desperate prayers." He reached out and placed his hand on the other man's shoulder. "Brother Mather, the plague has returned to Salem."

Justice Mather nodded curtly. "I fear the same," he said. "But we must proceed as best we can. Dress yourself. We must do our best to nip this evil in its hellish bud. If we act with the conviction that God be with us, then so shall He be."

"We will do what we can," said Hawthorne.

"We must fetch the brothers," said Mather. "There is no better pair for tonight's work."

"As you say," said Hawthorne, turning back into the house and beckoning Mather to follow him. "But even the brothers have their limits."

Chapter Four

The house was off the beaten path. It was a rough-hewn but well-built hodgepodge, a canny construction of wood, cut stone, and thick pond reeds. The chimney was a seemingly precarious pile of rough brick from which smoke belched out to thicken the darkness.

The man standing in the light of the doorway peering out was huge and lumbering, more like a bear than a man. His left eye was covered with a thick leathern patch that had once been dyed black but now had faded. His gray hair and lined face suggested he was in his sixties, but his thick and well-muscled body would have seemed to have been borrowed from a younger man were it not for the scars that crisscrossed his hands and arms. He squinted out into the darkness a moment more before grunting and returning inside, clapping the door shut behind him.

Dean Magnus walked to the fire, over which the carcass of an animal hung on a spit—a deer perhaps. The meat was blackened and charred on the outside but when he cut into it with his knife and sliced off a chunk of flesh, the inside was still bloody, nearly raw. He began to eat, tearing off mouthfuls of it, the juices and blood of the meat flowing down to stain his already-filthy beard and drip onto his shirt.

Behind him, sitting at a small wooden table whose surface was nicked and charred, was his brother Virgil. The family resemblance was clearly visible, despite Dean's eye patch and the fact that a good half of Virgil's face was torn by deep scars, the result of the swipe of a bear's claws. The bear's skin was lying on the packed dirt floor beside the table, and Virgil rested his feet on its head. Beside it, next to the table, was a goat chained to the wall, eating from a large bale of straw. On the table before him was a battered pewter plate in which sat part of a haunch of meat, charred on the edge and raw in the middle.

"Anything?" asked Virgil. He reached out and caressed the goat, which *baa*ed once, then continued to eat its straw.

Dean shook his head. "Something's happening," he said, "but not too close. Maybe nothing much."

Virgil nodded. "You're starting to see ghosts," he said.

"Aye, brother," Dean said, and continued to chew on his chunk of meat, stopping only to spit out a bit of buckshot still lodged in it.

Virgil turned back to his plate, slicing off a bit of the haunch and swallowing it all in one gulp—gristle, tendon, and all.

"I noticed," said Dean, and then swallowed deeply before continuing. "During morning services, I noticed the Widow Parsons was looking my way again. I think her mourning period might well be coming to an end."

Virgil shook his head. "Hallucination of a lustful mind, my brother," he said. Then he laughed. "That widow will be mourning 'til you are sleeping in a dirt hole feeding worms."

Dean regarded him with irritation. "Don't be so sure," he said. "I'll take down that woman just as I did this young doe. Once I set my sights, brother, my aim is true."

Virgil smiled. He shook his knife at Dean, the piece of meat impaled on the end of it shivering. "I doubt Widow Parsons would be as delicious to the taste as this blackened flesh," he claimed.

Dean relaxed a little, even smiled. "Don't be so sure," he said. "Nothing more delicious than a healthy woman craving meat."

"True," said Virgil. "Too true."

There came a loud pounding at the front door. Both brothers

froze. Dean finished his piece of meat and then wiped the blade of his knife clean on his trousers.

"Not ghosts after all," said Virgil.

"No," said Dean. "Told you there was something out there."

"Maybe it's the widow come a-calling, ready to be courted. Either that or someone just realized they're missing a goat."

"Mark my word, the widow awaits behind that door. The stench of finely roasted meat has done its job and brought her hither."

But Dean did not pocket his knife as he approached the door, instead holding it casually but at the ready in his hand.

Behind the door were Hawthorne and Mather, both dressed in black traveling garb now. Mather had lifted his cane again, was preparing once more to rap on the door with it. He stopped when Dean opened. The latter smiled, wiped his beard with the back of his hand, the other hand quickly sheathing the knife.

"Greetings," he said. "And to what honor do I owe this nocturnal intrusion?"

"It is time," said Hawthorne.

For a moment Dean stood there motionless, a questioning expression on his face. And then suddenly his expression changed, his eyes narrowing.

"You are certain? When we wanted to proceed before, you preached caution. What has changed?" he asked. "You have proof?"

"As much proof as we need," said Mather. "I have seen the red smoke."

Dean turned again to Hawthorne, who simply nodded. "Now is the time to act," he said.

Dean nodded, turned, and called back into the room, "Virgil!"

"Aye, brother," said Virgil, still slowly eating the haunch of meat.

"Our brothers in God are here. Reverend Hawthorne claims it is time."

"Time for what?" asked Virgil. But when Dean didn't answer he pushed back from the table and stood. "I see," he said.

"Sharpen the tools," said Dean. "We're going hunting."

"Already have, brother, already have," said Virgil. "A dull blade is of no use to anyone."

Dean turned back to the door. "Well, Reverend, we shall be the Lord's instruments of just destruction, his means of righteous anger. Direct us toward the demons and we'll gut their bellies as we would any fatted hog awaiting slaughter."

Chapter Five

They moved quietly through the night, the four of them traveling along the forest path single file. They all wore dark cloaks. Two of them had their faces hidden within their hoods. And they all had faces that were covered by dark masks emblazoned with rough-sewn death's heads. *Memento mori*, remember that you will die. Moonlight caught the death's heads and made them stand out faintly against the darkness, and with their otherwise dark clothing it was as if disembodied skulls were floating slowing down the path. It caught, too, on the blades of the weapons that a pair of the masked figures held: two huge splitting axes slung over their shoulders.

Even from a distance, they could make out the red smoke rising from the hovel's crude chimney. It had an unearthly glow to it. Yes, this was the Devil's fire.

They entered the clearing that contained the hovel and slowly spread out. Hawthorne approached the door silently. He depressed the latch lightly with his finger and then placed his hand against the door and pushed. The door, apparently barred from within, did not budge.

He slowly circled the house, the others following him as he examined the walls. After a moment he stopped, examined a section of wall up and down, and then nodded. He gestured and the masked Magnus brothers came forward. Together they heaved up their axes and began to chop.

The first few blows did but little, but after a moment the wooden wall began to splinter and crack, slowly coming asunder. Would they simply make an opening, wondered Hawthorne, or would the zeal of the brothers collapse the hut? Perhaps the easiest way to resolve this, he thought, would be for the hovel to collapse and for the witches to die beneath its weight.

But soon the hole was large enough for the Magnus brothers to shoulder their way in, Hawthorne and Mather following close behind.

What Hawthorne saw filled him with dread. The only one of the women on her feet was Margaret Morgan, who stood stock-still, her legs quivering, playing a simple haunting melody on a violin. The fire was high and strange, the color wrong, and around it, writhing at Morgan's feet, were the rest of the coven. They were naked, their bodies painted with strange symbols, and they moved over and across one another, moaning with ecstasy. They embraced one another but tried, too, to couple with the ground, and one even had blackened and burning fingers where she had thrust them into the fire. With one or two it was as if their skin was covered with unnatural shadows that moved and twisted back and forth in a way not canny with the light cast in the room itself. On the sole bed in the corner was the body of a slaughtered woman, trussed to the bed, gutted, most of her abdomen missing, the bed and dirt floor beneath it slick with her blood. He recognized her: Krista Seward. She had been pregnant. He cast his eyes around for the child, but could not find it.

He felt his skin crawl. Any doubt that he'd had that these were witches, that this was a coven, immediately vanished.

The Magnus brothers went straight for the fire, kicking aside the convulsing witches in their path. With their axes they scattered the coals, stamping their way through the flames and kicking sparks and embers onto the witches around it. Some of them seemed to come back to themselves, brushing off the embers, ceasing their writhing and crying out, and becoming conscious of their surroundings. Others, however, seemed not to notice even as the embers burned their hair and flesh and the room filled with the stench of it. There was a roaring sound coming from the fire and it suddenly and impossibly rose up again from the scattered ashes, and Dean Magnus's death's head mask smoked and caught fire. He tore it off, laughing, sparks sizzling in his beard, and beat the flames out against his leg. He and Virgil continued to kick and hack apart the fire until with a whoosh the fire diminished, its color returning to normal.

"Battling devils is sweaty work," claimed Dean, beating out his smoking beard. Through his mask, his brother gave a muffled laugh. The writhing of the women had slowed now. They were beginning to look stunned and confused, many not entirely sure of where they were. Some had begun to cover their nakedness, seeing the Magnus brothers leering down at them now that the fire was taken care of.

"Don't lose your heads, brothers," Hawthorne cautioned the Magnuses.

Dean brandished his mask, the death's head damaged and partly burned through. "But I already have," he claimed, shaking it. "I already have!"

Hawthorne frowned. The line between the good that they were trying to preserve and the evil they were hoping to stomp out was murky at times, and he could not help but feel that the Magnus brothers remained straddled there, one foot on either side of the line. They were willing to be God's instruments, but had things been just a little different, the brothers might have tipped in the other direction and served the Devil. Better not to think of it, Hawthorne told himself. Better to simply accept the pair for what they had to offer.

Margaret Morgan still stood there, playing her violin, seemingly oblivious to the brothers or Hawthorne or Mather. What was that melody? Where had he heard it before? Why did he feel so sleepy, as if he had no desire to move? It was haunting, seemed to draw him deep within himself, and as she played it he felt dark shadows begin to flit around him, gathering closer. Mather, he saw, standing beside

Morgan, was similarly affected, but Hawthorne watched him reach out with a great deal of struggle within him and drag the violin away from her.

As soon as the melody stopped, Hawthorne felt himself again, and control over his limbs returned. He strode forward as Mather broke the violin on his knee and tossed it to the ground.

"Margaret Morgan," he said in a loud voice. "I, together with my brothers in Christ Jesus, Dean Magnus, Virgil Magnus, and Samuel Mather, bear witness against you for consorting with the Devil."

Margaret Morgan stood motionless, unblinking, her face as slack and expressionless as if she were sleeping or dead. Hawthorne reached out and shook her shoulder, found her body as rigid as if it were made of wood.

"Margaret Morgan," he said again. "In the name of God and his angels, I call upon you to confess your crimes and turn away from the Devil and his minions."

This time she turned her head and blinked once and then smiled. "Satan will not desert me," she said. "You shall see."

"Satan!" shouted Mather, his eyes darting all around him. "We command thee to leave this place!"

"It is too late!" said Morgan. "We have unleashed him and you cannot confine him again. It is too late!"

She began to wave her hands and speak in a guttural, unknown language, and suddenly Hawthorne again felt a great, overwhelming tiredness. He could not move. He tried to reach his hand toward Morgan but it seemed to move so slowly that he could not believe that it would ever arrive. For a moment, Mather beside him was shouting but then he suddenly trailed off, his voice dying in his mouth. Morgan opened her eyes wide, and Hawthorne saw they were sparking with a reflected fire even though the fire in the pit was now out. *Or an inner fire,* he thought. *From Hell.* She opened her mouth and smiled, a wicked, hideous smile.

Then Dean Magnus struck her in the back of the head with the haft of his ax and she collapsed in a heap. And Hawthorne found he could move again. He took a deep breath.

"Did you kill her?" he asked.

Dean shook his head. "Just unconscious," he said. "Do you want me to?"

Hawthorne shook his head. "No," he said. "We'll bring them back for a proper trial. We will follow God's laws and give them that."

"Wouldn't it be better to kill them now?" asked Mather. "We know they are witches. We know what we have seen."

Hawthorne shook his head. "They will die as witches," he said. "That is beyond question. But even witches must be given a chance to confess and repent before they die." He turned to the Magnus brothers. "Bind their hands and gag them," he said. "And be certain that the gags are secure." He gestured to the floor, at Margaret Morgan's crumpled body. "Especially for that one," he said.

Chapter Six

The building had only one entrance, a heavy door in bound iron, which was now barred. Inside, it was lit by torches and there were no windows, no other way out besides the door that you entered by. That door was colloquially called the Portal of Judgment. Those who passed through it with their hands bound were rarely allowed to leave alive.

There was only a single room, a long beaten metal trough running down the center of it. The trough was heaped with dry sticks and tinder. Affixed at intervals within it were wooden posts. To these were bound the members of the coven, sometimes alone, sometimes two to a post, all of them tightly gagged. They were positioned to face a forged metal throne. It had jagged spikes in place of the seat and arms and straps to hold the condemned in place. The spikes and the metal itself were stained reddish brown with dried blood. The accused were made to sit on the chair, gently at first, the spikes pricking the skin and making it bleed, and then the straps were drawn tight and as the accused screamed and cried and begged for mercy the spikes were forced deeper and deeper. It was the Chair of God, though what went on in it could hardly be considered godly. Yet sometimes, Hawthorne told himself, you had to inflict suffering if you were to cleanse this mortal coil of sin and perdition.

Beside him stood Judge Mather, a sheaf of papers in his hand, his death's head mask still on but rolled back now to reveal his face.

Hawthorne wore his the same way—it was tradition, a way of acknowledging that the witchfinder and the judge were one and the same. These were, Hawthorne knew, the charges. Always the same, only the names having changed. He knew what was coming, remembering from the last time the plague had struck: *Found guilty of commerce with the Devil. Condemned to death by the very fire that shall be your eternal dwelling in the Hell that you have embraced and that awaits you to consume you.*

It was very late, hours past midnight but still well shy of the beginnings of morning light. But Mather had insisted that the trial be held that same night, immediately, before the witches had a chance to gather themselves and call evil down upon the town. Hawthorne, having felt Margaret Morgan's power, had to agree. This was a coven to be reckoned with. Better if they were done away with directly, before they could do any further damage.

Still, wouldn't it be better to wait until morning, to consider all afresh and with clear eyes in the daytime? Wasn't the night the Devil's favorite haunt, and did not God rule with the iron hand of justice in the cold light of day?

But what was done was done, Hawthorne told himself. The trial had begun. There was no stopping it now.

Beside him, Mather cleared his throat and began to read, his voice stentorian and charged with holy indignation.

"To the honor of Salem, Massachusetts, be it this day of sixteen September sixteen ninety-two. Clovis Hales, Mary Goodwin, Abigail Hennessy, Sarah Easter, Martha Bishop, and Elizabeth Jacobs, you stand guilty of granting permission to Satan..."

His voice dipped for a moment when he said the unholy one's name. When he continued, his voice was more solemn, less thunderous.

"...and other unholy spectral beings to be engaged in unholy alliances with such apparitions upon your specific persons."

Before them the bound witches struggled and tried to cry out through their gags, their eyes dark and angry with displeasure. Hawthorne's gaze moved from angry face to angry face. *No*, he thought, *there is no remorse here. There shall be no forgiveness either. They shall all rot in Hell.*

"Therefore," Judge Mather continued, "the accused are deemed self-afflicted to the crimes of witchcraft and accepting the Devil."

This was Hawthorne's cue. He took up a basin of water beside him and stepped forward. It was pure spring water, gathered fresh each day and prayed over by the Worthy to be an instrument of God's will. Not exactly the holy water that the Catholics used, for that would be idolatry, but consecrated nonetheless and purified of the mixture of sin and filth that threatened all things. With his hand, he splashed the first witch in the face, watched her recoil in horror. He was of two minds about it: Was it simply the cold of the water that made her recoil? Or was it the purity of it, the fact that it was about as far distant from the Devil as mortal substance could be.

"In the Name of Jesus Christ, Our Lord," he prayed, "we drive you from us, whoever or whatever you may be. We command you to depart, unclean spirits, all satanic minions and powers, all infernal invaders, all wicked legions!"

He moved on to the next witch, splashed her as well, careful not to get water on the tinder, careful to do nothing that would prevent her from catching fire later. He continued forward, splashing each witch and uttering his prayer, until he came to the end of the line and to Mary Goodwin. She was so young, barely thirteen, still a child. Hawthorne could not believe that she hadn't been led into temptation by one of the other women. Perhaps there was a spark here of goodness, something that he could blow on and fan into a flame that would lead to her salvation after this life.

When she saw him looking at her, her angry eyes went soft and pled with him. She tried to say something, but whatever she said was lost within her gag.

"Young Mary," said Hawthorne. "You have cared for my very

children in their hour of sickness. Is there anything you would like to say before God, angels, and these witnesses, my child? Now is the time to make your peace with Heaven and Earth."

Mary nodded, her eyes still pleading. *At last*, thought Hawthorne, *one who desires salvation.* Carefully, he set the basin of water down on the ground. Behind him, he heard Mather call his name in warning, but he ignored it. He reached over the metal trough and around Mary's neck, then loosened the gag and pulled it from her mouth.

When he stepped away, she smiled at him sweetly, and then in an instant her face was contorted and shouting and she was screaming.

"Satan, save us!" she screamed. "Save us from this world of misery! Bring us home to the glory of your everlasting love! I will die for you, O great master of darkness!"

Hawthorne was flooded with disappointment, which was quickly transformed into righteous anger. "Silence!" he shouted. "Silence!" He slapped the girl once, hard, and then crammed the gag into her mouth until she was almost choking and then tied it tightly behind her head.

He was just finishing, just beginning to calm down, when the iron-bound door swung open with a boom. He turned to see the Magnus brothers, cleaned up a little now. As was customary, Virgil still wore his mask, though like Mather and Hawthorne, he had pushed it up to reveal his face. Dean's face was bare, his scorched and flindered mask hanging in tatters from his belt. They entered pushing a wheeled metal cage crudely in the shape of a human. Inside was Margaret Morgan. Here was the ringleader, here the high witch who had led all these other women astray, who had removed so many souls from God's presence and introduced them to their own perdition.

"Bring the witch to me," Judge Mather said.

They pushed her forward, the crude wooden wheels squeaking beneath the weight of the cage. Her face was bruised and bloody. She'd been beaten. Once again the Magnus brothers had exceeded their authority.

And worse still, Hawthorne realized, she was no longer wearing a gag. Even caged as she was, unable to move her arms to practice her incantations and spells, Morgan was a dangerous woman. He turned to Mather to recommend she be gagged before they proceeded, but Mather, caught up in his just role, was already moving forward.

"Margaret Morgan," Mather stated solemnly, "I find you guilty of witchcraft, sorcery, and conjuring the very Devil himself for the purpose of eternal fornication with the darkness. Bow your head and admit your crimes, and acknowledge Jesus Christ as your Lord and Savior."

From within the cage, Morgan barked, her bruised and broken face twisting into a grimace. It took Hawthorne a moment to realize that she was smiling, that her barking was laughter.

"I reject your false God!" she said. "I worship the only true savior: Lucifer—the God of this world, the Father of Lies, the glorious Prince of Darkness."

Expecting no less, Judge Mather nodded curtly. "You shall be held by the Chair of God until such time as the demonic presence has been driven from your body," he said.

What was to follow Hawthorne did not relish. The screams of the damned woman as the spikes would penetrate her flesh and as she would beg for mercy until the moment when she was either left to die in slow agony or renounced Satan and his works and was given mercy by being killed quickly.

Mather had begun to turn away when Morgan hissed something. When he turned back to hear her, she spat in his face. But it was not ordinary spit, Hawthorne saw, but a black liquid, the vile substance of the pit. Mather stumbled back, clawing at his face, trying to wipe it off, clearly very frightened, perhaps even in pain.

"Enough!" said Hawthorne, feeling righteous indignation rising again within him, along with a certain amount of dread. Every moment that Margaret Morgan was allowed to live was an indignity to God, and put their lives at risk. "Commend her to the chair!" he shouted.

The Magnus brothers smiled. Virgil unlocked the cage and pulled it open. Dean reached in and grabbed Morgan and hauled her out. The cage clanged shut and together the brothers dragged the struggling Morgan toward the chair. She scratched and bit and nearly broke free. Then Dean, like a bear, cuffed her on the side of the head. For a moment she was dazed. He smiled.

"The Chair of God will break the fight of Satan in this one," said Dean to Hawthorne, noticing his stare. Yes, thought Hawthorne, if past experience held true, it probably would.

Morgan still resisted, but now focused her energies less on breaking free and more on trying to meet the eyes of the other members of the coven.

"Sisters," she said, "let the love of our blessed father set you free." She struggled, and when she spoke again, it was not to the coven but staring at the meetinghouse floor. "Satan," she cried, "release me! I am yours to bleed! Take me!"

The brothers held her now before the chair, one to either side of her. She was ready for the chair, but Hawthorne suddenly realized that something had changed. Morgan was no longer Morgan. Or rather, she was Morgan but also something else at the same time. Her face was transformed, her defiance coupled now with a dark contempt and confidence. There was no hint or trace of fear in her. She had made her body a vessel for the unholy one, and he was there within her now, insinuating himself into her flesh, testing her, feeling the limits and confines of her body. The brothers had not noticed. They stood holding her immobile, laughing at her suffering and enjoying themselves. Even Mather, normally so perceptive of the presence of evil, had not noticed, caught up as he was in his role as a judge. But Hawthorne could feel it. He knew.

There, trapped between the two brothers, on the verge of the torture that was the chair, she stood and laughed. But the laughter that came out of her throat was not hers—was not even a woman's laughter. It was dark, deep, and hollow and seemed to Hawthorne to issue from the very depths of Hell. He could feel within it the screams of a thousand consumed souls, the suffering of the damned. He could feel a demon clasping a young priest's head with one hand, sinking his bloody nails through his skin and deep into his skull and then hurling him into the abyss. He could feel a grim group of three men as they held a newborn child over a fire and slit its throat, the gap in the neck like a malevolent smile that grew broken and spread in a bloody sheet down its chest. He could feel a devil's careful flaying away of the skin of a Pharisee, the awful weight of Judas's betrayal, and many more tortures besides. But worst of all, he could feel in it the sound of all his own sins, small and large, the way the laughter called them from where he had pushed them down and hidden them within his brain, pretending they did not belong to him.

Judge Mather was shouting, his face dark red. "Remove her rags! I shall not have even the thinnest veil impede the righteous pain of the chair!"

Hawthorne nodded. God must penetrate deep into her flesh to find passage into her blackened soul. The Devil must be driven out and allowed no other body as a new proxy, and then the tainted flesh that had welcomed his dominion must be destroyed.

Dean had moved behind Morgan now. He held her in a headlock, lifted slightly off the ground, as Virgil tore the scraps and rags away from her body. Beneath the rags she was bruised as well, her thighs bloody. From the Devil? wondered Hawthorne fleetingly. Or from the Magnus brothers?

Suddenly the torches flickered and guttered, a wind rushing through the room. For a moment Hawthorne thought the door had been left open, but no, it was sealed. And then he realized with a shudder that the wind seemed to emanate from Morgan herself, rushing and swirling all around them. He felt it snatching and grabbing at him, tearing at his clothing. The bound and gagged witches writhed as if in ecstasy.

When Morgan again spoke, it was in the same voice as the laughter, a deep and hollow, demonic voice. She was looking right at him as she spoke, her eyes steady.

"Come to me, dear Hawthorne," she said. *It* said. "You have always desired to serve me." He could hear the voice grating within his skull, as if it were being uttered inside of his head.

"Get thee behind me, Satan," he said.

Morgan laughed. "Lick between my legs and taste the vile stench of your daughters!" she said. "For they shall belong to me as well." The demon was trying to provoke him, he knew, but even knowing this he found it difficult not to allow the anger to rise within him. And she knew it, he could tell. She looked him straight in the eyes, licked her bruised lips, and said, "Lick me as you pray to the cock of your false God!"

"Enough!" said Hawthorne, outraged. "Put this whore of Babylon in the Chair of God!"

"Gladly," said Dean, and he and Virgil threw her back into the chair, pushing her down hard into the seat. The sharp metal spikes cut deep into her legs and buttocks, blood already beginning to drip from the seat and onto the floor.

"Give me more!" said Morgan in her devil's voice. "I bleed for you, Lord Satan! My whole body bleeds to welcome you!"

"Bind her tight," said Dean to his brother. "The Devil is a wicked craftsmen and a keen trickster, and he will have at us if he can."

Together the two brothers bound Morgan's chest, neck, and arms to the chair with the thick leather bands. They grunted and pulled them as tight as they could, driving the spikes deeper into her legs and arms.

And yet Morgan seemed to welcome the pain. She did not scream. She even smiled and pushed against the straps to force the spikes deeper into her flesh.

"Hawthorne," she said in her hollow voice. "Yes, destroy the flesh of this my servant. Her blood and her body are the unholy sacrament that will bring about her revenge upon you! With each spike thrust into her flesh, you inflict pain upon you and yours."

"No more, vile demon, no more!" cried Hawthorne.

The others had finally realized something was wrong. Virgil and Dean were no longer laughing, their faces having grown taut and frightened. Mather, too, had taken a step back. He seemed to be hesitating, unsure of what to say or do.

Morgan hissed. "Revenge will be ours!" she screamed in her unholy voice. "The descendants of this town of Salem will fall to my power! I will rape the children of your children... I will claim them as my own, whores into eternity!"

Slowly, impossibly, the heavy chair rose, creaking, from the floor. It hovered there, a few feet off the ground. Virgil and Dean, terrified, tried to drag it back down, but it refused to come. Virgil let go and reached out to clasp his hands around Morgan's neck.

"The Devil is here!" he cried. "The Devil has—"

Suddenly he let go and dropped to his knees, clutching now at his own throat. He tried to gulp in air, but somehow couldn't get anything in. His hands scrabbled at his own throat, tearing at his own flesh, trying to tear away an unseen assailant. And then his own hands locked tight around his windpipe and began to squeeze.

Dean rushed to help him, prying at his fingers, battling to pull his hands away, but the grip was as firm as iron and though he could loosen it momentarily, he could not break the hands away.

"I can't breathe...," Virgil said in a suffocated voice. "I...I..."

He began to choke. Blood spilled from his mouth, long, dark strands of it.

"Virgil!" shouted Dean. "Virgil!" He turned to Hawthorne, his face full of panic for his brother. "Hawthorne!" he said. "The demon has entered his body! The demon is destroying his soul!"

That Virgil could be possessed by the demon suggested what Hawthorne had long known, that though he served good, Virgil's heart was far from pure. Hawthorne fell to his knees, raised his eyes to the heavens, and began to pray aloud. What else was there to do? Would God listen to them? Would he save them?

"Lord hear me!" he said. "Purge our brother Virgil from this Bringer of Death! Set us free from these serpents of Hell that have invaded our beloved Salem!"

"Sisters!" said Morgan to the coven, her voice no longer imbued with the demonic tones that had overtaken it but once again her own. "We are the true believers! The true masters shall return to avenge us! We shall live again!"

Mather kneeled beside him, joining Hawthorne in prayer. Near the Chair of God, Dean still fought to save his brother. He broke several of Virgil's fingers, but Virgil would not let go of his own neck, and even the broken fingers continued to cling to his flesh.

"In the name of the creator of the world," Hawthorne and Mather repeated together, "the king of kings, I command you to kneel before the power of God! Kneel before the power of God...Kneel before the power of God!"

Morgan laughed. "We would not kneel, even were we free to do so. We shall not submit to your false, weak God. He is worthy only of contempt."

Hawthorne and Mather ignored her words, continuing to chant, over and over again, "Kneel before the power of God." Hawthorne heard Dean cry out and he let his gaze fall from the heavens an instant to see Virgil gasp for his final breaths, his chest heaving but still unable to bring any air in.

Hawthorne's prayer slowly died in his throat. For a moment Mather went on without him and then stopped as well.

As they watched, Virgil's damaged hand fell away from his throat and dangled as if dead. His other hand, however, tightened even further, the nails of his fingers this time gouging their way into the flesh. Dean was blubbering and screaming, and Virgil's eyes were pleading, but otherwise his body seemed not to be his own. And then the hand tightened further and in a single, violent jerk ripped his throat out, spattering his brother with blood. Virgil swayed there a moment, blood pulsing through the ragged hole in his neck, and he then pitched forward, falling limply into his brother's arms.

Dean cried out his brother's name again and hugged the body to him. They had now lost one of their number. How many more would they lose before the nightmare was complete?

Mather was staring at Morgan with hatred. "By the power of the holy ghost and the blessed savior, your skull shall be drained of Satan's black blood!" he said.

"Bring me the helmet!" Hawthorne cried.

But Mather was already ahead of him. He had the wooden box there beside him, ready for use. He opened the lid and removed a roughly forged greased iron helmet made to cover the whole face. It was scattered with holes, two under the eyes and several spread in an arc across the forehead. The surface was stained with what looked to the untrained eye like rust but that Hawthorne knew to be the life-blood of past witches.

When Morgan spoke, it was again with the Devil's voice. Blood now was running down the sides of chair, pooling on the ground. She laughed. "Take joy in my momentary pain," she said. "For the blood of my death shall be the ocean by which we sail and you, my dear Reverend Hawthorne...your lineage shall be the vessel by which the Master completes his journey!"

"I shall have nothing to do with you," hissed Hawthorne. "Nor shall my heirs."

Morgan smiled in a disjointed, hideous way. "No, Hawthorne," she said. "We shall be Salem's everlasting plague."

These last words she repeated and then repeated again, *Salem's everlasting plague, Salem's everlasting plague*, the words said over and over again to become first a chant and then a kind of drone. Hawthorne struggled with the helmet. A wind rushed through the room again and the witches were suddenly ungagged, their screams joining the whistling of the wind. With a snap he managed to open the helmet. It split along a hinge in the middle, separating into two halves.

He stood and rushed to the chair, securing the back half of the helmet behind Morgan's head. Despite Virgil's death, despite Dean weeping and holding his brother and apparently unable to be of use, he felt at last hopeful. The end of the nightmare was in sight. He drew himself straight and fumbled to get the front half of the helmet into place. Morgan's chant was a distraction.

"Recite as you wish," he said. "There is no escape from the true Word of God! There is no resurrection from the pits of Hell!"

And then he had it right and had closed it over Morgan's face. He slid the iron hasp into place to lock it closed.

Behind him, all the witches shouted, as if one: "Satan's everlasting plague!"

"So be it that under our blessed God we are judge, jury, and executioner this night. Set the fires...Purify Salem from this curse!" shouted Hawthorne.

But Dean still stayed bent over his brother, holding his body.

"Dean!" shouted Hawthorne. "For God's sake, the fires!"

The bearlike man seemed to suddenly come to himself. He let his brother fall gently to the floor and lumbered toward one of the torch sconces. He grabbed a torch and trailed it along the trough. The tinder caught flame, a wall of fire quickly spreading down the trough. The witches began screaming, a veritable symphony of agony as the flesh of their legs burned and bubbled. The smell of burning flesh filled the air.

The wind began to rise again. "The nails!" Hawthorne shouted.

Mather stepped forward. In his hands he held five metal spikes and a wooden mallet. Hawthorne grabbed hold of one of the spikes and the mallet. One by one he drove the spikes through the openings in the mask.

He drove them into the eyes first, pounding them just far enough to blind Morgan and lodge them painfully in her sockets. Her body thrashed awkwardly, the veins standing out on her neck, her head immobilized. Then he drove one into the left side of her forehead. The spike, he knew, would tear away the flesh on the side of her temple and slowly gouge through the bone and then slip painfully along the exposed brain, tearing the tissue there just a little. The spike into the right side of her forehead would do the same, and the two together would reduce the little movement she had within the mask to nothing. Her body continued to thrash and her muffled screams echoed inside the helmet. It was terrible to hear, but never before had Hawthorne been so convinced that God's will was being fulfilled.

Perhaps now, now that the pain was so great, if asked to renounce Satan and his minions she would do so, Hawthorne couldn't help but think. But no, a sterner and more severe part of him thought. She had had her chance. Now it was too late for her. God's mercy would not be granted her.

Ignoring both Morgan's screams and the shrieks of the burning witches behind him, ignoring the stink of burning flesh and the smoke billowing up the chimney, Hawthorne positioned the final spike in the hole in the center of the forehead.

"You have sold your soul to the Devil," he said. "And to the Devil you shall now go."

He waited the briefest moment and then slammed the mallet hard onto the head of the spike, driving it deep through the bone and into the witch's head. Blood gushed uncontrollably through the holes in the mask and Morgan's body began to thrash violently, and then suddenly she fell still.

Dead at last, thought Hawthorne, and he turned away, trying not to think of her final threats toward him and his children. *What had she meant that they would be Salem's everlasting plague?* No, best not to think about it, he told himself. These were the rantings of a deranged woman in fear of death. Just as before, as always, God had protected him. God would continue to protect them, he thought, and tried not to look at Virgil's corpse. He told himself, not altogether convincingly, that they had nothing to fear.

PART TWO

SALEM, MASSACHUSETTS
PRESENT DAY

Monday

Chapter Seven

The town of Salem had changed much over the years, the dirt paths and wagon tracks replaced now by paved roads. The waterfront, once so bustling and lively with the spice trade, was now filled with shops for the tourists who came to Salem year-round, interested in the town's past. The only three-master in the harbor was a replica and was now a museum. There were still a few fishing boats, but the majority of the trade had moved a little way away, to the more commercial town of Gloucester. The customhouse that Hawthorne had once worked in was still there, a stately redbrick building with white pillars that resembled a schoolhouse. Near where the witches had been killed was now a paved pedestrian downtown: tourist shops, witch museums, witch tours. Next to a cart selling hats and T-shirts, two women with tags reading "I'm a Wiccan" were prepared to answer any and all questions.

But just a few blocks away from the center of town, the character of Salem changed. The streets became quiet, the tourists all clinging to the waterfront and the museums downtown. Here, the neighborhoods were old and historic, the houses painted traditional slate blue or dark red. The newer ones were New England late Victorians, large, impressive structures that these days were often split into multiple apartments. But there were among them federal houses with mullioned windows and hipped roofs, with the facades covered in wide, flat board siding. Less common, but still present, were the earlier Georgian colonials, wooden and barnlike in structure, with gambreled roofs, flat fronts, and double-sashed windows. Rarer still were the old saltboxes from the colony's early years, high on one side and low on the other, with very few windows, and these filled with a series of small diamond-shaped panes. On these streets, you could see the whole history of Salem's past and imagine the original colonizer standing shoulder to shoulder with their descendants, and could even convince yourself, if you were standing in the right place, before the right house, that the past was not past after all.

There was little about the house on the outside to suggest what Heidi Hawthorne's apartment looked like on the inside, or to give any clue to the kind of person she was. Outside it seemed a typical mid-Victorian house on a quaint street in this perfectly maintained and varied historic neighborhood, though this particular house was slightly less perfectly maintained than the others around it. The white paint had faded and the drab green shutters gave the house a less vibrant feel than the others. It wouldn't be long before the paint started to peel and the landlord would be paid a visit from the Salem Historical Society, reminding her that a responsibility to the community came with owning a historical home and encouraging her to properly maintain it unless she wanted a fine.

Inside, Heidi's apartment was anything but historic. The wall behind her bed was covered with a mural of a wasted-looking Keith Richards, with Richards leaning against a sign proclaiming "Patience Please. A Drug Free America Comes First!" The bed was overwhelmed with pillows, with the blankets disarranged and curled up around her.

She was lying facedown in it. Her hair was bleached white and dreadlocked and hid her face. Her slender bare body was covered with vibrant tattoos, a swirling water scene complete with fish and octopi crawling in a sleeve up one arm. The other arm was all skulls, outlined in black and rendered gold, chewing on one another and deliberately smearing into one another. An image of leathery, tattered bat wings ran along her shoulders and hung folded down her back.

Her dad would probably roll over in his grave if he had a chance to see her tattoos. Her mother told her this sometimes—not to be mean, really; she just couldn't help herself. And perhaps because she thought that it might keep Heidi from getting more tattoos. The first one she'd gotten she'd kept hidden from her mother for weeks, only wearing long-sleeved shirts when around her, but then her mother and she had accidentally crossed paths downtown and that was it. And her mother had been more upset that Heidi had hidden it than about the tattoo itself, so Heidi stopped hiding it. Though there were things she still hid from her mother.

But I wasn't a bad kid, Heidi thought. No, she'd been pretty much normal, maybe slightly geeky at first, but that all had changed as she got older and grew into her looks. Over the course of her freshman year, she went from being the kind of girl who didn't get noticed to the kind of girl who got almost too much attention. Yet the way it happened made her mistrust it, made her always think that it was just a fluke and that from one day to the next people could stop paying attention to her again.

When the clock radio clicked on, blasting metal, Heidi roused herself and rolled over long enough to turn down the volume. Her body was svelte yet shapely. She hadn't bothered to wash off her dark eye makeup from the night before and it had run a little.

She reached over and turned the alarm off and then pulled herself up to a sitting position. On the bedside table was a pair of cat's-eye glasses, which for a second her hand groped for and then found and put on.

She sighed. Another long night. She'd planned to have just one drink and then come home, go to bed early so she'd be up and rested by the time she had to go to her shift at the radio station late in the day. And now it was already midafternoon. She remembered the one drink, but then there had been another, and another after that.

Then things got a little hazy. Luckily, she'd managed to set her alarm before going out; otherwise she probably wouldn't have woken up in time for her shift.

Near the foot of the bed, wagging his tail, was Steve, Heidi's large Lab mix. When he saw her looking at him, he started wagging his whole body and came around near the side of the bed where he could get closer. Heidi yawned.

"Steve...," she said, and made a halfhearted attempt to pat his head. At the sound of his name, Steve's ears pricked up. "How's about you making me breakfast for a change?" she asked.

Steve wagged on.

"Nothing fancy," said Heidi, beginning to wake up a little more. She yawned. "Eggs Benedict, a little freshly squeezed OJ, and above all some coffee."

For a moment Steve stared at her attentively, waiting, but when nothing more happened he turned once in a circle and lay down beside the bed. Heidi just watched him.

"I'll take that as a polite fuck you," she finally said.

She untangled herself the rest of the way from the blankets, stepped out of bed, and stumbled toward the bathroom. Halfway there, she stopped and steadied herself against the wall.

God, she was hungover. She really shouldn't be drinking like that—not a smart idea in any case, considering that this time last year she'd been far from clean. And if it hadn't been for Whitey she probably would have lost her job, and then where would she be? She'd hated him when he'd placed the call and forced her to check in to the clinic. She had said some pretty unforgivable things, but she was grateful now. No, she had to be careful—one drink too many and then who knew what she'd do?

She waited for a minute for the throbbing to relax a little before continuing along.

The bathroom was less distinctive than the bedroom, though a WXKB bumper sticker had been stuck to the top of the toilet tank.

The sink was littered with brushes and parts of several makeup kits, a hair dryer balanced precariously on a towel bar. Heidi approached the mirror reluctantly, apprehensively. Her dark eye makeup was smudged and smeared.

"Jesus, Steve," she said. "I'm a fucking raccoon."

Hearing his name the dog slowly padded into the bathroom. He stared expectantly at her.

"Why didn't you tell me I forgot to take off my makeup?" she asked him.

When Steve tilted his head in confusion, she shooed him out and shut the door. She sat on the toilet, leaned her head against the cool porcelain of the sink next to her, and gave a little groan. Her head really hurt. No, she had to stop telling herself she'd just have one little drink. One drink was never one drink anymore. Peeing, she stared at the side of the tub, her eyes slowly losing focus, and a moment later, she found herself beginning to slip off. *No sleeping on the toilet*, she told herself. *Sleeping on the toilet bad.* How late had it been when she'd gotten in? Three? Four? Too late in any case, especially when she had to work the next day.

She was already starting to lose herself in her thoughts again, her eyes beginning to blur and sleep threatening to come. She lifted her head away from the sink and then reached over and turned on the water, splashed some in her face. It was cold enough to make her catch her breath. *There, that ought to do it*, she thought. But a minute later, her eyes were blurring again. She needed more sleep. But there wasn't time. She needed coffee, then, something to perk her up, something to make her feel better.

And when she thought that, *something to make her feel better*, she had a brief flash of the needle pushing in her arm again. The way it had felt back when she used to use, when she'd draw back just a little and watch her blood drift into the cylinder and then depress the plunger and tear the tourniquet off. The way it would hit her all in a rush, all at once, and how much better that made her feel. The way it felt to nod off and float into it. Until the moment it wore off and she felt not good but anxious, unable to wait for the next time, the next rush.

And that was enough to wake her up. No, she was out of that, wasn't even in touch with any of the people she'd known in that world. Not all of them were still around, in any case. Some had moved away, some had quit just like her, and at least one was dead. Her friend Griff, dead, heart just stopped. No warning, just didn't wake up. Just lay there for a day and a half until someone stumbled across him. She'd known him since junior high, back when they'd both been just normal kids. He'd always looked out for her. How he'd started using, how she had, it was a little hard to say now, and didn't make much sense. She'd had okay parents, good friends, had grown up going to church. Sure, she'd rebelled a little, but didn't everybody? And she didn't understand the steps that had led her from that to using. Griff's death should have been a wake-up call for her, but even with that, it had taken Whitey checking her in to get her to stop.

She thought about using every day, couldn't help it most of the time—the ex-addicts who had helped her break the habit had told her that those thoughts were natural, that they would go on for a while, maybe forever. But thinking about it wasn't the same as doing it. She could feel a craving for it but still not do it, and as long as she stayed clean, the craving would diminish little by little. Or at least that's what they said. She still felt it quite often and quite strongly. And when she did, she tried to remember Griff. She didn't want to end up like that. And now, thinking back, she remembered feeling it most strongly just after her first drink. Which is maybe why she'd had her second drink, as a way of not thinking about it. And her third. And her fourth. Maybe this is why that same group said that alcohol was also a drug and would lead her right back to where she was before. They claimed she must abstain from all drugs in order to recover. And yet most nights she found herself back at the bar.

She flushed the toilet and then stood in front of the sink, scrubbing the makeup off her face until she was satisfied, beginning to move out of her thoughts and out into her day. *Put on a happy face*, she told herself. *Act okay and maybe you'll be okay; maybe you'll get back to what you know you are.* Shuffling into the bedroom, she saw that Steve had jumped up onto the bed, was curled up in the blankets where she'd been sleeping. She quickly slipped on shorts and a T-shirt. She whistled once and he lifted his head.

"Come on, buddy," she said. "Let's eat."

At the word *eat*, Steve bounded up and off the bed and rushed toward the kitchen. With a laugh, she followed him.

Chapter Eight

She refilled Steve's water and poured him a bowl of kibble. He immediately began wolfing it down. She dumped the used coffee filter out and put in a new one, filled it with fresh grounds.

After starting the machine dripping, she stayed leaning against the counter a moment, listening to the sound of Steve crunching up his food. Her head felt like it had been filled with wet sand. *No more drinking*, she promised herself again, but knew that as the day went on she'd take it back. *Powerless.*

She sighed and went to get the paper. When she opened the door it wasn't on the mat and for a moment she thought it hadn't been delivered. She stepped out and peered down the long drab hall and there it was, halfway between her door and the next one. *Would it kill him to put it on my mat?* she wondered. Sighing, she made her barefoot way out into the hall to grab it.

She'd just bent down and picked it up when she felt the air out in the hall shift and change. She had the sudden feeling that she was being observed. She looked up and saw that the door to the apartment at the far end of the hall was ajar now, though she hadn't heard it open. The apartment had been unoccupied as long as she'd been in the house, and it was a surprise to think that the landlady had finally managed to rent it. Maybe they'd left it open because they were in the process of moving in. Or maybe the apartment wasn't rented after all and the door had simply come unlocked for some reason, had been left open when someone had walked through it looking at it or when a repairman had come.

For a moment she considered walking down and closing the door but as she straightened up she realized that there was something strange about the doorway. The darkness wasn't consistent within it.

As she peered closer, she realized with a start that there was a man standing there, motionless. He wore dark clothing, was mostly hidden in shadow, but he was there. And he was watching her.

"God," she said. "You startled me."

The man didn't say anything. Didn't even move. Just remained standing there with his arms crossed, just within the apartment. *Weird*, thought Heidi. *Fuck him.*

But maybe there was an explanation. Maybe he hadn't heard her. Or maybe he was just shy. She decided to make an effort to be neighborly and try again.

"Hello," she said, moving a step closer. "Are you the new tenant?"

Still he did not answer, did not even move. Was there really someone there? Was it some sort of optical illusion and she was seeing things? No, she could see him, could even, if she paid very close attention, tell that he was breathing.

"I live here in number two," she said, her voice losing its friendliness now. "My name is—"

Before she could finish, the door slammed shut. The man had moved so quickly she had hardly seen him. It was as if one moment he was there and the next not; one moment the door was open and the next closed. She stared at it in astonishment. So much for the new neighbor.

Shaking her head she returned to the apartment and poured herself a cup of coffee. What an asshole. If Lacy was going to rent it to someone like that, it would have been better if number five had remained empty.

She took a sip of the coffee and groaned. God, it was good. Maybe she could survive her hangover after all.

She'd have to call her mother, she thought, taking another sip. It had been a while since they talked, and she'd be worried, and ever since her dad had died, she didn't have anyone to talk to.

She sat down at the table and opened the *Salem News*. She'd always found the little icon of a witch riding a broom past the moon on the paper's masthead ridiculous. Why would a town cling so tightly to an awful history of witches and murder? If she had to bet, she'd say the majority of women executed in the Salem witch trials hadn't done anything at all, had just been in the wrong place at the wrong time. But being on-air at a radio station in Salem meant that she had to play along with the witch business in the same way that so many of the businesses around here did.

Even less going on around town than usual, if the paper was to be believed. She sighed and took another sip of her coffee and her thoughts turned back to toying with the idea of a fix. She shook her head and steered them away. She thought about the man in apartment five. His face had been difficult to read, expressionless as it was, and she had a hard time knowing why he'd reacted as he had. Maybe she just hadn't gotten a good look at his face. But now it was difficult for her even to imagine what he had looked like. Was he some sort of recluse? Or a mute, maybe? She'd have to ask her landlady about him.

She took another sip of coffee, yawned, and looked at the clock. Steve was already standing near the door, staring at it. Was it that time already?

"Buddy," she said, "I don't want to go to work today."

Steve gave a halfhearted wag of his tail but didn't turn away from the door. After a moment he began to whine.

"Hold your horses," she said, and took another sip. "Why can't you learn to use a toilet like those dogs on TV?"

Steve was silent for a moment, and then began to whine again.

"Come on, man," she begged. "Let me get half a cup down before we hit the streets."

Chapter Nine

She had thrown on her faux fur coat, a cute scarf she'd "borrowed" from the lost-and-found bin at the station, and black two-ring, knee-high boots. When she went out and bounced down the hall stairs with Steve, she ran into Lacy.

Lacy was a cute woman in her late fifties, still well-preserved. She was wearing a batik dress, a kind of hippie wraparound that Heidi had always suspected could be tied in different ways to become a shirt or a skirt instead, or even left untied and used as a shawl. Her manner was relaxed and easy. She had blond hair streaked through with gray that she left down and let go wild. She was standing in the entrance near the mailboxes, sorting through her mail. She looked up briefly and smiled when she saw Heidi, absently nodded.

"Hey, Lacy," said Heidi.

"Hello," said Lacy slowly. She was half-distracted, still thumbing through her mail. She gave Heidi only the smallest glance.

For a moment Heidi started to edge past her landlady, and then she remembered the man in the door.

"I see you finally rented number five," she said.

Lacy looked up momentarily, a strange expression flitting across her face. "I wish, babe. I wish," she said. "For some reason that apartment is a total dog." She stopped long enough to bend over and address Steve. "No offense, Steve," she said. Steve wagged his tail.

She looked back at Heidi. "Nobody wants it," she said. "I don't get it. I've looked around town. I know the price is right."

What? thought Heidi. Then who was the man she had seen? When she spoke again it was hesitantly, in a confused voice. "But I just saw someone, like, ten minutes ago standing in the doorway," she said. "Strange guy."

But Lacy had found the piece of mail she'd been looking for and had begun to tear it open. "Finally, took long enough," she said. "Of course when they owe *you* money it takes forever." Abruptly she stopped opening it, having realized that she'd been ignoring Heidi. "Huh? What were you saying, dear?"

"I was talking about the person in apartment five."

"Apartment five?"

Heidi nodded.

Lacy shrugged. "I don't know what you mean," she said. "I hate to break it to you, but there is no person in apartment five."

Heidi looked at her. Nobody in apartment five? But she had seen someone; she was sure of it. Was she wrong or was Lacy being cagey? Maybe Lacy was just confused by the question. Or maybe she herself was more hungover than she realized.

"Anything wrong, sweetie?" asked Lacy.

"Well, I definitely saw someone in there," said Heidi. "But when I said hi, he slammed the door right in my face."

Now it was Lacy's turn to give her a long look.

"You sure?" she asked. "Honey, nobody's even asked to see the place in a week."

Steve, feeling it was past time for his walk, whined.

"I think so," Heidi said. "Maybe...," she started, but unable to figure out how to go on with it, she let the sentence trail off unfinished.

"It doesn't make much sense, but I'll check it out if it'll make you feel better."

Heidi nodded. "Thanks," she said.

Steve barked, rubbing up against Lacy's leg. Bending down, Lacy patted him on the back and addressed him in a baby voice.

"Good morning, handsome boy. How are you today? Did you get a good sleep last night?"

Heidi rolled her eyes. "All right," she said. "Time to walk this handsome boy before he does some ugly business right here on the porch. Bye."

Lacy smiled. "Have a good one."

They started off but hadn't gone more than a few steps when Steve wanted to stop and sniff the bushes. Heidi glanced back to see Lacy there, frozen in the act of locking her mailbox. She was staring up the stairs. There was something strange about the way she held herself. Then Lacy finished closing her mailbox and hurried into her apartment.

Chapter Ten

W hat is it I feel, Sister?" asked the first nun.

"It is the same that I feel," said the second. "The time is coming." She made a gesture as if to cross herself, but the symbol she made was different and more complex: the cross was there, but once she had made it, she topped it with an upward-curving semicircle and drew a downward curving semicircle through its base as well. So, a cross, but not a cross. A cross perverted into something else.

The other sister made the same gesture.

They knelt together in the back pew in the deserted Saint Peter's church, in the darkest part. The nuns were both quite old. The portion of their heads and faces not hidden by the cowls of their habits seemed as wrinkled as dried apples, almost sexless. Their hands, resting against the backs of the pews in front of them, were bony and liver spotted and nearly translucent, quavering slightly.

"The time comes at last," said the first nun. "And we shall embrace it."

"Yes, we shall," said the second nun. "The promised time has come and Salem shall be reclaimed."

After a long moment, the first began to pray, a slow chant in what seemed at first nonsense. "Nema," she said. "Reve rof d'na won sruoy..." The other nun joined in. "Era ylorg eh-t d'na..."

Had anyone been listening, it would only slowly have dawned on them that it was not nonsense after all but some language, even if an unfamiliar one. Someone paying very close attention might have eventually realized it was not an unfamiliar language at all but a familiar one turned on its head and running in reverse. From there it would be only a matter of time before they deciphered that what the nuns were doing was reciting the Lord's Prayer backward.

They were interrupted by the appearance of a young priest beside them. He stood there with his hands clasped, smiling.

"Father," said the first nun in a voice that was flat and neutral, nodding her head.

"Father," said the second, imitating the tone of the first exactly.

"Sisters," said the priest. "I don't believe I've met either of you before. Am I mistaken? Are you newly arrived? Have you just been transferred to join us?"

"Not exactly," said the first nun.

"We are from another...parish," said the second nun.

"We are just passing through," said the first. "A little traveling."

The priest nodded. "You are most welcome," he said. "If I can be of service to you, please don't hesitate to call upon me."

Both nuns nodded. The priest stood there a little longer, waiting for them to speak, then after a moment wandered away. They watched him go, following him with narrowed eyes down the aisle. Once he was out of earshot, they began to pray again, continuing their act of desecration.

"I feel him," said the first nun.

"Who?" said the second nun. "Mather?"

"Hawthorne," said the first. "Though he has been dead these many years, I feel him."

"It is not he whom you feel," said the second, "but his kin. His blood."

The first nun nodded. "His blood still beats within her veins."

"But the time is coming," said the second.

"The time is coming," the first agreed.

They traced once again the symbol over their chests, then stood and left the pew. Leaning against one another, they hobbled their way down the aisle and toward the doors of the church.

"I feel him," whispered the first nun, angrily. "I feel him."

"We shall have our revenge," said the first. "And it shall be sweet."

And then they were out of the church and in the morning sun. They stood on the steps, sniffing the air.

"There," said the first nun. "There he is."

"Yes," said the second. "I can feel him. I can *smell* him."

Halfway down the narrow, redbrick sidewalk was a woman in a faux fur coat, leading a large Labrador retriever. She had stopped to let the dog sniff a lamppost. She was looking idly around, her eyes wandering. After a moment she tugged on the leash, but the dog braced its paws. It wasn't ready to be pulled away.

Her gaze was slowly drawn to the nuns. They stood there on the steps, motionless, their habits blowing in the wind.

"He sees us," the first nun said.

"No," the second nun said. "It is Hawthorne's blood but it is not Hawthorne. It is a she. And she does not know what she sees."

The first nun nodded. "She will not know what she sees until it is too late."

Chapter Eleven

The large African American man stood on the front steps of the apartment trying to stop himself from pacing. He was dressed in a way that made him stand out from other residents of Salem, that made him seem like a throwback to the seventies. He wore glittering white Adidas shoes, a black-ribbed T-shirt, and a white-leather suit coat. His pants were white as well, tight-fitting slacks that looked like they'd been tailored to fit him. He was in his late fifties, but still relatively fit. He took a cigar out of his coat pocket, stared at it, then put it away again. A moment later he had it out again and had bitten off the ends and was lighting it.

Might as well enjoy myself if I have to wait, he thought, puffing on the cigar and turning it in the flame until the tip glowed evenly. *Where is she?* he wondered. Late again. He tried not to worry about Heidi. When he'd knocked on the door, nobody had answered and that'd made him a little anxious, but Steve hadn't barked, which meant wherever she was she was out with Steve. Which meant the chances that she'd started using again and hadn't come home the night before were slim to none. She was okay, he was pretty sure, but he couldn't help but worry about her, because he'd seen how bad things had gotten for her last time. He didn't ever want her to go through something like that again. But he also didn't want to have to be the one to pull her out the next time; once was enough. He'd been happy to do it, happy to be there for her, but it'd been hard on both

Rob Zombie

of them, and the way she'd cursed him out when she realized he was going to check her into the clinic, well, that just wasn't something easy to forget. He'd put his own job on the line convincing the station to hire her back, which was why he made a point of picking her up and getting her to work on time, of making sure she didn't start fucking up again.

He took a long draw on the cigar. He loved the way the smoke changed the inside of his mouth, numbed it just a little but also changed the texture of it almost.

The curtains behind one of the windows on the ground floor were pulled back and he caught a quick glimpse of a woman's face before it quickly fell again. Landlady, he told himself. What was her name? Heidi had introduced her but he'd be damned if he could remember. Probably the old hippy chick didn't approve of him smoking cigars on her steps, but if that were the case she'd have to come out and tell him to his face. He knew that there were very few people willing to stand up to him, to Herman Jackson, and he suspected that she wasn't one of them. He wasn't a jerk—he'd stop smoking if she asked nicely and without being prissy—but as far as he was concerned he was outdoors with nobody else in smell range. He wasn't bothering anybody. And if he was, they could let him know nicely or grin and bear it.

"Hey," someone said.

He turned to see Heidi walking back toward the apartment building, leading Steve. Yeah, she was okay. He shouldn't have worried. It made him a little ashamed that he had, a little angry at himself, but a little angry at her, too, for putting him in a position that made him feel like he had to. But no, that was stupid. She was a good kid, trying just like anyone else, and mostly doing all right.

She reached him, Steve wagging and trying to jump up on him. He pushed the dog away, but gently.

"Hey, Heidi," he said.

"Did you pick up the new headshots?" Heidi asked.

"Headshots?" Herman said. He leaned over and scraped the coal off his cigar and then put it back into his pocket for later. "You're worried about headshots?" he asked. "You got any concept of what time it might be, girl?"

Heidi straightened up, puckered her lips. When she spoke again it was with a bad French accent.

"What is this time? I have no understanding of this time of which you speak."

Herman shook his head, keeping his face flat and trying not to smile. He looked at his watch. "Well then, Frenchie LaRue," he said, "let me put it in straight-up boots-on-the-ground all-American speak. It's half past get your fucking ass in the car."

Heidi gave a wicked smile, but he could tell from her eyes that she was tired and in no mood for playing around. "Let me just grab my shit," she said.

"Well, giddyap," said Herman. "The meter on my chariot is running."

She could mess around, Herman thought, but when she put her mind to something she got it done in good time. It had only taken her a minute to run Steve in and clamber into his car. He hadn't even had time to think about the half-smoked cigar in his pocket and light it again.

He flipped a U-ey, ignoring the double yellow line, something sure to scandalize Heidi's uptight neighbors. Why she wanted to live in the heart of the historical part of Salem, hell if he knew. Once, when she was drunk, she'd talked a little about her heritage, that she was descended from one of the early Salem witch hunters. But hell, that seemed like it might be a reason *not* to want to live in Salem rather than a reason to live there. And Heidi stuck out like a sore thumb in this neighborhood—nobody else around here under fifty. Not as much as he would have, being black and being a natty dresser, but still...

The crucifix dangling from the rearview mirror was still swinging from the U-turn. It kept catching flashes of sunlight and sending them into his eyes. He reached out and steadied it.

"It always does that," Heidi said, watching him. "You should just take it down."

He shook his head. "I'm not taking it down," he said. "That's God looking out for me."

"You know what they would have said about that in Old Salem?" she asked.

"What?" he said.

"They would have called you an idolater," she said. "Probably they would have burned you as a witch."

"Yeah, good times," he said. "But I'm keeping it where it is."

They drove in silence a moment, until Heidi, remembering, suddenly gave a little jump.

"Okay, so where the photos at?" she asked.

"Again with the photos." He waited a minute for her to riposte, and when she didn't he gestured over his shoulder. "Backseat."

"And...how do they look?" she asked.

"Wrong," said Herman.

"What do you mean, wrong?"

Herman didn't answer, preferring to let her see for herself.

She reached over the seat and shuffled aside a pile of clothes. Underneath were several boxes. The one on top was full of books.

"Christ, you need to clean your fucking car," said Heidi. "You are a hoarder."

God, she knew how to push his buttons. "Don't tell me what I need to do," said Herman. "And I ain't no hoarder."

"I'm going to get you an intervention on that show for hoarders," she said. "*Hoarding Emergency* or whatever."

"I ain't no hoarder," he insisted again.

She ignored him. She pushed the box to one side, opened one of the boxes under it. It was the right box, Herman saw with a glance in the rearview mirror as she opened it. She pulled out an 8″ by 10″ promo photo and then settled back into her seat and examined it.

When they had to stop at a light, Herman snuck a glance, curious to see if it was as bad as he remembered. "Big H Radio Team," it read along the bottom. And there he was. Yeah, his clothes looked good, as usual, but his head didn't look like that, did it? No, no way it could. It just wasn't natural. Heidi looked good, though, in her tattered Ramones shirt and her torn jeans, and totally at ease as well. But he, there was this problem with his head, probably some kind of Photoshopped joke, and plus he just didn't look relaxed. The third member of the team, Whitey, didn't look as bad as him, but didn't look half as good as Heidi either. He was a gangly man with long hair and a huge, bushy beard and he wore mirrored sunglasses that looked straight out of the seventies. Like he'd stolen them off an aviator. Just beaten the fuck out of an aviator and then taken his glasses. Yeah, Herman had to admit Whitey looked okay. A little creepy maybe, but still. Maybe he should have worn sunglasses, too.

"We look pretty cool," said Heidi. "What's so wrong?"

"My head!" said Herman, exasperated. Couldn't she see it? "My head looks too fucking big! It's got to be the fucking lens that asshole was using. I knew he snuck on a wide-angle lens, some kind of fishbowl thing. I know my head ain't that big."

"You look fine," said Heidi. "God, you are worse than a fucking chick."

"Fine? Fine is your polite-ass way of saying, 'Herman, he got a big fucking beach ball head.' I look like Charlie Brown."

He examined himself in the mirror. No, his head wasn't that big. No way it was that big.

Heidi put her hand on his arm, spoke in mock consolation. "Don't worry," she said. "You're still a stud."

"Yeah?" he said. He smiled, looked at himself in the mirror again. "Yeah, I do look good, don't I." She was all right, Heidi was.

Chapter Twelve

Just goes to show you, you think you've seen everything and then they go and pull out some new horror show, thought Cerina Hooten. *I got to get myself a new job.* She sat at her receptionist's desk, tapping her pencil against the desk's edge. How could she be expected to work under these conditions? Okay, musicians were eccentric, but this was too much. And couldn't they have the decency to sit down somewhere else in the waiting room rather than taking the chairs right across from her, facing her? What happened to common courtesy? She reached up and ruffled her bushy Afro. No, no. She couldn't be expected to type something up with them staring at her the whole time, no matter how urgent the station manager said it was. He was lucky she was even bothering to answer the phones.

She had their publicity photo on the desk and a Sharpie out. She'd thought the photo would be labeled, but it wasn't, which meant that she'd have to talk to them and ask them who was who or else Chip, the station manager, would complain. She looked closely at the photo. They looked just as bad in that. Ugh. Hideous. Why would anyone want to dress up like someone dead? She shivered. It was just plain morbid.

"Umm, excuse me," she said.

Neither of them looked up. Maybe they weren't aware that they were being addressed, but how could they not be? They were the only two other people in the reception area. They were foreign, right? Norwegian, maybe. Maybe they didn't even speak English.

But no, she thought a moment later, if they didn't speak English, why would they be here for a radio interview? They were just being difficult.

"Hey, you," she said. "The ghoul reading *Highlights*." *Highlights?* she wondered. *Wasn't that a kid's magazine?* The man looked up. He was wearing pale white face makeup, except for his eyes, which were lost in a pool of black. His lips were bloodred and smeared wider than his actual mouth, and blood or something that looked like it seemed to have dripped from his chin to stain his chest. Leather thongs bristling with nails formed a sort of headgear for him. A kind of black leather harness covered with larger spikes, what she saw as a sort of pervert's idea of lederhosen, was his only clothing. She couldn't help wondering what the spikes were doing to the vinyl chair he was sitting on. Who was going to pay for that?

"Which one of you is Count Gorgann?" she asked.

The musician reading *Highlights* lifted one hand in a Satanic salute, pointer finger and pinky lifted, his two middle fingers bent to touch his palm. He waggled his tongue and tipped his wrist to point his salute at his own face.

"All righty then," said Cerina. She turned to the man next to him. "Which I guess makes you Dr. Butcher," she said.

This one had apparently painted his face black first and then applied white face paint over it. It made his face look like a broken skull with darkness seeping out from behind it. The more she looked at it the more unsettling it seemed. His mouth had been painted in blood in a drooping frown that reached the side of his jaw. *What must their monthly face paint bill be?* Cerina asked herself, which made her wonder if she should check her own makeup. His arms were covered from wrist to elbow with leather bracers, with rusty iron spikes on them. *High tetanus risk*, Cerina couldn't help but think. He had more clothes on, a black T-shirt with the sleeves torn off and black jeans, but over the jeans he'd affixed a kind of codpiece with dozens of screws jutting tip-first out of it. He lifted his head briefly. He opened his mouth wide to show black-stained teeth, then returned to his magazine.

"I'll take that as a yes," she said.

You gotta be shittin' me, she thought, carefully writing each name in Sharpie beneath the correct image. *Damn, I really got to get a better job.*

"Are you serious?" asked Heidi. "I'm the problem?"

"You know you're the problem," said Herman. "Don't make me explain it to you."

He pulled into a parking spot behind the studio, turned the car off. He'd opened the door and was starting to step out when she put her hand on his arm and stopped him.

"Excuse me," said Heidi. "Just how am I the problem?"

He turned back toward her. "Well," he said. "For one, if you weren't always all dolled up and striking some glamour pose, me and Whitey wouldn't end up looking like ebony and ivory mutants."

"I've got news for you," said Heidi. "You'd look like ebony and ivory mutants whether I was there or not."

"Thanks a whole lot," said Herman.

They got out. Herman opened the back door and began unloading the boxes of promo photos, stacking his arms full. Heidi grabbed the last one.

"I'm the one all dolled up?" she said. "You dress like that pimp on TV Land, Teddy Bear."

Herman pretended to be offended. "I believe you mean Huggy Bear," he said. Then shouted, "My man Antonio Fargas!"

Laughing and shaking his head, he headed toward the station door, Heidi close behind him.

Cerina had turned away from the two black-metal ghouls, ducking a little underneath the desk as she spoke in a low voice into the phone.

"I swear to Jesus I got Satan times two sitting right across from me." She curled the phone cord around her finger, listened. "I don't know...," she said. "Some kind of heavy metal bullshit." She snuck a glance at the two band members. They were both still reading their magazines, waiting calmly. "Norwegian, I think. Norwegian Satanists." She listened again. "I think it's near Russia or something. Let me Google it."

She was tapping into her laptop, phone now held in a shrug between her shoulder and ear, when the stained-glass front doors rattled. Through them she saw Herman, arms stacked with boxes, trying to get in. She watched him, making no move to get up. A moment later, Heidi scooted around from behind him and held the door open.

Herman nodded in a way that could be interpreted as a thank-you. That was Herman all over, Cerina thought, her lips tight. Always prickly, never going out of his way to make anybody feel good about herself unless he wanted something from her.

He was talking to Heidi, speaking over his shoulder. "I should just walk these straight to the toilet and give a good flush," he said.

Just what does he have in those boxes? Cerina wondered, curious. "Hold on," she said into the phone, and covered the mouthpiece with her hand. When she spoke she was careful to look straight at Heidi, pretending that Herman wasn't even there.

"Sweetie," she asked, "you need any help?"

"No, we got it," said Heidi.

Fine, they don't need me. I've got better things to do anyway. Cerina nodded and uncovered the phone. "Oh, speaking of bullshit," she said, a little louder now, "I caught that bitch Jessica in a straight-up lie...Yes, sir, right to my face."

She took the photo of the band with the names marked on it and held it out across the desk, shaking it at Heidi as she passed. For a moment, Heidi simply ignored it and then she regarded Cerina with an inquiring look. When the latter nodded vigorously, she took the photo.

"Uh-huh," she said into the phone, beginning to rant now. "Then the nervy bitch tells me she's too sick to babysit my Reggie. No, she wasn't sick…Bitch posted pictures on Facebook of herself doing Jell-O shots at Charley T's…Of *course* I said something. What am I? I'm not her mother…"

She let her voice trail off. Heidi had stopped at the inner doors, had held them open for Herman but still hadn't gone through herself. She was staring at the black-metal musicians. Both of them had put their magazines down and were staring back, still and unblinking. Their gaze was emotionless, but very attentive. Then Heidi put her hand against her forehead and lowered her eyes and a moment later was through the doors.

For a long moment, the musicians continued to stare at the doors, almost as if they were willing her to come back out again. Then they both made a weird gesture, kind of like they were crossing themselves, but with the motions all wrong. *Weirdos*, thought Cerina.

Chapter Thirteen

Whitey was on the far side of the break room, filing CDs on one of the racks. He nodded once at Herman as he entered and then kept on with it. Chip MacDonald was there as well, but standing at a little distance, clearly watching Whitey. Chip's hair, the little of it that was left, was a mess, sticking straight up on the top of his head. *He should just go on home*, thought Herman. *He don't need to be here to watch us; we're old pros. Man's never gonna learn. He's just gonna make Whitey anxious and get himself all worked up in the process.*

He'd just lowered the boxes onto the table when Chip made his move.

"No, no," he said, moving to the rack and plucking out a CD Whitey had just filed. "Rod Stewart goes under S, not R. Can't you understand the concept of filing under last name first?"

Whitey shrugged. "Eh, we hardly ever play that CD. Doesn't really matter."

"That's not the point!" said Chip. "The point is that there's a proper way for things to be done."

Whitey shrugged again, seemingly confused. "But I don't need to find it."

"But what if you did?"

Herman just shook his head. "But I don't."

Chip raised his voice. "What you need to find is none of my concern!"

"Then why are we talking about it?" asked Whitey, genuinely confused.

"Calm it down, Chip my man," said Herman. "No need to start World War Three over a Rod Stewart CD."

Chip turned to him, his finger raised and pointed. "And you," he said. "You're worse than this guy. At least this knuckle dragger *attempts* to file the catalog."

That's what I get for trying to help, thought Herman. *Remind me never to do that again.* He sniffed, raised his nose in the air. "That, my dear fellow, is intern work," he said.

But Chip didn't get the joke. "Need I remind you?" said Chip. "This is a rock station. We don't have interns. You want interns? Go work for a Latino station. They've got all the pesos."

If the boss wanted a fight, Herman would give it to him. "Exactly," he said. "So you can sympathize with my quandary. No interns to do interns' work. It is quite perplexing."

"Ladies, please," said Heidi, rolling her eyes.

Chip turned on her. "And that's another piece of business I want to discuss. Please stop referring to everyone as girls or ladies. People are starting to get the wrong idea."

Heidi plastered a look of mock concern and innocence on her face. "Wait, what people? What idea?"

"That we are all…" Chip stopped, perplexed at how to continue. "Fancy…," he said, and then shook his head. "No, just drop it."

"Fancy?" said Heidi, her eyes wide. Herman couldn't help but grin. Chip should have seen it coming, he thought. But even when Chip saw it right there on the sidewalk, he couldn't help but step right smack in it. Had to almost feel sorry for the guy. Heidi looked left and right and then came a step closer to Chip, her hand cupped to her mouth. She said in a stage whisper, "You mean homosexual?"

"I…," said Chip. "Look," he said. "Let's just drop it. It's just confusing, is all."

"You feel a little confused, do you?" said Heidi. "Having thoughts and feelings that you're not quite sure your pastor would approve of?"

"I, no," said Chip, beginning to blush. "I'm not..."

"It's okay, Chip," she said, patting his cheek. "We'll still love you whether you're in the closet or out of it."

Okay, thought Herman, *good enough.* She'd started out teasing and fun, but it was turning a little mean. If she kept it up, Chip wouldn't know if he was coming or going. And then he wouldn't be much help with the show. "Hey," he said, breaking in. "What's with the Groovy Ghoulies in the lobby?"

Chip turned toward him, relieved to have something else to discuss. He smiled, tried his best to be hip. "Those strapping young vampires are your first guests," he said.

Herman smiled. He began to dance, a bumbling off-kilter softshoe, and then to sing in a deep, off-key voice: "The freaks come out at night, the freaks, the freaks, here they come."

"Be nice," said Heidi.

Be nice? he thought. *Girl, you probably should take your own advice.* But Chip seemed already to have forgotten about his ribbing and was going back to business as usual, watching Whitey out of one corner of his eye, waiting for him to misfile another CD.

Chapter Fourteen

At first something seemed to be wrong with the video. When they started it, the monitor stayed black and there was no music to be heard.

"There seems to be a problem," Heidi said, and reached out to restart the DVD. "Technical difficulties," she said into the mike. "Nothing we can't handle. Banter, guys."

"Um, did you guys give us some sort of foreign-coded DVD? PAL or whatever?" asked Whitey.

"There is no problem," said Count Gorgann, in a falsely deep voice and with a heavy Norwegian accent.

"But I'm not seeing anything but darkness," said Heidi. "And there's no music."

"Yes," said Count Gorgann. "This is it exactly. Darkness. And silence."

"So let me get this straight, man," said Herman. "You recorded darkness and silence. Kind of like John Cage."

"Who is this caged man named John?" asked Count Gorgann.

"Yes," said Dr. Butcher. He had a similar accent, slightly less thick. "Exactly like John Cage, if John Cage was a worshipper of Satan."

"Okayyy," said Herman. "Whitey? Anything to add? Or should we sit here watching darkness and listening to silence?"

"I got nothing," said Whitey.

"Heidi? What you got for me?"

"You want me to start this thing up again or not?" asked Heidi.

"It is the darkness and silence of the infernal regions," said Count Gorgann, matter-of-factly.

"Is it now?" said Herman. "Sounds cozy."

Whitey laughed.

"Real funny," said Herman. "We got anything else of theirs to play, Heidi?"

"This is it," said Heidi. "I think their production company was supposed to send something, but nothing has arrived. We only have this DVD because they brought it."

"Excuse me, it is not only the darkness and silence of the infernal regions," said Dr. Butcher. "First, it is such silence, to set the tone, and then we deploy our instruments to capture the torments of the damned."

"So there's music," said Herman. "Eventually."

"Yes," said Count Gorgann. "It is so."

"Well, why didn't you say so?" said Herman. "Heidi, roll tape."

"You got it," said Heidi.

The video started up again. At first, again, there was only the darkness and silence. "How long does this part last?" asked Whitey.

"Shhh," said Count Gorgann. "You must listen."

Whitey tried hard to repress his laughter.

"I think I see something," claimed Heidi. Count Gorgann tried to shush her. On the monitor, the darkness was still there, but it had become a little more variegated. Vague shapes were beginning to appear. Then the music began.

At first it started as a single highly distorted note on a lone bass guitar, strummed over and over until it began to seem like a kind of drone. Then a second bass joined in, and a third, the three of them riffing off one another, punctuated by the aggressive thumps of a bass drum. Each time the hammer struck the bass drum, a flash of light came. These left the stage for the most part veiled in darkness, with brief images captured on the video here and there. Glimpses of the band members flashed on one by one, a drifting smoke rising and obscuring them, even when the lights were on them. They were dressed in black, their faces dead white, spikes sprouting not only from their bodies but from their guitars as well. The music was almost thrashy, very fast and discordant, and the singer sounded like he'd been possessed by the devil. The words were sometimes in Norwegian, sometimes in an English that was badly enough pronounced to be almost incomprehensible.

And then suddenly the stage disappeared, to be replaced by news footage of a church burning. The music continued.

"What's this?" asked Herman. "Video's over? New video?"

"History of the struggle," said Dr. Butcher. "Now please be quiet."

Herman raised his hands in mock surrender.

The footage suddenly cut out, going back to the concert again. The singer had run the spikes on his wrist along his side until he started to bleed. *Watered down Stooges*, thought Heidi dismissively. Then it was back to the burning church. Or another burning church, she realized, not the same one. What was the story there? she wondered. She remembered vaguely a controversy in the nineties surrounding the burning of a series of churches in Norway, and the assumption that it had been tied to black metal, maybe even had been done by members of a black-metal band, but she couldn't remember the band's name and she wasn't really sure what the whole story had been. Herman had said something about it on the way over, but she hadn't really been listening. She'd failed to do her homework for the interview, and there'd never been any question of Whitey doing much—he did better just playing off of whatever Herman said, harassing him mildly. Which meant Herman would have to carry them.

When they shifted back to the concert again, the lead singer's demonic singing had deteriorated into a series of screams. Heidi winced. The lights flashed on and off faster and faster as the music crescendoed into something that Heidi did have to admit sounded like what she imagined the shrieking of the damned would sound like.

And then with a burst of fire, the stage lit up all at once and all four members of the band were finally revealed, their faces now dripping with what looked like blood. The last chord was cut off abruptly, and the stage was plunged into darkness again, leaving Heidi unsure whether the video had ended or if they'd run through the end of the recorded tape.

"That's it?" said Herman. "We're done now."

"Again there is silence and darkness," said Count Gorgann. "We have returned to the primordial chaos."

"So wait," said Herman. "Is the song over or not?"

Count Gorgann shrugged.

"I think it's over," said Heidi. "For us, anyway."

Herman shook his head. "I'm with you, girl," he said. "If you're just tuning in, we are here with Leviathan the Fleeing Serpent and the song you just heard and we just saw was 'Crushing the Ritual.'" He turned to Count Gorgann. "I must admit, I'm a little..."

Whitey pretended to cough. "Old," he said.

"...more into the classics," said Herman, giving Whitey a dirty look. "Led Zeppelin, Motörhead, Black Sabbath, that sort of thing when it comes to heavy stuff. So I don't exactly understand your music, but I do understand your passion. I see the passion...I get the passion. Can you explain the philosophy behind your music?"

"Yes," said Count Gorgann, in his heavy accent. He leaned his elbows on the table and tented his fingers, a posture that clashed oddly with his makeup and manner of dress. "It is very simple," he claimed. "Our philosophy is to expose the lies of the whores of Christianity and Jesus, the true bringers of death. We believe this way of life should be erased from the earth. More souls have been lost because of this war...God's war. We fight this in our music."

Herman looked like he'd swallowed something that tasted awful. "Whoa, all right," he said. He glanced down at the handful of notes he'd brought. Heidi could see they were largely Internet printouts, most of them from the band's own Web page. "So, are you for or against the church burnings that were taking place in Norway back in the early nineties?"

Dr. Butcher leaned forward. "We believe all churches should end in smoldering ashes," he said.

"You do?" said Herman. "Really?"

"We are not of the cowering flock," he said, his voice thick with contempt. "We are not the crying sheep of God. We are the mighty goat."

"But we can agree that you're a farm animal?" asked Whitey.

"Pardon me?" asked Count Gorgann.

Herman looked flabbergasted, unsure of what to ask next.

"The goat," said Heidi, trying to help Herman out. "That's interesting. Why the goat? What makes the goat different from the sheep?" *Do I really want to know?* she wondered.

"The goat has free will," said Count Gorgann, smiling his bloody smile. "For this reason, he will always be punished by the oppressor God…God must die. God is the unholy pig. We serve the butcher."

Wow, sheep, goats, and pigs, too, thought Heidi. *Pretty soon we'll have a whole barnyard. And wait, why would the goat gang up with the butcher? How did people get like this?* she wondered. *What made them go wrong?* If they just reeled time back a decade or so and stripped away the body paint, would they see innocent, ordinary kids, like her and Griff in high school? She saw Whitey smiling, preparing to make some joke, and motioned him off. No need to get the two black-metal guys ranting any more than they already were.

She looked to Herman, waiting for him to pick the interview up, but he was staring over the heads of the band members and at the window of the booth. She followed his gaze, saw Chip standing there looking even more frazzled than before, his remaining hair on end, drawing his finger repeatedly across his throat in an effort to get them to stop the interview. *Yeah, figures,* thought Heidi. *Talk of burning churches and killing God isn't likely to go down well with our sponsors.*

Herman gave a brief nod to Chip. "Okay, well," he said. "There you have it. Again the band is Leviathan and the Fleeing Serpent and the album is called 'Possessed by the Master's War with the Knights of Korgaron.' Any particular track you want us to hear?"

"Track four...," said Dr. Butcher. "'Cleansing the Skin of the False God.'"

"Okay, track four it is," said Herman. "I know you have to head over to sound check, so thanks for coming in and good luck with the show."

Whitey queued up the DVD to track four and it started again. At first there was only silence. Heidi glanced at the screen; again everything was black. Maybe they always started with darkness and silence, she thought. And then death metal started pouring into her headphones, even more frenetic than before. Herman, she saw, was wincing. He didn't keep the headphones on for long.

Chip was already opening the door and ushering the pair of ghouls out of the studio before they could do any more damage. He was nodding and smiling, telling them how much he appreciated them coming and he was so sorry they had to go so soon.

"But we don't have to go yet," said Count Gorgann. "We are happy to stay and speak more of the goat."

Chip just politely ignored him and moved them down the hall and out until they were gone. It was something that Chip was surprisingly good at, considering how easily he stuck his foot in his mouth on other occasions. Heidi took her headphones off, looked at Herman. Behind them, Whitey was still listening and watching the video, rocking his head slightly up and down.

"What was that all about?" asked Herman. "That what passes for music these days?"

Heidi shrugged. She hadn't liked the ghouls any more than Herman did. There was something about them, Dr. Butcher especially, that was creepy. Not white-makeup creepy but much more serious than that, something deep and dark and mangled. Why had they been staring at her the whole time? Or had she just been imagining it?

"What happened to the good old days?" asked Herman. "I remember this one time, Marc Bolan was here, must have been just a year or two before his death, back when I was first at the station. All of T-Rex was here, in fact. They must have—"

"Track's nearly over, dude," said Whitey from behind them.

Heidi put her headphones back on again and was surrounded again by the screams of Leviathan and the Fleeing Serpent. She tried to ignore it, ready to go on with the rest of the show.

Chapter Fifteen

It was late now, the Big H shift winding to a close. Cerina sighed. Hardly made any sense for her to wait around until the shift ended; nobody ever came in this late, but that was the way Chip wanted it. And what did she care? She was getting paid, wasn't she, and paid basically to do nothing.

She was flipping her way through the latest *Cosmo*. Not really her thing, but hell, someone had left it in the reception area and it was something to do, better than the *Highlights* the ghouls had been leafing through. After they'd left she'd gone through the issues of *Highlights* to make sure they hadn't left satanic messages for children to find later, but no, they were clean. At least there was that. She shivered. She was glad to have them out of her hair. Couldn't hardly focus with them staring at her.

The reception area was empty and quiet. Sometimes at night it felt almost a little too quiet, but tonight the problem was different. She kept hearing things, a noise, a rustling here and there, nothing she could quite put her finger on, but it made her jumpy.

When the phone rang, she nearly fell out of her chair. It was the babysitter telling her that her son had said that it was okay with her to order the sports package.

"Say what?" said Cerina.

"The sports package," the sitter said. "He said just go on and order it up. I thought I better call you first. But that boy, he definitely loves his hockey."

She felt herself getting angry. "I don't care how much he loves it," she said. "I am a working mother and I work my nails to the bone and I am *not* paying extra for the sports package. My goddamn cable bill is high enough. You should know better."

"What about HBO?" said the babysitter. "He told me to add that on, too."

"It's already on," said Cerina.

"So I should get rid of it?" asked the sitter.

"Oh no, HBO stays," she said. "You know I love my *True Blood*."

"*True Blood*," said the sitter. "That's hardly a vampire show at all. It's more a show about men taking their shirts off."

She sighed. "I know...I know," she said. "It's all garbage anyway. I don't even know why I own a TV."

A moment later she had hung up the telephone. *Sports package,* she thought, shaking her head. *Any babysitter worth her salt would have known better.*

She had flipped to the end of the magazine while on the phone. She was turning it back to the beginning again when she caught something out of the corner of her eye and realized that there, on the edge of the reception desk, was an antique wooden box.

Now where did that come from? she wondered. It hadn't been there a few minutes ago, and she'd been at her desk all night. She hadn't heard anyone come in or go out, and she hadn't seen anyone. Didn't make any sense that it would be there at all, and yet there it was. *Weird,* she thought.

There was a note on top of it, which she moved aside for a closer look at the box itself. Carved into the lid was a strange symbol. A circle, in the center of which was a cross, the head of it surmounted by a U to form an empty horned head. At the bottom was an upside-down U, the tail of the cross splitting its center. It looked like a humanoid figure, the kind of thing you might find on the wall of a cave. In addition, at the extremes to either side of the crosspiece were two dots, which gave the symbol the appearance also of being a strange face. So either a crude figure within a circle or a face or both.

Weird, thought Cerina. Probably some publicity stunt by some band, but how they smuggled it in without her seeing it, damned if she knew.

She picked up the note, opened it. It was written in old-timey script, long spidery letters. *For Adelheid Elizabeth Hawthorne*, it read. *From THE LORDS.*

But how did it get here? she wondered.

Easy enough to figure out, she decided, and used her laptop to access the station's security cameras. There was one in the reception area that showed most of the room, including the desk. All she had to do was take it back a few minutes and all would be revealed.

And why not? She didn't have anything better to do. It wasn't like she didn't have time to spare.

She went to the digital files and ran them back a few minutes, to a place where there was no box on the desk, and then watched. No box, no box, no box, and then suddenly a box. She must have blinked, must have missed it. She took it back again, and watched it slower this time, making sure she was paying attention, but again the same thing happened. The box wasn't there and then, suddenly, and inexplicably, it was.

She watched it frame by frame. Same thing.

That's impossible, she told herself. And then began to justify it. *Somehow the digital file has a flaw in it, skipped over a bit of time. I'm just not getting the whole story.* But there was nothing about the image to suggest that that was the case, no flash or cut or break to indicate a time shift.

It creeped her out a lot, particularly coming as it did on the tail of those two ghouls. It was as if the box had simply appeared out of thin air. *No,* she told herself firmly. *There's always an explanation, even if I don't know what it is.* It was ridiculous to think the box could have come out of nowhere.

She looked at the card again. *Adelheid Elizabeth Hawthorne.* Must be for Heidi. *Oh well,* she thought, *not my problem,* and made a conscious effort to go back to her magazine.

Chapter Sixteen

Herman sighed. It had been a long shift, and what they'd been given to work with made it seem longer. First the ghouls from that death metal band show up and start spouting nonsense about the goat. The goat, what was that? And then Chip ushering them out only to come back later and lecture them. *Wasn't my fault*, Herman had started to say. *I didn't set up the interview. You or one of the publicity people did.* But that wasn't what Chip was saying. He wasn't accusing them of setting up the interview, only telling them that any time somebody started going off about Satan or destroying God or burning churches they should have the good sense to pull the plug on the interview.

"If I hadn't been here," he said, "who knows how long it would have gone on?"

Herman sighed. Just one more reason for Chip to feel like he had to micromanage everything and everyone. "Wasn't my fault," Herman said again.

"This is Salem," Chip had said. "The whole town makes a living by making historical witch burnings interesting and using them as an excuse for fun T-shirts that say things like *My Other Car Is a Broom.* But that only works because people think of witches as being in the past and maybe even as not being real. If people start feeling that devil worship is too close, things get very bad."

"How bad?" asked Whitey.

"We lose sponsors," said Chip.

"Always comes down to sponsors," said Herman.

"Well, yes," said Chip, adjusting his glasses. "I'm afraid it does."

"What I'm here for is the music," said Herman.

"Well, so am I," said Chip, nodding. "I like music, too. It's just that we also have economic—"

"Track's ending," said Whitey. "Out of the booth, Chip. We've got work to do."

But after that band, Leviathan and whatever the fuck they were, and Chip's mini-lecture, they'd never quite caught their rhythm. Which made the night drag on a lot longer than it should have. Plus, there was the Fantastic Film Fest to push, and Chip there periodically at the glass holding up a scrawled sign to remind them to mention it.

Which was what Heidi, with the show coming to an end, was doing right now, even managing to sound enthusiastic about it.

"And don't forget Thursday night at the Cabot Theater," she said in that throaty voice of hers. He'd always been told that hot radio voices never had a beautiful body to go along with them, but Heidi proved that theory dead wrong. "WXKB's Fantastic Film Fest continues with a special midnight screening of *Frankenstein versus the Witchfinder*."

The what? Herman thought. Just when you think you've seen all the Frankenstein movies, a new one surfaces.

Whitey, working the board, played a quick audio clip from the film.

"I curse the day you came to this village, devil Frankenstein!" cried a man's voice.

"Please tell me this is based on historical fact," said Heidi.

Whitey began to read off the film's publicity page. "The year is 1645. Matthew Hopkins, an opportunist witchfinder and his dwarf assistant, Carlo—"

"Carlo?" interrupted Heidi.

"Yes, Carlo," said Whitey. *Must be an Italian dwarf assistant,* thought Herman. Whitey continued. "Hopkins and his dwarf assistant, Carlo, visit village after village, brutally torturing confessions out of suspected witches...that is, until they come face-to-face..."

He stopped and fumbled at the board until he found a music cue, a few ominous notes.

"...with the Frankenstein monster."

"Other than Carlo, it sounds amazing," said Heidi.

"What's wrong with Carlo?" asked Whitey.

"No fighting, you two," said Herman, "or I'll have to make one of you ride in the front seat with me."

"Are we there yet? Are we there yet? Are we there yet?" said Heidi.

"We won't get there any faster if you keep asking," said Herman.

"Are we done yet?" asked Whitey. Herman looked over at him. He was feeling it, too, ready to cut and run.

"I know I am," said Heidi.

"Oh God yes," said Herman. "Let's get the eff out of here."

"Language," said Heidi, shaking her finger and smiling. "The FFA has a big jar and they fill it with money every time someone like you swears."

"I said eff, didn't I?" said Herman. "I didn't say—"

"It's Monday," said Heidi quickly, "so you know what that means...ladies' choice...in other words..."

"Rush," said Herman and Whitey together, in an exhausted voice. And with that Whitey started up "The Spirit of Radio" and the show ended.

They filed out. Bill Ambler, the lone guy who took the post-midnight shift and who knew more about music than everybody else in the station combined, stepped to one side and huddled near the door as they made their way out.

"Any issues?" he asked.

"Nope," said Whitey. "Board's working fine."

"You should be fine," said Herman, "as long as two Norwegian black-metal dudes don't mistake the radio station for a church and burn it to the ground."

Ambler looked confused. "What?" he said. "Is there something I should know?"

"It's a joke, Bill," said Heidi. "Don't worry about it."

Ambler looked confused a moment more, then nodded briskly, started to arrange his things.

A moment later and the Big H team was in the break room, starting to relax. Heidi stretched. Whitey sat down and put his feet on the table. Chip would hate it if he saw him doing that, thought Herman, but didn't worry about it long. Instead, he went after the bottle of wine he'd hidden earlier, found the corkscrew, and began to open it.

"Not our best show," he said.

"Not every show can be our best show," said Whitey. "If that happened, one day we'd literally just spontaneously combust."

"Like a drummer," said Heidi.

"Like a drummer," said Whitey, and smiled.

What are they talking about? wondered Herman, not for the first time. The cork came out with a ripe pop. Now all he needed was something to pour the wine into. He looked in the cabinets but all he could find were coffee cups. They'd have to do.

"I hate to admit it," said Heidi, "but those two kind of freaked me the fuck out."

"Eh, weird accents always make shit like that sound more intense. If I said that crap you'd laugh at me." Whitey cleared his throat, tried on a Norwegian accent. "I murder in the name of Satan's goat."

"I thought Satan had a dog," Heidi said.

"Yes, he has a dog as well," said Whitey. "His name is Cujo. But I do not murder in the name of Satan's dog. I murder in the name of Satan's goat."

"And what's his name?" asked Heidi.

"His name is Ralph," said Whitey.

"Satan's goat is named Ralph?"

Whitey shrugged. "Sure, why not?" he said. "Gotta be named something."

Herman poured the wine into the coffee mugs, half a mug for Heidi and Whitey but almost full for the mug he'd kept for himself. After all, he'd been the one to buy it. He should get something for his money.

"God-hating motherfuckers is what that was all about," he stated.

"You don't think it was just an act?" asked Heidi.

"Nope," said Herman. "Now Alice Cooper, that's an act, and a damned good one. But those two drank the Devil's Kool-Aid, fo' sure. Like that other metal band. What're they called again?"

Heidi stared blankly at him.

"You know, the cannibals," said Herman.

"Mayhem," said Whitey, staring down at the table.

"What'd they do?" asked Heidi.

"They were always talking about cannibalism," said Whitey, "pushing it as a good idea. And then one band member killed himself and maybe one of the others, well..."

"Ate him?" asked Heidi, her eyes wide.

"I don't think so," said Whitey. "Or not much of him anyway."

"I think he made a stew out of his brains," said Herman.

"You're joking," said Heidi. She looked shaken.

"I think that's just a rumor," said Whitey. "Nobody ever proved it."

"Yeah, they definitely drank the Devil's Kool-Aid," said Herman. "Speaking of Kool-Aid, who's in?" He held up the cups.

Whitey yawned. "Always thirsty for dinner," he said.

"Hand it over," said Heidi.

"A team that drinks together stays together," said Herman. He passed out the cups of wine.

He'd just settled down and begun to drink when Chip stuck his head through the door. When Herman and the others ignored him, he rapped on the wall to get their attention.

"Drinking at work again, I see," he said. When nobody chose to answer and Herman didn't rush to offer him a mug of his own, he turned to Whitey. "So, we're good for tomorrow, I take it?"

"Good for what?" asked Whitey.

Chip looked startled. "Please tell me he's fucking with me," he said. He turned to Heidi. "He's fucking with me, right?" Heidi just shrugged.

He turned back to Whitey. "Francis Matthias...," he said, and waited. Whitey's face remained blank. "The witch book guy..."

Whitey shook his head. "No clue," he said.

"What do you mean no clue?"

"Dude, you've lost me."

"For the Fantastic Fest promotion," said Chip, and motioned with his hand for Whitey to pick up the thread.

But Whitey just continued to look blank. Chip's expectant face slowly took on a frown.

"You son of a bitch," he said. "You forgot to book him." He grabbed his head with both hands. "No, it's even worse," he said. "You forgot I even told you to book him. I knew it! You're the one always screaming, 'Let me book some talent. Give me some responsibility!' Jesus!"

Whitey had brought his feet down off the table, was squirming awkwardly in his chair. He started making excuses. "I was gonna... I just had to...this thing came up and..."

"Oh, Whitey," said Heidi.

Herman took a sip of his wine, trying to keep from smiling.

"Fantastic Fest is important to me," Chip said. "I need asses in seats or I can kiss it good-bye. I need gimmicks to promote! That is why I asked you to go down to the book signing and book him in person. 'No prob,' you said. 'You can count on me.'"

"That doesn't sound like something I'd say," said Whitey. "I don't remember any of this."

And then Herman could see that Chip was really going to blow.

Enough fun and games, he thought. "Don't worry," he said. "I already booked him."

"You did?" said Chip. He shook his head. "Why do you cover for this fool?"

Herman shrugged. "It's what I do," he said. "And you're damn lucky it is. What, no 'Thanks, Herman. I couldn't live without you'?"

Chip gave a little cry of frustration and stormed out.

Herman took a sip of wine and waited. Once he was sure Chip wasn't coming back, he turned to Whitey, gave him a hard look. "You know how he gets with that film festival shit," he said. "You owe me, man."

Whitey shrugged, already returning to his usual lackadaisical self. "What else is new?"

They drank their mugs dry and then clanked them against the table like convicts until Herman sighed and got up and brought them some more. As usual, he took more for himself, but Heidi didn't care; he was the one, after all, who always bought the wine. And he was older, so maybe he needed it more. And as she'd proven last night, maybe she didn't need any at all.

She was sipping from her mug, letting her gaze drift around the familiar break room, when she saw it. Something wooden, the wood lacquered but somewhat distressed, had been crammed into her mail slot, on top of some magazines and other mail. An old box of some kind. Where had *that* come from?

"What's that?" she asked, and pointed.

"What?" asked Herman. "Where you pointing?"

"The mail slots," said Whitey, in a way that made it hard for Heidi to decide if he was joking or serious. "They've always been there."

She stood up and went over to the slot, grabbed the box. It was antique, or at least had been made to look like it was. Crazy the things a band would do to get noticed. A folded note was taped to it, and on the top of the box was a symbol. A rough circle, a small upturned half circle within its top and a small downturned half circle in its bottom half, the two connected by a line that was in turn cut across by another line with a dot at either end of it. *Pretty cool*, she thought. *Blixa Bargeld would be proud.*

"Check this out," she said, bringing it back to the table.

"Cool promo," said Whitey. "Who is it?"

Heidi plucked the note off the box's lid, read it. "Some band called the Lords, I guess," she said.

"Never heard of them," said Herman.

"That's because they're not from the seventies," said Whitey.

"Ha-ha," said Herman. "Very funny."

Heidi looked for a way to open the box. She could tell the lid from the rest of the box by a shift in the grain of the wood, but there were no hinges, no hasp either. Maybe it wasn't locked at all. She tried to push it up with her fingers but something held it closed, some hidden latch.

"Let me try," said Whitey.

"I got it," said Heidi, slapping his hand away. She ran her fingers along the line of the lid, looking for something, not quite sure what. Other than the symbol on the top of the lid the box was unadorned, with no marks or carvings of any kind. It really did look antique—whoever had put the promo box together had done a great job of making it look distressed, as if it had been buried for a few hundred years and was just now being seen again for the first time. It even smelled old, and the groove of the wood grain had turned gray in places from what looked like dust.

But what was the point of having a promo that nobody could figure out how to open? Heidi wondered why she should bother, why she shouldn't just throw it in the trash. The band probably wasn't all that good anyway—they seldom were. Herman and Whitey were already starting to lose interest, might even have left the table if there hadn't still been wine to drink.

She let her finger trace the symbol on the lid and then, on a whim, placed a finger on each of the two dots at the end of the crosspiece. Something clicked and the lid of the box came suddenly loose.

"Cool trick," said Herman.

She carefully worked the lid off and set it to one side. Inside was a record. She cradled it by its edge and lifted it out. It was black and oddly heavy, and when she looked at it from the side it seemed strangely thick. She saw Herman staring at her with a skeptical look.

"Sure as shit...it's shit," he said. He drained off what was left in his mug and poured some more.

"Just for that I'm going to take it home and give it a listen," said Heidi. She lifted it back into the box and placed the lid back on. It clicked into place and once again the lid was latched on, the box impossible to open without pressing on the dots. Then she shoved it into her messenger bag. *Should I really bother?* she wondered.

Herman raised his glass in a toast. "Here's to you discovering the next Earth, Wind, and Fire," he said.

Just for that, I will bother, thought Heidi. *And if it's good, I'll figure out some way to tell Herman "I told you so."*

"You got to update your references, dude," said Whitey.

Herman stared at him with narrowed eyes. "I don't have to do nothing," he said. He stared back without blinking. They held the look until it was too much and they both burst out laughing. Herman got up and opened another bottle.

By the time they were walking out of the station, all three of them were pretty loaded. Heidi was carrying the bottle and drinking straight from it. Outside it was dark. The air, which had been crisp before, was now windy and freezing. Herman shivered.

"Goddamn!" he said, fumbling at his coat's zipper. "It's fucking witchy titty cold out here. Man, I hate this time of year." Still unable to get the zipper to go, he wrapped his coat tighter around his body and crossed his arms over it. "Anyone care for a lift?" he asked.

"My head is spinning," said Heidi. "If I get into a car, I think I just might puke."

"All the more reason to get in Herman's car," said Whitey.

"Real funny," said Herman. He bowed. "Enjoy the walk. The fresh air will do you right. Good for the lungs, I hear. Not that I'd know from experience."

"Thanks," said Heidi. She took a drink from the bottle and then passed it along to Whitey. Whitey drank as well, wiping his mouth dry with his sleeve after.

"I'll walk with you," he said.

Heidi smiled. She stumbled a little, rested her palm lightly on Whitey's chest. "All right," she said. "Probably a good idea."

"Well, la-dee-fucking-da," said Herman. "I'm freezing. This gentleman is going to try and get home to the warden without racking up another DWS. If you know what I mean."

"Yeah," said Whitey, turning toward him. "You mean DWI."

"Naw, DWS," said Herman. "Driving while sexy." He thrust his head back and gave a James Brown shriek. Spinning around, he soft-shoed off toward his car. How he could manage to do that after having had so much to drink, Heidi wasn't sure.

"Good luck," called Heidi after him.

"See you suckers later," said Herman. Then he shouted, "Fuck, it's cold!" and jumped into his car.

Whitey and Heidi watched him drive off and then they started walking toward Heidi's place. For a while they walked in silence, trying not to shiver in the cold.

Whitey was the first to break the silence. "You think Herman's wife knows he calls her the warden?" he asked.

"No way," said Heidi. "And he doesn't mean it. He's a pussy cat around her."

They walked along again in silence. The wind was blustery, sending the autumn leaves skittering across the empty street and over the sidewalk in front of them. Heidi shivered, concentrated on walking straight. She'd had a lot to drink, as usual, but not as much as the night before. *I'll probably be okay,* she thought, *as long as I don't keep on drinking once I get back to the house.* She wrapped her faux fur coat tighter around herself, snuck a glance at Whitey. His forehead was wrinkled, as if he was trying to think of something to say.

They stopped at the steps of Heidi's building. Heidi reached out and grabbed his arm. In a pretend flirty voice, she said, "You want to come up and see what's cooking in my kitchen?"

"Really?" said Whitey.

From the overexcited way that he said it, she knew she'd stepped wrong. He apparently couldn't read the difference between flirty and pretend flirty.

"Really?" she said back, imitating his tone. She rolled her eyes. "I didn't mean come up so I can suck your dick in the kitchen. I mean come up so I can make us some pancakes or something."

"I knew that," Whitey pretended, back to his old non-eager self, but still not quite meeting her eyes. He looked at his watch. "Hmmm? It's getting pretty late," he said.

Can't let him go home with his feelings hurt, thought Heidi. "Come on," she said. "You got something better waiting than pancakes?"

If it'd been Herman, he would have figured out how to turn that one into a joke, but Whitey didn't. Maybe they both had had too much to drink. "Ya know," he said, "the sad thing is...I never have any place better to be."

Heidi nodded. "Exactly," she said. "So what's stopping you?"

He looked at his watch again and then shook his head and smiled, followed her in. Things were back to normal, Heidi thought. Well, if normal was what they'd actually been before.

They were inside and on the inner stairs leading up to her apartment when a door on the first floor opened. *Fuck,* thought Heidi, *we've woken the landlady up.* She kept walking. From behind her, she heard Lacy call her name.

She turned, putting on her nice company face, trying not to look too drunk. Whitey hesitated a moment, but turned with her. Lacy was standing there, still wearing that same batik wrap, her hair no longer loose now but instead gathered in a ponytail.

"Hi, Lacy," Heidi said. "Sorry if we woke you up. I'll try to be quieter next time."

Lacy just shook her head and smiled. "I'm a night owl," she said. "You didn't wake me."

Then what does she want? Heidi came down a few stairs, lifted her eyebrows expectantly.

"So, I took a look at five," Lacy said.

"Yeah?" said Heidi. "And?"

"And everything looked just as expected," said Lacy. She came a little farther into the hall, to the very base of the stairs. "Dusty as hell and full of cobwebs," she said, "but normal. No sign of any intruders...alien or otherwise." She smiled.

What? thought Heidi. *But I saw the door open, and there was someone there. I know it.*

"I'm positively sure I saw somebody standing in the doorway," she said. "My eyes are bad, but I'm not blind."

Lacy shrugged. "I'm sorry, honey," she said. "I don't see how it's possible. The place was locked tight and I have the only set of keys. And even the dust on the floor hadn't been disturbed. I'm afraid nobody was there."

"Wow," said Heidi. She thought for a moment. Could she have imagined it? Maybe. She'd been hungover, after all. Or could there be someone there but for some reason Lacy didn't want her to know about it? No, that was crazy—Lacy was a nice old hippy lady. She didn't have any reason to hide someone and then lie about it. What reason could there even be to do so? She shook her head. "Okay, well, I guess I'm seeing things...again," she said. She smiled, turning it into a joke, but was worried that Lacy would see the fear in her eyes. "It's been a while since I've had that problem."

Lacy nodded and smiled back. She crossed her arms over her chest. "It happens to the best of us," she claimed.

But Heidi felt less sure than she sounded, and she knew she didn't sound all that sure. Something weird was going on, maybe inside of her. "Yeah, I guess," she said. She turned to start up the stairs again, saw Whitey hovering above her. *Almost forgot*, she thought. "Lacy," she said. "I should introduce you. This is White Herman. He 'works' at the radio station with me." She made artificial quotes with her fingers as she spoke the word *works*.

"White Herman?" she said. "What kind of name is that? Some weird family thing?"

Whitey came down a few steps and held out his hand to her. She took it and shook it briefly. "Well," he said, "we have two Hermans on the Big H team and the other is an African American guy. We kind of figured that Black Herman sounded a bit...you know." Heidi had to stop herself from feigning innocence and saying, *What? No, I don't know.* But it wasn't a good idea to do that in front of her landlady, particularly when she was drunk. Whitey continued: "Most people just call me Whitey," he said.

Lacy nodded. "Nice to meet you, Whitey. Good night," she said, but made no move to go back into her apartment.

"Good night," said Heidi. She turned and headed with Whitey up the stairs. When she reached the top, she looked back. Lacy was still there, at the bottom. She seemed to be watching them closely. Heidi waved once, but Lacy didn't wave back, nor did she look away. *What's wrong with people today?* she wondered. And then shaking her head she went to unlock her apartment door.

Chapter Seventeen

Whitey tried to take the apartment in. It was both like he'd expected it to be and different from what he'd imagined. It felt like Heidi all the way through—same kind of eclectic mix of objects and items that he would have guessed, considering the way the girl dressed, same sorts of things dragged in from thrift stores, but not just anything. She'd been pretty careful about what she'd chosen, but there was a lot of it, and things were scattered pell-mell. There was what looked like some kind of antique fainting couch, the upholstery beginning to fray and wear through so that the stuffing poked out. She'd thrown over that a striped, fringed blanket that looked like it had been picked up from a street vendor in Tijuana. Next to that, on the end table, was a lamp with a hula girl for its base, complete with faux grass skirt—the kind of thing you would find in a bad Hawaiian restaurant called Tiki Joe's or something. The whole apartment was like that, carefully chosen objects that clashed in a way that you couldn't help but like. Or that he, anyway, couldn't help but like. Heidi he couldn't help but like either. She didn't care all that much about what people expected her to look like—she just dressed however she wanted and that was what you got. But that was all right with Whitey.

Everything was jumbled and mixed, except for the milk crates. She had dozens of them, stacked floor to ceiling on either side of the stereo and filled with old records. The stereo setup, too, he had to admire. She wasn't messing around there. It was good-quality gear, great speakers, plus several turntables, a couple of CD players, and a top-of-the-line eight-track tape machine. And the eight-track looked brand new rather than something from a salvage yard. Sure, Whitey had an eight-track, but it was something he'd pulled out of a junked car, and it sat on the floor next to his stereo with wires running every which way. But hers was a home stereo model and didn't look more than a year or two old. *Didn't even know you could still get those,* thought Whitey. Maybe she'd had it for years and just took great care of it. Fuck, hot and knew her electronics, too—that was not only rare: it was downright impossible.

"Where'd you get the eight-track?" he asked.

"Huh?" she said. "My dad."

"Was he a DJ, too?"

She shook her head. "No," she said. "He just liked his music."

"You see him much?" he asked.

"No," she said, her eyes a little absent. "He died."

"Oh," he said. "Sorry."

"It's okay," she said, and gave him a sad smile. "It's been a while now. I'm getting used to it."

She went into the kitchen. After a few minutes of looking the stereo up and down, he started in on the vinyl. Great collection. Lots of stuff he used to have before he dumped his own vinyl, and lots of stuff he wished he still had. Good taste.

"Like what you see?" she asked when she came back from the kitchen. He swallowed, then nodded.

"You are the only chick I've ever met with such a killer rack," he said, gesturing at the stereo, and then wincing when he realized what he'd said.

"What was that about a killer rack?" she asked in her dumb-blonde voice from behind him. If he turned around, she'd probably be standing there with her hips canted and one knee bent like some Miss America contestant. He decided to ignore it.

"Man," he said, continuing to thumb through the albums. "Seeing your collection really makes me miss my vinyl. I can't believe I sold all my shit."

"I warned you," she said.

Well, maybe she did, but that was no reason to lord it over him. "Yeah, well," he said, a little defensively. "I mean, CDs do technically sound better, but they're dead, too."

She came around to where he could see her, gave him an exhausted stare.

"Fuck that." Her voice, too, was exhausted and didn't have much fight to it, but she wasn't going to concede. "You and every other muso miss the point," she said. "Everything sounds the same, but my records only sound like my records. The pops and scratches are my pops and scratches, you know. They belong to me."

"I guess I never really thought about it that way," he said. He sat staring at the albums in front of them. Yeah, she was right. It was like the way your car, as it got older, became even more your car: the key you had to jiggle just right, the window that wouldn't roll down all the way, the ceiling fabric that came loose and brushed your head while you drove—all the little problems that gave it personality. "Fuck," he said. "Now I'm really depressed. I've destroyed my entire musical history. What was I thinking?"

She had gone back into the kitchen. He cast a glance over his shoulder, saw her flip a pancake.

"You weren't thinking," she claimed. "Just walking off the cliff with all the other lemmings." Then she laughed. "Don't worry, these will make you forget your troubles."

Whitey shook his head. "I doubt it," he said. Though it was true, the smell of the pancakes was already making his mouth start to water. "Mind if I play something?" he asked.

"Go for it," Heidi said, "but choose wisely."

Choose wisely? Was this a test? "Oh no," he said, shaking a finger at her. "You're going to make some judgment based on my choice, I assume?"

Heidi flipped the pancake out of a pan and onto a plate. "Don't assume," she said.

He couldn't decide if she was serious or joking. That was always the problem. It wasn't like he was a stupid guy, only that when it came to people like Heidi, girls he liked, it was like some switch turned off in his brain and he found himself doubting how he should read them. With Chip it was different—the way that guy thought was just too boring and predictable to follow. His mind rebelled against that. But with Heidi it was probably that he listened too closely and worried he was hearing things that weren't really there.

He flipped through the records, found the Velvet Underground & Nico's self-titled album. Shit, she actually had the early edition, where the banana peel was still a sticker, and the sticker was still on. Not bad. That, and wondering where the pops and scratches would come on Heidi's copy, was enough to convince him to get the record out of the sleeve and put it on one of the turntables, side one up. He started the table spinning and carefully lifted the needle, placing it on track four.

The sound of "Venus in Furs" filled the room. When he turned, Heidi had her wrist balanced on one hip, the spatula balanced loosely in the other hand. She was giving him a wry look.

"What?" he said.

She rolled her eyes. "Nothing," she said.

"Too obvious?" he said. He liked her, so what? It wasn't like he thought playing "Venus in Furs" was likely to get her to invite him into the bedroom.

She shrugged and began to sing along to the record. After a moment, he joined in as well.

Chapter Eighteen

Steve made his appearance as soon as the pancakes were served. How he'd known food was on, and why he hadn't come before when he'd first smelled them, Whitey didn't know. Steve was like that. A much smarter dog than he let on. Kind of freaky, if you thought about it.

But there Steve was, begging bites of pancake until they'd finished their first round and got their second and Heidi told him to go lie down. He did, with a kind of exasperated noise, crawling up onto the fainting couch where he quickly fell asleep. "He's not supposed to be up there," Heidi confided to Whitey, but she let him stay anyway. Considering how unhesitatingly Steve had hopped up there, Whitey would guess that probably happened a lot, that Steve had her wrapped around his little finger. Or whatever it was that dogs had rather than fingers.

"This is one sweet apartment," said Whitey, carving off another bite of pancake. "The rent must be insane."

"Only three hundred bucks a month," said Heidi.

Three hundred bucks? He was paying basically double that for a shit hole. "How is that possible?" said Whitey. "What's the catch?"

Heidi shrugged. "Weird story," she said. "I was walking Steve and ran into my landlady. We got talking, just chatting about nothing really, and she told me she thought she was going to have an apartment open and asked if I was interested. I was perfectly fine where I was, so I told her no, but then she told me how little she wanted and how could I say anything but yes?"

"You couldn't," said Whitey. "Not if you were sane."

"Right," she said. "But she's kind of a freak, too. When we were talking, very first time we met, she grabbed my hand and stroked it like it was an animal or something. For a while she wouldn't let go. I was on the way to getting creeped out when she told me I could have the place for three hundred bucks a month. I couldn't believe it."

Whitey shrugged. "Old ladies have different rules about how long they can hold your hand. My grandma was that way. And for the price, you're just lucky," he said. "That's probably all it is."

Heidi smeared her syrup around her plate with her fork and shrugged. "I think maybe my landlady has the hots for me," she said. "That probably explains it. You saw her. She's kind of got that hippie free-love vibe going on. I mean, she's sweet, but...I don't know."

"My place sucks ass," said Whitey. "I'm paying a fortune for absolutely nothing. My landlord is some asshole Russian guy, Kazmir Yakov...total cunt." He pulled himself straight and tried to imitate his landlord. "Vitey, Vitey, you got my rent? In Ukraine, rent is due when landlord knock on door. If landlord have to knock twice, then KGB knock next."

But Heidi wasn't listening. She wasn't looking at him but at some indefinable space beyond him. "Dead air," she said.

"Huh?" asked Whitey.

"Music," said Heidi.

Oh, right, thought Whitey, *the record ended*. He got up and took the record off the platter, slid it back into its sleeve, and then kneeled down to put it away.

"You manage to file things right over here," said Heidi. "Why can't you do it at the station?"

"What?" asked Whitey. "Oh, here it matters," he said. Inwardly, he winced. What was that supposed to mean? *She must think I'm an idiot.*

He flipped through the closest stack of records, looking for the next thing, his mind wandering. How was he supposed to choose something when she'd make assumptions about him from anything he chose? Heidi's bag was right there as well, leaning against the side of the milk crate. It was half open, the wooden box sticking out of it. *There we go*, he thought. Neither of them had heard it, so it wouldn't say anything about either of them if he chose it.

He put on his landlord's accent again. "How about this? In Ukraine, music always delivered in wooden box. Like dead body."

"Sure, whatever," said Heidi.

Whitey took out the box and tried to open it, but it seemed stuck. He could tell where the lid stopped and the box started, but there didn't seem to be any latch or hook to separate one from the other. How had she done it again? Embarrassed, he pried at it.

"See those two dots in the symbol on top?" said Heidi. "Press them at the same time."

"What for?" asked Whitey, but when she didn't answer, he pressed them. The box clicked and the lid became slightly loose. "Clever," he said. He carefully lifted the lid off, removed the record from inside.

He held its edges against his palms, still speaking in mock-Russian. "Ah, very thick vinyl...strong like bear."

Actually, it *was* unusually thick, and strong, too. He stood and laid the record down on the turntable.

He lifted the needle and set it in place. But as soon as he let go, it immediately slid across the entire record. *What the fuck?* he wondered.

"Whoa, sorry," he said, lifting up the needle and hoping Heidi hadn't been paying too much attention. "Let's try that again."

But when he replaced the needle, the exact same thing happened. He set the needle in place and released it and it fled to the center of the record, as though it were blank. But he could see the grooves, which meant something was pressed on it.

"That's weird," he said, reaching out for the needle again. "The needle keeps jumping to the other side of the..."

But before he could lift the needle, the record began to play, the needle moving slowly backward across the vinyl, from the center toward the rim.

"Huh?" said Heidi. "The other side of the track?"

"Well, I was going to say 'that's weird, the record won't play,' but now it's playing..."

"So what's the problem? Why don't I hear anything?" asked Heidi.

"It's playing backward. Look at this. I've never seen anything like it."

Heidi got up and went over to the stereo.

"What the fuck?" she said. "How is that even possible?"

Whitey just shook his head. "It's not," he said. "The motor doesn't work that way, unless you've made some weird sort of mod on it."

"Why would I do that?"

Whitey shrugged. "I'm just trying to explain it," he said. "I'm not accusing you of anything."

Together they looked down at the needle moving in reverse. No, it shouldn't be able to do that, but there it was, doing it. *Damn*, Whitey couldn't help but think. *This isn't Heidi messing with me somehow, is it?* But she seemed as confused by it as he was.

"I guess it's blank," said Whitey. "I don't hear anything."

"Why would it be blank?"

"I don't know," said Whitey. "Some kind of joke?" He began to reach out for the needle, ready to pluck it off the record.

"Hold up a second," Heidi said. She reached down and cranked the volume all the way up. And then Whitey could hear something, a sort of faint moaning sound. But how Heidi had been able to hear it with the sound turned down to normal levels damned if he knew. Maybe she hadn't been able to hear it and had just made a lucky guess.

It was moaning voices, he was pretty sure, a bunch of them, or the same voice overlaid a bunch of times. It sounded strange, definitely. Gradually the sound grew louder, melding with a rhythmic and repeated booming sound. The booming was repeated three times in succession, followed by a fourth strike at a higher pitch, then repeated again. Together with the moaning it was almost hypnotic, and as Whitey continued to listen he heard something else. What was it, exactly? A kind of crackling noise, like a fire, or like twigs being snapped, but not quite either of those things. And there, far beneath the other sounds, was the strange discordant noise of various primitive instruments, a flute or a kind of pipe, a screeching from some sort of stringed instrument being played wrong, a sound like someone blowing through a long tube, a sound like sand being thrown against an echoing surface: *spat, spat, spat.* It was all pretty chaotic, but it definitely added up to something. Not really a song exactly, more a kind of drone or chant, the music (if it was properly speaking music) wandering and shapeless. But there was a note pattern there, too, if you listened for it, a structure of repetition beyond the rhythmic boom of the drum, but one that seemed to have little interest in resolving itself. There was something there, too—it was hard for him to put his finger on it since so many aspects of the music were so different—that reminded him of the tracks they'd played from Leviathan and the Fleeing Serpent earlier. Maybe a tone? Even just a repeated gesture, something very slight? Very hard to say. But yes, there was definitely a connection. Was it just the fact that both that and this kind of made his skin crawl?

"Man, this is really fucked-up sounding," he said. He looked at Heidi but she didn't say anything, just stared at the turntable. "I'm going to take it off," he said, and when she still didn't say anything, he reached out and lifted the needle.

"We should Smash or Trash it tomorrow and see what happens," he said.

But Heidi still didn't answer. She seemed lost in thought, standing almost like she was paralyzed over the turntable.

He reached out and touched her arm. "Heidi," he said.

"Huh?" she said. She looked up at him, disoriented and a little scared, almost like she didn't know who he was.

"Just for the fuck of it should we Smash or Trash this tomorrow?" Whitey asked.

"Yeah, sure," said Heidi.

He waited for her to go on, but she didn't. "Or not," he said.

Heidi put her hand to her forehead, rubbed her temples. "Whew, I am suddenly really tired," she said.

Maybe he'd outstayed his welcome. Not a good thing to do on his first visit, particularly if he wanted to come back. "Yeah," he said. "I should get the fuck out of here anyway. I've got to walk all the way back to the station to get my car."

"You didn't have to walk me home," said Heidi. "Thanks."

"No problem," he said. "Besides, I got paid in pancakes."

Heidi wasn't playing along, though. She really must have been tired. "You can crash on the couch if you want," she said, but he could tell by the way she said it that she was just being polite.

"Naw," he said. "I should go." She just nodded. Still holding her head, she led the way to the front door and let him out.

Chapter Nineteen

What the fuck was that all about? wondered Heidi. *Did I drink more than I realized?* No, that couldn't be it. She'd been just fine, having a good enough time, eating pancakes and talking with Whitey, listening to music, a little tired, and then suddenly everything had changed. It had been that record, the one by the Lords. Why had the needle done that? It shouldn't have been able to do that.

She massaged her temples. And then when the record started playing, why had Whitey been unable to hear it? It hadn't been loud, true, but even when Whitey was claiming the record was blank, she could *feel* it. Not hear it exactly, but feel it somehow pulling somewhere deep within her body, tugging at her guts. Was that music? It wasn't the way she normally thought about music, but it was true there were songs that felt like they took place inside of you instead of outside. Maybe it was a little like that, but a negative version of that. It didn't feel good exactly. It had made her feel almost nauseous.

But once she'd started to feel it, she'd been unable to stop herself from reaching out and turning up the volume. And then the moans had started and Whitey could hear them, too. But from there, things had gotten strange.

She couldn't remember exactly what the music had been like, simply knew that it was strange. But what she did remember was seeing something. And not simply seeing it—experiencing it almost. There was blood; she remembered that. Blood everywhere, and flashes of bare flesh, but they were so distorted it was hard to see. And that symbol on the box as well, but not carved in wood, instead drawn on flesh in something dark. Maybe paint. Or maybe blood. Or maybe not drawn exactly but cut into the flesh. Hard to say—it all had come in bits and pieces, in flashes, and was hard to put back together again. She groaned. There had been something else, a fire, and women swaying, their bodies naked and grimy, moaning and clutching at one another and—

Maybe I'm getting confused, she thought. *Maybe that fucked-up black-metal video we watched earlier had some subliminal shit in it, and now that I'm tired it's rising in flashes to the surface.* Again, just like earlier that day, she felt the craving for a fix. She pushed it aside. She sighed, again rubbed her temples. *Best thing you could do for yourself,* she thought, *is crash and go to bed.*

Chapter Twenty

The apartment was dark throughout, or almost so, the only light being the television's pulsating blue glow. Heidi lay in bed, trying to fall asleep, half watching the program in spite of herself and despite her own exhaustion.

On-screen, a man in a black hood was discussing his time as a hit man for the Mafia.

"You indicated you used a shotgun," said the interviewer from somewhere off-camera.

When the hit man responded, it was in a digitally distorted voice, unnaturally deep, almost demonic. "Not just any shotgun, a sawed-off," he said. "He was at a red light and I pulled up alongside him and fired both barrels. He never saw the green. I wasn't expecting the blast to tear his head off."

And then, for just a moment, the screen seemed to shift as she watched, flashing strangely, giving her a glimpse of something else. In the place of the hit man she had a brief glimpse of a human skeleton, several holes broken through its skull.

She blinked and it was gone, the shadowed hit man in its place.

She groped for the remote, but couldn't find it. She closed her eyes, tried to trick herself into sleep but it wasn't working. She heard, from the TV, in that same distorted voice: "I expected them to die...But I didn't realize I would grow to enjoy the killings."

She opened her eyes and looked at the TV, but instead of the hooded hit man, she saw a filthy room. Hanging from the ceiling was a wrought-iron cage, crudely made. A chicken had been crammed into it. The creature filled the cage so fully that it was unable to move or turn around. Its feathers bowed against the cage's bars or poked out. Only its head and neck could move. Its head darted desperately around, its movements shaky, its eye darting about. And then suddenly there was a rapid movement, a flash on the screen and the chicken was gone, the cage bent and torn open and half gone, with blood dripping slow down the bars.

Did I change the channel? she wondered. But the voice that was speaking over the image of the cage was that of the interviewer, rambling on. Maybe something was wrong with the TV.

Or maybe something was wrong with her.

And then the camera angle slowly shifted to reveal a strange face very close to the lens. It didn't look quite human. It was oddly colored, almost brick red. *Maybe a trick of the light,* she thought, and then thought, *What the hell is this?* The face smiled and the teeth the open mouth revealed were long and sharp, filed. No, definitely not human. Some sort of network problem where two signals had gotten crossed.

"After a while," said the distorted voice—and strangely enough the demonic mouth on the screen seemed to be moving in time with it, as if it were actually the one saying the words—"I started taking a few liberties. I wasn't killing just for hire. I did that, but I'd also just drive around until I found someone and if it was safe, well, I had my sawed-off handy."

The eyes were red and glowing like two coals. The whole time the voice was talking, these eyes seemed to be staring straight at her. Like they saw her through the TV. It felt like they were trying to suck her in.

Fuck, she thought, *what's wrong with me?* She groaned, searched again for the remote. When she didn't find it, she rolled over and reached for a glass of water on the bedside table. She drank from it, but there was almost nothing in it, just a half a swallow.

"Fuck," she said. Still thirsty, she got out of bed and stumbled to the bathroom, turning the TV off on the way.

The bathroom light nearly blinded her. She stayed still, blinking and staring down, letting her vision adjust, then moved to the sink. She filled her water glass and took a long drink. *Forgot to call my mom,* she realized as she drank. She filled the glass a second time and then exited the bathroom.

But on the way back to the bed, something felt wrong. The space felt different. It *was* different. There was something different that she couldn't quite put her finger on for a moment and then she realized what it was: no dog smell, no dog noises, nobody rubbing up against her leg and asking to be petted when she was on the way back to the bed. Where was Steve?

She whistled but Steve didn't come. She looked around the bedroom and then wandered out into the front part of the apartment. But Steve didn't seem to be there either. And the apartment door was open.

"Aw, man, what the fuck?" she said.

Just to make sure, she went through the apartment again, whispering his name. But he wasn't there. So she threw her faux fur coat over her pajamas and stepped out into the hallway.

Steve was there. He had gotten out somehow, or maybe the door hadn't latched all the way when Whitey had left. He was at the end of the hall, scratching at the door to apartment five.

She leaned out in the hall and hissed at him. "Steve," she whispered, "get over here... Get over here!"

But Steve ignored her. He just kept scratching at the door.

She tried a few more times and then gave up, began tiptoeing down the hall toward her dog.

"What the fuck, man?" she whispered to him once she was there. "You're scratching up the wood. Lacy's going to kill me."

Steve whined and tucked his tail down but wouldn't look away from the door. She bent down next to him and grabbed him by his collar.

"Buddy, how did you get out? Let's go back to bed."

She tugged on his collar and slowly pulled him away from the door. He didn't seem to want to go, and at first braced his legs. But after a while she got him moving. He kept whining, though, all the way back to the apartment.

She was just reaching her own door when she heard something behind her, a slow creaking sound. She turned to see the door to apartment five slowly sliding ajar, finally falling fully open. Was there someone in there after all? Yes, there was definitely a light, dim but there, and pulsating a little, and reddish as well. She couldn't see the source of the light exactly, just the throwback of its glow. The source of the light itself was somewhere deep within the apartment, out of sight.

She stayed staring at the open door for a long while, wondering what to do. After a moment she realized she was still half bent over, still gripping Steve's collar. Steve, though, she realized, was no longer whining. Instead, tail between his legs, he was shivering.

"It's okay, boy," she said. Quickly she opened up her apartment and thrust him inside, closing the door after him. Immediately, once he was in, he began to scratch at the door and whine. Heidi ignored him, instead turned to face apartment five.

Yes, a reddish glow, but the glow somehow didn't seem to illuminate the apartment. She could see the light, but somehow it didn't make it easier to see anything in the apartment. It was almost like darkness, a reddish darkness that hid things rather than revealed them.

Heidi took a step forward. Then another. She found herself drawn toward the apartment on the one hand, and repelled by it on the other. She hesitated, but felt one foot, almost in spite of herself, slowly lift from the floor and slide forward, dragging her closer. And then again.

As she neared the apartment, the red glow grew stronger. *I shouldn't do this*, she told herself. *I should go back into my apartment and wait for morning to come, then talk to Lacy*. But she was too curious to know what the light was to be able to stop now.

As she came closer she slowed down, barely moving now, staying close to one wall. The glow was still there and now she could see a little of the apartment in it. What she could see of it was bare, empty. She came closer, and then slowly leaned around the door frame and peered in.

The glow wasn't even coming from the apartment, she realized, but from a window in the back corner of the apartment, from something behind the window that was partly covered by ragged curtains.

It was a relief to know the source of the light wasn't within the apartment, but she still couldn't help but wonder what it could be. There wasn't anything out there that she could remember that would glow like that. Maybe an ambulance light or the light from the top of a police car? But if that were the case, wouldn't it be flashing rather than pulsating?

For a moment, she hesitated. She almost returned to her apartment, called it a night, and curled up with Steve. That would be the smart thing to do rather than wandering around in a strange apartment at night. *Or at the very least,* she told herself, *I should go down and knock on Lacy's door, get her up here to have a look, too. Safety in numbers*. It was late, sure, but this was important.

She stayed there on the threshold, hesitating, holding to the edge of the door frame. But then curiosity got the better of her and instead of turning around and leaving she went in.

Inside, she could smell the dust. The air, too, was thick and stale, as if it had been trapped there for too long. She shuffled in slowly, crossing the room and moving toward the pulsating light.

She reached out and parted the curtains, brought her face close to the glass so she could see. There, on the back of an old brick building, was a flickering red neon *Jesus Saves* sign. She stared at it. No, that was wrong, she told herself. It couldn't be there. She knew what was behind the house, and it wasn't that. Something was wrong.

And as soon as she began to think this, the *Jesus Saves* sign began to change. It almost seemed to melt, the words beginning to shift and change, the neon staying lit but flowing like water along the wall to become a series of strange, incomprehensible symbols. *What the fuck?* she thought, beginning to feel apprehensive. She rubbed her eyes, but when she opened them the symbols were still there.

I've got to go, she told herself. She turned from the window and made for the door, but before she could reach it she heard a rustling from the shadows. There was something there, or maybe someone.

"Hello?" she said, but nobody answered.

But something was moving there, she could hear it, and as she stared, something came stumbling out and into the red light.

It was not a person, though it had once been one. Now the face was charred and burned, little more than bone, the body mere bone as well, though bits and pieces of withered and charred flesh still clung to it here and there. It was dressed in nothing but a few blacked scraps of tattered fabric. It stared into her eyes—or at least would have if it had had eyes. Instead, it turned two blackened sockets in her direction. Its jaw clicked and then opened. When it did, a black liquid began to spill from the mouth.

Heidi just watched, horrified, paralyzed. She couldn't breathe, felt like the wind had been knocked out of her.

Then the creature hissed and lunged at her and she came to herself enough to stumble back and away from it. But there was another one behind her, this one charred but with more flesh, a woman obviously, her body still warm and smoking as she clawed at Heidi and made a noise a little like someone suffocating might make. Black fluid was pouring from her mouth as well. Heidi struggled to get away, feeling both creatures tear into her with spastic motions, almost as if they were puppets or sleepwalkers. They shredded her clothes but didn't stop there, continuing to rip and tear at her, deeply slashing her skin with their charred and bloody hands. She cried out in pain, struggled to get away. The sharp nails of a hand clawed deep into her forehead, tore her scalp partly off.

She cried out again, pushed and shoved violently and managed to break free. She ran toward the light of the open door, but before she could reach it something struck her hard in the side and knocked her off balance. She missed the door and hit the wall hard, unable to stop, and quickly the hands were upon her again, dragging at her, pulling her down onto the floor as she screamed and cried. She could feel them clawing at her, caught glimpses of their hideous bodies and burned flesh, their strange fleshless grins, as they set upon her.

She lay there. She didn't know how long she had been unconscious, nor, to tell the truth, whether she was alive or dead. She wasn't sure when they had stopped tearing at her, nor if they were still there, hovering over her, just waiting for her to move before setting on her again.

The floor was wet all around her, her body wet, too, but it took her a moment to realize that it was with her blood. She rolled to one side and felt her whole body blaze up with pain. She stopped there, hesitating, but there was no movement in the apartment, no sign that they were still there. Perhaps they had thought her dead and had retreated to their shadows. Or had gone elsewhere to make others their victims.

Very carefully she got her limbs under her. She felt something tear painfully in her arm, a wound ripping open again. She thought of standing up, but no, she wasn't sure she could manage, and she worried she would be too visible. No, she needed to be as inconspicuous as possible, needed to try to make it out before they realized that she wasn't dead after all.

There it was, the door to the hall, light coming through it. She put one hand out in front of her and dragged her way a little closer to it. Then she waited. When nothing happened, she pulled herself with the other hand and then managed to get her legs partly under her and begin to crawl.

It didn't seem like she was the one crawling. The pain made her feel so distant from her body that it felt like she was a ghost hovering above herself, somewhere near the ceiling, watching someone else crawl. She kept the body below her moving toward the door, trying not to feel its pain, trying just to keep it moving.

Her fingers crossed over the threshold and pulled her partway out. *I might survive after all*, she thought. All she had to do was drag herself the rest of the way out and down the hall and into her apartment and call 911, then staunch her wounds and try to stay alive until they sent an ambulance for her.

Then she was all the way out and into the hall. She came back from where she was hovering like a ghost over her body to occupy the body itself and had to stop herself from screaming in pain. But being in the body made her feel more capable as well. She could feel the adrenaline pumping within her and she managed to crawl up the wall and pull herself to her knees. From there, with a tremendous effort of will, she stumbled to her feet and stood there, braced against the wall, out of breath. The wall was all bloody, she saw, from where it had touched her, and she knew if she turned around she would see a swath of blood along the hallway floor as well from where she had dragged herself. *Don't look back*, she told herself. *Move forward*.

She would have done it, too, only when she looked up she saw a woman standing there, a tall woman with an austere face and dark eyes and a cruel mouth. She stood dead center in the hallway, blocking Heidi's path.

The hallway suddenly seemed bled of sound. Heidi couldn't hear the rustle of the wind outside, nor the settling of the house, nor even the sound of her own breathing. It was as if the whole hallway had been swaddled in cloth and removed from the world, as if nothing beyond this hallway existed. She could not feel her body either, but it wasn't as if she was above it now, only as if she was in it but unable to feel it. She felt strangely at peace. There was even a comfort to this, but a comfort, she couldn't help but think, that must be like the comfort you might find in being dead, if you could be aware of being dead. And it was as if she was under a spell.

She stared at the woman in the hallway, wondering whether she should try to go around her, not even certain she'd be able to move. Before she could make her decision, the woman began to speak in a soft, almost inaudible voice.

"I am Margaret Morgan, child. I glimpse you through the ages, for such is the power of my Dark Lord. You have done nothing, and yet you shall suffer. And yet you, too, are chosen."

Heidi looked past the woman, at her own door. She tried to hear the sound of Steve scratching there, but the hall still seemed absent of all sound apart from Morgan's soft, oddly soothing voice.

"Feel the earth...taste of the air. Hear that?" asked Morgan. She cupped her hand to her ear. Heidi listened, but still heard nothing beyond Morgan's voice. "The sound of the clouds and the scent of the wind...all becoming one. The whores of the deceivers will gather before us and bleed us a King. You, my beloved sister, are the knife by which we strip the skin of Salem's daughters."

As she spoke, smoke began to rise around her. Then flames. Then, though her voice remained soft and did not change at all, she began to burn. Her skin reddened and then began to boil and crackle, then blacken.

"All will know the sister's pain...," she said to Heidi. Slowly, her voice became more broken, more labored, and she began to hesitate between the words, her eyes filling with anguish. "My pain...the pain of feeling flesh cooking within your body...They will feel what I felt...They will..."

But Margaret Morgan couldn't go on. Her hair caught fire, and her face as well. She seemed to want to speak again, seemed to be struggling to say more. But when she managed to open her mouth again, her head engulfed in flames, it was only to let out a terrible scream.

Chapter Twenty-one

She sat straight up, gasping for breath. Where was she? In the hallway, watching that woman catch flame? No, she was in her bedroom, in bed, the TV still on, the Mafia hit man on the screen. She must have dozed off and then stumbled into some sort of bad dream.

But she could still see, in one corner of her mind, the red light illuminating the room, could still almost smell the burning flesh in her nostrils. That was fucked-up, a woman going up in flames like that, so suddenly. On the one hand, she could recognize that it must have been a dream, that it hadn't happened. On the other hand, though, it still felt so real that it was hard to believe it *hadn't* happened.

She sat there for a moment, her heart beating hard, and then she groped around until she found the lamp on the bedside table. She clicked it on. She kicked back the covers and examined her arms and legs, looking for marks from the attack, but there was nothing there. *Of course there's nothing,* she told herself again. *It was only a dream.* But still she kept touching her body, looking for marks or cuts. She could feel them there, gashes and abrasions on her skin, even though they weren't visible. Like they were there psychically even if physically there was nothing.

She shook her head. What was wrong with her? Was she going to start having bad dreams now? Wasn't her life tough enough as it was? What had happened to the old days when she hadn't had to worry about anything, back before her life got complicated?

Her mind wandered a little, her eyes returning to the screen.

"What did you want them to think as they died?" asked the interviewer from off-camera.

"Nothing," said the hit man, whose face was covered by a sack. "I just wanted them to see my face. I wanted them to realize I was Death."

Fuck, she said. *No wonder I'm having bad dreams.*

And then suddenly she saw it, two eyes glowing in the darkness below her. She almost screamed before she realized it was just Steve.

"You scared me, buddy," she said, her heart thumping again. "And just when I was starting to calm down. Go lay down." But then, before he could, she reached out to pet him. He pressed up against the side of the bed and bent his head to get it at the angle he wanted scratched, just like he always did. It made her feel a little better, having him there with her. And he was calm, too, which was a good sign.

She clicked the TV off and lay back in bed, one hand still idly trailing along her dog's back.

How was she supposed to read it, this dream? She still felt like there should be marks on her body, cuts and scratches and even gashes. But there was nothing. She took a deep breath, trying to calm down. And what had been up with apartment number five in her dream? What had been in there? What was it exactly that had attacked her? Something not human, though it had been human once. Or no, there were two of them; maybe they weren't the same thing. Undead or ghouls or God knows what.

But what was she talking about? They weren't real, after all. It was a dream. There was no point trying to think about them as if they were real. She could see how it might happen. Those two black-metal ghouls in the studio earlier in the day didn't help any, obviously. They'd gotten deeper into her head than she'd realized. Plus, that video of theirs, the "darkness and silence of the abyss," or whatever they'd called it, that was odd stuff, probably chock-full of subliminal bullshit that was just waiting for her to fall asleep so that it could surface. That must be the explanation. She hadn't ever had a dream like that before. And she hoped she never would again.

She felt a little cold. She realized the bedroom window was open, a light breeze ruffling the curtain. Had she left it open? She couldn't remember having done so, and it was hardly the right time of year for it, considering how cold she was, but who knows. She'd been drinking. Maybe she'd been flushed when she went to bed. She sighed and stood up to go shut it.

As she was about to slide it closed, she noticed across the street a fat man standing just inside his own window, facing slightly to the side, messing with something just out of sight. He was naked, his belly and thighs spilling out to hide his privates. Somehow that looked more obscene to her than if his cock had been visible. There was something wrong with him: he had a clear plastic mask strapped over his face. She followed the tube leading off it back to an oxygen tank. *Ugh*, she thought. And then he turned toward the window and looked straight at her. Caught off guard, she met his gaze. For a moment they just stared at one another, and then he lifted up a hand that seemed strangely red, as if stained with blood, and slammed a set of iron shutters closed.

Excuse you, she thought. *Didn't hurt to look, did it?* Or maybe it did a little, if that guy was what you had to look at.

She was starting to feel a little better. She went back to the bed and crawled onto it, lying facedown. Turning out the light and closing her eyes, she tried to get back to sleep.

When the light was on, when she had walked through the room, when she had looked around, it simply wasn't there. Or if it was there, she somehow couldn't see it. Somehow looked right through it. Would someone else coming into the room have seen it, or when the light was on was it simply not there?

But there in the dark above her something slowly coalesced. At first it was little more than an unsteadiness in the air; then it became a blur, then, slowly, more and more substantial. It took on form. A line of deeper darkness running down from the ceiling became, slowly, the links of a greased iron chain. At the end of it hung something that at first seemed solid but then separated into gaps and bars, becoming a wrought-iron cage. It was empty, but the bars were stained with blood and stuck with feathers and the door did not latch. It swung slowly back and forth, creaking. But rather than slowing and stopping, it swung more and more regularly. It seemed propelled by an unseen hand, the hand soothing and coaxing some unseen or invisible thing in the cage.

Beneath it, oblivious, Heidi moaned and struggled and tried to sleep.

Tuesday

Chapter Twenty-two

Though broken into apartments, there was nothing on the outside to reveal the house to be anything but a single-family home. It had been painted a deep indigo typical of the colonial period, one of the colors approved by the Salem historical society. Unlike most rentals, the tiny lawn was neat and tidy, not a leaf in it. A small knee-high fence ran around the yard, wrought-iron bars with spikes at the end of them, maybe enough to keep a dog in if it was a small dog, but little more. The porch, too, had been carefully swept, and the walkway had been scrubbed until the cement almost glowed.

Only once you went inside and saw the doors with names on them did it became clear it wasn't a single-family dwelling. There was a door just inside the front door with the name *Savage* on it, and a table covered with mail split into three stacks. A staircase wound upward to the second floor and another door, another name on it. A narrower staircase climbed farther, to a shorter, smaller door that led to a converted attic.

Inside this last door, a man with slicked-back white hair paced through his living room. He was old, near seventy, but thin and spry. He was dressed in a simple black suit, old but in good condition. He stopped before a full-length mirror beside the door and began fixing his tie. He regarded himself with a sour look.

"What the hell's wrong with my hair today?" he asked. He waited for a response and when none came he continued. "Should I shave?"

When there was still no response, he half turned from the mirror. "Alice?" he said.

Alice Matthias, a silver-haired woman with perfect bone structure, stepped nearer and gently pulled his hands away from his tie. "You're just making it worse, dear," she said. When his hands began to move back to it, she said, "Francis, let me do it." She undid the tie and then smoothed the ends out, began tying it again. Francis fidgeted a little but let her do it.

"There, Francis," she said. "I think that looks good, don't you?" She patted him softly on the chest.

"What about the hair?" he asked.

Alice gave him a scolding look. "You do realize that it's radio," she said. "Nobody's going to see how you look."

"I know," said Francis. "I want to…" He hesitated, and then admitted, "I don't know what I want."

Alice patted his chest again. "Don't be so nervous," she said. "You'll do fine."

Fine, thought Francis. *I want to do better than just fine. And why did I ever agree to do this in the first place?* He'd been feeling good when the guy from the station had suggested it—after all, he was at a bookstore and signing a bunch of his books: who wouldn't feel good about that? But then he'd made the mistake of listening to the program last night and realized that the Big H team wasn't going to exactly be scintillating talk and conversation. He'd be lucky if they'd even *read* his book. No, he'd be lucky if they'd even read a *chapter* of his book. And last night there'd been an interview with some odd Satanic rock group. It was demeaning to follow on the heels of something like that.

"I'm a little nervous," he admitted as Alice continued to rub his shoulder. "I can't believe I let myself get talked into these things. I hate things like this."

She stood on her tiptoes and kissed his cheek. "Calm down," she said. "It will be fun and you yourself were just complaining." She pulled back and did her imitation of him—he hated when she did that, but if he was honest with himself he had to admit she was pretty good at it: "I need a way to sell more books, Alice. I need to get the word out."

Well, he had said that, and he did need it. His book was good—he knew it, really solid historical writing. But it just wasn't getting into the right hands. But there was no way the Big H team and their listeners were the right hands.

"I don't sound like that," he lied. "I didn't say that."

"Whatever you say," said Alice. "Oh, make sure you get some passes to the film. I want to see it."

"What film?"

"You've already forgotten? *Frankenstein versus the Witchfinder*."

"You really want to see that?" he asked. "I thought you were joking. It's undignified. Alice, you know how I feel about those historically inaccurate portrayals of—"

She cut him off with a look. "Be a dear and get me my passes," she said.

"I'm not going to ask them for—"

"Just do what the wife says and nobody gets hurt," she said.

Francis sighed, nodded. "Yes, dear," he said.

Chapter Twenty-three

A few hours later and he was there. Yes, Alice had been right; there was no reason to dress up. None of the Big H team were wearing suits—one of the men hadn't managed to find a shirt with buttons and seemed to be wearing a promotional T-shirt, a sparkly gold thing advertising a band named Mattress. What kind of name was that for a band? The fellow was also wearing a cowboy hat and sunglasses—indoors! What was the point of that? And he had a beard that would have made Santa Claus jealous. The other, the one named Herman—or wait, that was confusing too because they both were named Herman it turned out, but he was supposed to call the other Herman something else. What was it? White Herman? Were they pulling his leg? What kind of a name was that? Anyway, this other Herman, the African American guy, he was dressed like an extra from a seventies Blaxploitation film, was even wearing a purple pimp's shirt with gold buttons. Fool's gold, probably. Francis didn't know quite how to take it. Had Herman been dressing that way since the seventies or was it just some sort of hip thing that was so gauche that it had become fashionable again? The third one, the woman named Heidi, looked all right, though a little bedraggled, like she'd just gotten out of bed despite how late in the day it was. She had dark circles under her eyes and didn't look like she'd slept much, but she seemed the nicest of the three. The most normal anyway.

It made him jittery just being there. No, these three were hardly his audience. And they clearly hadn't read the book—not even a page! They hadn't even said anything about the specifics of the book to him. Herman, who had spoken to him the most, had gotten the title wrong. It was all Francis could do not to groan when that happened, but he'd held back and just gently corrected him, just like Alice would have told him to do. No, this was already a serious disaster.

There was a commercial on, for Anderton Auto. Those crooks! He couldn't imagine that anybody who would be interested in his book would get their car repaired at Anderton Auto. Even the commercials were telling him he shouldn't be here.

Someone tapped him on the shoulder. He turned over, saw Herman's face. Man, that guy had a big head. "Ready?" Herman said.

He shrugged, not sure what to say.

"Calm down, man," said Herman. "We ain't gonna bite. Just be yourself. It's gonna be all right."

The commercial wound down, slowly fading into the background. The woman, Heidi, put on some headphones, leaned toward her mike, and began to speak.

"That's right," she said, her voice expressing an enthusiasm that couldn't be read in her face. "Anderton Auto is now open on Sunday. Anyway, if you're just tuning in, we've got a guest in the studio. We'll be chatting with Francis Matthias, author of the book"—she paused, looked down at the book in front of her—"*Satan's Last Stand: The Truth about the Salem Witch Trials.*"

At least she'd gotten the title right. Maybe it'd be okay after all.

"Hello," said Francis. "Heidi, I am happy to be here." He winced. Two minutes in and he already sounded stilted and uptight, like he had a stick shoved up his ass.

"Heidi, may I?" asked Herman.

Heidi rolled her eyes. "Yes, you may," she said, her voice revealing nothing of the eye roll.

Herman grinned, turned toward Francis. "So, Francis, tell me exactly how many people were actually executed during the Salem Witch trials."

He opened his mouth to answer, but that other Herman, White Herman, cut in. "And more important," said White Herman, "were any related to Dr. Frankenstein?"

He felt his blood start to boil—they just weren't taking this seriously! But Alice, he knew, would want him to keep his cool. He took a deep breath and then responded.

"A good question, Herman," he said. "Approximately twenty-five in all if you include accused witches who died while in prison..." He thought he might end it there, but both Hermans were looking at him, waiting for him to go on. *Ah, what the hell,* he thought. "And as far as I know, none were of any relation to Dr. Frankenstein."

Whitey laughed. "Twenty-five? Are you serious? I thought there must be hundreds. I have to admit I'm disappointed by that number and especially by the non-Frankenstein lineage."

How was he supposed to answer that? He just stared at the microphone.

"Professor Matthias," said Heidi, "correct me if I'm wrong here, but wasn't Dr. Frankenstein only a fictional character?"

"Yes," he said, thankful for the correction. "Yes, I believe he was. And the book *Frankenstein* didn't appear until nearly thirty years after the Salem Witch trials."

"So what you're saying is that the book *Frankenstein* was based on the Salem Witch trials?" said Whitey.

"Um, no," said Francis, confused. "I wasn't suggesting that at all. There's no relation between the two."

Whitey laughed. *Am I being toyed with?* wondered Francis. *Or is this man just an idiot?* He wondered if he should have said something else, or if he should go on now, but Heidi was already asking a new question.

"Hang with me on this, because it might seem like a ridiculous question," she said. *Oh no,* he thought, *not a promising start.* "Were there any quote unquote 'real witches' in Salem in the seventeenth century?"

He cleared his throat. "Well, today we have a large group of practicing Wiccans living in Salem, which is a positive, earth-centered religion. They sometimes refer to themselves as white witches. It might seem strange to think they would gather here, at a site where witches were persecuted in the past, but they claim to be curing the place of the evil that took place here. But I assume you mean…"

He let his voice trail off. He wasn't sure he wanted to get caught up in this sort of conversation. It wasn't really what his work was about. It was a historical examination, for God's sake, not some hippy-dippy mystical speculation.

"You know," said Heidi, "classic witches with actual powers of some sort? Any of those?"

He shook his head. "Sorry, no. There is no such thing as witchcraft. Witchcraft is nothing more than psychotic beliefs brought on by a delusional state of mind."

"So, nothing."

Hadn't he said just that? Couldn't they move on to something else? He sat there staring at her, shaking his head, but she wouldn't ask another question. He imagined Alice at home listening. She'd be disappointed. He wasn't playing the game; he was messing it up.

He made an effort. "Nothing," he said.

But the woman wouldn't let it go. Maybe he'd been wrong. Maybe she wasn't the nice one after all.

"Not even the teeny-weensiest incident of supernatural activity ever occurred?" she asked. Even the way she asked he found belittling, an assault on his dignity. No, it had been a huge mistake to come on the show. He could see that now. He never should have agreed to do it.

When he spoke again, there was a harshness he couldn't keep out of his tone. "I thought I was quite clear the first time you asked," he said. "You can ask me again, but the answer is still no."

But still the girl didn't stop. What was wrong with her? "How can you be so sure?" she asked. What was she, someone with aspirations to witchhood? He was losing his temper now.

"I can be sure because I am a reasonable person," he said angrily. "I do not believe in supernatural nonsense any more than I believe in Bigfoot or the Loch Ness Monster." He turned toward Whitey. "Or Frankenstein for that matter."

"Whoa, my brother," said Herman. "Don't be ragging on Frankenstein. I've got film fest tickets to move."

But Frances was going now and couldn't stop. "In fact," he said, stabbing his finger toward Heidi, "the idea of 'real witches' as well as the mindless cinematic trash like *Frankenstein versus the Witchhunter*—"

"Witchfinder," interrupted Whitey.

"Witchfinder, whatever," said Francis. He took a deep breath. "This inane garbage completely undermines the social importance of the witch trials themselves. Can't you see that? That is exactly the problem with this country. Everything has to be a joke or a headline. History means nothing anymore."

His anger was starting to run out of steam. He tried to calm down and wind it up. "History isn't about the past," he claimed. "It's about defining who we are in the present."

When he finished there was silence. Maybe he'd gone too far. He felt a little stab of regret; he'd promised Alice that he'd get her the tickets she wanted, but there was no way he could do that now, not with the tirade he'd just given them. There'd be hell to pay when he got home.

Heidi was looking at Herman, who was looking back at her, gesturing for her to go on. She lifted her shoulders and shrugged, gestured back to him. White Herman was deliberately not looking at either of them, staring down at his soundboard. No, he'd gone too far.

Finally Heidi spoke. "So which are we, then?" she asked. "Descendants of witches or descendants of murderers?"

For a moment a dull anger rose up in him. She was still trying to play the game, still trying to get him to say something sensational and irrational. But another part of him told him not to get angry. It wasn't her fault—she was just doing her job, trying like so many people in Salem to sell something by using their history of destruction and violence. It was indicative of a problem with the country at large, but it wasn't her fault. Probably it hadn't been her who had insisted on interviewing him. Probably it hadn't been the idea of any of them— hey, they just worked here. They were just as much victims of it as he was. And getting angry like that just made him tired.

"Both," he said wearily. "We are the descendants of witches, and we are the descendants of murderers."

She stared at him, a little surprised by his answer, and then White Herman jumped in and took over. "I could have told you that just by looking at the crowd at Dunkin' Donuts this morning," he said. "And speaking of defining who we are in the present, I think we need to define some present...It's time for..." Whitey reached out and hit a button on the board. A recorded intro of a drumroll began to play, followed quickly by the sound of glass being smashed.

"Smash or Trash!" said the intro tape in an unnaturally deep voice.

That was it, then, thought Francis. His five minutes of radio fame were over and they were moving on to some novelty segment. Smash or Trash, whatever that meant. He'd made a fool of himself, probably came off as a pedantic old idiot. Oh well, what else was new?

"Today I think Heidi is going to provide us with the victim," Herman was saying.

The victim? wondered Francis. What were they talking about? They weren't going to start doing prank calls, were they?

"That's right, Herman," said Heidi. "This one is a little different from most. I have no info about where this came from. Strange handmade box with a weird symbol on it that just showed up in my mailbox here at work, no return address, nothing, and with an unmarked record inside. All I know is the group is called the Lords."

"The Lords," said Herman. "I assume they are from around here, so we'll just call them the Lords of Salem."

The Lords of Salem? Francis was a little shocked, not sure he'd heard right. Was this another joke they were playing on him? Had they read his book after all?

"Excuse me," he said. "Did you say the Lords of Salem?"

Herman looked over at him, a little annoyed. "Yes, I did," he said. "Francis Mattias, ladies and gentlemen. You got to remember, Francis, we're still on the air."

Probably just a coincidence, Francis told himself. *I'm sure plenty of bands out there would take a name like that.* And it wasn't exactly the band name either—they were just the Lords, right, and it was Herman who had tacked "of Salem" onto them. *No, it was just a coincidence. Nothing to worry about.*

"The phone lines are now open, so get ready to smash or trash!" said Herman.

Or maybe it was the Lords of Salem, thought Francis, but the band had been founded by someone who had read his book, who knew what the name meant. Yes, that was a possibility, too. The book was just out, but bands were changing their names all the time. Maybe they had put together their album and decided on their name at the last minute…

On the other side of the studio, Whitey started the record. Initially he put the needle at the end of the record rather than at the beginning and then seemed surprised when nothing happened. Maybe he really was an idiot, thought Francis. He tried it twice that way and then put the needle where it was supposed to go. The music started up right away, and everyone took their headphones off.

"Hey, it's going the right way," said Whitey to Heidi, gesturing at the record. "What do you make of that?"

"I guess your turntable is possessed," said Heidi to Herman.

"Not my turntable," said Herman. "Last I checked that was how records played."

"Yeah," said Whitey. "That's what I said. It's going the right way. Last night it wasn't. It was playing backward."

"Backward?" said Herman. "Nah."

"I shit you not," said Whitey. "Ask Heidi."

Herman turned to her. She nodded. "I know it sounds weird," she said, "but that's what happened."

Herman stared at her a moment, then shook his head. "Naw, you guys are both messing with me," he said. "Or you just had too much to drink last night."

Backward? wondered Francis. *What were they talking about? And what was it about the music that was making his skin crawl?*

Chapter Twenty-four

A sound like women chanting, but distorted. Instruments that sounded damaged and as if they were deliberately being played wrong. Maisie Mather was naked in bed with her gangly boyfriend Jarrett when she heard the song on the radio.

Maisie was a WXKB girl, born and bred. It was the only Salem-based station that played classic rock, and it had stuck to that for years. She had curly black hair and was petite, not bad to look at but no raving beauty either. But she liked the way she looked; she was comfortable with it, and with herself. Maisie had lived a charmed life. She'd lived in Salem all her life, had even lived on the same block with her parents until finally moving out a few years back and into her own place. She'd grown up feeling loved and protected, and the knowledge that her family was old-Salem blood had given her a sense of privilege and belonging that she'd come to rely on. Her parents had accepted that privilege but had always played down her ancestor Judge Mather's relation to the witch trials, and she had at first, too. But once she was older she'd embraced it, deciding that she might as well accept it rather than run from it. That was why she'd gotten involved with the Witch Museum, why she'd made a gift to the museum of Judge Mather's papers once her parents had died.

It was still hard for her to think about their death. It had been so unnecessary, and the officer at the scene had said it was a hundred to one shot, that the wreck wasn't all that bad and that they should have survived. Indeed, the people in the other car had all walked away without a scratch. She was still getting over that, and she never got into a car without thinking about it and wondering if, had she been in the car, she would have died, too.

She'd gone to college at Boston University, commuting every day from Salem. At the time, she'd told herself that once she graduated she was done with Salem and with Massachusetts in general, but no, apparently not. She didn't know if it was inertia or an unwillingness to abandon her parents even though they were dead or what, but every time she got up the nerve to leave, something happened to keep her here. Last time, she'd even had a job arranged in California, had bought the plane ticket and everything, when she'd gotten a call to say that the company had been taken over and the job no longer existed. After a while, she started thinking of it as fate and figured she'd be here pretty much forever.

At first she didn't pay any attention to the song, just kept kissing Jarrett, encouraging him, trying to get him into it. His blond beard and long hair kept on getting in the way, poking into her eyes, tickling her neck or snaking its way into her mouth, but whatever, that was how it was with Jarrett, something you had to live with if you wanted to have sex with him. And if you could get over that, well, he wasn't such a bad lay.

Or okay at least. She had to admit, the last few weeks' sex with Jarrett had been feeling a little routine. She had a hard time keeping her mind on things. She kept drifting away, thinking about what she had to do the next day, wondering whether she'd put the trash out, if the cat litter needed to be changed, whatever. Not a good sign, and probably an indication that Jarrett and she weren't likely to be an item for all that much longer.

But today her mind was catching on something, on the song coming from the radio. At first it seemed just weird, nothing worth paying much attention to, but there was something about it that kept hooking her. Hooking her, tugging at her, reeling her in. She kept imagining that: a hook sliding into her flesh and then pulling at it, the feel of it as it went in, the sharp pain of it, and then the anxious buzz of it as, once affixed, it began to tug. *Why am I thinking that?* she wondered briefly. It should have grossed her out. But weirdly enough, it was kind of a turn-on. It was like the tug of the hook and the music and the movement of their bodies were all the same thing, all mixed up in a way that made her crazy, but in a good, transgressive way. *A really good way,* she thought. It had been years since she'd felt this turned on. What was this music anyway? What was it doing to her? And how could she get it to do more?

"Turn it up," she said, midthrust.

Jarrett stopped, breaking the rhythm. She pushed him from his side onto his back and climbed on top of him, slid him into her, took over. There it was again, the hook, piercing her skin. Only the music didn't feel like a hook exactly anymore. It was thicker and harder, more like a nail or even a spike. And instead of feeling like it was hooked into the flesh of her body, it felt like it was being pounded first through one eye and then through the other. It was like she was being blinded by desire. Why should that feel good? *What's wrong with me to have a fantasy like that, some fucked-up mutilation thing?* she wondered, and for a moment she tried to break away from it. But the music: something about it was too insistent, and it kept drawing her in, flooding her body and mind.

She gave a kind of gasp.

"Oh my God!" she said. "Turn that up... Turn it up! I have to hear it louder!"

Beneath her Jarrett lost his rhythm again, but she just kept going, faster and faster, listening to the slick thwip, thwip, thwip her movement made. "Huh, um, okay...," he finally said. "Okay." He reached to one side, tried to fiddle with the knob of the radio, but he wasn't finding it fast enough.

"Louder!" screamed Maisie Mather.

And then he found the knob and had cranked the music as loud as it would go. The radio's tiny speaker began to fuzz out, but Maisie didn't care. Somehow that made the music even better. And she was beside herself now, no longer even quite sure who she was anymore. The music was a kind of discordant off-kilter metal, but with a tribal beat hidden somewhere inside it. It flowed into her and through her, and beneath it she could hear something else, a kind of chant, a kind of spell almost, but running backward. There were voices there, and they were calling out to her. She could almost hear them, could almost hear what they were saying to her, what they were telling her to do.

"Louder!" she screamed again. "Louder!"

"Dude, chill," said Jarrett. "That's as loud as it'll go!"

She moved faster and faster, grinding harder and harder. Even if she'd wanted to stop, she probably couldn't have. Beneath her Jarrett just tried to hold on. She sunk her nails into his chest and he cried out, a little hurt maybe, but she didn't care. She just kept going, the music rushing through her.

Inside of her, a sleeping beast reared its head and became attentive. It came and pressed its ear against the side of her skull, listened through the music to the reversed chant hidden within it. A chant she didn't even hear until the beast did. She could feel it slavering within her, and then it opened its mouth and began to speak.

"Maisie Mather," it said, and she felt her own name echo darkly within the confines of her skull. Its voice was the voice of an animal, and the words came out crippled and unnatural, but she could still understand them, could still hear her name. And once it said it, she realized that yes, this was one thing the chant was saying: it was calling to her, calling her name. And something inside her, some bestial thing she didn't know was there, had heard the call and was answering for her, and now was listening to what was hidden in the music, to what the music was trying to say.

Suddenly she was very afraid.

But the part of her that was afraid was caught in a dark tide that swept through her whole body. It was as if her body no longer heard now; it was moving fast and hard and almost without her. The beast that had reared its head was fully awake now, and she could hear it slowly stretching and spreading within her, its limbs sliding through her arms and legs until it filled them, its chest expanding to fill her own and even push it out farther until her ribs threatened to crack. Below her Jarrett was a little astonished, maybe even a little afraid, but enjoying himself, enjoying the way she kept going and going and going. *Help me,* the part of her that was still left tried to say to him, but the only thing that came out of her mouth was a moan that mixed pleasure with pain. The creature snuffled through her skull and slowly pushed its way along its edges until its own head filled it, and the person who had been Maisie Mather was now relegated to a little imaginary island deep within her brain where she could feel things a little, could look out the eyes a little, but couldn't move, couldn't act. She was where the beast had been. And now the beast had taken her place.

Oh God, she thought, *what's happening?* She tried again to cry out, and did cry out inside, but outside she felt her lips curl into a smile. The beast was enjoying her body, enjoying having control of it, and wasn't likely to give it up willingly. How had she released it? It wasn't her fault. It wasn't what she wanted. No, it had been the music. The music had done it. *Turn off the radio,* she tried to say to Jarrett. *Turn it off before it's too late!*

But even as she struggled to say it and failed, she knew it was already too late.

She felt her body grinding and flexing, felt the beast pushing it harder and harder. Jarrett's chest was red and scratched by her nails and maybe she'd hurt him a little. She could still hold the beast back a little, couldn't stop it but could brake it a little, slow it down slightly. But that was fading, too, and she was afraid of what it would do to Jarrett, or to herself, if she lost control. The song was coming to an end, she hoped, building to a crescendo anyway, and if she could just hold on, could just keep some measure of control, maybe once it was over she'd be able to get hold of herself again and force the beast back asleep. She fought it, fought it hard, and the beast felt her fighting and snarled at her and clawed at Jarrett using her hand, and grinded even harder.

The demon let her go just enough that she could really feel how it felt. Oh God, it felt good to let go like that. The beast was her and not her. She could feel herself—things she had done, ways she had given in to her desires and impulses over the years—in it, in what it was doing now. But it was frightening, too. It wouldn't stop, she knew. It would go too far. She'd always felt she had that in her, the desire to go too far—maybe everybody had it, maybe she wasn't the only one with a beast, but most people could keep it in check. She had always been able to keep it in check, too, but that had been because she was in charge—she would wake the beast up just a little, let it join in the fun but keep it groggy, and knock it unconscious again right after. But the music, something about that song, had pushed things the other way, so that now it was she who felt groggy and almost overwhelmed as desire swept through her. It felt so good! Maybe she could just let go a little, just a little more, and then still get back in charge after, push the beast back down. Or maybe the song would end and that would be enough and she'd get back in charge before the beast did something really rash and slaughtered Jarrett.

Because that was where this was heading, she suddenly knew. It was great having sex with Jarrett, the beast was thinking, but how much better would it be just to go a little further, to let Maisie's nails not just scratch their way along his chest but gouge out his eyes and pop them, tear his throat out, beat his head in until it was a wet pulpy mass, not only fuck him but kill him, and then once he was dead see what else she could do with him? With what was left of his body.

Inside, she recoiled, started screaming. But she wasn't in charge. No, the beast was in charge.

The song has got to end soon, she told herself. *Please, dear God, let this song end.*

Back in the radio station, the whole bank of phone lines had lit up. The song was still playing, with Francis and the Big H team waiting for it to end.

"Total Christmas tree," said Herman, gesturing to the phone bank. "I guess this crap struck a nerve. Either that or the FCC is calling to pull our license."

Francis, on his way to the door, stopped and turned around. He touched Heidi lightly on the shoulder. She jumped a little and then looked at him questioningly.

"I wanted to apologize. I'm very sorry I overreacted to your question," Francis said. "I take everything so seriously. God, I must have sounded like such an ass."

Heidi shrugged it off. "All good," she said. "We should have gotten a better sense of you and your book first, I guess. It was a dumb question anyway."

He was tempted to say, as he'd said in his classes back when he taught, that there were no dumb questions. But he didn't exactly believe that. Never really did. And the apology wasn't really why he'd stayed around. "You'd mentioned that, for the movie...," he said, then let his voice trail off.

"Yeah, sure, man," said Herman from next to her. "Pick a couple up at the front desk on your way out, tell the receptionist there I said it was cool."

Francis nodded his thanks, but didn't look away from Heidi. "May I ask you," he said to her in a quiet voice, "where exactly did this music come from?"

She'd already turned back to the papers in front of her, getting ready for the next segment. "Huh?" she said. "The receptionist said it just appeared with nothing but a note for me. Probably somebody dropped it off while she was out to the bathroom or something."

"So it was specifically sent to you?" asked Francis.

"Yeah, very specifically," she said. "Check this out." She reached into her pocket, removed the crumpled note, and handed it to him. He took it, and then took out his reading glasses to get a better look at it. The paper was handmade rather than mass-produced. Strange script, too, he thought. A very good imitation of seventeenth-century handwriting, and probably done with a quill, too, or something very much like it. *For Adelheid Elizabeth Hawthorne*, it read. *From THE LORDS.*

"Adelheid Elizabeth Hawthorne," he said. "That's you?"

"Yeah," she said. "I didn't even think anyone knew my real name. A little creepy, right?"

"A little," he said. He held up the note. "Do you mind if I take this?" he asked.

She looked a little surprised, but shrugged. "Whatever. Go ahead," she said. "Why do you want it?"

He weighed in his mind whether to tell her the truth. No, he decided, it was silly in any case, no point in alarming her with some wild story, particularly not after having come out so strongly against irrational ideas and the supernatural. He faked a smile. "I collect examples of interesting handwriting," he lied. "Just a hobby of mine."

When Maisie came she *saw* things, had visions almost. They flooded her and crowded in on the little space that was left to her, over-whelming her. She saw Jarrett lying there with his throat cut, the bed soaked with his blood. She saw him strangled, her hands locked around his neck. She saw him tied to the posts of the bed and then slowly pricked, over and over again, with needles. She saw him with his eyes gouged out and she crouched over him, slicing off his genitals with a razor and letting the blood spurt warmly over her belly. She saw herself claw his chest bloody and then claw deeper and push her hands in through his flesh and tear out his heart, then slowly begin to eat it. It was rubbery and hard to chew, like poorly cooked calamari.

She saw herself standing in a circle around a fire, her body smeared in the blood of a newly slain infant, a symbol inscribed on her chest. A circle, with an upside-down cross in it, the top of it touched by a crescent moon, the bottom of it cut across by a hillock of ground, two stars lying at the extremes of the arms of the cross. Beside her, standing in the circle with her, were other women, like her but not like her. Their clothes were outlandish and old, as if they were from another time. And as she watched them, they stripped their clothing off and collapsed one by one, moaning and writhing, giving themselves over to libidinous pleasure, the same pleasure that her body felt when, in the real world now, with Jarrett, she came so hard it nearly tore her head off.

After that, lying exhausted next to Jarrett, she expected the beast that had filled her body to disappear, to curl up and go back to sleep and let her take over again.

But it did not disappear. And it did not let her take over again. It was as if she had lost the right to do anything with her body. She could see out through her eyes, but nothing more. She no longer had any sort of control.

Help! she cried silently to Jarrett, trying to plead from behind her eyes. *Help me!*

But Jarrett was lying there out of breath, covered with sweat, exhausted.

The beast within her licked its lips. Licked Maisie's lips, rather. It was still hungry. She could feel it taking the imagined images of a slaughtered Jarrett into its mouth and rolling them around on its tongue. Yes, they tasted good to it, and since she was there with it, she could taste them, too, could taste what it wanted her body to do to Jarrett next.

"Whew," said Jarrett. "What was up with that?"

Jarrett, she cried silently. *Run!*

She felt her body throw off the covers. Carefully, as awkward as an automaton, she stood and walked jerkily out of the room.

"Babe, I meant that in a good way!" she heard Jarrett call from the bedroom behind her. *Please,* she prayed. *Please, dear God, let this be a dream.*

The song was ending. Heidi watched the old writer, Francis whatever his name was, leave, still a little perplexed. Strange turnaround there at the end. Why the sudden interest in the Lords, and in the note? He didn't exactly seem like the type to be a headbanger, but it took all kinds, she guessed.

As the song faded, Whitey clicked over to the first caller.

"Okay, are we dealing with a smash or a trash?" he asked.

"Come on, dude," said a gruff male voice. "I'm at work right now listening and it's making my day worse. That is fucking shit!"

"Whoa!" said Herman. "No F bombs or S bombs please. One for trash. Next caller."

Whitey clicked over to the next one. "Smash or trash?" he asked.

"What?" said a voice that might belong to a man, might belong to a woman. "I just wanted to make a request. Air Supply's—"

Whitey cut the call off, went on to the next line. "Smash or trash?" he asked.

"Trash!" said another male voice, angrily. "Total trash! My band Tuesday Weld Overdrive kicks ass over that! We are playing—"

"We already did a smash or trash on Tuesday Weld Overdrive and the verdict was trash. Next!" said Heidi, just as Whitey cut the call.

"Trash it or smash it?" asked Whitey.

"Oh my God, it's beautiful," said a woman. Her voice was breathy, almost fluttery.

"Beautiful?" said Herman. "Lady, you might like it, but there's no way in hell anybody can think of that crap as beautiful."

But the woman didn't take the bait. "Keep playing it . . . Please play it again . . ."

Who is that? wondered Maisie briefly, feeling sluggish and then thought, *Oh God, it's me.* She was looking out at her body all right, staring at her reflection in the mirror. Only it didn't quite look right, didn't quite look like her. There was something wrong; the lines of her face were a little off, the tilt of her head different than normal. Something glowed in her eyes, too, something that she'd never seen there before. Her naked body was holding a small porcelain cat, stroking it very slowly, as if it were real. It kept running its hands over the cat's surface, nails clicking against the porcelain.

She tried again to take control of her body, but now that the beast had tasted freedom it wasn't about to give that up. It kept its thumb pressed to her, holding her firmly pinned, making her squirm.

She watched her reflection in the mirror as if through a red haze.

In the background, the radio rambled on.

"Smash or trash," said Herman's voice.

"Smash!" screamed a woman's voice. "Smash! I love it!"

Yes, she heard the beast think: *Smash. Time to smash.* Her hands swiveled and held the cat out over the hardwood floor. For a moment they held it there and then they let go.

The cat tumbled end over end and then struck the floor, breaking into thousands of pieces.

"What was that? Are you all right, dude?" she heard Jarrett call out. She didn't answer. Instead, she tentatively lifted one foot, brought it down among the broken bits. She ground the foot down, feeling the pieces cut into her flesh. She brought it away and then stepped down on it again, and when she lifted it the beast within her was pleased to see the red stain that was left behind. She watched her body smile, and then watched it open the top drawer in the dresser below the mirror and reach in. Within her, the beast smiled. In the reflection, her face smiled in exactly the same way.

When her hand came up, it was holding a pair of scissors. It lifted them slowly, lethargically, turning them, examining them, watching how the light caught and glittered on them. Her hand spread them open and snapped them together. And then she watched her reflection open its mouth and give a short, barking laugh.

Slowly, her hands lifted the scissors and opened them, then put her neck in the V the spread blades made. *No*, thought Maisie, and she heard the beast laugh inside her head. She felt the blades tighten, felt the pressure on either side of her neck, her carotid artery pounding against the sharp blade. Her hands left them there a moment and then slid them away. In the mirror she saw where blood had beaded on one side of her neck. Slowly, it formed a drop and slid down. The beast used her mouth to lick its lips.

Her hands lifted the scissors again, higher this time, and began to cut away her black curls. She watched her locks fall down, all her lovely hair going away.

The cutting continued up and around the back until her hair was shorn down nearly to the scalp in some places, irregular and a little longer in others. She looked like a mental patient. It was a look the beast liked. Again her mouth smiled.

I'm dreaming, she told herself. *I'm dreaming. Soon I'll wake up.*

But there within her she heard the beast chuckle. *No*, it said in a deep voice. *You're not dreaming, child. You belong to me.*

She tried again to struggle, tried again to take control of her body, but the beast held her effortlessly. It laughed within her, and she saw the laughter bubbling like blood from her own mouth. No, there was blood, too; the beast had bitten partway through her tongue and she could feel the new cut in it. If she bit again, she'd probably bite it clean through. Her mouth was full of blood. She could taste it, distantly. As she watched, it began to slip out of her mouth and down her chin, spattering over her bare breasts.

Her hands opened the scissors and held them spread, bringing one point down close to her chest. It hesitated there, over her heart, and then pushed slowly against the skin until it was uncomfortable to breathe. She could feel the blade there, just on the edge of her breast, tight against the skin, and then she saw in the mirror a drop of blood form on the end of the blade, then a line of blood begin to flow.

All I need to do, she heard the beast within her say, *is push this a little farther, then a little farther still, and then that will be the end of you.*

She waited for the beast to do just that. In her head she felt it watching her, smiling, waiting.

But, Maisie, it said, *that would bring an end to all our fun. No, I have so much more in store for you.*

Her hands lifted the scissors away and then brought them down again between her breasts, cutting deep through the skin this time. It carved a slow, meticulous channel through the skin as her mind filled with pain. The face in the glass stared at her the whole time, smiling.

Feel that? asked the beast. *Are you having fun now? Self-mutilation is always the heart of the party.*

When the scissors were lifted away, she saw that the beast knew exactly what it was doing. It had hurt her, had done permanent damage, but had not carved deep enough to incapacitate her. She was bleeding, yes, lines of blood now oozing down her stomach, and the muscles in her breast hurt, but she wasn't going to die any time soon. At least not from these cuts. No, it wanted her to suffer before it killed her, wanted to light her mind up with pain. And each time she experienced pain, she realized, the creature seemed larger within her, seemed to have grown in size and in confidence.

It smiled again at her with her mouth, and then lifted the scissors again.

May I have this dance? it asked her. And then, without awaiting a response, began to carve again. A straight, vertical line starting just above the midpoint of the circle and descending through it to close the bottom of the circle. Then a crosspiece near its top, painfully tearing through the muscle. Then a kind of head, but open at the top, a U, and legs, too, with the bottom of the vertical line of the cross like a tail between it. The pain was almost unbearable. She felt it, could hardly stand it, but her body seemed not to notice it at all. Inside, she was screaming and panting, trying not to lose consciousness. Outside, she was calm and collected, almost meditative, as she carved the symbol into her own chest.

The beast stopped for a moment, regarded its handiwork in the mirror. Then it smiled. Very carefully, near each end of the cross-piece, it used the end of the scissors to bore a tiny round hole. Her chest was slick with blood now, but even with all the blood, the symbol was still visible, its lines darker, more definite. She watched her mouth twist, then smile again.

"You belong to the Lords now," the beast whispered with her voice, her mouth, to her reflection. Or maybe it was the reflection whispering to her.

"Maisie, where are you?" she heard Jarrett call from the other room. "Are you coming back or what?"

She heard the beast within her prick up its ears. It had forgotten about Jarrett, but now that it had been reminded, it felt hungry. It licked her lips.

"Coming, honey," she called back. Or the beast within her called back.

But there was something weird about her voice, something strange about the way the beast used it. It was too deep, not right somehow. Jarrett heard the difference.

"Are you all right?" he asked. But she didn't answer. Instead, she closed the bloody scissors, took a firm grip on the handle, and went back into the bedroom.

It's fucked-up, thought Whitey. Sure, there were always disagreements over whether something should be smashed or trashed, particularly when they did local music and the bands tried to get their friends to call in and support them, but it never was as wide a range as this. People either loved the shit out of this track or they hated it and wanted to crucify the Lords. No middle ground.

And it was still going, still a line of people queuing on the phones, wanting their opinions to be heard.

He took the next call. "Smash or...," he started, but then let his voice trail off.

The woman on the other end was weeping. *Shit*, he thought, *some psycho*, and reached to disconnect her.

"Please play it again...," she managed to say before he cut her off. "I need to hear it again."

Shit, he thought, her voice, the longing in it. She'd heard the song only once but it was like she was already addicted to it. Was she crying out of disappointment that the song had ended or out of joy that she'd been lucky enough to hear it? It was like all the crazies were coming out tonight.

"The chicks love it," Whitey said. Yeah, that was right. Every woman who called in loved it. That was weird. Every man who called in seemed to hate it. That was weird, too.

"I guess it's a girlie smash," said Heidi. *Girlie smash*, he thought. That was a good one. He'd have to file it away and use it sometime himself.

"What can I say?" said Herman. "It's obviously the new 'Sexual Healing.'"

Little different sound, though, thought Whitey. A lot more aggravated—hardly a good track for bedroom fun, unless you happened to be Jack the Ripper.

He reached out and connected another line. *Let it be a woman who hates it,* he said. *Break the pattern.* It was a woman all right, but she didn't hate it. As usual, being a woman, she loved it, thought it was a smash. *Messed up,* he thought, *and a little creepy,* and then he went on to the next call.

He'd turned over, was lying on his side now. He was still naked but he was covertly checking his phone, something she hated him to do after sex. *Look up!* she silently begged. *See what's happened to me, and then run.*

But he didn't. He kept checking his phone as she came slowly in and clambered into the bed and spooned him from behind.

"Mmm," he said. "Back for more?"

She didn't say anything. Her body started kissing him on the shoulder, the neck, leaving bloody mouth prints with each kiss.

"Feels great," he said. He arched his back a little, rubbed his shoulder blades against her breasts. She felt the symbol carved on her chest tear a little, the wounds bleeding more freely. But her body pushed back, acting as though nothing was wrong.

"Are you wet?" he asked. "Splash yourself with water or something?"

She didn't answer, just reached around him and put her hand on his cock, began to rub her thumb up and down its shaft. That distracted him a little, made him worry less. He tried to turn around and get where he could kiss her, but she kept holding on, tightening her hand around his cock and squeezing. *Shhh*, the beast said through her. The whisper sounded a little weird, but not so weird that he noticed.

"Okay, okay," he said, giving up. "We'll do it the way you want to do it. But honestly, I don't know if I have another go in me quite yet. But sure, why not, we can play around."

She kept rubbing his cock, rubbing her body up and down his back, tearing her wounds open. Everything was getting bloody. Everything was growing wet with blood. The beast inside her took a deep breath through her nose, enjoying the smell of her blood.

"Why are you sticky?" Jarrett asked. "Did you get something on your chest? Honey or something? Is this part of the game?"

"Sure," the beast said. He stiffened a little. He knew her voice, knew something was off with her, something was wrong. Now he'd turn around and see what she'd done to herself and realize what danger he was in.

"Why are you talking like that?" he asked. "It really isn't funny."

Run, Jarrett! she was screaming inside. *Run!* Her hand, though, had left his cock and was groping through the bedsheets, looking for the scissors. She felt her fingers brush by them and tried to will them to keep moving, to not stop. Jarrett was trying to turn and she had let go of him enough that he mostly could. But instead of looking at her body, he saw only her head.

"What the fuck have you done to your hair?" he asked, drawing back.

Her hands found the scissors again and closed around them, and then swiftly she drew her arm back and brought them down hard and sharp into his neck.

He cried out once and tried to rear up, the scissors having cut through his flesh to lodge in his windpipe. Blood was coming in a kind of spray out through the wound, and the throat, too, was hissing from the hole, air escaping. He struggled and tried to turn around, and struck out and hit her hard on the side of the head. The beast inside of her laughed. Jarrett tried to sit up, made it partway, but then fell back, the color already drained from his face. He groped weakly at the scissors in his neck and managed to close his hands around them and tug at them. They came partway free and then his hand stopped moving and his eyes slowly glazed over. Slowly the hand released them and the scissors slid out on their own. Maisie's hand was there to catch them.

She stared at them in her palm. Inside her head she was huddled, weeping, but unable also to stop herself from looking out. But the beast made her look. The beast showed her the scissors, turned them in her hands, watched the light glint off them.

Put them down, she told herself. *Put them down and call the police.*

The beast used her mouth to smile. And then her body began stabbing Jarrett's corpse, over and over and over again.

Slowly the sheets grew sodden with blood. Inside of her the beast roared, swelled. She cowered, covered her head. No, she didn't want to be here, didn't want to have anything to do with what had just happened, nor anything else like that. She'd prefer dying to having to watch someone she cared for being killed.

The beast seemed to hear her thoughts. In some sort of space within her head it came over and crouched beside her, sniffed her. *You're no fun*, it said. And then, *So be it. I can have more fun without you.* It stood straight and placed a red, clawed foot on her imaginary head, but still she felt it somehow in her real head. It began to press its weight down. She felt the pressure build, and then, all at once her skull cracked and the scaly heel made a mess of her brains.

Outside, she stiffened and collapsed. For a moment she was like that, seemingly lifeless and then she stretched and stood and gave a terrible laugh.

And then for a long time there was nobody left inside of her except for the beast, who began licking her lips and set her hands to carving up the body beside her. He started with the face, flaying the skin back and then cutting the muscles away to get down to the bone of the skull. He lopped a few of the fingers off, almost at random, and then started onto the elbow joint.

Once he left his residence in the body, there was nobody left inside her at all. Her body lay there, eyes wide, unable to move, no longer Maisie, no longer the demon, unaware that she had once been human, no longer really anybody at all. Then the injured woman within her skull began to slowly gather herself, pushing her brains back into her imaginary skull, slowly regaining consciousness, slowly coming to realize what she'd done.

Chapter Twenty-five

All the way home he couldn't help but think about it. The Lords of Salem. He took the note out of his pocket, looked at it again. Yes, the handwriting had characteristics that made it representative of a style of script common in the late seventeenth century in the New England colonies. But so what? The paper was handmade but not old. It was obviously just someone having fun. Why had he taken the note? Did he really want to compare it to samples of handwriting that he had? Whose? Margaret Morgan's? That was crazy, exactly the kind of thinking that he'd discouraged that young woman from. What was her name? Heidi? He looked at the note. Adelheid Elizabeth Hawthorne. John Hawthorne had had a daughter named Elizabeth, if he remembered correctly, and another named Adelheid. With a name like that, she had to be a descendant of his.

When he reached home and climbed the stairs, he found Alice standing by the open apartment door, arms crossed, waiting for him. Seeing her was enough to bring him back to the present. Inwardly, he groaned, thinking of what a disaster the radio show had been. He took off his coat, hung it on the hook while she watched him with a concerned look.

"Did you listen?" he asked. "How was it?"

"Did I listen?" she asked. "Of course I listened, Francis. You were wonderful." She was lying; he could tell. She uncrossed her arms and leaned forward and gave him a kiss. It was bad, he knew, anything but wonderful, but she was trying to protect his feelings. He let her lead him to the couch.

"Would you like a drink?" she asked.

"Don't bullshit me," he said. "Seriously, tell me the truth. How was I?"

"You were completely...fine," she suggested.

Fine, he thought. *Well, he hadn't even been that, to be honest.* "Fine?" he said. "What does *fine* even mean? Can we back things up? What happened to *wonderful*?"

Alice's smile was a little strained now. "How can I put this?" she said. She looked away from him, her eyes focusing on the radio. "Well, you got a little weird with that girl when she asked you about real witches."

"Was it that obvious?" said Francis. "I hate that question. And she kept asking it, no matter how many times I said no."

"But you recovered," said Alice. "I taped it so you could listen back. It'll make you feel better."

God no, he thought. Last thing he wanted was to live through that again. "No thanks," he said. "I can't stand the sound of my voice."

Alice patted him on the knee. "Think how I must feel," she said, and smiled. Her smile was genuine again.

"Very funny," he said. "But no, I don't think I want to listen to it again. I had to live through it, remember?" He grabbed his head with his hands. "What a disaster."

She put her arm around him. "There, there, dear," she said, her voice soothing. "It's not as bad as you think. You don't have to listen to it now, but it'll be waiting whenever you're ready."

He just shook his head. She'd let go of him and was standing up when he thought of something. "Was it just me you recorded?" he asked.

"Of course not," she said. "I had to record the people who were asking you questions, too."

"No, no," he said, shaking his hands in frustration. "That's not what I mean. Did you happen to record the music they played afterward?"

"Ugh, yes," she said. "I didn't know if you were done or were going to come back on again, so that's there, too. I can't believe the awful noise that masquerades as music these days. What was up with those girls?"

"Girls?" he asked.

"They kept calling in, saying how much they loved the music, almost weeping over it. One after another after another."

"I don't know," he said absently. "I was gone by then." *I've got to hear it again*, he was thinking. *Something about that music really bothers me. Especially what she called it...* "The Lords of Salem," he said, softly.

"What, dear?" asked Alice.

"What?" he said. "Oh..." and then shook his head.

She waited for him to go on, and then when he didn't she shrugged. "Also," she said, "you got the tickets, right?"

"What?" he said. "No."

"No?" she said, her voice rising.

"Well, yes. They said I could pick some up on the way out. I just forgot. I'll go back for them tomorrow."

She patted him on the arm. "That's fine then. You hungry?" she asked. "I can reheat the leftover pasta."

"Huh?" he said, already lost in his thoughts again, eager to turn on the tape and take a closer listen to what was there. He felt his pocket, made sure the note was still there. "Sure," he said. "Pasta's fine."

Chapter Twenty-six

The parking lot was largely empty, the pavement cracked and the air frosty. A cold wind whistled, rattling the handicapped parking sign and rippling the awning, and a handful of fallen leaves skittered their way over the asphalt. They stayed together, all in a bunch, whirling around one another, around and about, but not separating. They scuttled back and forth across the parking lot, almost as if waiting for someone.

Then the station door opened and all at once they scattered, blowing every direction. Heidi, Herman, and Whitey came out all at once, talking and laughing. They walked over to Herman's car, gathered there a moment, shivering but not yet ready for the evening to end.

"All right, children," Herman finally said. "I will see you tomorrow." He turned to Heidi. "And *you* get some sleep, would you? I'm sick and tired of worrying about you. You look exhausted."

"Thanks a lot," she said sarcastically.

"You know what I mean," he said. And from the way he searched her face, she knew he was nervous that she was up to something stupid. Like using again. But he didn't keep it up long, and Heidi didn't mind—she wasn't using and it was kind of good to think that he was still watching out for her.

He turned to Whitey. "You ready to go?" he asked.

Whitey nodded, opened the passenger-side door. Herman moved around to his own door.

"You get some sleep now, hear?" he said to Heidi.

"Fear not," said Heidi with false bravado. "I have a plan. I'm going to implement the red wine method tonight. Never fails to bring sleep."

"Sounds vaguely similar to my scotch on the rocks plan, if I can sneak it past the warden. You want a lift?"

"No, thanks," said Heidi. "I need the exercise."

"Fuck exercise," said Herman. "It's cold. And we're all gonna die someday."

"Nice philosophy," said Heidi. "But no thanks. I should walk. It'll help me sleep."

She walked through the streets. Salem was a little creepy at night, all the old houses that looked fine during the day starting to seem sinister. There was hardly any crime here, so she was pretty safe, but still it freaked her out just a little, probably because of the town's history. Maybe she should have taken the offer of a ride from Herman.

But she had to walk a little, had to calm herself down. She'd had a terrible sleep and that Lords track had done something to her. Whoa. It had given her a headache to listen to it again. And she couldn't understand why it had played backward in her apartment the night before but played normal at the station. The music seemed different, too. Had she really been drunk enough last night that she hadn't had a clear idea of what was going on? She might've thought Whitey was playing a joke on her, but he was hardly the type to let it go on for this long. No, he was a good egg. He'd have told her. Something was weird. And that, with the darkness and her lack of sleep, had jangled her nerves. Better to get a good walk and calm down a little. Maybe that would help her sleep.

It was cold, though. Herman was right: this time of year was hell. You could never tell if it was going to be cold or warm and no matter how you dressed it was usually wrong. Her faux fur coat was helpful, but she was still cold. She'd be chilled by the time she got home.

She reached into her pocket and pulled out her earbuds, put them in, then plugged the cord into her iPod. When she pressed PLAY it random-shuffled her to a How to Learn French album that she didn't even know she had on her iPod and she thought, *Why not? Here I am, walking through the streets of Salem, learning how to speak French, improving myself, taking control of my life. What could make for a better evening?*

"How much do I owe you?" a Frenchman asked her. *"Combien est-ce que je vous dois?"*

"Combien est-ce que je vous dois?" Heidi repeated absently, her mind already starting to wander.

"Could you speak more slowly?" asked the Frenchman, and for a moment she had the impression that the tape was speaking directly to her. Then he continued: *"Pouvez-vous parler plus lentement?"*

"Pouvez-vous parler plus lentement?" she repeated.

And then she suddenly realized where the album was from, that Griff had downloaded it to her computer a few years back. The idea had been that they'd get clean, listen to it, learn French, then go to Europe together, a good vacation, just the two of them. But when it came down to it, neither of them ever had any money, and they'd never gotten around to listening to the album. Griff talked about it for a while, and then he stopped, and then he was dead. Leaving only her. She was lucky to be alive, she knew, but she couldn't help but feel guilty.

She shivered and skipped to the next track, which turned out to be a Tom Waits song about Suffolk's red barn murder. Better. It didn't have any memories associated with it.

It was fucking cold, her fingers and wrists aching, her breath clouding up in front of her. She was about halfway home, maybe a bit more, and was just passing the big red double doors of Saint Peter's church. They had been left slightly ajar, a light shining inside. Surely the priest wouldn't mind if she just went inside for a moment to warm up.

She slipped quickly in. The light that was on was just inside the doors, the main light for the vestibule. The rest of the church, though, seemed dark. She could see the vague outlines of the pews and the aisle, the ghost of the lectern and altar at the front, but very little else. Probably the door had been left open by accident and nobody was meant to be there. That was okay; she wouldn't stay long. She'd just warm up for a few minutes and then she'd be on her way.

She slipped out her earbuds—it seemed disrespectful to be listening to a song about a murder while standing in a church—and began to chafe her hands. They were already feeling a little better. *Combien est-ce que je vous dois*, she thought. *How much do I owe you?* And felt again a little stab of guilt.

She stood there a moment, and then suddenly realized she was hearing something. It was soft, almost inaudible, a sort of low mumbling sound. And then she realized it had been there ever since she'd taken out her earbuds.

She peered out in the darkened church. It seemed to be coming from there, somewhere in the pews. Mice, maybe? Or rats? No, it wasn't quite that, but something different. More like someone whispering.

Curious, she took a step forward, out of the entranceway, through the pillars, and into the church proper. She felt suddenly vulnerable, knowing she must be outlined against the light behind her, and she stopped for a moment and listened. No, the sound hadn't stopped. It was still there, and sounded all the more like someone whispering.

When she moved forward it was while trying to be as silent as possible. She moved down the aisle slowly, trying to follow the sound. Just a few pews up, the sound no longer seemed to be coming from in front of her but more from one side. She eased her way into the pew, began making her way down the row.

The sound grew louder and louder. Yes, definitely voices. Why would they be hiding in the dark, though?

She almost didn't see them until she was right on top of them. They were dressed in black, faded into the darkness, and if they hadn't been whispering she might have walked right smack dab into them. As it was, her foot scraped and they heard her coming and stopped talking, rapidly turning to face her. Then she saw the white fabric around their faces and the faces themselves. Very hard to see, but from what she could make out in the darkness they looked really old.

"Oh hey, sisters," said Heidi. "Sorry. I didn't see you. Was just looking for a place to warm up from the cold."

The two nuns regarded her without saying anything. Just stared.

"I didn't mean to disturb you," she said.

"You're not disturbing us," said the first, in a creaky old voice.

"No, you're not disturbing us," said the other. "We were expecting you."

The first elbowed her.

"Expecting me," said Heidi. "How could you be?"

"She doesn't mean that," said the first. "We were expecting someone, but not you. How could we be expecting you?"

"Yes," said the second, her eyes shining in the dark. "How could we be?"

"Um," said Heidi. "I'm warm now. I probably should go."

She turned and started back down the pew.

"Wait," said the second nun. "What fragrance do you wear?"

"Fragrance?" said Heidi. "Perfume, you mean? No, I'm not wearing anything."

"But you smell so good," said the second nun. "Almost good enough to eat."

"Sister," said the first nun. "Think before you speak."

"Well," said Heidi quickly, "I should go."

She almost ran the rest of the way to the doors of the church and was only really comfortable once she was outside, in the cold again. *So much for a good night's sleep*, thought Heidi. Shaking her head, she hurried the rest of the way home.

Chapter Twenty-seven

Her fingers were aching by the time she reached her front door. First it was hard to get her keys out and then, once they were out, to make her fingers find the right one and get the door open. She checked for mail, and then headed for the stairs.

Lacy's door was wide open, light spilling out into the hallway. The sound of voices and scattered laughter came from inside. She groaned—last thing she wanted tonight was company. She'd have to go past on her way to the stairs. She'd just go quickly and quietly, she told herself, and hopefully not be seen.

She was halfway past when she risked a glance in. Lacy was there, a glass in her hand, sitting in a high-backed chair that looked almost like a throne. She was rapt, her attention turned to a sharp-nosed woman, with a huge, tangled mass of brightly dyed red hair, around Lacy's age, sixty or so, who was speaking. On the other side of her was a cute, perky woman with short, choppy blond hair, maybe a little younger. The latter turned and looked straight at her, and smiled.

Heidi hurried past. She'd put her first foot on the step when she heard Lacy's voice ring out.

"Heidi!" she called. "Come meet my sisters."

Heidi took a deep breath. Last thing she needed was a landlady who wanted to be her friend, too. She gathered herself and returned to the door. She put on a fake smile, poked her head around the door frame, and waved.

"This is Megan," said Lacy, gesturing to the woman with red hair. "And this is Sonny," she said, gesturing to the blonde. Funny, thought Heidi, they didn't look like Lacy's sisters. She couldn't see much family resemblance. Maybe Lacy was adopted?

"Hi," said Heidi. "Nice to meet both of you."

"Nice to meet you, too," said Sonny. "Come on and join the party. We don't bite."

Megan simply nodded and held up her wineglass.

Lacy smiled. "Please come join us, Heidi," she said.

"Oh hey, thanks," said Heidi. "But tonight's not so good for me. I got held up at work and I'm not feeling so great, so maybe a rain check."

Lacy nodded. "One glass?" she said.

Well, she had told Herman and Whitey she was going to practice the red wine method, and they definitely had red wine here. But still she resisted. "I really should call it a night and get some sleep," she said.

"One itsy-bitsy spider of a glass?" wheedled Lacy.

What? thought Heidi.

"She broke out the good stuff for a change," said Sonny in a stage whisper.

Heidi gave a tired smile. She was too exhausted to fight. "All right," she said. "One drink. But first I have to feed Steve."

She trudged up the stairs. She shouldn't have glanced in, should have pleaded exhaustion. Probably if she hadn't, she would have managed to get by without them calling to her. But now it was too late. She'd have to go talk to them.

At her apartment, she couldn't help but glance down at apartment five. For a moment she thought the door was open and did a double take. But no, it wasn't open after all. It was just the way the shadows fell. She resisted the impulse to go down the hall and check to make sure it was locked.

She opened the door on darkness, heard Steve whining.

"I know, buddy," she said. "I'm late. I'm so sorry. Hold on, give me a second."

She flipped the kitchen light on, but when it came on it flickered a little, and kept flickering. *Bulb must be going out,* she thought. She took off her coat and tossed it into the living room. She dropped her bag.

Steve was acting odd, whining a little. He greeted her, but not very enthusiastically, but once she filled his bowl with food he began eating right away, wolfing it down and growling as if he expected someone to take it from him.

"Stop being weird, Steve," she said, feeling a little hurt. "I wasn't gone all that much longer than usual."

She watched him for a moment. Gradually, his growling seemed to fade away. Maybe she'd forgotten to feed him before she left. She grabbed a bottle of wine off the counter and opened the apartment door, stepped out into the hall.

"Okay, buddy," she said. "I promise I'll be back quick. I'm just going to go have a quick one with the old ladies downstairs." *How do I get myself roped into these things?* she was wondering.

She stood in the doorway watching Steve eat a moment more and then shut the door and went out into the hall. She glanced again at the door to apartment five and again had the impression it was open, but this time stopped herself from turning around to look at it. It would be, she was sure, the same as it had been before: just an illusion. Nobody was in apartment five, she told herself. The door was certainly closed.

She continued toward the stairs without turning back around, feeling the skin prickling on the back of her neck.

But the door was open this time. And there, in the door frame, half consumed by shadow, stood a thin figure. As Heidi moved toward the stairs and down them, the figure moved out of the doorway, gliding silently down the hall.

When it came into the light it revealed itself to be so thin that its bones were showing through its skin, vividly outlined. There was no flesh to the figure. It was hard to believe that it belonged to a living body and not a corpse. There was something wrong with its face, something about the skin—it looked as though it had been torn free, torn loose, and only imperfectly reattached. It hung wrong on the skull, as if ready to slough off at any moment, and the mouth and eyes didn't seem lined up quite right.

It seemed drawn forward, step-by-step, moving in time with Heidi's movement down the stairs. When she stopped and rapped on the door frame of Lacy's apartment below and said "I'm back," it pretended to rap on Heidi's door, mimed her speech.

"Come on in," said Lacy downstairs, and the figure bowed low before Heidi's door. It reached out and tried the handle, found it locked. The flesh on its hand, too, was less like skin and more like a glove, loose and pulpy, and it left damp stains on the doorknob and the door beside it.

The figure gave a strange lopsided smile. It put both hands up against the surface of the door and then pushed. For a moment the door tightened in its frame, the wood creaking, and then, suddenly, its hands slipped through the surface of the door. It thrust itself forward and the arms slid through the wood as well until its face rested against it. It pushed its face against the wood and the skin of the face stretched strangely and sloughed to the side, laying bare for one moment a raw and fleshless expanse of pinkish skull. And then with a wet squishing sound the face thrust through the door and disappeared to the other side. Neck and body followed. Slowly the figure wormed its way through and into Heidi's apartment.

When it was done, the door was still one piece. All that was left was a wet stain the size and shape of the figure, and very quickly that began to fade away.

From inside came the sound of Steve whining. And then of him scratching at the door, trying to get out.

*   *   *

Just as always, one drink had become two, which had become three and then four. *Those old ladies sure can slam it back,* thought Heidi, feeling a little buzzed. She'd made short work of a plate of cheese and crackers as well, but maybe should have had another plateful, enough to soak up all the wine in her belly.

Sonny was there beside her with an inquiring look on her face, holding up the bottle, ready to pour. *What the hell?* thought Heidi. *One more won't kill me.* She held out her glass and Sonny filled it, emptying the bottle.

"And that ought to do it," said Lacy. "Another dead soldier." She reached out and took the bottle from Sonny and saluted it. "Sir, you served your country well."

"Thanks," said Heidi. She took a sip. So far the evening had been the old ladies quizzing her down on everything under the sun, from boyfriends to her job at the radio to her Christmas plans. She'd answer a question and then be barraged by two more. But, she realized, Lacy's sisters had said almost nothing about themselves. And Megan had said almost nothing at all.

She turned to Megan. "So what do you gals do?" she asked.

But it was Sonny who answered. "Well," she said. "I'm what you might call a self-help guru. I guide people who are lost in the art of finding oneself."

"I think I could use a little of that," Heidi said. That wasn't exactly true. She'd mostly been doing okay lately, but the last few days had been rough for some reason. She hoped it'd get better soon.

Sonny reached out and patted her hand. "Everyone can, dear…," she said. "And Megan here…Well…"

"I read, darling," said Megan. Her voice was sharp and powerful, deeper than you would think it would be from looking at her.

"Read?" said Heidi. "I'm sorry, I'm not sure what you mean exactly. Read books? And you get paid for it?"

But Megan didn't answer, just kept looking at Heidi with a steady, steady gaze. *Did I say something wrong?* wondered Heidi.

There was an awkward silence, which Lacy finally broke.

"Megan is quite the palm reader," she said.

"Oh," said Heidi. She didn't know what else to add.

"Most readings are surface-level observations," said Sonny. "But Megan here...she sees very deep into the world beyond." As she said it, she moved her hands back and forth as if pretending to cast a spell. Heidi shot a quick glance Megan's way to see if she minded her sister teasing her, but her face remained as placid as ever.

"She's very good at it," said Lacy.

"Really?" said Heidi. "I've never had my palm read before. I always figured it was a scam." She turned to Megan. "No offense," she said.

"Actually, my dear," said Megan. "I do take offense. Great offense. But not at you. At all those who demean the true gift with their false substitutes. Plastic gypsies with crystal balls and neon signs have destroyed the value of my true gift."

At the mention of neon signs, a memory flashed up in Heidi's mind, a flickering red neon sign that read *Jesus Saves. Where was that from?* she wondered. Where had she seen it?

"Give her your hand," said Lacy.

"What?" said Heidi. "It's late, maybe another time. I've got to—"

"Heidi, give her your hand," said Lacy, a little more insistently. "Come on, it'll be fun." When Heidi still hesitated, Megan reached out and took it.

"Um, okay," said Heidi.

"The hand and the brain are one," said Megan. "The hand is controlled by over three hundred muscles, tendons, nerves, bones, and arteries. One-quarter of the motor cortex in the human brain is devoted to the hand. Did you know that, darling?"

What, now I'm getting a science lesson from a palm reader? "No," Heidi said. "I can honestly say I did not know that."

She watched her hand resting in Megan's bonier, older hands. Megan turned her hand palm up and spread the fingers. With one hand she held Heidi's hand in place. With the other, she began to run her fingers gently over the lines of Heidi's palm, up and back, up and back. It was a little weird, slightly sexual, and reminded her of the way Lacy had held her hand so long the first time they'd met. The light touch made her skin tingle and seem to come alive. All the women were leaning in now, peering at Heidi's palm.

"The lines are formed at a subatomic and cellular level," said Megan. "These are the lines of your life."

"I thought these lines were just from the stress of my life," quipped Heidi.

Beside her Sonny pointed to her forehead. "No, these are stress lines," she said, and smiled.

"Please, sister," said Megan, and Sonny fell silent. Megan's fingers continued running over Heidi's palm, up and back, up and back. "No, no, these are formed in the womb and continue to control the thoughts," said Megan. "Give me your right hand. The right hand is the future."

Heidi drained the glass of wine in her other hand and set the glass down on a rickety old wooden end table. She held out her right hand and Megan released the left and took it. She took her hand and ran her finger up the center of the palm.

"Is that the life line?" asked Heidi.

"No," said Megan. "This is the fate line. This is the only line of concern to me. The length of your life is inconsequential. It is what you do with your time here that matters."

She saw Lacy and Megan exchange a strange look. What was going on? Were these women messing with her somehow?

"Oh, okay, so tell me then, what is my destiny?" she asked. And then she turned it into a joke. "Please don't tell me that I'm going to meet a tall dark stranger? I've had more than enough of those lately."

But the sisters didn't laugh. "It reads your fate, Adelheid," said Sonny. "Not your destiny."

How does she know my full name? wondered Heidi. "Is there a difference?" she asked.

"Yes," said Lacy, quite serious now. "A crucial difference."

Heidi was tempted to pull her hand away, but she felt Megan's grip tighten on her wrist. "With destiny you participate in the outcome, but fate...ah, fate leaves you no choice. It is predetermined by outside forces greater than ourselves."

No, thought Heidi. What the hell had been going on the last few days? She couldn't even walk into her own house without someone trying to freak her the fuck out. It was like the whole world was conspiring against her. "Oh, I don't think I like that," she said. "I've changed my mind. I don't want to know. I'll keep my fate a mystery. A mystery to me, anyway."

She tried to pull her hand away, but Megan held on. *Freaky old bitch,* thought Heidi. Megan was staring at her, trying to look deep into her eyes. She turned away and saw that Sonny was staring hard at her as well. So, on the other side, was Lacy.

"You must make peace with your subconscious desires," said Megan in a slow, deep voice.

She pulled at her hand again, but Megan wouldn't let go. She was starting to feel trapped. If she didn't get out of there soon, she was likely to start yelling. Or screaming even.

She pulled again. "What desires?" she asked, hoping just to get it over with.

"The wicked thoughts burning inside your head and exploding in the juices between your legs," said Megan, her voice perfectly controlled. "The darkness inside your very soul, Adelheid. The only reason you exist."

What the fuck? thought Heidi. Megan suddenly slackened her grip and Heidi pulled free, more than a little stunned by Megan's words. She started to stand, nearly tipping the chair over, knocking the end table askew so that Sonny had to dart forward to keep her wineglass from falling.

"Um, maybe I'll make peace with those desires later," she said, already backing to the door. "Right now, I better get going." She turned to Lacy. "I really should go back upstairs. I have to get some sleep."

"Pleasant dreams," said Megan.

Fuck you, too, thought Heidi.

Lacy followed her out. "Sweets," she said. "I'm sorry if Megan upset you. She is a little...adamant about things sometimes. And she can be a little intense."

"And a little wasted," shouted Sonny from within the room, humorous again. Whatever had been off about the mood of the room had broken now. Had she just imagined it? Or had something shifted there? Had something odd happened?

"It's nothing to worry about," said Lacy. "Don't pay any attention to what Megan says if it bothers you."

Heidi pressed her hand to her forehead. "No, no, I'm fine," she said. "I just need to get a decent night's sleep. Haven't had one in a few days for some reason, and I've got a couple of crazy days ahead of me."

"Yes," said Lacy. "I'm sure you do." Her tone was a little odd, too, thought Heidi, but maybe it was just a result of the drinking, or of Heidi herself being a little rattled. Lacy's expression was polite but otherwise unreadable. "Good night, then."

"Good night," said Heidi.

Half smiling, Lacy slowly closed the door, leaving Heidi alone in the hall. Alone, she slowly let out her breath. *What the fuck?* she wondered.

Chapter Twenty-eight

The handle of the door was sticky. Maybe she'd touched it when her hands were dirty or something. She wiped it off with the corner of her shirt and opened the door. She went in, her head reeling a little, and stumbled into the bathroom. Steve was nowhere to be seen. Probably curled up and sleeping already, she thought, or sulking and mad at her for leaving him.

She switched on the portable television on the counter. She turned the tub faucet, the water hot enough that the room began to fill with steam.

On the television was a black-and-white film, the tube of the TV casting it slightly blue. Two people danced around an arena. The image was far from crisp and kept fuzzing out. Heidi reached for it, and when her hand got close the image became sharper, the man becoming Fred Astaire, the woman Ginger Rogers. She drew her hand back and the image went fuzzy again, making it hard to tell who was who. *Ah well,* she thought, maybe once she was in the bath it'd come in clear. Usually it worked that way.

She poured herself a glass of wine and set it on the sink next to the TV, then carefully tied up her hair, watching herself in the mirror as she did so. *Tough day,* she thought. *And yesterday, too.* But now she could just relax, wind down. The day was over.

She turned off the tap and then slipped out of her clothes. She took one last moment to position the TV and then took her wineglass and climbed into the water. Wow, it was really hot. For a moment she just stood in it, letting her legs get used to it, and then she slowly eased her way in.

She lay in the water, the steam rising up around her. Yes, now that she was in the bath the portable TV was doing better. Picture wasn't perfect, but she could make out who was who at least. She watched Fred and Ginger twirl their way around the dance floor. Beyond, she could see the open bathroom door leading out into her dark apartment. She should have closed that, she realized, to keep the heat in, and to keep Steve out. Not that he was likely to come in anyway, considering how asleep he must have been when she came in.

She watched the movie for a while, sipping the wine, but then the dance number ended and the sound wasn't quite loud enough for her to follow the dialogue. It took too much attention. She took a washcloth and dropped it into the water near her belly, watched it slowly grow sodden and begin to sink. When it had taken on the heat of the water, she wrung it out and draped it over her face. Ah, it felt good. Finally she could relax.

Across the room, something changed. Heidi, washcloth still draped over her face, remained oblivious, unaware. At first it was only a change in light, a strange thickening of the darkness somewhere within the frame of the door. And then the bathroom itself started to feel cut off from the rest of the world, the sounds of the outside world—the wind outside, the settling of the house, the noise of the landlady and her sisters still laughing downstairs—were simply gone. Heidi didn't notice. Steve was awake and in the kitchen now, scratching at the outside door and whimpering, but Heidi couldn't hear him. She continued to hear from the TV the sound of Fred and Ginger continuing to chat, filling time before their next dance number. But if she'd taken the washcloth off her face, she would have seen that the images on the screen were no longer the same.

Instead of the two dancers, the TV depicted a strange hovel-like structure surrounded by woods. In front of it was a roaring bonfire, around which danced a ring of women who one by one stripped off their clothing until they were dancing naked. Their bodies were covered with symbols, written on their flesh in paint or blood, and they cavorted around and finally fell into one another's arms and began to rub themselves and writhe in the dirt, attempting to couple with the ground or with each other. One of them came too close to the fire and her hair caught flame and she ran howling and mad and foaming at the mouth around the hovel until that, too, caught flame. She fell on the ground and came up again with her hair burned away and the fire extinguished and her scalp blistered and smoking, a crazed ecstatic smile on her face. The hovel was soon roaring with flame and from it stumbled a figure whose body seemed made strictly of fire and who stood there in the door of the hovel, calmly burning, in the shape of a man but larger than a man should be. The women around the fire stopped dancing and prostrated themselves before the blazing figure, crying out something that could not be heard as Fred and Ginger's voices talked calmly on.

And then the darkness in the bathroom doorway solidified, slowly coming into sharper and sharper focus. At first it was a kind of black smoke that billowed around itself and then it gathered and whitened and grew pale. It slowed and solidified and became flesh, and became a woman. And then became Margaret Morgan.

She was stark naked. Her skin was pale, unnaturally so, and crusted over, as if it were flaking and rotting away. She stood completely still, her posture stiff and unnatural, as if possessed. She stared into the room, her gaze wandering slowly here and there before coming to settle on Heidi in her bath.

Her lips parted to show her teeth. She lifted her arms and the skin at her joints cracked and began to seep a white liquid, a pus or ichor of some kind. Her lips were moving, as if reciting something, but no noise came out of them. She stayed there, swaying slightly, eyes on Heidi, but did not move forward.

Suddenly there was movement behind her and a small hand snaked its way along her thigh and up onto her belly. A body followed it, belonging to a small humanoid creature with a sickly swollen head and huge bulbous red eyes. It was deformed and almost fetus-like, but nearly three feet tall, much too big to be a fetus. And though it clung to Margaret Morgan's leg, it moved with an awareness and intelligence that Margaret's body did not seem to have. It, too, turned its eyes on Heidi in the bath and watched her carefully and attentively, licking its lips.

The creature pushed Morgan forward and she moved jerkily into the room. Slowly and silently, she approached the side of the tub. Soundlessly, she lifted her leg and stepped into the water. Heidi, behind her washcloth, neither heard nor felt her. The creature lifted the other foot and stepped in, standing now between Heidi's legs, and then she began to crouch, bringing herself lower and lower, somehow still managing not to touch Heidi despite the lack of space. It was as if the tub was much deeper for her than for Heidi. She folded in on herself, hunched, and descended until she had vanished under the water's surface. She was gone. From the doorway the creature watched, smiled.

She lay there, the steam rising around her, listening to the slow drip of the tap into the bathwater. On the television, the static stopped, to be replaced again by images of an iron mask, clearer this time. It was being affixed over someone's head, a woman's, and was like a kind of cage. The woman's eyes darted back and forth as strong hands held her in place and forced the mask around her face. She was screaming. You could tell by the way her throat kept clenching and releasing, but her mouth was invisible within the metal mask.

A hand holding a spike moved forward into the shot. It brought it up to rest just above the hole in the mask for the right eye, and then held it there, just millimeters away from the eye itself. The eye below it darted back and forth, desperate to get away. But suddenly a mallet came down hard and drove the spike in. The eye burst in a spurt of jelly. The mallet struck again and the jelly was followed by a slow puddling of the socket with blood.

A moment later the hand appeared with another spike and brought it to rest just above the other eye.

On the wall high above the tub a drop of blood formed, seemingly out of nowhere. Slowly it began to slide down the wall, becoming a streak of blood and growing larger and wetter the farther it traveled. A foot or two from the tub itself it suddenly thickened, becoming a dense mixture of not only blood but ground organs and flesh, a sort of slurry of bloody flux and disjecta. The stream of bloody goo slid farther down to slop into the tub, where it slowly began to spread through the water. It curled and wound its way through the liquid almost like the tentacle of an octopus feeling its way tentatively forward. It touched Heidi's leg and looped carefully around it, then wound past it to curl slowly around her body, crissing and crossing on itself until slowly the water became nothing but a murky red stew. Heidi, washcloth still over her face, half sleeping, noticed nothing.

The television burst into static again, silent this time, and then an image formed, this time of a woman in a tub. The tub seemed identical to the one Heidi was in, and the woman in it had a washcloth draped over her face, and the water, too, wasn't water but a slurry of blood and flesh. But the arms were too drawn and skeletal to be Heidi's arms.

Very slowly the woman lifted the washcloth off her face and revealed herself to be Margaret Morgan.

She seemed to be looking out of the TV screen and at Heidi in the actual tub, and then, on the screen, bubbles started to plop up through the bloody water, as if it had started to boil. Slowly, something began to rise between Margaret Morgan's legs, but only gradually did it become clear that it was the misshapen head of the small creature with bulbous red eyes that, a moment before, when she had stood in the doorway, had been gripping her leg. It opened its mouth and smiled, bloody water running off its head and plopping grotesquely back into the tub.

Then, very slowly, both Morgan and the misshapen creature slid lower in the tub and disappeared beneath the water.

And then suddenly the TV switched itself off.

Chapter Twenty-nine

The bathroom was silent except for the noise of Heidi's breathing. She lay in the tub, soaking, trying to relax.

After a moment she sighed. Her hand fumbled blindly for the glass of wine balanced on the edge of the tub, without finding it. She groped again, but the wineglass didn't seem to be there. Maybe she'd put it on the floor.

She reached up and pulled the washcloth off her face. She was already half turning and reaching to search for the wineglass when she stopped, seeing the water gone murky and bloodred all around her. *What the fuck?* she thought, and then thought she must be hallucinating. She closed her eyes and opened them again, but the tub was still brimming with blood.

She scrambled back, the bloody water sloshing all around her and slopping over the sides and onto the floor. She was trying to get her feet under herself to get out of the tub but they kept slipping, the blood spattering her face and hair.

She opened her mouth and let out a piercing scream, but as she did something erupted out of the bloody water, spattering blood everywhere. It was, impossibly, another woman, somehow in the tub at the same time as she. But something was wrong with her, her arms bone thin and seemingly bloodless beneath the skin, her eyes darting madly about in the sockets. Heidi scrambled back, trying to sit up, trying to get out, but the woman was already upon her, grabbing Heidi by the throat and beginning to squeeze.

Heidi felt her body tense, felt the woman's thumbs digging into her neck, cutting off her windpipe. She kicked and thrashed, trying to break the woman's grip, bloody water sloshing up and over the sides and going everywhere. Bloody water was in her mouth and eyes. She tried to scratch out the madwoman's eyes, but the woman hissed and turned her head and she couldn't quite get to them. Heidi beat on her arms, then tried to pry her fingers away, but they wouldn't come loose.

Her vision was beginning to blur. *Oh God,* she thought, *I'm going to die.* And then the woman came closer and hissed again, smiling this time, bloody water dripping from her mouth.

Heidi made a last effort and turned her body hard, dragging on the woman's arms at the same time. With a bang, the woman's head crashed into the wall, cracking the tile, but the movement made Heidi slide lower in the tub, the water lapping against her chin now.

The woman's grip loosened a little and Heidi gasped in some air. Before the woman could recover, Heidi did it again, as hard as she could this time, and this time the woman's head struck violently enough to leave a splash of black blood on the wall. She gave a hideous unearthly scream, and a thick black liquid began to spew out of her mouth, getting in Heidi's eyes, blinding her. She struggled to break the woman's grip, but still she wouldn't let go, and instead bore down hard, making Heidi slip even lower in the tub, forcing her head underwater, knocking it repeatedly against the tub's porcelain bottom. Heidi struggled, tried desperately to break the woman's grip, tried to get her head up and above the water, but the woman held on, bore down even harder. Heidi could hear her continuing to scream, the sound muffled beneath the water but still audible. She opened her eyes and tried to see, but could make out nothing beyond the redness of the bloody water.

And then, suddenly, the screaming stopped and the pressure eased.

She shot up from the water, still struggling, still fighting to break free, and gasping for breath. She braced herself for another attack, her fists cocked.

But somehow the woman was no longer there. Heidi's gaze darted around, her heart pounding rapidly, coughing up the water that had gotten into her lungs. The water was no longer bloody. It seemed completely normal. What the fuck had happened? The fluid that had splashed all over was normal water as well, nothing unusual about it, and the woman simply wasn't there. The tile splash guard above the tub was uncracked, no sign of blood anywhere. The TV channel was back to normal, showing the same Fred Astaire movie, and reception was perfect now.

Had she imagined it all? Dreamt it? But then why did her throat hurt? Was it simply that she'd swallowed water? No, she could still feel the woman's thumbs on her throat, was sure that if she got up and looked in the mirror she'd see the bruises they had left.

But if it had been real, wouldn't Steve have been in here barking his head off? Come to think of it, where was Steve? Why hadn't he come when she'd been splashing and gasping for air?

Her head was still spinning and she was still out of breath, adrenaline coursing through her body. She tried to stand up and leave the tub but she was too dizzy and had to sit back down again, splashing back into what little water was left in the tub. She gathered her knees to her chest and leaned against the wall, shaking, trying and failing to make sense of what might have just happened.

Chapter Thirty

After a while, she'd gathered herself enough that she could drain the tub and climb out. Dazed and still shaken, she stumbled from the bathroom to collapse facedown on the fainting couch. She lay there for a few moments, catching her breath, and then lifted her head and crawled toward the phone sitting on the table just beside the couch. Trembling, she picked up the receiver.

But who could she call? Herman maybe? His wife would be pissed if she called in the middle of the night but Herman would do his best to help her—he'd done that before. Her dealer? He'd be glad to hear from her, but his idea of helping her would probably be fronting her some product and gear, just to get her going with him again. No, that was out. Whitey? He'd probably come and sit with her awhile, but that'd be using him in a way that she didn't feel comfortable with. The police? What would she tell them? *I've been attacked in my own bathroom, by some sort of corpse thing, nearly drowned, but there's absolutely no evidence.* They'd think she was crazy. Maybe she was.

She should just throw on a robe and go down and knock on Lacy's door, she told herself. She could make up some story to tell Lacy and Lacy would probably let her crash on her couch. As long as she wasn't alone, she'd be okay, even if Lacy and her sisters had ended up freaking her out as bad as anyone.

But she usually wasn't alone, she told herself. Usually, she had Steve.

Where the fuck *was* Steve, anyway?

"Steve?" she called. "Steve?" She whistled, but he didn't come. She put the phone down and stumbled into the kitchen, looking for him. He wasn't there, but the floor was dotted with bloody paw prints. And she was only now realizing she hadn't seen them when she'd come back from Lacy's—had she been that drunk? She'd assumed he'd been asleep but she hadn't even checked. What kind of dog owner was she?

The paw prints mostly milled around near the door, and the door was splintered where Steve had been scraping at it. One set of bloody tracks, though, led away from the door and through the living room, toward the bedroom.

No, a part of her cautioned herself. *Don't go in there. Whatever is in there, it's not something that you want to see.* But another part of her, a stronger part, was too concerned about her dog, too curious to know what had happened to be able to hold back.

Near the bedroom door there was a slick patch of blood, as if something had died there. She stepped over it with her bare feet, trying not to slip on the blood, and went in.

There was something in the bed, a shape there. She called out her dog's name, but he still didn't answer. Slowly, she approached the bed, tried to see what was in it, but whatever it was it was completely covered by the blankets, was impossible to see.

She reached out and took hold of the edge of the blankets. She pulled them back.

In the bed was a woman with blond hair who resembled her in every particular except that she was dead. Her wrists had been slashed and her skin had started to go gray. A syringe hung loosely from the vein in one of her arms, empty. She reached out and brushed the woman's hair back, but it still looked exactly like her. *But it can't be me,* she told herself. *I'm still alive. I'm here.*

She pulled the blankets back farther, and there, near this false Heidi's feet, was Steve. He was covered in blood, and the fur and skin had been stripped away from his head, leaving it a pulpy bloody mess, a slick and shiny skull poking through here and there. His paws, too, had been severed and placed in a little pile near his belly, as if they were puppies ready to feed. He snarled when he saw her, his eyes mad with rage or pain, and when she reached out to him, he snapped, bit her.

Oh God, she thought. *Oh God*, and stepped away from the bed, backing toward the door. Her mind was fleeing in a thousand different directions at once, and she slipped on the blood in the doorway and fell, hard. She crawled her way back into the living room, as quickly as she could manage, dry heaving, and pulled herself onto the couch. She reached again for the phone, this time dialed 911.

She was just raising the phone to her ear when something cuffed her hard on the side of the head, making her ears ring and sending the receiver flying. Standing over her was the woman she had hallucinated meeting the night before. Margaret Morgan, she had said her name was, and seeing her like this now, her skin unnaturally white, water dripping off her, Heidi realized as well that this was the woman who had tried to kill her in the tub.

For a moment they just stared at one another, neither moving, Morgan's eyes calm but hard. And then Heidi tried to scramble up and Morgan shoved her back hard with one hand, seemingly without effort. When Heidi started to struggle up again, Margaret screamed, her mouth opening unnaturally wide to reveal a shining black mouth, darker than Heidi thought possible. When Heidi struggled to get up a third time, it was not Morgan who kept her back but rather a long pitch-black arm; it held her, wrapping tightly around her waist. It seemed to shoot up from the couch, pushing up through the middle of a cushion, and she couldn't see a body attached to it. She struggled to break free, but just as she did so another pitch-black arm pushed its way through another cushion and clamped onto her thigh, digging clawed fingers in. Then another, pulling on her shoulder, and another still, this one clamping over her mouth.

She tried to cry out, all sound muffled by the hand. She struggled to break free, but there were too many arms, a dozen of them now, each of them grabbing hold of her body and tugging at it, restricting it, pinning her to the couch. And then there were several dozen pitch-black hands clinging to her everywhere, arms looping around her like darkness, tightening, cutting off her breath, dragging her back tight against the couch. She kept fighting, but then a hand clamped over her eyes and there was nothing but darkness. She could hear the sound of her muffled breathing, her muffled cries, and then something settled over her ears and all she could hear was the sound of breathing inside of herself and the furious beating of her own heart.

She felt herself lifted, propelled into darkness. The hands holding her began to feel less and less distinct, slowly thinning and changing into something else, something still restrictive, and at times disappearing altogether. The pressure on her mouth went away and she found she could breathe freely again. It slowly vanished over her ears as well and she could now hear her own panicked, desperate breathing. And then it faded over her eyes, but she still could not see. She blinked. No, there was nothing covering her eyes, but she was surrounded by darkness.

She tried to move her arms, her legs, but they were held fast, held spread far from her body. She struggled, but whatever held them was too strong and secure for her to escape from. She tried to calm down, tried to slow her own breathing, and slowly and gradually she did, listening to the sound of it easing and relaxing until she hardly could hear it at all.

But that was a mistake as it turned out. For as she slowed her own breathing, she began to hear an awful sound. It was a deep, vibrating sound, the kind of inhalations an animal might make, and it seemed to be wandering at some distance from her, slowly moving closer. *What is that?* she wondered. As images of a slavering mouth filled her mind, she tried desperately not to imagine the body that could be attached to it. It came closer still, the breathing very loud now, and she could feel its hot, fetid breath against her bare skin.

A crackling sound came from overhead, and a red light began to flicker. There, far above her, in the midst of darkness, she saw a neon *Jesus Saves* sign begin to flicker, bringing her surroundings to her in flashes of light. Only there weren't any surroundings. It was as if she were floating, suspended in an abyss, darkness pooling all around her. She was lying on a wide, long board that seemed to slowly tilt back and forth. Her arms, she saw, were strapped to the top corners of the board; her feet were spread wide and strapped to the bottom corners. She watched her body flash in and out in the strobe, as if it were deciding whether or not it would continue to exist.

The animal breathing had receded again, but she could still hear it, somewhere in the darkness, circling around her. In a flash from the malfunctioning sign, she thought for a moment she saw Margaret Morgan standing there beside her, a circle of women joining her and surrounding Heidi, but in the next flash they were gone again and there was nothing but her, the sign, and the darkness.

Slowly, very gradually, the breathing grew louder. She lifted her head, trying to locate its source. A flash of light came and she caught a glimpse of something monstrous, like a man but much larger, and bent over and deformed, and lumbering toward her.

The light flashed on again, and it was there, closer now. She could make out its deformed head, one large eye and one smaller one, two horns winding up from its skull, one of them to twist back down and burrow into the bone. And then it was close to her. She could hear the breathing as loud as the wind now, and could feel its hot breath and smell its fierce musky odor. When the *Jesus Saves* light flickered on again, the creature was standing between the sign and her, blocking it, so that all she could see was its silhouette, huge and monstrous and looming over her, and the strange reddish glow of its large and small eye.

It stood there watching her. She opened her mouth and screamed as loud as she could but the sound seemed just to drift off into the darkness and vanish. And once she had finished screaming, the figure opened its own mouth wide and offered a resounding, demonic laugh.

Chapter Thirty-one

When she regained consciousness, it was with the impression that she was hanging upside down in the air, clinging to the ceiling. If she moved at all, she worried that she would lose her grip and fall down, and perhaps would never stop falling.

But slowly she began to realize she was wrong, that she was disoriented, that something had gone wrong with her perception. Her face was pressed not against the ceiling but against a dusty wooden surface that, she started to realize, was a floor. She moved her hand and didn't fall. No, she was not hanging in the air but lying on the floor.

What had happened to her? She had been suspended in darkness, her arms and legs pinned. She had seen the creature and it had approached her and it had laughed at her and then she had felt herself exiting her own body, falling off into the darkness. But what had happened after that, and how she had made her way back to her body afterward, and why she now found herself here, unbound and lying on a floor, she couldn't say.

What happened? she asked herself again. But a part of her, a very large part of her, did not want to know what had happened.

She groaned. She was sore all over, her stomach and thighs especially, as if they had been beaten with a stick. Slowly, she lifted her head and pulled herself to her feet.

She was, she suddenly realized after glancing around, in apartment five.

It was empty and dark, lit only by the cast-off light of a streetlamp from outside and by the glow coming in from the hallway through the open door.

How the hell did I get in here? she wondered. And then thought, *I have to get out. Now.*

She stumbled out of the apartment and into the hallway, steadying herself against the wall. Her clothes, she realized once she was in the light, were torn and there were scratches and bruises visible on her sweat-drenched body. What had happened to her? A dream? Was she still having one?

Slowly, she made her way toward her apartment. Behind her, she heard a whispery noise and she turned to catch sight of something pale and white flitting through the depths of apartment number five. Though, no, she wasn't exactly sure she had seen anything. Maybe it was just the light. She backtracked and closed the door to the apartment, just in case.

By the time she was approaching the door to her own apartment, she was starting to get her mind around things. Her clothing, looking at it again, didn't seem torn exactly, only rumpled, and what she'd thought were scratches and bruises were instead just lines and creases from sleeping on a bare floor. Plus, she could hear Steve scratching on the inside of the door, which meant that he was okay, that there was nothing wrong with him, that it had all been just a bad dream.

The only question she had was, if it had been a dream, why had she woken up not in her own bed but in apartment number five? There was definitely something wrong with her.

She was just opening the door when she heard a creaking down at the end of the hallway. Despite herself, she turned to look. The door to apartment five was open. And there was something strange about the darkness of the doorway itself. It was almost as if, when she looked hard enough, she could begin to see someone standing there.

Very quickly, heart pounding hard, she entered her own apartment, locking the door behind her.

Steve was okay, still had all his paws anyway. He was definitely a little skittish, but maybe she was just passing her own mood along to him. *Talk about a fucked-up dream.* But she felt like she hadn't gotten any sleep, and like she wasn't likely to get any. She was reluctant to go back into the bathroom, but when she did everything seemed normal. There was a little water on the floor, puddles of it here and there, but nothing out of place. It was just an ordinary bathroom.

But still she felt unsettled. She sat on the toilet and held her head in her hands, and then she began to shiver and shake. Once she started shaking, it was hard to stop. It just kept coming. She stayed there for a moment, jittery as hell, then *Fuck this,* she thought, and she stood and grabbed a bottle of pills, quickly downing several. She slumped back on the toilet, waiting, hoping they would have some effect.

Wednesday

Chapter Thirty-two

Francis yawned, still tired. He was curled up on the couch, still wearing his pajamas and robe, despite it being late in the morning. He'd been more worked up than he'd realized after the radio program and then he'd allowed his research to get the better of him. What time exactly it had been when he finally closed his books and came to bed, he wasn't sure.

"Do you want more coffee?" asked Alice. She was sitting in the armchair, feet propped up, reading the *Salem News*.

"Excuse me, dear?" he said. He looked down at his cup, which was still more than halfway full. To be honest, he'd forgotten he was holding it. "No," he said. "I'm fine."

He lifted his cup and took another sip, turned his attention back to the television. An old Western was playing on it, something he vaguely remembered having seen years ago, perhaps even when he was a child.

He cleared his throat. "Do you think there is anyone under the age of a thousand who still remembers Randolph Scott?" he asked.

Alice turned her page. "Nope," she said.

"Shame," said Francis. He took another sip. "Do you remember... what was it... *Ride the High Country*?"

"Nope," Alice said. She suddenly paused, put the paper down. "Hey, weren't he and, um... Cary Grant a couple?"

Were they? wondered Francis. *Why am I always the last to know?* "I don't want to think about that before lunch," he said.

Alice gave a curt nod, raised the paper again. For a while she read in silence. Francis turned back to the TV, tried to watch the Western again. A man in buckskin was crouching behind a rock. Every time he tried to poke his head out, someone fired a shot and a puff of dust rose on the stone a few inches from the man's head. No, he'd be trapped there for a while. Was he the villain or the hero? If he was the villain, probably eventually he'd make a run for it and then keel over, shot in the back or, if he was lucky, the leg. Then there'd be a death-bed scene if it was the back, an arrest scene if it was the leg. If he was the hero, then he'd hold out, cling to his rock until the villains shooting at him ran out of bullets or the cavalry showed up. Usually you could tell which it was pretty quickly but in this case he was having a hard time figuring it out. Man didn't look like a villain nor really like a hero, just like some ordinary bastard who was about to die.

"I see they've released the identity of the murder victim and his killer," said Alice, lowering the paper again.

Without fail, thought Francis. *I start getting caught up in the show and she has to say something to pull me out of it.* "Not interested," he said. "I don't need to know." But it was too late; his concentration was broken. He was no longer lost in the movie anymore. He felt irritated. "I don't *want* to know," he added. "Murder as gossip does not concern me."

Alice gave him a hard stare over the top of her glasses, but as usual she didn't rise to the bait. How could she always remain so calm? It was something he couldn't help but envy a little. "I thought this might interest you, Francis," she said. She ruffled the paper and was hidden behind it again. "Says here the murderer was named Maisie Mather."

"Mather?" said Francis. It was like his research was haunting him. First that radio woman in all likelihood related to Hawthorne and now a descendant of Justice Mather, Hawthorne's crony.

He held out his hand. "Give it here," he said.

Alice folded the paper over, handed it to him. He took it and tried to look at it a moment at arm's length, but the print was too small. He fumbled his reading glasses off the end table and began to read.

MURDER VICTIM IDENTIFIED

The victim in the murder that rocked Salem, MA, yesterday has now been identified as Jarrett Perkins, 33. His body had been dismembered and mutilated, though the degree and nature of the mutilation has not been released by the police.

Early this morning, Maisie Mather telephoned the police station. "I want to confess to a murder," she said. "I killed my boyfriend."

"She seemed calm and collected," according to the 911 operator she spoke to. "When I asked her how she was sure her boyfriend was dead she said, 'Because he no longer has a head.' When I asked her for the address, she gave it without hesitation and added, 'Please come take me away before it happens again.' "

When police arrived, they found Perkins dead and Mather weeping, sitting in a pool of his blood.

Perkins, originally from Trenton, NJ, moved to Salem nearly a year ago. He is reported to have met Mather at a local music show shortly after arriving and had, according to friends, been seeing her ever since.

Mather, a lifelong resident of Salem and descendant of Judge Samuel Mather, a man notorious for his role in the Salem witch trials, has fully confessed to the murder of Perkins. She has, however, claimed not to have been able to control her actions.

"Clearly she is laying the groundwork for a non compos mentis plea," said Prosecutor Michael Stewart, a plea otherwise known as not guilty by reason of insanity.

When asked if the state would encourage such a plea, Mr. Stewart shook his head. "Considering the brutality of the crime itself and the nature of the mutilation, we have no choice but to pursue the maximum penalty."

That penalty would be multiple life sentences. Massachusetts abolished the death penalty in 1984.

According to her own confession, Mather was engaged in intimate acts with Perkins when an uncontrollable urge struck her. She got up, shaved her head, carved a symbol into her chest, and then killed Perkins with a pair of scissors.

When asked why she had done it, she claimed she didn't know. When asked what the symbol meant, she also claimed she did not know. Police have not released a description of this symbol.

Mather is described by her former employer Brian Conn as "a normal, ordinary person. I never would have expected anything like this to happen in a million years. I can't even believe it was her." Neighbors describe her as "sweet" and "generous to a fault."

Mather has no history of mental illness.

Francis sighed. What was life coming to? What happened to the good old days when you could just hide behind a rock and, as long as you stayed there, you wouldn't get shot? Never any dismemberings in a Western. At least not that he could remember. There was a picture next to the article and he took a close look at it. Yes, the face meant something to him. He could see a resemblance to the old paintings of Judge Mather of course, but it was more than that.

"Hmmm," he said.

"What?" said Alice.

"She looks familiar," he said. Where was it? Where had he seen her before? "I remember this girl."

Alice rose and went over and stood behind his shoulder, looking down at the picture. "I don't think I know her," she said.

Francis snapped his fingers. He had it. "She came to that summer fund-raiser we had at the museum last August. She was a sweet kid," he said. "Didn't seem the type to go in for dismembering."

"What do you think would drive a girl like that to do something so dark?" asked Alice.

Francis kept studying the picture. The resemblance to Mather was there, but with very little sign of Mather's intractability and cruelty. No, at the fund-raiser she'd been completely normal, really a lovely person. It just didn't make any sense. "Hell, I don't know," he said, feeling depressed now. "I don't know why anyone does anything anymore."

Alice put her hand on his shoulder, squeezed it. For a while they were silent, staring at the picture of the girl.

"It isn't like she just woke up one day and thought, 'I'm going to shave my head and murder the first person I see.' "

Francis shrugged. "Maybe that's exactly what it was like," he said.

Chapter Thirty-three

God, her head hurt. Her awareness of the night before was blurring now. Weird shit, that was what it was. She felt like she was really losing her grip. She had screamed herself awake—how fucked-up was that? And now she was walking in her sleep as well? What the hell? She'd woken up in the hall, pounding on the door to apartment number five. Or thought she had. She wasn't even sure of that anymore now that it was light outside. The nightmares she'd had seemed so real, so vivid, and that shit of falling asleep in the bath and that fucked-up dream were the worst of all. How could she have gotten to sleep after that? To top it off, she had had too much of Lacy's wine, so when she wasn't busy screaming herself awake or listening to her heart beat louder and louder in her ears she'd been queasy and could feel the room spinning around her. And there was a period, she wasn't sure if it was real or another dream, when she'd been kneeling on the floor and vomiting into the toilet, with Steve, sweet dog that he was, wagging his tail next to her and licking her face and trying to cheer her up. Or maybe he was just trying to get a taste of that vomit, who knows? Gross.

With all that, she felt more tired than she had when she'd gone to sleep. It was like each night was worse, like every night whittled away another thin sliver of her sanity. She'd been doing well over the last year, been holding it together. But she needed something to relax her, mellow her out a little, or there was no way that she was going to make it through the day. She wasn't going to do something extreme—she wasn't going to call her dealer up. And she definitely wasn't going to get some gear. No, just something to relax, something harmless. Relatively so, anyway.

She stumbled her way to the dresser. She began digging through the top drawer, piling underwear and socks on top of the dresser until the drawer was empty. Shit, it wasn't there. She'd been sure it would be there, remembered putting it there just as backup, just in case. But it wasn't there now. Maybe she had the wrong drawer? She bent lower and opened the next drawer down and this time she simply pulled the whole thing out and dumped it on the bed. Her hands quickly pawed their way through the contents, searching, tossing clothing left and right. She was just about to give up when…

Ah, there it was. She knew she had one. It was the butt of a joint, half smoked or so, really dry shit, something like a year old and likely to be more than a little harsh by now, but what the hell? It'd still have some kick.

She stepped back. Steve was there, lying on the floor, staring at her. "What?" she said to him. He kept staring at her, ears flattened a little. "I just need a little something to steady my nerves today," she said. "Don't worry, I'm not getting into all that shit again." *What, now I have to justify myself to a dog?*

She took the lighter off the counter and flicked the flame on, sucked on the joint. She drew the smoke deep into her lungs, held it. Ah, it felt good. Too good. *Gateway drug*, she thought. The NA guys definitely wouldn't approve. Though they wouldn't approve of the wine either, so what difference did this make? Anyway, this wasn't what she'd been addicted to so it didn't matter. Steve was still staring at her, probably thinking much the same thing that the NA guys would have, she reckoned.

She let the smoke out slowly. She ashed the joint and shook it at Steve. It was already short enough that she could feel the heat coming off it against her thumb. "Now, don't you start judging me," she said to Steve. "That's the last thing I need."

                              *   *   *

Yeah, it wasn't bad. She felt pretty good. Part of her was already feeling guilty about it—doing shit like this opened a kind of hunger in her, just made some monstrous part of her stretch and begin to wake up and start craving what she'd had before. But no, she couldn't get into that again. Last time, it had gotten bad enough that she was lucky she came out of it alive. Griff hadn't, after all. Did she feel guilty about that? Guilty about surviving?

But maybe, something in her said hopefully, *maybe this time it'll be different. Maybe it won't be any trouble for me at all.*

No, no next time. But the thoughts were already getting fuzzy. She was losing track of them, letting them slip away from her. Which, she told herself, was what she wanted—to not worry, to relax a little, to be able in some way or another to face her day.

Time slipped a little. It got slow, as if it wasn't passing at all and it seemed like each moment was being stretched further and further. Maybe she slept a little. And then suddenly it sped up again and Steve was there, whining, licking her arm.

"What is it, Steve?" she asked him, and when he kept whining she hauled herself to her feet and stood. Wow, she was dizzy. She leaned against the wall for balance and navigated her way into the kitchen, poured Steve some food.

He immediately wolfed it down, clearly hungry. Had she remembered to feed him the night before? She wasn't sure. Maybe, maybe not. God, she was terrible, starting to really fall apart.

No, she told herself, *don't think like that. You're doing okay. You just have had a couple of bad days. Talk to your friends and they'll help you.*

Shit, the joint had made her moody and paranoid instead of relaxing her. Go fucking figure.

The bowl was empty but Steve was still whining, staring at her. Her head hurt a little. What did he want now?

It took him going over to the front door and pressing his nose against it before she figured out what she should have guessed immediately: he hadn't been out yet.

"All right," she said. Feeling like she was wading through knee-deep water, she found his leash and attached it to his collar and then led him out the door. She headed toward the stairs, but as she moved around the railing and started down she caught a glimpse of something and couldn't help but stop.

No, she told herself. *Don't look.*

But she couldn't stop herself from turning around and looking down the corridor at apartment number five.

The door was open. And despite the fact that it was daytime, it remained dark, almost black, within the apartment. It was impossible to see anything.

Fuck me, she thought. For a moment she thought about going down the hall and looking in, see if there wasn't someone there after all.

But no, she'd had so many nightmares about apartment number five that she knew it'd be a mistake. And she was stoned. Even if there was nothing in there, she still might get freaked out.

So she forced herself to turn back around and start slowly down the stairs.

But all the time, with every step she took, she could feel the room there, behind her, looming as if waiting for her. And about halfway down she thought she heard a strange rubbing sound, like bare feet sweeping along the hall's wood floor. In her head, she saw unnaturally pale and unnaturally thin legs, the feet at the bottom of them slightly twisted, the nails blackened, following her. In her head they were just that: disembodied legs with a strange darkness surmounting them, hiding whatever was above.

And then she heard a creaking that sounded just a little too much like a high, tittering laugh. She bolted, taking the rest of the steps two at a time, making a run for the door.

*   *   *

Once she was outside, she felt a little better. She could breathe again anyway, could relax a little, and even though she was stoned it was okay now since she was out and walking. She took the usual route for a while until Steve did his business, and then decided to take the scenic route.

She headed down a long set of stone steps that looked as if they'd been there for hundreds of years. They were cracked here and there, covered with moss on the edges. They led to a bridge with wrought-iron sides that passed over a pond. On the other side was the heart of Greenlawn Cemetery. She crossed the first of several rolling hills, she and Steve slowly following the winding cemetery roads and gravel paths. The graves were well-kempt, the stones often ostentatious with many family plots that offered a central monument with smaller graves circled around them.

Her father's grave was in the front part of the cemetery, among the newer stones. Usually she avoided it, but today, well, something drew her there. It was a modest stone, but long. The grave had her mother's name on it as well, even though her mother was still alive; it was just waiting for someone to carve in the date of her death. Her mother sometimes spoke about that, said there was a "bed" waiting for her in the cemetery. Kind of creepy, Heidi thought, but also kind of romantic. Her mom and dad had really gotten along, really cared for each other, which had made her dad's death all the harder.

And here she was, stoned to the gills, not sleeping, staring at her father's grave. She'd had all sorts of advantages in life: parents who loved her, education at a good school, good friends. So why was it that she was where she was today? Where had she gone wrong? How had she slipped off course? How could she get back to being the person she wanted to be?

She moved away, into other parts of the cemetery. If you knew where to look, you'd find the older graves, some of them with stones so old and eaten away by time and the elements you could no longer read them. There, the stones were often not straight, sinking into the earth at odd angles as time had settled the ground below them.

She walked her way through the graveyard and out the edge of it, going a few blocks down to Saint Peter's church. She had started past the old stone building and was near the huge red doors at the front of it when Steve stopped to sniff around a little. A little religion might not hurt, she told herself, though she also promised herself to take off if those two creepy nuns appeared.

Chapter Thirty-four

She found a small sapling and tied Steve's leash off to it. He sat with his ears perked up, watching her leave. One of the red doors was slightly ajar and she pushed it open enough to slip in. She moved through the vestibule and into the main hall.

The church looked much different than it had at night, with a rich amber light now pouring through the stained-glass windows and making the air dance with motes of dust. An ornate crucifix hung over the altar, either gold-plated or bronze. Inside, the church was completely empty. She found a pew in the back that was warm from the sunlight, and she sat down, trying to take the atmosphere in, trying to relax. Did she want to try to pray? No, that seemed false— she could come share the comfort of a place like this, but she could hardly pass herself off as a believer. She hadn't been to church in years. Still, she closed her eyes and tried to empty her mind of all bad thoughts.

When she opened her eyes, it was because she heard the sound of a door somewhere. She glanced up and saw that a smallish door to the right of the altar was ajar. As Heidi watched, a priest passed through it. Slowly, he began to walk down the central aisle, his footsteps ringing against the stone.

He had his hands behind his back and seemed lost in thought, his face half frowning. He didn't seem to notice her.

He was almost past Heidi when she said hello and smiled at him. The priest stopped, startled at first. Slowly, he focused his gaze on her, squinting, almost as if he had difficulty seeing her.

"Why are you here?" he asked, his voice low and hoarse.

"Why am I here?" she asked. Good question, actually, if this was the kind of reception she was going to get. "I don't know," she said, straightening a little in the pew. "I was walking by with my dog and I thought I would just come in and sit for a moment. Is that okay? Are you closed?"

"You brought your dog into a house of worship?"

"No, of course not," said Heidi. "He's tied up outside."

The priest nodded in curt acknowledgment. "No, we're not closed," he said. "The Lord's house never closes. God is always open and ready to listen."

"That's good to know," said Heidi. "I've been having some problems lately and thought..." She looked up. Something about the way the priest was looking at her bothered her. *Fuck it*, she thought. "I don't know what I thought," she said. "I guess I just needed to sit."

"Sit," said the priest. "Hell, don't mind if I do." And with that he sat down next to her, close enough that their shoulders rubbed against one another.

Not very priestly language, thought Heidi. She felt crowded and was tempted to move away, but she was worried about offending the man.

"Yes, it is a nice place to just come and sit," said the priest. He had turned his head toward her and she could feel his breath as he spoke. There was a strange smell to it, like spiced meat. As she watched, she thought she saw a fly slip out of his mouth. *I'm still stoned*, she told herself. *I'm hallucinating. There was no fly.*

He reached out and gently placed his hand on her shoulder. Very gently he began to massage her there.

"You're very tense, my child," he said.

Another fly slipped out of him, from his nostril this time. *I definitely saw that*, Heidi thought. It crawled along his lip and over his cheekbone and then burrowed into his ear. The massage was less gentle now. Slowly, he slid his hand up behind her neck. *What the hell?* she thought.

"Um, yeah," she said. "I feel better now. I think I should be going."

His hand paused momentarily on the back of her neck and then gripped it hard. Just when she was about to cry out, he let go. She started to stand but when she did he wound his fingers into her hair and tugged hard, dragged her back down. When she tried to pull away, he sunk his fingers deeper and pulled harder so that her head was being cranked backward over the back edge of the pew, leaving her throat bare and exposed.

"Ow, what the fuck?" she said.

"What the fuck indeed," said the priest, seemingly unperturbed. He reached out and kissed her on the throat, and then opened his mouth and clamped it around her windpipe. She could feel his teeth exerting pressure, constricting her breathing just slightly. She struggled, but he had, she suddenly realized, shifted his body to pin one of her arms and when she tried to strike him with the other arm he first batted the arm away and then caught her wrist in one thick hand and squeezed. She cried out in pain, and when she did he bit her hard on the throat, hard enough that when his mouth came away there was blood on his lips. He let go of her wrist and began fondling her breasts, knocking her hand back effortlessly when she tried to push him away.

"You have a lot to learn," he said. "And I'm going to teach it to you."

"Let go of me!" she yelled.

But he did not let go. Instead, he brought himself a little closer, looming over her. When he spoke, his voice was strangely flat and calm, perfectly cold, which frightened her more than if he'd been shrieking at her. "You have to understand there is a war waging in Heaven," he said. "Michael and his angels fought against the dragon and his serpents. But God does not spare angels when they sin. He sends them to Hell."

She heard the sound of him unzipping his fly. Suddenly the hand that had been pulling her head back pushed it forward hard, nearly bending her double and forcing her facedown into the priest's lap. She felt his cock slide against her cheek, warm and semitumescent and smelling of standing water and oil.

"You are a filthy whore of Satan," he claimed. "Christ cannot save you. Only I can save you." His voice had begun to change, becoming harsher and deeper, and he had begun to lose his composure now. His breathing was growing more and more heavy. He shifted his hips and forced himself into her mouth, pulling hard on her hair when at first she refused to open.

"You must no longer offer worship and sacrifice to the goat idols to whom you prostitute yourself," he was saying.

He forced her head up and down. She choked and tried not to gag and wished for it all to be over. He began to moan, and she felt his thighs begin to tense. She felt humiliated, but quickly the humiliation shifted to anger. Rage filled her. She tightened her mouth and bit down until her teeth were tearing into the flesh of his cock and her mouth tasted of blood. But the priest, rather than protesting or hitting her, seemed to enjoy it. She tried to get her hand that was trapped behind his body free but it was wedged too firmly. She tried to strike him with her other hand but bent over like that, it was all but impossible. He just laughed.

He was panting heavily now, his hips bucking as he forced himself farther down her throat. "You must," he said, "understand what the Lord...has done for you...and how...he has supreme...dominion... over your soul."

Suddenly he gave a scream and Heidi expected him to come, but nothing happened. Instead, she felt something wet on the back of her head and neck and he let go. She pulled her head back quickly, saw that his eyes had rolled up into his head. From his mouth spurted a

black, viscous ichor, spraying into her mouth and eyes as she tried
desperately to get away.

She woke up suddenly, feeling someone shaking her. She raised her
hands to defend herself before realizing it was a priest.

"Miss...wake up," he said. "Wake up."

She looked at him in horror. He was the same priest as in her
dream, though the lines of his face were different, softer, his expression anything but cruel.

"I believe you fell asleep," he said, leaving his hand on her shoulder. "I'm afraid you must have been having some kind of nightmare.
You kept calling out. I felt it my duty to awaken you."

Heidi rubbed her face with her hands. "Oh, sorry," she said. "I,
um...I gotta go."

"Are you all right?" he asked. "Do you need someone to talk to?
God is always open and ready to listen."

Hearing the same words as in her dream, she recoiled and pushed
his hand away. He hovered there at the end of the pew, confused.
"No," she said. "I'm just fine." Quickly she gathered herself together,
pushed past the priest, and fled the church.

Steve had managed to get himself tangled and could hardly move.
How long had she been asleep in there? Fuck, she was going to be late
for work if she wasn't careful. It never seemed to stop. Hands shaking, she untangled Steve and the two of them started quickly off and
away.

She couldn't stop herself from casting a glance back over her shoulder. She expected to see the priest standing by the open doors, but
he wasn't there. Instead, there were the two old nuns just standing
motionless, watching her.

It's like the whole world is out to get me, thought Heidi, and then,
No, that's just the joint making me paranoid.

But it was more than that. It had to be. Those dreams started before she had smoked the joint and everything had seemed weird before that. No, the world was fucked-up. Something was very wrong. It wasn't just her.

She crossed the bridge over the pond and started up the stairs. She was still rattled, jittery enough that it was hard to walk. She stopped a few steps up and sat down, then begged a cigarette and a light off a passerby. Another gateway drug, another return to old habits. Her hands were shaking so hard that the man had to take it back from her to get it lit.

She took a deep puff, tried to calm down. Maybe the cigarette would do it. And if that didn't work, there were always anxiety pills. And if those didn't work, she could get drunk again. And if that didn't work? Well, she didn't want to think about that.

She tried to relax, letting her eyes wander. The pond was placid, the light just mellow enough that the reflections of the trees and hills in the water seemed almost more real than the actual trees and hills.

There were shouts and she turned her head to see, perhaps one hundred meters away, children wearing flowing white ghost costumes running around some of the graves, an older grouping of them, with cracked and dilapidated headstones. She watched the costumed children run, laughing at one another, playing tag or something.

And then suddenly, in unison, they stopped. Slowly, they began to turn until they were all facing her. *What the fuck?* she wondered. Steve began to whine. The children in ghost costumes stood there motionless, watching her, waiting.

Chapter Thirty-five

He'd waited at the curb, and then honked a few times, but the only thing that had happened was that that bitch who was her landlord came out and gave him the evil eye. Or maybe she was just checking him out. Hell, he was dressed nice, as usual, and he knew that even old chicks dug guys in fine-ass threads. She could look, but she couldn't touch—Herman knew the warden wouldn't tolerate that.

So he sat in the car a bit and then he got out and went up to the porch and rang Heidi's bell about ten times but there was no answer and no sounds of anything stirring inside. He took out a cigar and rolled it between his fingers a bit, thinking that she'd come out right as soon as he started to smoke it. But even after he clipped off the ends and started puffing on it, there was no sign of her. He smoked it about halfway to ash. When one of the other tenants came out, he left it balanced precariously on the railing of the porch and grabbed the door before it could close and clomped his way down the hall and up the stairs to her door. *Pound, pound, pound.* Still no answer. And no whining or barking from Steve either, which meant that she probably was just out with her dog and had forgotten the time.

Still, he couldn't stop himself from turning the door handle just to make sure. It wasn't locked, and he couldn't resist going in. *Just to see,* he told himself. *Just to make sure.*

But what he saw didn't reassure him. An empty container of prescription pills rattling around in the sink of the bathroom. Not even in her name, but from someone named Griffin Lawe. He read the label on it—naproxen sodium, 500 mg. Not anything he'd ever heard of. Could be a painkiller or a sleeping pill but could also be an acne medication or something relatively harmless. *Don't judge in advance*, he told himself. *You shouldn't even be in here.* Records out and scattered all over the floor in the living room, some of them broken. The fainting couch had been turned over and was lying on its side, and several of the drawers of her dresser had been pulled out and dumped on the bed. Not nearly as bad as the time when he'd had to rescue her, admittedly, but something was wrong. She wasn't keeping her shit together. Was she using again? There wasn't anything besides the empty pill bottle in the sink to suggest that she was, and even that didn't really prove anything, but still. He couldn't help but be worried.

He went back outside, easing the door shut as he left. On his way toward the stairs he realized that the door to the apartment at the end of the hallway was open. Probably whoever lived there hadn't pulled it quite shut when they left and his opening Heidi's door had made that door come open, too. He was momentarily tempted to go down and pull it shut, do someone a good turn, but then thought, *Not my fucking problem.* No, he had to get over the idea that he was put on this earth to look out for other people, particularly if it was true that Heidi was using again. Last fucking thing he wanted was to get caught back up in that shit again.

Once back outside, he had to relight the cigar. He puffed on it patiently, feeling the impatience grow inside of him. Cigar gone, he ground it out and waited around outside a few more minutes, as long as he possibly could without being late. When she still hadn't shown up, he just shook his head and climbed into the car.

He sighed. Maybe she'd already gone to the station and he'd meet her there. Maybe he'd been worried for nothing.

But no, he thought as he pulled a U-turn and started toward the station. She has Steve. She'd have to come home first.

Still, by the time he got to the station, he'd convinced himself that she might have brought Steve to work with her, that she'd be there waiting for him. But the only person in the break room was Whitey.

"Yo," said Herman.

"Yo," said Whitey back. He was holding a cup of coffee that was already mostly empty. Whitey had been there for a while. Which meant it must be later than Herman thought.

"Where you been?" asked Whitey. "You're never late."

Instead of answering, Herman turned to the refrigerator. He opened the door and looked inside, shuffled around a few items. At first it had been just to avoid answering Whitey, but when he realized what was missing, he began to get seriously pissed. But he wasn't sure if it was real anger or just redirected shit over Heidi's absence.

"Goddamn it! Who the fuck is stealing my Slim-Shakes?"

Whitey shrugged. "Not me," he said. He patted his belly. "I'm trying to *gain* some weight. Got to be one of the overnights. Ambler maybe. He's looking pretty fit these days."

Herman just shook his head, closed the fridge. He pulled out a mug, poured himself some coffee. "Where's girlie at?" he asked.

"Heidi? She didn't take them. She's not even here yet."

"Are you fucking kidding me?" Herman glanced at his watch. Shit, they'd be on any minute. "What the hell, man? I knew it. I could see something in her eyes the other night. She better not be fucking up again. I laid my balls on the line to get her back on the air."

"Chill, man," said Whitey. "It's all good."

"It's all good? You call this all good?"

"Mellow," said Whitey. "She's just late, is all. It's no big thing."

"I swear I'll jam my size thirteens up her butthole if she repays me by throwing my ass under the bus."

Whitey didn't bother to answer. After a minute Herman sat down at the table and started drinking his coffee.

They were like that, listening to the sound of the news announcer playing low on the station speakers in the background, waiting for Heidi to make an appearance, for a minute or two. Finally Herman heard the sound of footsteps coming down the hall and thought, *She's finally here* and began to relax. But it wasn't Heidi who came in the break room door. It was Chip.

He was carrying a large wooden box and seemed to be out of breath. He set it down on the table between them with a loud thud.

"There you go, boys," he said. "All yours."

"What's this?" asked Herman.

Chip smiled. "Free money."

He pulled the top off the box. Inside were stacks of identical records, all of them in a simple black sleeve with that creepy-ass Lords symbol on it: a kind of weird, fucked-up Neanderthal face or whatever.

"Lords promos," said Chip.

"What for?" said Whitey.

Chip turned to him, gave him a disgusted look. "What for? Are you sure you work in radio? For promotion, obviously. It seems this bunch of musical geniuses is coming to town and we're the presenting station."

"We're standing behind that shit?" asked Herman. "Seriously?"

"Like my impending triple bypass," said Chip. "So, in other words, the Lords of Salem are now off-limits to your wisecracks. No more jokes about this garbage. You play that record in heavy—and I do mean heavy—rotation and keep your snarky comments to yourself. And give all but one of these records away," he said. He reached back into the box and pulled out a sheaf of tickets, shook them at Whitey. "And make sure these are all gone by Saturday."

Whitey gave him a confused look. "What's Saturday?" he asked.

Chip rolled his eyes. "Again, are you sure you work in radio? What do you think? The concert."

Whitey, Herman realized, was getting ready to ask *What concert?* To head off Chip's imminent explosion, he held out his hand and said, "Hand them over." When he did and Herman looked at them, he did a double take.

"Um, there's a mistake here," he said.

"What do you mean, a mistake?" said Chip.

Herman pointed to the venue listed on the ticket. "The Salem Palladium? Correct me if I'm wrong, but I don't think there's been a show at that dump since around 1983. Isn't it abandoned?"

"Was last time I checked," said Whitey.

Chip shrugged. "Technically, yes, but who am I to argue? If they want to have a show in a rat-infested hellhole, well then, God bless."

"You sure it's not just a mistake?" said Herman. "Where did these come from anyway? What did the rep say about them?"

"No rep," said Chip.

"No rep? How'd you get them then?"

"They just showed up," said Chip. "Were waiting for me when I got in this morning."

"Who's the contact?" said Whitey. "Let's check with him about the venue."

Chip ruffled through some of the promotional papers. "No name or number," he said. "Not very professional."

"Someone's taking you for a ride," said Herman. "It's a joke."

Chip shook his head. "No," he said. "They already paid. Envelope of cash was included with the promos."

"Doesn't that seem fucked-up to you, Chip?" asked Herman.

But Chip was ignoring him. He was shuffling his way deeper into the papers. "Palladium, Palladium, Palladium," he said. "If it's a mistake, then they've made the same mistake the whole way across the board. It's not our fault. We run with it."

"That place is huge," said White Herman. "You're telling me this band is gonna sell enough tickets to fill it up?"

Chip turned toward him, a look of irritation immediately on his face. "I'm not telling you anything except get rid of these tickets," he said. "These comps are the only tickets."

"Weird," said Whitey, looking at the stack. "That's not nearly enough to fill the place. It's going to be super-sparse. Even empty."

"What the hell do I care?" asked Chip. "If they want to play to an empty hall, then let them."

"A classic underplay," said Herman. "Sounds like a big money loser to me."

Chip pulled a small poster out of the box and unrolled it, showed it to Herman. On it was the same symbol as on the record, but it looked like it had been carved into the flesh between a woman's breasts, the wound brimming with blood and beginning to drip. Below, it read, in a gothic script, *THE LORDS ARE COMING*.

"Not a money loser for us," he said. "We're being paid just to push it. And money loser or not, the Lords are coming and it's our job to spread the word."

Chapter Thirty-six

Herman still was thinking about Heidi with half his mind, wondering if she was okay, wondering if she'd get there. But so far no Heidi. Whitey looked like he wanted to say something or ask about her, but Herman put that don't-mess-with-me look on his face and Whitey read it loud and clear and swallowed his words. Even when it was time for them to go on the air neither of them said anything about her absence, just gathered their things and went into the studio.

Just as they were getting ready to start, Chip came in. "Where's the final member of Big H's holy trinity?" he asked.

Herman thought for a second about what he should say. He could say that he didn't know, which would just make Chip anxious. Or he could say that she was fucking up again, which would get Chip angry not only at her but also at him. Or he could lie and just pretend like things were okay and then later let the chips fall where they would. The warden would be pissed at him about that last one—she was always telling him that he needed to look out for number one first—but he was built how he was built, and he was going to do what he was going to do.

"She called," he said. "Said she's going to be a few minutes late."

"What's wrong?" asked Chip. "Is anything wrong?"

"We got it covered," said Herman. "No worries."

"If you need me—" Chip started.

"We got it covered," Herman said, more firmly this time than he felt. It was enough for Chip, who nodded and went out.

Which left him and Whitey alone to get their things together as the commercials wound down.

"I didn't know she called," Whitey said.

"Shut the fuck up," said Herman. "You're putting me in a bad mood."

Whitey was silent for about four seconds. "Could have told me she called," he said.

"She didn't call," said Herman. And when Whitey opened his mouth to speak again, he lifted a finger, stopped him. "Focus," he said. "Show's starting."

They stumbled through it for ten or fifteen minutes or so, both of them worried in their own way, but just trying to go forward with the show. And then they relaxed into it and it was okay. As per usual, Whitey offered up one of his various family dramas, fucked-up things from his childhood that were probably all made up but that the listeners seemed to like to hear. Was there a grain of truth in them? Hell if Herman knew. He'd stopped wondering about that about a hundred stories back. It was his job, he knew, to seem incredulous, and then let Whitey make the story wilder and wilder. And then, cut to a commercial or a song.

"I'm sorry, man," he said, after Whitey had finished his first rendition of the story, "but I don't believe it. That story sounds like complete b.s."

"What's so hard to believe?" asked Whitey. "I'm on a cruise ship with my grandparents, and my grammy gets seasick. So she leans over the side to puke...and pukes out her dentures right into the ocean. No joke."

"Disgusting," said Herman.

"Oh, it gets worse," said Whitey. "Later that night, I walk in on a butt-naked, toothless grammy giving Grandpa a blow job."

"Butt-naked, eh?" said Herman. "That's the last thing you want to see."

"Well, not quite naked. Actually she had a sombrero with the words 'Aye, Chihuahua' embroidered on it."

"Excuse me?" said Herman.

"What, did I forget to mention it was a Mexican cruise?"

Herman just shook his head. They were definitely skirting the edge of what Chip would see as appropriate. Any moment he might pop up at the studio window and give them the signal to tone it down. But still, he couldn't resist saying, "I guess Grandpa didn't have to worry about teeth that night."

"Are you calling my grammy a whore?" asked Whitey. He made sure the listeners could hear the smile in his voice so they'd know he was joking. "Don't talk about my grandparents like that."

There was movement in front of the glass of the booth and he thought, *Chip, right on schedule.* But when he glanced up it was to see Heidi. Very quietly she eased the door open and then slipped in. She made it to her chair, a little unsteady on her feet and slid in behind her microphone.

She didn't look good. Her eyes were glassy and bloodshot and surrounded by dark circles, like she hadn't slept in weeks. She was a walking disaster. Goddamn, why had he covered for her?

"Well, look who's ready to join the party," he said, his voice indignant.

When she spoke into the microphone it was with a mellow, throaty voice. Yeah, he had to admit, she had a great radio voice. You could hear sex dripping off it. "Did I miss anything?" she asked.

"Another nonsensical Whitey childhood memory," said Herman.

"Nonsensical?" protested Whitey. He put his hand over his heart. "Every word of it was true. If I do say so myself, it was a fascinating tale of my slutty grandma and some missing teeth."

Herman bit back the impulse to scold Heidi on air. "Anyway, since you're here, I guess we can make our big announcement. Fanfare, please, Igor."

Whitey hit a switch on the board and played a flourish of off-key trumpets and kazoos.

"That the best we can do?" asked Herman.

Whitey shrugged. "I can play it again if you want," he said, and did so. Heidi, meanwhile, was resting her chin against her hand, eyes half closed, about to nod off. Herman gave her a dirty look, but she was too out of it to even notice.

When the fanfare ended, he began to speak in stentorian tones. "The Lords are coming to Salem for one night only."

At that Heidi perked up a little. Opened her eyes anyway.

"The Lords of Salem? Really?" she said in a half mumble. "When?"

"You've got to start coming to the meetings," said Whitey.

Heidi gave a lazy smile and flipped Whitey off.

Herman began singing, Bay City Rollers style. "S-A-T-U-R-D-A-Y night! And we've got the tickets. In fact, we have all the tickets. You get them from us or you don't get them at all. Plus, the show is free."

"Did you say free?" said Whitey in a fake excited voice. "Now I know there's gotta be a catch."

"Why does there always have to be a catch?" groaned Heidi.

"I don't know," said Whitey. "There just always is."

Chip wasn't going to like that if he heard it, thought Herman. No point in making the audience paranoid. "No catch at all," he said. "Just call in and get your tickets or come on down to the station and get them. Any way you slice this meat loaf, it is free, baby."

He gestured to Whitey, who put the needle on the album. The Lords track started off. Hell, he liked it even less than the first time he'd heard it. He made a face and then turned to dress Heidi down.

Chapter Thirty-seven

Virginia Williams sighed, her hands deep in the dishwater. She was tired, but she always felt tired these days. How had life gotten away from her? Last thing she remembered she'd been, like, twenty, and then she blinked and now suddenly here she was, fifty-one. Not even fifty, but fifty-fucking-one. And still with Keith, for Christ's sake. And on top of that, she had to put up with this crap. Had Keith ever even washed a single damned dish in his life? To hear him tell it, he was the one who did all the work and kept things going. If that was the case, then why was the porch about to rot off? It was hardly even safe to go out there these days. And why was it that every time she turned around he was sucking down another beer?

Okay, Keith wasn't sucking down a beer right now, but he was damned sure digging through the fridge looking for one. He was way over the hill and halfway down the other side, almost sixty compared to her fifty-one. No hair on the man's head to speak of, and why did he still insist on wearing a wifebeater? The only hair he had left was his chest hair, which was a stiff dirty white that was better left covered up. But could she get him to put a nice shirt on at home? Hell no. She sighed. It was lucky, she supposed, that he was willing to throw on a tank top. If she had to see even an inch more of his pasty white flesh, well, she didn't know what she'd do.

He surfaced from the fridge again and sure enough this time he had a beer in hand. He twisted the lid off and flicked it at the trash where, as usual, it bounced off the side and skittered across the linoleum. Was he going to pick it up? Not a chance. She'd be doing that later, as soon as she was done with all these dishes.

On the window ledge over the sink, the radio was playing. The Big H. They were the best that Salem had to offer, which wasn't, she had to admit, saying all that much.

"I guess it's time," said one of them. Whitey, his name was.

"Oh, it's time, baby," said the other one, Herman. "Give it up for the Lords of Salem."

And then the music started. It was some far-out stuff, all right, hardly even music, not like the stuff she grew up with anyway: REO Speedwagon, Donna Summer, Earth, Wind, and Fire. But there was something to it, something was pulling at her, dragging her into it.

Keith was saying something to her, jabbing a finger at her as he spoke, just kind of crouched there beside the sink, watching her, drinking his beer. Couldn't he just leave her alone? Couldn't she be allowed to do the dishes and listen to the radio in peace for once? Was that really too much to ask?

She'd missed most of it, but she caught the word *daughter* and realized he must be talking about his granddaughter's birthday party. He'd been griping about it for days now.

"Why should I?" he was saying. "I might as well stay home."

"Well, I don't want to go either," Virginia said harshly. "But guess what? You can just suck it up because we're going."

It just bounced off Keith. It usually did. He was the kind of guy who thought an argument was just two people's normal way of communicating.

"It's so stupid," he said. "The fucking brat is one year old. She doesn't even know it's her fucking birthday."

"Hey," she said. "It's your family, not mine."

He gave her a disgusted look. "Trust me, I know," he said, and walked out of the room.

And then, mercifully, she was alone. Just her, for once. Or her and the music. There was something about it, something about the song, that she could feel humming in her bones. She liked it. It made her feel like she was somewhere else, and that was exactly how she wanted to feel. Anywhere but here. She reached out and turned it up just a little, her wet hand giving her a little shock when she touched the knob. Yeah, that was better, a little louder. What did it remind her of? Something, she couldn't quite put her finger on it, but yeah, it was familiar somehow. The music was calling to her, whispering to her. Wow, she hadn't felt that way about a song for years now, decades even. It made her tingle all over.

The plates were done. She reached into the dishwater and groped along the bottom of the sink for silverware. She was scrubbing off utensils, moving them from the soapy water to the clean water when something caught her eye. What was that through the window above the sink, that shadowy shape staring at her?

With a start, she realized that it was her own reflection against the dark glass. But it didn't look like her, did it? Who was that old, fat, bedraggled woman? That wasn't her. She knew she wasn't really that way. This was the universe playing tricks on her.

But maybe, a voice inside her said, *it's time for you to start playing tricks back.*

Who was that? she wondered. She looked at the strange shadowy reflection of herself in the pane of glass, the image that both was and was not her. There was something different about it, and it wasn't just that the image was backward. She looked different than she had. A sly smile had begun to curve on her lips.

"What kind of tricks?" she asked her reflection.

"Did you say something?" shouted her husband from the other room.

She ignored him.

Well, it whispered back, *we could start with a makeover…*

A makeover! She'd always wanted a makeover. She'd begged her friends to put her name in for one of those TV shows, the ones where the women went in looking dumpy and came out looking beautiful. She'd be perfect for one of those shows; she knew it. There was a beautiful woman hiding inside her. All she needed was for someone to let it out. But nobody ever took her seriously about it. And most of those friends were gone now anyway, driven away by Keith. She should have left him long ago. If she had, she'd probably still have friends now.

"Shall I go get my makeup?" she said to her reflection. She began to dry her hands off, getting ready to go into the bathroom.

"Are you talking on the phone or something?" Keith shouted. "Who you talking to?"

She just ignored him. This was between her and her reflection—Keith had nothing to do with it. If Keith got involved he'd just wreck things, like he always did.

No makeup needed, said her reflection. *You've got an innate natural beauty. We just need to bring it out a little.*

Yes, that's right, she thought. *I do have an innate natural beauty. I'm ravishing.* She lifted up her dripping hands and ran her fingers through her stringy hair.

You just have to bring it out, said her reflection.

But how was she to do that? And without makeup? She looked around on the counters but there wasn't much there. A half-empty box of cereal, a grapefruit, some tomatoes. Two dirty shot glasses that somehow she'd missed washing. A rack with spices on it. Other than that, there were only the things now draining in the dish drainer. A bunch of plates, some plastic cups, some utensils, a carving knife—

—a carving knife, said her reflection. *Well, that might come in handy.*

It just might, she thought. She saw her hand slowly reach out toward it, her fingers closing around it. It felt good, had a good heft to it— why hadn't she noticed that about it before? She turned it slowly in her hand and watched the reflection of the overhead light enter the flat of its blade and then slide off and then slide back on when she turned it back. It was like the knife was winking at her, like there was a secret between her and the knife. She glanced up at her reflection and saw that it was winking at her as well, the sly smile having been transformed into a leer. A part of her was a little horrified by what she saw, but a larger part of her was delighted. Yes, Keith had spent so many years stamping her down, controlling her. How wonderful it was to finally be able to stretch out a little bit and show her inner self.

"We're in charge now," she whispered to the knife. She turned it just right and lo and behold she saw her reflection in it, stretched a little, cut off at the top of the head, but still there. She was seeing herself in the knife now. She was the knife.

Now what are you going to do with me? her reflection asked, the knife asked. *Use me?*

She gave a low laugh. It came out sounding a little funny, like something was wrong with her vocal cords. A part of her registered that and filed it away, but most of the rest of her didn't care. It felt so good to be free.

She let her gaze drift away from the knife and back to the window. Her reflection was there, too. She watched the reflection slowly lift the carving knife and begin hacking off her hair. Strands of it drifted down into the sink and onto the counter. A new Virginia began to come out, a woman with short hair, thatched in places and in other places cut close to the scalp. She looked tough. And more than that, she looked dangerous.

She reached up to feel her new head, was shocked when she felt the hair still there. The actual knife hadn't moved—her reflection was somehow not following her, was instead showing her what to do. Now it was gesturing to her, telling her it was her turn.

She brought the knife up and grabbed a fistful of hair. In the window, her reflection was behaving. It had gone back to being her reflection, was showing her what she was doing again. She watched as the hair began to fall, felt the tug of the knife as she sawed the blade through her hair, trying to crop it as close to the skull as possible.

Her hand slipped and she jabbed her head, making a gash near her temple. It began to throb and bled feebly for a moment. In the window she saw her reflection reach up and touch the cut, then bring a blood-covered finger to its mouth. It licked the finger clean, its eyes crinkling with pleasure.

A few moments later she had finished. The water in the sink had gone cloudy with blood. She looked at her reflection. She looked beautiful, her head shorn nearly bare, little lines of blood dripping down here and there where her hand had slipped or she had cut too close. Yes, she was gorgeous.

In the window, her reflection smiled. Then it carefully shucked its shirt and dropped it out of sight. It took off its bra, its breasts now dangling loose, sagging. It took the carving knife and very deftly began to cut into its own chest. It traced out a circle on its chest, then drew a cross within it, then an upward facing semicircle at the head of the cross, a downward facing one through its base.

Wow, she could become even more beautiful.

It gestured to her. Was it her turn now? It was!

She lifted her shirt off and dropped it onto the floor. She unhooked her bra and let that go, too. It fell into the water and floated for a moment before slowly becoming sodden and beginning to sink. She brought the knife to her skin and pressed it against herself until it broke through. It hurt a little, but it was a pain she enjoyed. It was the pain of letting go, of becoming something new, something that could be controlled. Panting, she brought the knife around to form a ragged, bloody circle. The upright of the cross was hard since at times it almost scraped bone, but soon she'd finished it.

It hurt. God, it hurt a lot, more than anything she'd ever felt. Even more than that time when Keith had gotten drunk and hit her until she had to go to the hospital. But when she was done carving, she looked amazing. Like some sort of demonic goddess standing there with a shaved and bloody head and her chest radiating fire from the symbol she had made.

She started to put the knife down on the counter, but then she caught sight of her reflection in its blade.

Not yet, Virginia, it said.

"Not yet what?" she asked the reflection.

I don't think you're done with that yet, it said. *Do you?*

Not done with it? What else could she do with it? Maybe carve another symbol? She pulled the knife back closer to herself until all she was seeing was the image of her own eye, flattened and wavering on the blade. Then the eye, slowly, winked.

Watch me, she heard the reflection in the window say. She looked up and saw her slightly askew image, watched it put its fingers to its lips and then turn and walk away from the sink, walking step by step out of the kitchen. It was gone a long time. She just stayed there, staring at the window, waiting for it to come back. When it finally did, the knife and the hand that held it looked as if they had been soaked in blood and there was blood spattered over its body, too.

Now your turn, it said, and gave a twisted smile.

Yes, she thought, smiling back. *Now it's my turn.*

Whitey had left the Lords playing on the in-studio speakers instead of shutting it off. Heidi felt like she wasn't just hearing it; she was feeling it, as if it had become part of her body. Her skin buzzed and her stomach twisted. She broke out in a cold sweat. *Jesus, I must be sick*, she thought. But it felt like it was the music doing it to her, like the music was making her ill.

She tried to take a few deep breaths but it wasn't helping. Her head was pounding now, too. She tried to get out of her chair, nearly knocked it over. She stumbled toward the door.

"Excuse me a second," she said.

"Just where the hell do you think you're going?" asked Herman.

But Heidi didn't answer, just careened out of the room.

Herman shook his head. "Okay," he said. "It's on. This is getting fucking ridiculous."

"Maybe she just has to pee," said Whitey.

Herman gave him a look.

"Really? Maybe she just has to pee? Come on, she's practically nodding out right in front of you. You can't ever find fault with her, can you?"

Whitey just shrugged. "So what are you going to do?"

"Do? What am I going to do? I'm going after her."

"Dude, she's probably in the ladies' room."

"Well, she don't belong there," said Herman, standing up. "Because she ain't no lady."

By now she had used the knife to cut the rest of her clothes off her body, jabbing herself a few times in the process. Damn, that song was great. It was making her feel really alive. How had she been able to survive this long without it? She reached out and turned the music up, loud this time, her wet hand getting shocked again. Weirdly, it felt good. She turned it up as loud as it could go.

From the living room she heard Keith shouting at her. "Will you please turn that fucking radio down?" he called.

No, her reflection said. *I won't.*

She smiled at herself and then turned and moved stealthily toward the living room. Behind her, she imagined her reflection doing the same thing, going into the living room that lay within the reflection, killing its mirror husband. Or wait, no, it had already done that and had come back bloody, so maybe now it was just waiting there, staring at her, watching her. She turned around to have a look and sure enough there it was, watching her go, bright now against the black glass, and with eyes that glowed red. *Go on*, it motioned to her with the reflection of the knife. *Go on.*

She went on. She came to the doorway and slowly peered around it. There was Keith in his shitty La-Z-Boy, sprawled out, reading the sports page, beer on the table next to him. He hadn't even bothered to put the beer on the coaster.

She could see the back of his head and the bald spot on top of it. *Jesus*, she heard him say, and then he half turned and she ducked back behind the doorway.

"Christ!" he said. "Turn it the hell down! I can't hear myself think. If I have to get out of this chair and do it myself there'll be hell to pay!"

She stayed there against the wall until she heard the rustle of the papers again, just audible over the radio. She peered out around the edge of the doorway. He was reading again. Slowly she shuffled forward and around the doorjamb. Keith, fool that he was, didn't notice.

She made her way around the back of the room, clinging to the wall, until she was directly behind him and then fell to her knees and crawled across the shag rug. There she was, gently touching the back of the armchair, listening to him rustle his papers and grunt and burp just on the other side.

She felt her way along the fabric, locating where the wooden supports were hidden beneath. Carefully, she considered where he was on the other side and chose a spot.

In one fast motion she drove the knife through the back of the chair as hard as she could, letting out a shriek as she did so. Her husband gave a cry of surprise and pain and stumbled out of the chair to crash into the TV. He had one hand pressed to his back, blood already seeping out, and seemed unable to catch his breath. She gave a crooked smile. Maybe she'd punctured a lung.

She stood and came out from behind the chair, moved toward him.

"Virginia?" he gasped. "What the hell?"

There was fear in his eyes. He reached his hand out toward her and she flashed the knife forward, taking off two of his fingers at the knuckle. He cried out again and turned and clawed at the wall, tried to escape her by going through it and she brought the knife down again and took off one of his ears, opening a gash in his shoulder.

"Bit by bit," she said, in a strangled voice she could hardly recognize as her own—it was almost like someone else was speaking through her. "Just like what you did to my life!" And when he turned and looked at her in surprise, she struck out and cut open his cheek and took off most of his nose.

The knife was sharp and so the small bits were easy. After a while he was on his knees screaming for mercy. She smiled and tried to cut off Keith's hand, but it wouldn't come and he kept grabbing at the knife so finally she just stuck it hard and deep into her husband's neck. He burbled for a moment, even managed to get to his feet and reel through the doorway into the kitchen. He stood there swaying for a moment, then fell facedown and got blood all over the linoleum. *Once again*, she thought, *there he goes making a mess that he expects me to clean up.*

Once he'd been down a few seconds, he stopped moving. Now it was much easier to cut the hand off.

She sat on his legs and pulled his feet up and then unlaced his shoes and pulled them off. Hell, he was a mess. His socks didn't even match. She stripped the socks off, too, and then got to work removing the toes, going smallest to largest. She collected them in a little pile that she made just beside his mouth.

In the end she looked exactly as she had looked in the mirror, as if the knife and the hand that held it had been dipped in blood, with the rest of her body spattered in it. She returned to the sink and stood before it and looked at her reflection again. She waited for it to speak but it did not speak. Now they were the same.

She smiled. She'd never felt better in her life.

The only thing missing was that song by the Lords. She got up again and wandered around the kitchen until she found her cell phone. What was the station's number again? She would call them and beg them to play the song again. And if they didn't, well, they'd find she was a woman to be reckoned with. By hell, she'd go down there with her big knife and *make* them play it.

Chapter Thirty-eight

She was lying on the floor when Herman pushed his way in, the smell of vomit in the air. She'd made it into the stall but hadn't made it as far as the toilet, had vomited all down the tile splash behind it. Damn, she was bad off. He hated to mess with her, but well, somebody had to.

But he let her be for a moment. She just lay there with her head against the cold tile. And then as the Lords song finally wound down over the bathroom sound system she began to groan. A moment later, holding her head with one hand, she pulled herself up, stumbled to the sink, turned on the water, and splashed her face.

It was only then that she noticed Herman.

He expected some wisecrack from her, some sort of quip to laugh things off or try to make him feel that she was better off than she looked. But apparently she was beyond that now, through with joking around. Which made him think that maybe it was even worse than he had thought.

"What?" she said, her eyes dead, her voice flat, like she didn't give a shit.

It pissed him off. "What?" he said. "You want to play a little game called What? What is fucking going on? And I don't want to hear any more bullshit excuses about not getting enough sleep or food poisoning or motion sickness or anything like that. I want the real fucking deal."

Heidi sighed, eyes still dead. "What do you want to hear?"

"The truth would be a nice place to start this trip down bullshit road," said Herman. "Nice place to end at, too. Even though I'm afraid that you're going to tell me something I don't want to hear."

"What are you so afraid of?" asked Heidi.

God, her fucking nerve. She wasn't going to just come clean. She was going to make him say it. "What am I afraid of? Same old junkie business, baby."

For a moment her eyes stayed dead, hearing him without really taking the words in, and then they suddenly grew fiery, furious. Yeah, there she was. She still had some fight in her, Herman thought, and he couldn't help but think of that as a good sign.

"Fuck you!" she said angrily. "I told you I'm not doing that shit anymore." She pulled back her sleeve and showed him her arms. "You see any fresh needle marks?" she asked. "You want to check under my toenails and fingernails? That not enough? You want to test me? You can fucking watch me piss to make sure I'm not hiding a secret urine stash."

He took a step back. Whoa. "All right, then," he said. "Maybe I'm an asshole. But you fucking explain it to me. You owe it to me to tell me. What the fuck is going on?"

Behind them the door swung open. They both turned, expecting Cerina since she was the only other woman working that shift at the station, but it was Whitey. He came in but stayed near the door, hanging back.

"What?" said Heidi to him. "You too? Or is this the new break room and I didn't get the memo?"

Whitey didn't say anything. "You owe it to him, too," said Herman. "Come on, without us you would have lost this job a long time ago." He reached out and took her shoulders, shook her lightly, just enough to get her paying attention again. "Come on," he said. "Start talking."

Heidi pushed his hands off, turned away, clutching herself. "I don't know what the fuck is going on," she said slowly. "I wish I did. But I can't explain it."

"Try," said Herman.

She didn't speak for a moment. Herman just stood there with his arms crossed, waiting. Whitey, too, was silent, waiting.

"Well," she said. "I don't know. It started a couple of days ago. I started having these nightmares, but not regular nightmares. Not normal nightmares but, like, I don't know, sleepwalking nightmares. They don't even feel like nightmares exactly. They feel real. Last night I woke up in the empty apartment down the hall. I don't even know how I got in there. The thing is...there's bits and pieces of it, weird shit that doesn't make sense, but it's basically a total blackout."

If she's lying, thought Herman, *she's too good at it for me to be able to tell.* Maybe she was telling the truth. Maybe she hadn't started back into the shit after all.

"Were you drinking?" he asked.

"Yeah, a little," Heidi admitted. "But I never black out from drinking, Herman. You know that."

"Yeah," said Herman grudgingly. "I know that."

From behind him Whitey spoke, his voice quiet. "Sounds like night terrors to me," he said.

"Yeah?" said Heidi. "You think so?"

"What's that?" asked Herman, turning toward Whitey.

Whitey cleared his throat. "Night terrors...," he said. "It's like a nightmare you can't fully wake up from. I had a friend when I was a kid who had it. I remember sleeping over at his house for his birthday and he woke in the backyard drenched in sweat and screaming. I mean, he seemed to be awake and everything, but he wasn't. His eyes were open, but he was still asleep or, like, half asleep. He was just screaming and thrashing at something that none of us could see. But in the morning, he didn't remember anything."

"Maybe that's it," said Heidi. "But I've never had them before. Why would they start now?"

Whitey shrugged.

"Maybe I should see a doctor," Heidi said.

"I think you should most definitely see a doctor," said Herman.

Heidi made a face, getting a little annoyed again. "All right," she said. "I get the picture."

"And nothing else?" said Herman.

"What do you mean?" she said. "Besides getting the picture?"

Herman shook his head. "No," he said. "Besides the wine. You're not doing anything else to help you sleep?"

"No," she said. "I swear." But the way her eyes flicked to one side as she said it, he wasn't quite sure she was telling the truth.

"Cross your heart and hope to die?" he asked, just like he was a kid again.

She started to trace an X with her fingers in the center of her chest, then stopped, shook her head.

"What's the matter?" asked Herman.

"The way the dreams I can remember are going, there's no fucking way I'm going to say I hope to die."

He looked at her face. Yeah, she was really scared, he realized. Really messed up over all this. Okay, he wouldn't push it.

And then her expression changed. She was looking up, listening for something.

"Dead air," she said.

"Huh?" said Whitey.

Oh shit, thought Herman. The song had ended and none of them were in the studio.

"Dead air," she said again, and this time it clicked for Whitey. "Fuck!" he said, and rushed out of the bathroom.

Chapter Thirty-nine

In Heidi's building, upstairs, the hall lights began to flicker, going out one by one. Light still came up from the stairwell, but very dimly. Had anyone been there, it would have taken a while for their eyes to adjust enough to see that anything in the hall had changed. For as soon as the lights had gone out, the doorknob of apartment number five began to turn. Very slowly the door opened, just an inch at first, then another inch, and another, moving with a slow creaking sound.

At first that was all, just an open door. But then there was a brief flicker of movement and something small and gray, just barely lighter than the darkness, rushed out. A rat. It zigzagged down the hall before coming to rest, panting, near the top of the stairs. Another rat soon followed, then another, and suddenly they were coming all at once and far too quickly to count, first dozens then hundreds of them, the door swinging wide. They spilled down the hall, pouring over one another like water, rolling and tumbling and flooding down the stairs.

And then, as suddenly as they had been there, they were gone.

But the door was still open, the hall lights still extinguished. The doorway itself had a more palpable darkness to it. Something was not right.

And then the darkness moved and seemed to thicken. Until it became a black figure, a silhouette, like a man but larger. It was wearing a broad-brimmed hat that nearly brushed the top of the door frame. It seemed to have no thickness, seemed to be just a shadow, but was cast and reflected in a way that it should not be, on a dark, open space. Either it was just a shadow or it was so enwreathed in darkness as to appear so.

For a long time, it just stood there, unmoving. A strange odor filled the hall, the smell of something rotting. The only sound was the sound of breathing, a slow, huffing sound, coming from the open doorway, either from the figure standing within the frame or from something beyond it, deep in the room itself.

And then the figure took a step out into the hall.

Thursday

Chapter Forty

Francis had a stack of books out already, several dozen of them, and a bunch of crumpled photocopied articles as well, but he still hadn't found what he was looking for. There had been so much that he'd read when he'd been writing his own book, pages and pages, and so much that he hadn't been able to fit in—even with his computer files and index cards and scrawled notes it was anyone's guess where he'd find what he'd been looking for.

But he'd find it eventually; he was sure. It was here. It was just a question of time. He pulled another book off the shelf, a cheap paperback with a broken spine called *Mass Hysteria in Salem, Mass.*, and paged through it. He read some of his marginalia within it, and then thought, no, probably not that one, and shoved it back in. Another book, *Witches in Salem: A Cultural Anthropology*, he kept out longer, thinking it more likely, but no, nothing relevant in the index, and nothing revealed by a quick scan-through. Sighing, he dropped it onto the desk, as something to comb through more closely later.

He scanned farther down the shelves, pulled out a dark hardcover called *The End of the American Witch*. Maybe yes, it was this one.

And when he began to page through, he came right to it. He read for a moment, nodding his head, and then carried the book out of the room.

"Alice!" he called. "Alice?"

Where was she? Why could he never find her when he wanted to show her something. No, not wanted—needed. This was important.

He wandered out into the living room looking for her, but she wasn't there. Not in the kitchen either. Had she gone out when he wasn't looking? Maybe she'd told him and it just hadn't registered because he'd been looking through the books. Yes, that was possible. He had a hard time focusing on other things when he was caught up in his research.

"Alice?" he called again, a little louder this time, and this time heard her voice from inside the bedroom. "What?" she said. Only when he went into the bedroom she wasn't there. Had he misheard? What kind of game was she playing?

"Alice!" he shouted. "Can you come help me with something?"

"What?" she shouted back. She was in the bathroom. He should have realized. He went to the door and pressed his face close to it.

"I need you to play something," he said. "On the piano."

"I'm in the tub!" she shouted back.

What did that have to do with it? he wondered. He checked the doorknob and, finding it unlocked, went in.

The room was still steamy from the heat of the water. Alice liked her baths hot enough to cook off a layer or two of epidermis. His glasses immediately fogged up. He closed the door behind himself, shuffled over the honeycomb tile to the edge of the claw-foot tub.

"Francis!" she said, and covered her breasts with her arms. Why should she bother doing that? He'd seen her naked countless times before, and she looked great like that. There was no cause for her to be embarrassed.

"Look at these pages from John Hawthorne's diary," he said, and held the book toward her.

"Can't this wait five minutes?" she asked.

"Why?" he asked, surprised. He realized he had it turned to the wrong page, flipped through it until he found the right one. "Most of the books just give a transcript," he said. "But this one gives a facsimile."

He settled on the toilet seat, holding the book where she could see it. He pointed.

"Now look here," he said. "This book reprints a few of the surviving pages from Revered John Hawthorne's diary. A very fine reproduction, too."

"I thought that diary was considered to be the writing of a lunatic," Alice said. "You yourself told me that, didn't you?"

"Yes," he said patiently, drawing himself up a little. "It is true that many believe it to be the writings of a man in an advanced stage of dementia, but that's not important right now. My point is that he refers to this coven of witches as the Lords of Salem...then that DJ Heidi tells me that this music from 'the Lords,' the one they played after I spoke, was sent directly to her."

Exasperated, Alice chuckled. "So?"

"Let me finish," said Francis. "Heidi's full name, you may be surprised to know, is Adelheid Hawthorne. She is directly descended from Jonathan Hawthorne." He had her attention now, he could see. "On top of that, we have this incident of slaughter in which Maisie Mather butchered her boyfriend. Maisie Mather is a direct descendant of Judge Mather, who, according to Hawthorne's diary was directly involved with Hawthorne in the execution of this Lords coven."

For a moment they just stared at one another.

"Strange, no?" said Francis.

Alice nodded. "And your point is?"

Francis took a deep breath. "Well," he admitted, "I'm not exactly sure what my point is. That's why I need you to play something for me."

"This is ridiculous," said Alice, "but if you insist, let me get out of the tub and I'll meet you at the piano."

"I'd like that," said Francis. Satisfied, he stood back up, still scanning the book, and wandered out of the room. A moment later he was back. "How long do you think you'll be in the bath?" he asked.

"I just got in," said Alice.

"That doesn't answer my question," said Francis.

Alice sighed. "I'll be out soon, I guess," she said.

"Soon," said Francis. "Yes, that sounds good. Soon. Okay, I'll be waiting."

Heidi felt like she was sleepwalking, dead on her feet. *Maybe this is a dream,* she thought. Maybe she was still asleep, lying in her bed, waiting for the nightmare to begin.

But it didn't feel like a dream. It felt real. She was here, and the sun was out; the air was crisp but there was no wind. She was walking through the streets of Salem with Steve, and walking past people who seemed normal and real enough, and some of them were even people she knew. Some of them knew her and nodded as she passed or even spoke, and she did her best to nod or speak back, though from the way they looked at her, the concerned looks they gave her, she could tell that they knew she wasn't all there.

Why was she so tired? Last night, for once, she hadn't had any dreams. At least not any she could remember. Come to think of it, she hardly remembered anything after the radio show itself, and even that came only in bits and pieces. She remembered vomiting in the bathroom, remembered the embarrassment of Herman coming after her and dressing her down and accusing her. How dare he? She hadn't done anything wrong. Well, okay, she admitted to herself, maybe she hadn't told him everything, hadn't told him about smoking the joint, but she'd only done that because of the dreams, to calm herself down. It wasn't like it mattered—she'd told him the important things. After that, she remembered the show itself, remembered muddling her way through it, and then Whitey had put on the Lords again and something had happened. It was like she'd just phased out. And then she'd woken up in her own bed, hours later, sun streaming in on her. No dreams, no memories, nothing. But still, somehow, even more exhausted than she'd been the night before.

But Steve had to go out and so she'd groaned and heaved herself up and fed him and then they'd gone, and now here they were and she'd forgotten her sunglasses to boot, so she had to wince and squint. Hell of a start for what was sure to be a miserable day.

She let Steve lead her. She followed him to the green and gold sign that read SALEM WITCH TRIALS MEMORIAL, and then let him lead her down the brick path and along the stone wall. He went slowly, sniffing his way, occasionally lifting his leg to mark his territory.

By the time they came to the opening and the entrance Steve had already done his business, but something drew her on. It had been years since she'd been inside the grounds. Maybe it was time to go in again. Maybe facing up to Salem's history of witches a little would put things in perspective, would help the strangeness of the dreams she was having disperse.

She followed the path in, followed the wall to look at the memorials. SARAH GOOD, HANGED, JULY 16, 1692, she read. Someone had laid a flower on the grave, a red rose. REBECCA NURSE, HANGED, JULY 19, 1692. The stone of this one was mossy and harder to read. On Susannah Martin's grave someone had left a cornhusk doll with red string tied around the neck, wrists, and waist. There were words written on its dress, but rain had smeared them and she couldn't read them. Beside it was a wreath of white flowers. She wasn't sure what kind exactly. There was a candle, too, the wax having puddled on the stone.

She walked a little farther, found a slab of stone embedded in the ground, something she remembered her mother having shown her in her childhood. The stone was weathered now, the words mossy and faded but still legible. GOD KNOWS I AM INNOCENT, they read. She stared at them a moment, sobered by them, then moved to another stone, this one partly cut off by the walls surrounding the memorial, which had been laid on top of them. Strange thing to do, considering several of the witches had been killed by being pressed to death with heavy stones. She brushed the gravel aside. TO MY DYING DA-, it read. I AM NO WIT-.

She stayed looking at it for a long moment, until she felt Steve tugging at her, trying to get her to move on. Did it help her to come here? Did it make her feel better? Could anything make her feel better?

She didn't know. No. She couldn't say.

As soon as Alice came out of the bath, he was there holding her robe for her, helping her to put it on. She sighed, but let him slip it on her.

"I'll just put on some—" she said.

"No need," he said. "There's no law against playing the piano in a bathrobe. There'll be plenty of time to get dressed later."

She protested for a moment, then gave in, deciding that she'd waste more time arguing than in just getting it over with.

She allowed him to lead her by the hand out of the room and to the piano bench. His witch book was already there, open on the front of the piano, open to the entry for Hawthorne's diary for September 16, 1692.

Francis dragged his finger down to the bottom of the page. Tapped his finger at the end of a series of musical notes that were drawn across the bottom of the page. Next to them was a strange symbol, a circle with a cross and some other strokes in it. Two dots as well.

"That symbol," said Francis, pointing to it. "It was on the sleeve of the record they played."

"That exact symbol?" asked Alice. "Or just something that looked like it?"

Francis shook his head. "I'm almost certain it was precisely that symbol," he said.

"Almost certain," she said. "But not completely certain."

He ignored her, his hand drifting back to the musical notes. "Okay," he said. "Along the bottom here are a series of musical notes. Can you play them?"

"Of course," said Alice. "My mother didn't pay for twelve years of piano lessons for nothing."

"Of course she didn't," said Francis. "Let's hear it."

She looked more closely at the notes. There was only an upper stave, and it was a little strange. Instead of five lines it had only four, which meant she had to do a little guesswork about where things started, which line was missing. Maybe it wasn't even the same notational system. Still, she gave it a try.

"That's not it, is it?" asked Francis.

She shook her head. No, it didn't sound right. She moved her fingers a little farther up the keys and tried again. This time the first chord and the notes that followed were discordant, but they still felt intentional, like they were part of a larger structure.

"I think that's it," she said.

Francis nodded. He went over to the stereo, pressed PLAY on the cassette tape in its deck. It was the radio tape, Alice realized, the tail end of the recording of Francis's appearance on the radio show. Someone announced the Lords, and then music started.

He let it go for a moment, then shut it off.

"So is it the same?" he asked.

Alice furrowed her brow. She thought she already knew the answer, but she played the notes on the piano again anyway. Meanwhile, Francis rewound a little, and when Alice was done he played the tape a second time.

"Yes," she said. "Embellished, but basically the same. So?"

"Doesn't that strike you as odd?" asked Francis.

Alice laughed. "Not really," she said. "You said yourself this symbol was on the record. Somebody else obviously had this book and took the name, the tune, and the symbol from it. No big mystery."

Francis pulled a frown. He came over and sat down on the bench next to her.

"Play it again," he said.

Alice began playing the notes over and over. She sighed. It'd be afternoon, probably, by the time he'd let her get dressed.

Back in her apartment, Heidi found herself just sitting on her bed. How long she'd been there, she couldn't say. Every once in a while she'd come back to herself, think about getting up and going to do something, but by the time that happened she was already beginning to sink back into a stupor.

After a while, she realized she was looking up, trying to see something. What? She didn't know quite what. There was something hanging over the bed. She felt it, but no, there was nothing there, only empty air. But why did her eyes keep wandering up, looking to whatever wasn't there? There was something about the air there, something thicker than air should be. She couldn't see anything and yet, somehow, she still felt that something was there.

I've got to get up, she told herself. *I've got to leave.* And yet she didn't feel any desire to move. Any time she tried to budge, she felt as if all the energy had drained from her body.

She watched the sunlight slowly coming through the window diminish and then disappear entirely. Then night came, and the glass became dark. She stared up into the air above her, waiting for something to happen, for something to appear.

Francis sat with the portable phone gripped in one hand. He had the white pages spread open on his lap. He was scanning his finger rapidly down the page when Alice came in.

She was dressed now to go out, her hair and face done up, wearing a scoop-neck top, black tights, and a jean skirt. Francis took her in approvingly at a glance before letting his gaze return to the page.

Alice put her hands on her hips. "Who are you calling at this hour?" she asked.

"Huh?" said Francis, without looking up.

"Francis, who are you calling?"

"Oh," he said. "I was thinking of calling that girl Heidi from the radio station."

"What?" she said. "And what exactly did you plan on telling that girl Heidi from the radio station?"

"I was planning to tell her what I discovered about the music," he said.

"Why?"

"Why?" he repeated. He looked up, finally read her angry expression. "Well, it's only...I thought she might find it interesting."

"Interesting," she said, folding her arms.

"Yes, interesting."

She came forward and plucked the phone out of his hand. She carried it away, put it back on its wall charger.

"What's the problem?" asked Francis, genuinely surprised.

"You know what, Sherlock—let's drop it," said Alice. "This is getting silly. First an hour or so of having me play the same piece of music over and over again, and now this?"

"Really?" said Francis. "You don't think she'll find it interesting?"

"No," she said. "Honestly, I don't."

Francis sighed. He pushed the phone book closed, slid it off his lap and onto the couch. "All right," he said.

For a moment she just stood there, looking down at him, and then her expression softened and she came over to him. She moved the phone book over on the couch, snuggled in beside him.

"Maybe we should have a date night," she said.

"I thought date night was Friday," he said. He spoke as if slightly hurt, like he hadn't gotten a memo that he should have been sent.

"Yes," she said slowly, "usually we do go out on Friday, but that doesn't mean that we can't go out other days, too. I was kind of hoping that we could have a date night tonight and you could take me out."

"Um, sure," said Francis, still half distracted. "But isn't it a little late at night to be heading out on a date?"

"Well," she said, "you could take me to the midnight screening of *Frankenstein versus the Witchfinder*."

He stiffened a little. "Please tell me you're not serious," he said.

"Oh, I'm serious, my friend. Besides, you have free passes, right?"

He didn't answer, just hung his head.

"Wait a minute," she said, pulling back a little and folding her arms across her chest. "You didn't pick up the free passes?"

"It was just," he said, "with the way things went, I just couldn't. I meant to go back and get them, but…"

"Francis," she said sternly. "You promised."

"I know but—"

"Well we're going," she said. "Your treat."

Francis thought for a moment. "All right," he said reluctantly. "*Frankenstein versus the Witchfinder* it is."

Chapter Forty-one

One moment she was sitting on the bed, unable to move, staring up at the ceiling, and the next thing she knew she was wandering through the streets of Salem with no idea of how she'd gotten from one place to the other. It was strange. Suddenly there she was, walking through a seedy-looking industrial neighborhood that felt both familiar and unfamiliar, moving through a cloud of steam coming out of a vent. There on the side of the wall had been plastered a poster with that same symbol that had been on the box of that fucking record. *The Lords Are Coming*, the poster said.

She stumbled a little, kept walking, not sure what else to do until she figured out where exactly she was and how to get home. The windows on one side of the alley had been boarded up, some of the boards torn away, and the wall had been tagged. There was also, a little ways down, another poster. This one showed a terrified girl in torn clothes running through an open field, screaming, glancing back over her shoulder. Behind her was Frankenstein's monster, its arms stiffly extended. *Frankenstein versus the Witchfinder* read the top of the poster, in words that looked like they were dripping blood.

Who would post promotional posters here? she wondered. *Kind of a waste, right?*

And then suddenly she realized that she knew this place after all, knew it all too well. Her steps slowed, stopped entirely. For a moment she stood there, on the verge of turning around and going back, but then, almost against her will, she began moving forward again.

She approached a brown metal door in the side of a brick wall. Here she was. For a moment she stared at it. *I could still turn around*, she told herself. *I could turn on my heel and walk back to my life and still be okay.*

But she knew it was too late for that.

She knocked softly on the door. She waited a moment and when it didn't open she knocked harder, pounding this time. Abruptly the door opened a crack and Heidi saw a man's pale and unshaven face, his bloodshot, angry eyes. He looked her up and down, suddenly recognized her.

"Ah, Heidi," he said. "Returned to the fold I see."

"I wouldn't say that," she said.

"And yet here you are," he said. "How serious are you? Needle serious?"

She shook her head. "I just need something to make me feel better."

He nodded and grinned, showing a set of carefully filed teeth. "I know what you need. Have any love for me?"

She reached into her pocket, pulled out a carefully folded bill, pushed it through the crack in the door. She saw the man's three-fingered hand take hold of it and pull it in, and then the door closed.

She stood alone in the alley, shivering. She told herself again that she could leave anytime she wanted, but it hadn't been true the first time she'd said it and was even less true now. She thrust her hands deep into her pockets and tried not to think.

A moment later the door slid open and his hand shot out. She put hers forward and he shook it, leaving a tiny packet in her palm when he released his grip. Then the door closed and she walked away.

On the way home she passed through Leppin Park, deserted at this hour. She was surprised to see the monument there: a bronze statue of Samantha Stevens from *Bewitched* riding a broom across a crescent moon. *Wow*, she thought. *Start the day looking at memorials to witches and end it looking at bad sculpture of a TV sitcom witch. Only in Salem.*

She reached out and touched the statue's smiling face. The bronze was very cold, almost too cold to touch. For a moment, she had the impression of cold bleeding into her from the statue, running up her arm and wriggling its way deep into her bones. She held her hand steady a moment, cupping the face, and then slowly made her way home.

Chapter Forty-two

Francis grumbled a bit getting dressed, but finally gave in to the movie, beginning to enjoy himself. Alice was right—there was no reason that Heidi would want to know about what he'd discovered. It would just make her nervous, most likely. He had a hard time remembering sometimes that not everybody in the world was interested in knowledge for its own sake.

Despite his grumblings going out the door, Alice knew that it was a bit for show, so she let him do it, let him keep it up until they were almost to the theater and then she told him sternly he had to behave. But that was fine with him. He was having a great time, and even if he would be exhausted tomorrow from having gone to a midnight show, that'd be just fine.

He tried, at the ticket booth, just to have one more chance to be indignant. When it was his turn, he said, "I believe there are two complimentary tickets in my name, Francis Matthias." He felt Alice's hand tighten on his arm and he was getting ready for the ticket seller to tell him that he was sorry there were no tickets waiting for him when the man handed them over. He took them, a little surprised, and handed them on to a smiling Alice.

"Look at that," she said. "You'd gone ahead and arranged the tickets all along."

Had he? Maybe he had on his way out, or maybe he'd said something in passing at the beginning. He didn't remember. But since the tickets were free, Alice insisted on getting popcorn. The theater was pretty full, but there were two seats together right in the back, where they liked to sit because of his vision, and she snuggled up against his arm when the movie started.

So a good night. Or was anyway, until the movie started. It wasn't even an old B-movie, though it had been made to look that way. But he could tell it wasn't—the fashions were just a little off, modernized, and the hairstyles were definitely not right. He'd seen enough of the old Hammer films with Alice to know what a B-movie looked like, and clearly this guy had, too. It was, he had to admit, as smart or smarter than most of the Hammer films, and, if you could relax into it, as enjoyable, too. It was cheesy, a little bit, but there was something else there. The guy who played the Witchfinder was great, and he played it almost like the sheriff in an old Western. Or he seemed at first like the hero from a Western, and gradually he seemed to be more and more like a villain, and then he began to seem like the Devil himself. The monster went back and forth, too, between being sympathetic and being totally over the top and relentless, and that made it very hard to know what to think about it—which turned out to be good and to hold his interest. It reminded him of his feelings about the witch trials—were they evil men or were they just terribly confused men trying to do their best? One moment you saw the monster identifying with others, trying to make sense of what it meant to be human, and the next he'd torn a child's head off, just like that, without a second thought. He'd winced when that had happened, and Alice had tightened up, too, but what ran through most of the audience was incredulous and slightly nervous laughter. "Outrageous, dude!" called out one guy a few rows in front of him. Maybe he was too old for this, he thought for a moment, grumpily.

But people around them seemed to be having a great time, moving very quickly from laughter to fright and back again, and it was infectious. He found himself giving in to it, relaxing for once. Yes, probably better not to have said anything to poor Heidi Hawthorne. If he had he'd probably have terrified her and kept her from sleeping. Better to leave her alone and think of her at home, sleeping like a baby.

Heidi stared at the packet, wondering how long she would last before she opened it. Maybe just having it with her would be enough for a while, just knowing that she could fire it up if she wanted to, that it was there as her safety net.

But I'm already falling, she thought. *Don't I need the safety net now?*

Beside the bed Steve whined, his ears flattened.

"Don't worry, buddy," said Heidi. "It's going to be okay." But even she didn't believe it. She held the packet in one hand, just held on to it, and waited. Then she went into the kitchen and got out the aluminum foil and tore off a piece of it. She folded it smaller, then carried it back into the bedroom. She sat cross-legged on the bed, the tinfoil and the packet and her lighter just beside her, calling to her.

She switched on the TV and started surfing channels, but nothing was on. Absolutely nothing. She left it on one of the shopping networks, which was running an ad for huggable hangers. *Why the hell would you want to hug a hanger?* she wondered. Turns out they were fuzzy for some reason, and that the claim was that clothes would never slip off them. A woman wearing a pair of ugly slacks kept demonstrating them, showing how even if there were a major earthquake your clothing wouldn't fall off the hooks. They came in packs of twenty-four, and you could get them in sage, or bright gold, or black, or silver, or turquoise, or...

"And to complete your collection," said a strangely distorted voice, "meat hooks."

Her head snapped up. On the screen now was a bald man wearing an eye patch, half of his head covered with hideous burn scars. He was stripped to the waist and was grotesquely muscled, tattoos with intertwined demons winding over his chest and arms. In one hand he held a meat hook by its wooden handle. His other hand gestured around it, outlining the blade. The inside of the hook had sharp, smaller barbs lined backward along it.

"Now, most meat hooks, you get them hooked into a good chunk of flesh and wave them around a little and the meat just slides right off," said the man. His voice seemed to be subtly slowing down and speeding up, as if she were listening to a warped record. "But not this little baby. Once you get this one in, it just isn't going to come out."

He walked over across the stage, the camera slowly following him to a door marked five. He slowly opened it and entered. Inside was a poorly lit room where a man sat with his arms tied behind his back and his legs duct taped to a padded vinyl chair. His hair was rumpled and his face red, and duct tape had been stretched around his mouth to gag him, too. It took her a minute to recognize that it was Chip. Her boss was famous! He was on TV!

As the tattooed man approached him, Chip struggled and tried to speak through the gag, his eyes vivid with fear.

"Now, take a situation like this," said the tattooed man. "We've all been there. You've got a man tied up in a chair. You're not quite ready to dismember him, but at the same time he's at one side of your deserted factory space and you want to drag him over to the other side of your deserted factory space because you've got your dismembering and other torture equipment over there and, plus, the video camera is already set up. It's just more convenient to have him over there."

He bent over a little, pressed his hand against his back. "But your back has been acting up on you," he claimed, looking straight into the camera. "Not too bad, not enough so that you're going to have to let this guy sit for a few days, but enough that you don't want to have to bend over to pull him."

He raised the meat hook in the air, and the camera closed in on it, held it in close-up.

"Ordinary meat hook and a guy struggling as much as this little bastard's going to be in just a moment and it'll slip out maybe five, maybe ten times on your way over," his voice said from off-camera. "You'll have to put so many holes in the guy that by the time you get over there that it's hardly even worth it—he may even be dead by the time you arrive. And you won't have captured any of it on film. What fun is that?"

He put one hand on Chip's triceps, caressing it, examining it.

"But a meat hook like this," he said. "Well, it's special." He raised it high in the air and with one sharp, hard movement drove it through Chip's upper arm. Chip screamed into the gag, his eyes rolling. *Holy shit*, thought Heidi. "Now that," he said, grabbing the handle and jerking on it, "that's a meat hook that's secure."

She jerked awake. *Shit*, she thought. *More nightmares.*

Almost without thinking, she reached for her lighter.

Friday

Chapter Forty-three

It was close to noon before Francis got out of bed. Once up, he puttered around the house a while. He looked for Alice, but she'd left a note on the counter saying she had an appointment with her hairdresser and wouldn't be back for a few hours.

Hairdresser, he thought, somewhat amused. *How could a woman go revel in B horror movies by night and go to her hairdresser by day?* But maybe that was why he liked her.

He looked for the paper but it wasn't in the kitchen, not in the living room either. Maybe she'd taken it with her, but that didn't seem like something Alice would do. No, she knew he liked to read his paper in the morning. Admittedly, it wasn't actually morning anymore, but to him it still was. In a way.

He poured himself some cereal and sat down at the table to eat it, then looked around for the paper again. Maybe she'd forgotten to bring it in? He opened the door, but it wasn't on his mat. Sighing, he went back inside and put on a shirt and some trousers and then went down the stairs in his slippers, but it wasn't downstairs. And when he opened the door and looked out on the porch, it wasn't there either.

So he trudged back upstairs, irritated now, and put on his shoes and jacket, grabbed his wallet. A little walk wouldn't hurt him, he told himself. True, usually he took a walk at some point in the day, but why should he have to take it before he'd read his paper?

He walked out the front door and down the street. The low

autumn sun was out and shining. It was still cold outside, but not as cold as it had been a few days before. It was completely bearable. He walked down the street, through beautiful historic Salem. A little trash-ridden, admittedly, but still beautiful. He crossed the street and moved toward the downtown—probably likely to be crowded with tourists, considering it was a Friday and that Halloween wasn't all that far off, but he knew at least he could get a paper there. He'd just try to avoid all the somewhat irritating witch tourism. Or try, at least, not to let it make him angry.

He followed Mason Street as it curved along the perimeter of Mack Park. At the edge of the park he came to a Labrador retriever who had been tied off to a *No Parking* sign. The poor animal had gotten tangled up so much that he could hardly move.

"Are you all right, boy?" asked Francis. The dog just wagged its tail. He looked around for its owner, but didn't see anybody— probably off in the park somewhere. But if that was the case, why not take the dog along? Francis let his arm fall limp and brought it close to the dog, watching for signs of aggression, ears dropping back or lip starting to curl, but the dog just sniffed his hand and licked it.

"Maybe I can untangle you," he said. "How would that be?"

He knelt down and helped guide the dog's legs free of the leash until he was doing all right again. One of the dog's haunches was a little bloody and at first Francis was worried, looking for a wound, but no, there was nothing there. The dog wasn't cut; something had gotten blood on the dog. Maybe it had been in a fight with another dog? It didn't seem like the fighting type.

The owner hadn't come back by the time the dog was untangled. He looked at the dog's collar, but there wasn't an address, only a phone number and a name: Steve. Steve, what kind of name was that for a dog? He stood up, patted the dog on its head. Steve just wagged. Well, if it was still here when he came back, maybe he'd take it to the house and call the number on the tag. He chuckled. That would certainly surprise Alice, him showing up with a dog.

He continued down Flint Street and crossed over the river and the local train tracks, then from there went left on Essex Street until he was at the Salem Library. For a moment he thought he'd remembered wrong, but no, there it was, partly hidden behind the bicycle rack: a newspaper vending machine.

He put his coins in and opened the gate, took the top newspaper. He'd folded it up, put it under his arm, and was starting to walk away when he suddenly stopped stock-still, wondering if he'd actually seen what he'd glimpsed. He stood there on the sidewalk and unfolded the paper. The headline read:

SECOND NIGHT OF RITUAL MURDER IN SALEM

"Oh my God," he said aloud, and read on.

> For the second time this week, Salem was rocked by murder.
>
> Virginia Williams, 51, a lifelong resident of Salem, has been arrested for the murder of her husband, Keith Williams, 60.
>
> "I don't know what came over me," responded Virginia Williams to this reporter's question, "Why did you do it, Virginia?" She continued: "I mean, I really don't. I was resenting him or whatever and then suddenly things got out of hand. But I don't even remember that happening. It was like I just woke up in a pool of blood."
>
> Mrs. Williams is alleged to have repeatedly stabbed her husband with a knife, and then to have mutilated and dismembered the body.
>
> Friends of the Williams's report that Keith allegedly had a history of abusive behavior. Said one, who wished to remain unidentified, "I'm not surprised. He sure had it coming."

This murder is remarkably similar to the murder of Jarrett Parsons by Maisie Mather earlier this week. Police have speculated that there is a link between the two murders.

Said Chief of Police Jon Greenhalgh, "We have no doubt that a connection exists between the two murders, and even that Mather and Williams conspired in the killings."

When asked to be more specific, he mentioned that both women had carved the same symbol into their own chests before committing the crime.

According to another member of the police department who wished to remain anonymous, there is clear evidence that these murders are ritual in nature.

Police are not releasing more specifics at this time.

Another murder, thought Francis, *and this one identified as ritual*. Or rather as a second night of ritual murder, so that means the first was ritual as well. Williams, though—it was a common enough name, but not a name readily identified with the witch trials. Maybe Maisie Mather had just been a coincidence. But still, it was strange. And he was willing to bet that the symbol they'd carved in their chests was a symbol he'd seen before: the Lords symbol.

Lost in thought, he hurried home.

Chapter Forty-four

S teve?" Heidi called. She was lying slumped on the bed, a little confused. "Steve?" Where was that dog? She'd had him just a minute ago, had been walking him, and then things got a little blurry, a little fuzzy, and well, she was back here now, wasn't she, and so Steve must be around here as well. That made sense. No, Steve was a good dog. He was around here somewhere. She didn't have to worry about him. He probably was just in the kitchen or something, sulking. And she was okay now, too. All she needed was another hit or two, something to calm her down, and now she felt great.

The TV was on. On the screen a group of ballerinas ran down a staircase and fluttered by a giant devil's head with a gaping mouth large enough to swallow any of them. They clung to one another in fear. She pressed the channel changer and with a click the TV switched to local news, a picture of a woman in handcuffs being led into the police station. She pressed it again and the channel changed to the opening credits for *Bewitched*.

Fuck me! thought Heidi, giving a weird laugh. *I was just looking at your statue!* She tried to smile, but it didn't come off right. There was a dead look in her eyes and her mouth had gone slack. She stared at the screen, hardly seeming to see it. Meanwhile, her hand was feeling around next to her, first on the blankets and then on the bedside table. When it returned, it was holding her lighter and a small piece of tinfoil, and a glass tube.

She shook a little onto the tinfoil, then grabbed the square by one edge. She flicked the lighter on. Her eyes still on the TV she fired up the tinfoil, then sucked in the fumes with the glass tube. God, it felt great. She held the smoke in until she could feel her blood slowing down, beating slower and slower in her ears. Her vision had begun to go dark around the edges, and then she exhaled and fell back against the pillows.

How had she lived without this? Now she felt good again. Now she was sure everything was going to be okay.

From the other room she heard a knocking at her front door. She ignored it, began to drift off. When the knocking came again, she slowly lifted her head and gathered her lighter and the drugs. She felt like she was moving underwater, or in a dream. Thinking about dreams gave her, deep below the blissful surface she was riding on now, a stab of anxiety. Slowly, she slid the drawer of the bedside table open and dropped everything into it. Closing it was a little harder, but she managed.

The knocking came at the door again. Mumbling to herself, she managed to get her legs off the bed and her feet under her and wove her way across the room and into the living room. From there, she could move along the wall of records, dragging her hand over the milk crates to get to the kitchen and from there to the door.

The door turned out to be harder to open than she remembered. It was like they had made it more complicated since the last time she had had to use it. She played with the knob for a bit but nothing was happening. Finally, she remembered she had a peephole and slid her face up to it, found it, managed to get an eye to it. Outside was her landlord Lacy, and to either side of her those weird sisters of hers. What were their names again? The blonde was Sonny. She remembered that because the sun was yellow and Sonny's hair was, too. The other was named Morgan or Megan or Mona or something like that. Lacy was holding something, a small tray with a teapot and cups on it.

She moved her head back and tried the door again. Oh yeah, locked. She turned the dead bolt and now it opened just fine.

She swung the door open. "Hey," she said, her voice hoarse.

Lacy gave a big smile. "I might be wrong, but I had a feeling that maybe you could use some company," she said.

Heidi gave a slow smile back to her. *Wow*, she thought, *she can't even tell that I'm high. Or maybe she doesn't care.* "I definitely could," she said, struggling to keep them in focus.

And then she just stood there. It took Sonny coming forward and pushing her gently to the side for her to understand that she was blocking the door.

"What's that?" she asked, pointing at the teapot.

"This?" said Lacy. "Oh, just a little something I put together. Calming tea, I guess you could call it."

"Calming tea," said Heidi, and nodded.

Sonny suddenly popped into her vision. "But more important," she said, "there are chocolate chip scones."

"Nice," said Heidi. "You ladies know just what I need."

"Indeed we do," said the other sister, the one with the name she couldn't remember. She was the strange one, Heidi remembered, but she couldn't quite remember what made her strange. She took Heidi by the arm. "Now, let's see about making you comfortable," the woman said.

Chapter Forty-five

Francis had spent the day wondering about the killing, going through the meager article, looking for clues. He pulled down book after book, trying to find a link between the name Williams and the witch trials, or something to tie Virginia Williams in some way to Maisie Mather. But there didn't seem to be anything. The two women were different ages, lived in different parts of town, seemed to be from different social classes as well. But the link had to be there; he was sure of it.

Alice at first wouldn't talk to him about it, and then when he finally got her to listen she wasn't much help at first.

"It's not healthy, Francis, getting obsessed over a murder," she claimed. "You should just leave it alone."

But he couldn't leave it alone. That was the problem. There had to be a connection; even the police knew that. And everything about it pointed back to the witch trials.

"Maybe you wouldn't think that if you weren't a historian of the witch trials," suggested Alice.

"Maybe not," admitted Francis. "But that's what I am. There's got to be a historical link between the two women. There's a captain mentioned named Williams, but he wasn't involved in the trials as far as I can tell."

"You're looking for the name Williams?" said Alice, surprised.

"Yes, of course," Francis had said. "Shouldn't I be?"

"Oh, honey, isn't that her married name?" said Alice. "Shouldn't you be looking at her maiden name?"

Yes, of course, how could he have been so stupid? He must be getting old to have made such a ridiculously dumb mistake. But when he managed to track down her maiden name online in the marriage archives of the *Salem News*, it didn't tell him anything either.

It was only after poring over dozens of reference books that it occurred to him that her maiden name might not be the right name either. With Alice's help, he managed to find a website called FIND YOUR FAMILY TREE and after having paid a so-called nominal fee he had Virginia Williams's family history. He followed the tree back step by step until he came to the name Magnus.

"I'll be fucked," he said. "Dean Magnus."

There was the link. And yes, it was about the witch trials after all. Which meant that Adelheid Hawthorne, as a descendant of Hawthorne's, was no doubt in a whole hell of a lot of trouble.

"But you don't believe in witches," Alice said.

"No," he said. "No, I don't." He pondered. "But it could be something else. There could be a logical explanation for it."

"What sort of explanation?"

"I don't know," he said evasively. He was having a hard time reconciling his satisfaction of having discovered the link with his skepticism about witches. "Somebody setting these women up, maybe. Manipulating them in some way. I'll know when I see it."

Chapter Forty-six

On the television Elizabeth Montgomery twitched her nose and her husband found himself unable to get off the couch. It was like he'd been glued to it. The studio audience laughed.

They were watching the TV in Heidi's bedroom. Heidi had tried to suggest that they could sit in the living room, but one of the three women had said, "*Nonsense, dear, we should go where you'll be most comfortable,*" and they'd ushered her through the apartment and back to her bedroom. Sonny had helped her into the bed and fluffed the pillows behind her, and then had taken a seat beside her. Lacy had served Heidi tea and had put the tea service on the floor next to the bed. Then she'd climbed into the bed on the other side of her. It made her feel cozy. The other sister—Megan, it turned out her name was; why had she thought it was Morgan?—brought in a kitchen chair and sat off to one side.

"Have any of you seen my dog?" asked Heidi. "Steve?"

"I'm sure your dog is okay," said Lacy, patting her arm.

Yes, she thought. *He's probably okay. Good old Steve.*

"I just—" she started to say, but Sonny was touching her on the other arm now, lifting her arm up.

"Take a sip of tea, dear," she said. "It'll make you feel better."

"What?" she said, and then said, "Oh." She let Sonny lift her arm up, and then took over and blew on the top of the mug to cool the tea, and began to sip.

When she looked up, she momentarily had the impression that everyone was staring at her. But no, she thought a moment later, they were all watching the TV—she'd just gotten confused somehow. Why would they be staring at her?

On TV, Samantha's husband had succeeded in getting off the couch, but only by stepping out of his trousers. He went yelling through the house looking for his wife, but she was already back visiting her more witchy mother.

"God, she was really beautiful," said Lacy.

Who? wondered Heidi, and then realized she must be talking about the actress who played Samantha, Elizabeth Montgomery. "Yeah, I guess so," she said. Her voice, when she spoke, sounded really slow to her, like it was oozing out of her. "I never really noticed before," she continued, "but she really was."

"Is she still alive?" asked Sonny.

"No," said Heidi. "I think she died."

"Oh right, of course," said Lacy. "I remember now."

"More tea?" asked Sonny. "Another sip?" And again she helped Heidi raise the mug to her lips. *Why aren't they having any?* Heidi wondered. And a moment later she realized her voice was asking that very question aloud.

"No, sweetie," said Lacy. "None of us are thirsty. Besides, I made it specially for you."

Specially for me, she thought, and smiled, her thoughts beginning to drift in a way she had a hard time understanding. It was like Lacy was a mother for her. It was nice to have that. But wait, didn't she already have a mother?

The drift was interrupted when Megan spoke again. "I wonder, what would Elizabeth Montgomery have thought of that ridiculous statue of her?" she asked.

"I was just looking at that tonight on my way home," said Heidi. "Or maybe it was yesterday."

"It doesn't matter," said Lacy.

"No," Heidi agreed. "It doesn't matter."

"More tea?" asked Sonny.

Heidi shook her head. "I'm calm enough," she said. "I can barely keep my eyes open." She yawned. "Wasn't there some controversy about that statue?"

"Oh, not really," said Lacy. "Some of the locals thought it was in bad taste. The paper said it 'was like erecting a statue of Colonel Klink at Auschwitz.'"

"Huh," said Heidi. She yawned again. "I guess that's one way of looking at it."

"Don't mind us. Why don't you just lay back and get some rest?" said Lacy. "We'll be right here if you need us."

"What?" said Heidi, her eyes already half closed. "No. I'm not going to sleep with you guys sitting here."

Lacy leaned closer, brushed back Heidi's hair. "Why not?" she said. "Even big girls need to be babied sometimes."

For a moment, Heidi tried to protest, but she was having a hard time putting sentences together. Eventually, she just shook her head and moved lower in the bed, turning on her side. Almost immediately she fell asleep.

Chapter Forty-seven

For a time the three sisters just stayed in their places, watching the television, their faces expressionless in the pale blue light. They did not speak, hardly moved.

Finally Lacy prodded Heidi with a finger. When she didn't move, didn't respond to the prodding in any way, Lacy got up and went to turn off the television.

She stood there at the foot of the bed, in the light cast through the window. Her face, normally so friendly and relaxed, had taken on a different expression, as if a mask had been stripped away to reveal a true face underneath. Her mouth was tight, her lips pressed. Her gaze was cold. She stayed there, staring intensely at Heidi.

"Sisters," she said. "It is time."

"Yes," said Sonny and Megan in unison. "It is time."

Heidi slept on.

Lacy had just begun to move toward the door to the living room when the telephone on the bedside table rang. She stopped and waited, then made a swirling gesture with one hand. Megan, the one closest to the phone, reached out and answered it.

"Yes," Megan said, her voice level and calm.

"Hello," said the voice on the other end, speaking quietly. "I'm looking for Heidi Hawthorne."

When Megan said nothing, the voice said again, "Hello?"

"Who did you say you were?" asked Megan.

"I didn't say," he said. "I'm Francis Matthias, and it's urgent that I speak to her."

"And who were you looking for?" asked Megan.

"Heidi," said Francis. "Heidi Hawthorne."

"I'm sorry, darling, but there's nobody here by that name," said Megan. "You must have the wrong number. Please, don't call back."

She hung the phone back in its cradle and then unplugged it from the wall. Lacy left the room and moved through the living room and kitchen, went out the apartment door. From the room, you could hear the sound of her footsteps moving down the hall. Sonny and Megan had both stood now and were looming over the bed, staring down at Heidi. There was something strange about the room as well, a disturbance in the air that moved slowly about the bed, becoming finally a pale ghostly figure before fading back into nothingness and then becoming tangible again. Both Sonny and Megan noticed it, but showed no sign of anxiety or surprise. It walked toward the bed and then through it, pushing its legs through the mattress without disturbing it until it came out on the other side. Slowly, it made its way toward the corner of the room and then pushed its way through the wall and disappeared.

For a moment they were alone and silent, as if they were the only people in the world. And then came, very quiet at first and at a distance, a metallic squeaking noise. It stopped a moment and the apartment door opened and closed, and then it started again, the noise growing louder until Lacy appeared, pushing an old-fashioned wicker wheelchair.

It had large wooden wheels in back, with wooden spokes, like wagon wheels though not nearly so large. The front wheels were very small and made of wrought iron. The seat itself was frayed and coming apart and the basket to hold the invalid's feet had been awkwardly repaired with strands of wire.

She moved it near the bed and then nodded. Sonny and Megan reached down and heaved Heidi up to a seated posture but she still did not wake up. Her head lolled loosely, as if she were freshly dead. They dragged her over to one side of the bed, then moved her legs so that her feet were resting on the floor. With each of them grasping an arm firmly, they forced her to her feet and then pulled her over to settle her in the chair.

For just an instant her eyes wavered open slightly, and then they closed again. The two sisters busied themselves positioning Heidi's legs in the basket and crossing her hands on her lap, and then Lacy began wheeling her backward out of the room with her sisters following.

They went squeaking through the living room. Sonny and Megan darted out to hold the door open. Lacy maneuvered the wheelchair through and turned it sharply, directed its wheels toward apartment number five.

"Oh, Father," said Lacy quietly as she went, her voice just audible over the squeaking of the wheels. Her face had taken on an unearthly glow. "You give us the venom...fill us with your essence."

"Let it burn through our souls and our minds," said Megan.

"We trample on the cross," claimed Sonny.

All together, as if repeating a ritual, they intoned, "We spit upon the book of lies...We desecrate the virgin whore."

Lacy stopped just before the door to the apartment and bowed. She released her grip on the wheelchair and walked around in front of it. Removing a stub of chalk from her pocket, she proceeded to trace a circle on the floor. In the center of it, she carefully and deftly inscribed the symbol for the Lords of Salem.

"We blaspheme his holy spirit and rejoice in his suffering," she said, her voice thick with hatred now. She stepped back and bowed again, and then gestured. Megan came forward and stood in the middle of the circle, careful not to smear or obscure its design. From there she reached out and placed her hand on the doorknob. Slowly, muttering something inaudible, she turned it and opened the door.

The door opened not onto the empty rooms that belonged to the abandoned apartment five, but onto another place entirely. Through the doorway was a massive room, bigger than the house itself and lavishly furnished. It smelled of strange incense and burned hair, and of something else as well that was impossible to place, something fetid. Heidi's eyelids flickered open again, then closed. But her eyes kept moving back and forth beneath the lids, as if she were dreaming.

Megan raised her arms, her fingers spread wide. "Guide this child still in the shackles of the Oppressor," she said. "Help her break free from his tyrant ways." Then she stepped out of the circle and stood to one side of the door frame.

Sonny stepped forward and into her vacated place within the circle. She ran her palms over her breasts and down her sides to her hips. "Entice her to take that precious bite," she said. "From whence she shall be delivered." She stepped out of the circle as well.

Lacy had stuck her hands underneath Heidi's armpits. She hauled her to her feet and brought her stumbling into the circle, Heidi's feet erasing and distorting the symbol. Sonny and Megan reached out and steadied her, while from behind, just on the outside of the chalk line, Lacy performed an elaborate bow.

"You are the Dragon, Lord Satan," she said. "We hail the serpent and stand strong as warriors for you, both in this world and beyond."

Heidi groaned. Her head, drooping forward, came up for just a moment and then fell back down again. With Sonny and Megan dragging her and Lacy supporting her from behind, Heidi shuffled forward, her feet effacing the remainder of the symbol. Slowly, and with great care, all four of them moved through the door and into the well-appointed room beyond.

For a moment they stood there, just inside the doorway, Heidi still unconscious and the three sisters peering about themselves as if in wonderment. And then, very abruptly, the door was slammed shut by an invisible hand.

Chapter Forty-eight

They held a mirror to her face. She was awake now, but what she saw she didn't recognize: a dead white face, lips bloodred. They'd put a beauty mark on one cheek, a black pock. She was wearing an eighteenth-century gown, ribs of whalebone painfully constricting her waist and chest so that it hurt to breathe too deeply. The gown billowed out below the waist, quadrupling the size of her hips, crossing and interlacing, parts folded forward and back. She felt like Marie Antoinette, ready for the chopping block.

Where am I? she wondered. *What's happening to me?*

Last she remembered, she had been in the apartment building, in her own room. This definitely was not her own room. Stretching before her was a gigantic rococo cathedral, draped in a low-lying fog that made it hard to see the edges of the space, as if it might continue on forever. In the center of it was a red velvet staircase that led up to a black cross. There was something wrong with the cross itself, the crossbeam lying too low, as if it were upside down. Sitting in a slovenly fashion before the cross, in flowing white robes that covered not only their legs but also their ankles, were three judges. The robes had long angular hoods with inverted black crosses on them that completely obscured their faces.

As Heidi watched, a half-dozen white-skinned whores, wearing doll-like makeup and nude but for powdered wigs, descended the red velvet staircase. They moved lasciviously, stretching like cats with each step. Slowly, they approached Heidi, tilting their heads as if their necks were broken.

It was only once they were drawing close that Heidi suddenly wondered why she was standing there waiting for them. But by then it was too late. As they came closer, she realized there was something wrong with them: their apparent beauty began to collapse and crack, and up close their faces revealed themselves as diseased, scrofulous, and even deformed.

As she tried to move to turn away from them, they grabbed her arms and bound her to an elaborate and quite beautiful movable torture rack, accented in gold and armatured with silver spikes. Or not quite a rack, because when they strapped her into it, the straps bent and twisted her in ways that she did not realize she could be bent. It didn't hurt unbearably yet, but she could see the wheels and levers at the side and could already feel the pressure.

Where had the machine come from? Why hadn't she seen it before? They had attached her to it with chains, shackling her wrists and stretching her tight. Once she was secure, they rolled her toward the black cross, throwing bits of confetti and glitter in celebration as they went.

The device moved slowly, rolling forward on awkward stone wheels that made the stone floor below them crack and pop as the machine moved. In the end, as they got closer, all the whores had to abandon throwing glitter and push in a concerted effort to make the device move forward, but finally they stopped before the judges.

For a moment Heidi stared at the judges. Perhaps they stared back. It was impossible to tell because of their masks, and even more difficult to know what they were thinking.

And then, the two judges to either side reached over and took hold of the center judge's robes. They slowly drew their hands away, parting the robe as they withdrew and Heidi saw that what she had thought was a man was not a man after all.

Instead, beneath the robe were two stick-thin figures. Their skin was covered in a kind of mange. They were scabby and encrusted and looked more than a little sickly. They were wound around one another and hugged one another so tightly that it was impossible to tell where one began and the other ended. They were, so it seemed, humanoid, but not human—too thin and long for that, and they gave the impression, perhaps false, of having too many limbs. From their bodies sprouted two long twisting appendages, intestine-like but outside the body rather than inside it, phallus-like but too long to be phalluses, and too motile as well. The appendages writhed and whipped back and forth as if independent creatures. It was terrible to watch.

The whores, though, moved quickly forward and managed in teams to trap the whipping objects and wrap themselves around them, riding them like horses as they cried in ecstasy or wrapping their arms around them. Four of them held them steady while the other two manhandled a funnel-shaped object and brought it forward, forced the ends of the appendages into the large end of the funnel. They began to milk them, working their hands up and down until a thick black liquid began to ooze from them and fill the funnel, and then began to drip from the funnel's tip.

As soon as that happened, the whores became very excited. They gave off little shrieking noises and spoke in a language that Heidi could not understand. They brought the funnel close to her and began to tear at her clothing, slowly stripping her bare. She struggled, but shackled like she was there was nothing she could do.

Once she was naked, they forced the funnel between her legs. The appendages began visibly to pump, and as the black fluid began to fill her, Heidi's body began to thrash back and forth, threatening to tear itself apart.

Outside the door to apartment five, Lacy, Megan, and Sonny kneeled reverentially, apparently in prayer. After a moment, they joined hands and began to speak in unison.

"We honor you through our actions and our thoughts," they said together. "Each day we live upon this earth, may we grow stronger in wisdom and in our love for you, Dark Lord. You are our Father, our Teacher, our Muse, our Lover, our Destroyer. We have taken your mark in dedication."

The door creaked open, revealing an impenetrable darkness. The women let go of one another's hands and looked up, staring into the darkness, waiting.

Out of the blackness stumbled Heidi. She was expressionless and drenched in blood, perhaps her own, and she swayed as she came forward, barely able to stay on her feet.

The women rose and gathered around her, steadying her.

"You are transformed," Lacy said to her.

"You have met the dark bridegroom," said Sonny.

"You have become one of us," said Megan. "You have betrayed your ancestors and joined the Dark Lord."

Heidi didn't answer. Slowly, the women began to lead her back to her apartment, supporting her. Heidi had trouble staying afoot and would have fallen without them. Even with them, she managed only slowly.

Lacy opened the door. "I will hold her here," she said to the other two as she moved her head under Heidi's armpit and grabbed her opposite hip with her hand. "You shall clear a path."

As Lacy balanced Heidi in the doorway, her sisters entered the apartment, moving objects out of the way. They pushed the kitchen mats to one side, folded the carpet over in the living room. When they were satisfied there was a clear path to the bathroom and nothing that could be soiled permanently by blood, they came back out, nodded.

"Let her enter," said Megan.

Lacy nodded. Slowly, they moved into the kitchen, leaving a series of Heidi's bloody footprints behind. Lacy walked Heidi forward, Megan helping to hold her steady. Sonny came behind with a wet towel, swabbing up the blood.

They coaxed her forward, through the living room, past the bed, into the bathroom. They helped her climb into the tub. She was awake but not awake, not conscious but not unconscious. She knew something had happened to her, something terrible, but she wasn't sure what it had been. A moment later she heard the screech of the rings against the rod as the shower curtain was drawn closed, and then suddenly she was being sprayed with water, the women reaching around the curtain, touching her body, patting it down, washing the blood away, cleaning her. On the one hand, it felt comforting, as if someone was taking care of her. On the other, though, it felt as though she was being very casually molested.

She swooned and went down, striking her head on the rim of the tub. The women made clucking noises, gathered around her, pulled her up, getting wet themselves. Then one of them was there standing in the tub with her, naked as well, pressing her body up against Heidi's and whispering in her ear. For a moment she thought it was Lacy, but when the woman began to speak she realized it was Megan.

"What happened to you was a privilege," she heard the woman whisper in her ear. "Our Lord does not favor just anybody, only the precious few. Now you are one of us."

"One of you?" Heidi managed to say. "What are you?"

Megan chuckled. "Ah," she said. "That is the question, isn't it? We have always been here and we will always be here. No matter how they try to do away with us, we survive."

She felt Megan begin to lick the water off the back of her shoulder and then begin to kiss her neck. Megan moved her arm up and brought it down across her breasts, beginning to caress one of her nipples with her hand. Heidi struggled, but was too weak to do much. Slowly, Megan seemed to lose interest and then her arm slipped higher up, to wrap finally around Heidi's throat. It tightened gradually, until Heidi found that she could not breathe.

She clawed at the arm, tried to bring it away, but Megan would not let go. Her vision began to be shot through with whirling points of light, like a swirl of flies, and then began to go black.

And then she passed out.

When she awoke, she was still groggy. Her throat hurt. She was lying in her bed, naked now, but clean, her body freshly washed. Her hair was still wet. Three women were there. Who were they again? They looked familiar, but for the life of her she couldn't remember their names. Morgan, she was pretty sure one of them was called. One of the other two had hold of her blankets and as she watched she brought them higher, tucked them up around her neck.

"There," the woman said. "Now you'll be cozy." And then for some reason, the woman laughed.

The woman reached over and turned off the light. "Sweet dreams," she said, and then blew Heidi a kiss.

Each of the other women came forward as well. They bent over the bed one after the other and spoke a comforting word or two, and then kissed her on the brow. She could feel the kisses burning there long after they had stepped back. And then the three of them, waving to her, slowly moved out through the door and away. She heard them walking in a group through her living room, and then the change in the sound of their footsteps as they entered the kitchen, and then the sound of the apartment door opening and closing. And then they were gone and she was alone.

Only not exactly alone as it turned out. As she lay there, with the room blurring in and out around her, she began to feel that something was there, watching her. Her eyes drifted around the room, slowly coming to rest on the end of the bed. There was something there, at the foot of it.

Steve? she tried to say, but nothing came out.

Her eyes crossed, and the end of the bed doubled itself. She let one bed drift away from the other and then drift back again. When she blinked and they returned to being one bed again, she could see what was there.

She wished she couldn't.

Something was perched there, huddled at the end of the bed. It was small, hardly bigger than her forearm, humanoid in form but with skin that had the striated texture of bare muscle. It was blotchy and red, and in places oozed with pus. Wherever they touched it, the bed linens grew damp and filthy. Its eyes, too, were strange and protruding and seemed ready to burst.

It just stayed there, watching her. Not doing anything, just watching.

She was terrified. She tried to move, but she could not move. She tried to scream, but she could not scream. Her body no longer belonged to her. All she could do—all she would ever be able to do, she felt—was lie there and watch it watch her, and wait for it to move closer, inch by inch, until it was on top of her chest, taking away her breath.

Saturday

Chapter Forty-nine

Where was that book again? wondered Francis. He had just been looking at it yesterday. Now where had he put it? He searched through the kitchen, then looked around the living room, then the bedroom without finding it. But when he went back into the living room he immediately saw it, open on the piano, right in plain sight. Of course. He should have seen it right away.

He closed it and shoved it into his briefcase, momentarily glimpsing the cover illustration, which was of a hanging witch. Last night after getting the wrong number he had tried to dial again, but this time nobody answered. If Heidi was there, she wasn't picking up. So he'd made a note of her address. Assuming she hadn't moved, he'd be able to talk to her in person, which was probably the best thing to do anyway, considering what he had to tell her. He would take the book with him and show her the Lords symbol, see if she'd let him compare it to the symbol on the record. And if she had a piano or a keyboard or something maybe she'd be able to play the tune for herself. Once she did that, maybe she'd be ready to hear what he had to say.

He headed for the door.

"Where are you going?" Alice asked.

Almost instinctively he lied. "I have to drop by the museum for a second and check on something for the new exhibit." Feeling guilty, he added, "Should I pick up lunch on the way back?"

It wouldn't do for Alice to know where he was really going. She'd just tell him he was being crazy and that he should "leave that poor girl alone." But two of the female descendants of the men who had judged and slaughtered the Salem witches had been involved in ritualistic murders. Heidi was the only other female descendant he knew of, and she'd been sent a record with the Lords symbol on it, and thus she should be warned. He probably should tell the police as well, but that was a harder proposition. He didn't know what he could say to them without making them think he was a nut job.

"Can't someone else handle it?" she asked.

"Well, they could," said Francis slowly. "But they'd do it wrong and then I'd have to redo it and that would take twice as long. Better just to get it over with. I'll only be an hour."

"Unbelievable," said Alice. "You retire from teaching and suddenly you're busier than you've ever been. What are they going to do when you give up working for the museum?"

"Close up shop, I guess," he said.

And giving her a kiss on the cheek he headed for the door.

Chapter Fifty

Alone in her apartment, Heidi sat cross-legged on her bed, morning light pouring through the window. She stared blankly ahead as she raised a cigarette to her lips and took a long drag. Something was missing, she kept thinking, but no matter how much she wracked her brains, she couldn't figure out what it was. She kept staring straight ahead, trying to remember what it was, but it just wouldn't come to mind.

She got up for a moment, wandered through the apartment, her face still expressionless. The place was a wreck, and for some reason she'd moved the mats and the runner in the kitchen and folded the rug back in the living room. She couldn't remember any of it, not a fucking thing.

In the kitchen on the floor were a water bowl and a food dish. What were those doing there? She must have been watching someone's pet and forgotten to take them back. Probably they'd been there for a while.

She wandered a while more before suddenly finding herself in bed again. The cigarette hanging from her fingers was dead. Where had that come from? When had she started smoking again? She flicked it onto the floor and reached into the pack for another, got it lit, drew deep on it.

Her cell phone rang. She let it ring a few times, then reached out and flipped it open. Slowly, she raised the phone to the side of her head and pushed it against her ear.

"Hello," she said. Her voice sounded happy, perky. But her face remained expressionless, seemed almost dead.

"Hey, girl," said Herman.

"Hey," said Heidi. "What's up?"

"Oh, nothing," he said. "I'm just a worried Mother Hen checking in to make sure that everything is hunky-dory on the other side of the tracks."

"Yes, I'm fine," she said. "In fact, I slept really well last night."

Her voice was still animated and lively but her face remained a mask, her eyes continuing to stare off into the distance.

"Well, that's something anyway," said Herman.

"Yeah," said Heidi. "Hey, I'm sorry for being such a flake this past week. It's all good now. I'm all good now."

"I hope so," said Herman.

"So, did you touch base with the band yet?" she asked.

"The Lords?" he asked. "Negative. As far as I know, nobody has. Sounds like amateur hour to me. I guess we just basically head over there, go through the motions, and hope that at showtime someone actually turns up and does a gig."

"Well, worst case, I guess if they're a no-show, then we get an early night."

"Either that or a riot. Anyway, Whitey will swing by for you around five and then you can head over and experience this magical evening firsthand."

"Sounds like a plan, Stan," she said.

"So," said Herman. "He'll be over around five."

Heidi laughed. "Dude, heard you the first time. Don't worry. I'll be ready for him. Bye."

"Bye," said Herman.

She snapped the phone shut and for a moment sat motionless. Slowly, she raised her other hand to her mouth and took another long drag on the cigarette.

She let her eyes slowly cross, the room suddenly doubling itself.

She held her gaze like that for a moment and then slowly, very slowly, let it come back together.

When the image was singular again she realized that the apartment was not what she'd thought it was. The carpet was not a carpet after all but thousands of rats. Her blanket, too, wasn't a blanket after all, but rats. When she lifted her cigarette to her lips, it was not a cigarette she lifted, but a smouldering rat's tail. Rats were everywhere. *I should be upset by this*, she told herself, but no matter how hard she tried, she could not be. She watched them come and go, felt them move under her and around her, but made no effort to drive them away or to flee. She just stayed where she was, motionless, her face utterly expressionless, like that of a doll.

Chapter Fifty-one

Francis moved his briefcase from one hand to the other and then reached into his trouser pocket. Where was that piece of paper? He reached across his body, patted his other pocket but it wasn't there either. No, he had just had it. Where—and then when he reached into the breast pocket of his suit coat, there it was.

He unfolded it and straightened it, then compared the address written on it to the address on the house's steps. Yes, the same. He headed up them and peered at the buzzers until he found Heidi's name.

Just as he was about to ring the buzzer, he noticed a woman standing inside, watching him. It startled him so much that he almost dropped his briefcase.

She opened the door partway, looked at him. "Are you all right?" she asked. She was attractive, perhaps a few years younger than Alice. She was wearing a batik dress. She had a good head of curly blond hair, a little gray running through it.

"Yes," he said. "I'm fine. I wonder if you can help me. I'm looking for Heidi Hawthorne."

The woman gave him a strange smile. "Do you perhaps mean Adelheid Elizabeth Hawthorne?" she asked.

Francis nodded, smiled. "Yes," he said. "Actually, I do."

The woman looked him over more carefully. "You look familiar," she said.

"I do?" he said, surprised.

"Yes," she said. "You do."

"I work as a volunteer over at the Salem Wax Museum," he said. "Sometimes I walk by here on my lunch break. Maybe you've seen me then."

"Ah, the wonderful wax museum," said the woman. "Got to teach those impressionable kiddies about Salem's glorious past."

Here at last, thought Francis, *someone who understands.* He smiled, extended his hand. The woman took it, shook.

"My name is Francis Matthias," Francis said. "It's a pleasure to meet you."

The woman nodded. "Now, are you friend or foe?" she asked.

"Of Heidi's?" he asked. He pondered. "I wouldn't exactly say I'm a friend. I don't know her well enough for that. But I'm certainly not a foe. An acquaintance, shall we say?" He made an effort to withdraw his hand, but she kept hold of it. "And may I ask who you are?" he said.

"Lacy," she said. "I...I take care of Heidi." She let go of his hand.

"Can I see her?" asked Francis.

For a moment Lacy just stood there and blinked, but then she smiled. "I don't see why not," she said. "Please come in."

Lacy pushed the door open wider and ushered Francis past her. Smiling and nodding to her, he made his way in.

I should get up, Heidi was thinking, as she'd been thinking for the last half hour. *I've got to leave. I've got things to do.* But she felt like she didn't have complete control over her own body. It was as if she was living in her body but no longer filling it, like the person who was Heidi existed in a small place deep within the body itself and the rest was blankness and empty space. It made her body feel bloated, ungainly.

She managed with great effort to leave the bed and wander into the living room. Her boots were in a heap there and she sat on the fainting couch and pulled them on. Her faux fur coat had been balled up and thrown near the entrance to the kitchen, and she slipped it on and stumbled toward the front door.

But when she opened it, she found that it opened not into the hall-way but into another manifestation of her apartment. She walked out and found herself back in the same room, confused.

She closed the door, waited. When she opened it again, the apart-ment was still there on the other side. She walked through again, moving from her apartment into her apartment, and then stared around. It should have felt backward but it somehow didn't. It was the same apartment. She simply couldn't leave.

She closed the door and waited, counting slowly to one hundred. Her heart was beating faster and she tried to relax, tried to breathe deeply, and she did calm down a little. Then, gathering herself, she reached out and opened the door again.

It opened this time not onto her apartment but only onto a bricked-up doorway. The bricks were old and weathered and the mortar was dusty and filthy, as if the wall had been there for a very long time.

What the fuck? she wondered.

A little panicked now, she closed the door again and went to look out the bedroom window. Yes, everything looked normal out there, just the same old ordinary street.

An older man came down the sidewalk and stopped in front of the house and stared up at it. He looked familiar, but it took a moment still for her to place him. It was Francis, the guy they'd interviewed a few days ago, the witch guy. What was he doing here? Maybe he was coming to see her. That was good. Maybe he could help her get out.

She watched him until he began moving down the walk and toward the house and then she moved back into the kitchen, waiting for the doorbell to ring so she could buzz him in.

But the doorbell didn't ring.

Maybe the door downstairs was already open, she told herself.

Sometimes Lacy left it propped open, particularly on a nice warm day. If that was the case, he might just come up the stairs and knock on her door.

She waited. And then waited some more. But nobody rang the bell or knocked on the door.

What happened to him? she wondered. Maybe he hadn't come to see her after all, but if not, it was a weird coincidence. Probably he'd just run into Lacy and she was talking his ear off, she told herself. Probably he'd be up here soon.

She waited another ten minutes, watching the wall clock in the kitchen tick its slow way forward. No, she finally admitted to herself. He wasn't coming. What had happened to him?

She stared at the door. She reached out and placed her hand on the knob and then pulled the door slowly open.

This time it was a little different. Behind the door, flush up against it, was another door. There was a brass plate on it, with a number inscribed on it. The number was five.

"We can wait in my apartment," said Lacy. "Heidi stepped out for a moment. She is sure to be back very soon."

"She isn't here?" said Francis. "Well, maybe I should just come back another time. I don't want to impose."

Lacy smiled, touched his arm. "Nonsense," she said. "She'll be back shortly. Come in and have some tea."

"All right," said Francis.

He followed her down the hall and to her open door. He was surprised to find two other women already there, each of them holding a teacup. He *was* imposing on them, he realized, interrupting a conversation that they were already having, but when he tried to say as much and excuse himself, Lacy shook her head and dragged him in.

"These are my sisters," she said. "They don't mind. In fact, I'm sure that they're eager to have some company other than me." She picked up the tea service. "They'll keep you entertained while I brew us a new pot."

A little unsure of himself and still holding his briefcase in his arms, he sat down and introduced himself. One of the sisters, a blonde with short hair, was named Sonny. The other, with beautiful red hair that fell in ringlets, was named Megan. *What would Alice think if she could see me,* he wondered, feeling a little pang of guilt, *sitting here with three lovely women instead of adjusting wax figures at the museum?*

As if she could detect the current of his thoughts, Sonny asked, "Are you a married man, Mr. Francis?"

"Yes," Francis said, slightly startled. "Very happily married. Thirty-six years in November."

"Local girl?" asked Sonny.

"I'm afraid not," he said. "She's not a Salem native like me. She's a California gal."

"Any children?" asked Megan. Her voice was strange, a little vibrant.

"No, no. Somehow we never got around to it. Work was always my baby and Alice, well, she wasn't set on it and so…"

"Well, that's understandable," said Megan. "Children are a bit of a waste…Most are a total loss. So few have anything of substance to really offer us." She took a sip of her tea before continuing on. "But on the rare occasion, a special child appears."

A little flabbergasted, Francis wasn't quite sure how to respond. He chuckled nervously. "I never really thought about it like that before," he admitted. "I just didn't like the idea of changing diapers."

"Does anyone?" asked Megan. "Have you ever met anyone who said, 'If there's one thing I love, it's changing diapers'?"

Francis chuckled again. "Well, no," he said, "if you put it that way…"

Lacy came back into the room with the tea tray and a fresh setup for Francis. She held the tray before him as he poured himself some tea and dropped in a few lumps of sugar.

"Is it caffeinated?" he asked. "It won't make me jittery, will it?"

"No, no," said Lacy. "Just the opposite. It's very soothing."

She set the tea service down on the table next to him, freshened her cup and those of her sisters, then took a seat facing Francis. "I couldn't help but hearing from the kitchen Megan spinning her little philosophies on the value of breeding," she said. "Don't mind her. Megan lives in her own little bubble."

Megan gave an enigmatic smile. Almost sinister, Francis thought. He relaxed his hold on his briefcase, placed it on the floor beside his chair, and was surprised to see the eyes of all three women follow the briefcase to its new place. He took up his teacup, raised it to his lips.

"How does it taste?" asked Sonny.

"Very good," he said. Truth be told, it had a bit of an odd flavor, a kind of musty undertone to it beneath something more floral. That probably made it a good tea, gave it a complex nose, or whatever term one used with tea. But he didn't particularly care for it.

Lacy held her own cup and saucer in her lap, balanced on one knee. "Now, what's so important that you had to race over here to see my dear Heidi?" she asked.

"Hmmm?" said Francis. "Well, truth be told, really it wasn't that important. Just something about a record she was playing on her show the other night."

"Do you mind if I ask what record it was, Mr. Matthias?" asked Lacy.

"No, of course not. Trouble is, I don't have a name for it—I don't think there was a name on it, actually. But it was by a band called the Lords."

"Don't take this the wrong way, but you seem a bit old to be a typical listener of that station," said Sonny. "Sometimes looks can be deceiving, I guess."

"No, you're right. I don't listen to it," he admitted. "It was just... I was a guest on the program, and, well, I heard the album, and..." He let his voice trail off.

"Sonny dear, would you mind getting me some sugar?" asked Lacy.

"But there's sugar already on the tray," said Francis. "I got some when I got my tea."

A flicker of irritation crossed over Lacy's face but was quickly smoothed over. "Did I say sugar?" she said. "I meant sweetener." She patted her side. "I'm watching my figure."

Funny, thought Francis. She looked like a hippy type, the kind of person who'd be opposed to sweetener on the grounds that it wasn't natural. But of course looks could be deceiving, as Sonny had just pointed out.

Lacy was regarding him politely, waiting for him to go on. So he did. "Anyway," he said, "I just thought the information I have could be something she might find interesting."

Lacy gave a little laugh. "Something she might find interesting." She mimicked his voice in a way that Francis suspected was vaguely insulting. Then her face and tone suddenly became serious. "Mr. Matthias, you strike me as a man who would normally mind his own business."

He chuckled. "I do, do I?"

"I'm not laughing," said Lacy harshly. "Why are you? Is something suddenly funny?"

He stared at her dumbfounded. What had he said to offend her? No, he had imposed more than he'd realized perhaps—clearly she didn't want him here. "I think I should come back later," he said, his tone and bearing quickly formal. "I'm afraid I've taken up too much of your time already."

"Do you know what I think?" said Lacy. Her voice was still harsh, and as she spoke she seemed to bare her teeth.

"Definitely not," said Francis, reaching down for his briefcase. "And I don't imagine I want to know."

Lacy ignored him. "I think you are here to get inside the head of my dear little Heidi. Get inside her head and fuck her brain. Are you here to stick your nosey little cock inside her head and fuck her brains, Mr. Matthias?"

For a moment he couldn't believe he'd heard her properly. How was it possible that garbage like that was coming out of her mouth? He felt his face flush with embarrassment.

"I really should be going now," he said, stiffly.

"I'm afraid it's too late for that," said Lacy.

He stood and turned toward the door and was just in time to be struck in the face with the flat of a shovel's blade. He stumbled into the end table and upset it, spilling the tea and scalding himself before finally ending on the floor, staring up. Sonny was there standing over him, holding the shovel, her face impossible to read. He looked around to the other two women for help, but neither of them seemed upset or disturbed.

"Ah, my sugar," said Lacy, her voice calm. "Thank you, Sonny."

"My pleasure," said Sonny.

Francis, dazed, was having a difficult time figuring out what had happened. His head began to throb and his jaw felt numb and was perhaps broken. His face was cut, too, and blood was filling his eyes. He started to try to sit up, but Sonny struck him in the face with the shovel again, not quite as hard this time, but hard enough to break his nose and make him want to stay down.

He watched Megan calmly stand up. She lithely stepped over him and moved to an old record player beside Lacy, placing the needle on the record. Classical music began to play very loudly. Mozart's *Requiem Mass*, he dimly realized it was.

When she turned around and came back toward him, she was holding a butcher knife.

She closed the door and locked it. No way she was going through that door. She moved across the apartment feeling trapped, crossed from the kitchen to the living room and the living room to the bedroom and then back again, shuttling back and forth, hugging herself. What was she going to do? She had to leave. She had to get out, but how could she?

Maybe she could climb out the window, she thought dimly. But when she went and looked out the window she saw not the street that she had seen before but the back of an alley. Even though she knew it was still day, it was dark through the window, and the alley was cast in a red light thrown by a flickering neon sign that read *Jesus Saves*.

Shit, she thought. And for a moment she wasn't sure if she was in her own apartment or if she was in apartment number five.

She drew the curtains closed and moved away from the window, walking backward until she ran into the bed and sat abruptly down. *It's not real*, she told herself. *I got some tainted shit and am hallucinating. It's not real.* But it felt real; that was the problem. Maybe if she just stayed there, just waited, then eventually she'd come down off of whatever trip she was having and everything would be back to normal.

But before she'd sat there very long she started hearing strange sounds from below her. Lacy's voice, yelling and screaming, and then a thump, and then the sound of a man's hoarse voice, crying out for something. What the fuck was going on? She dropped to her knees and pressed her head against the floor and listened.

Lacy moved toward Francis, whose face was now puffy and swollen and who lay in a slowly growing pool of blood, leaking from his broken head and from where Megan had thrust the knife almost gently into his neck. He was alive, but not by much, and the life was slowly ebbing out of him.

She reached down and thrust her hand inside his suit coat, taking everything out of his inner pockets and dropping the items on the floor.

In his outer pocket was a folded newspaper. She removed it and unfolded it, saw that the headline read *Second Night of Ritual Murder in Salem*. She studied it, was particularly interested in the fact that Francis had circled Virginia Williams's name and written the name Magnus in the margin.

"Well, well, well," she said to the dying man. "Looks like you found yourself a real Hardy Boys–style mystery to solve." She smiled. "Let me guess," she said. "You, the gallant detective, were going to warn Heidi, perhaps? Funny thing is, no matter how many little notes you scribbled or dots you connected, there was nothing taking place here that you were ever going to manage to prevent."

She nodded her head sharply to Megan and the latter dropped to her knees to begin violently stabbing the dazed and injured man over and over. She started in his chest, trying to make him hurt as much as possible, then moved down and sliced open his belly. He grunted. He tried to cry out, but failed.

"Enough," said Lacy.

Abruptly Megan stopped. She stood up again, panting, the knees of her pants soaked in blood, blood spattered all over the rest of her body. From the floor a faint gasping sound could still be heard coming from Francis, and a hissing from where air was leaking from a wound in his chest. Lacy bent down beside him and knelt in his blood, giving him a smile.

"Some die so readily," she said, "giving up the ghost just like that and welcoming the devil that awaits them. But others, like you, cling to life long past the point where it's too late." She turned to Sonny, who was holding Francis's briefcase now, standing beside Megan.

"Well?" she said.

Sonny opened the briefcase and quickly looked through. "If it isn't my favorite fairy tale," she said. "*The End of the American Witch*." She dropped the briefcase and began to flip through the book. "I'll bet there are all sorts of juicy stories in here about big bad witches and the heroic deeds of the mighty John Hawthorne."

Lacy extended her hand, palm up, and Sonny handed over the book. She thumbed idly through it, then chuckled.

"I bet you'd love to tell our dear Heidi these spooky little tales of judgment day, hmmm?" she said. She dropped the book onto Francis's bloody chest. "But you see, dear Mr. Matthias, the judgment has already been made." She smiled. "Oh, and you have paid so dearly..."

Morgan handed Lacy her bloody knife. Lacy took the knife by the haft, blood oozing between her fingers. Francis's eyes had glazed over, and he was all but dead. Lacy spat into his face.

"...so, so dearly for the sins of your fathers," she said. "But the payment has only begun."

She lifted the knife high and slammed it down hard into Francis's chest, then pushed with all her might. Francis's body convulsed.

"Shhh," said Lacy to him, watching the last life drain out of his eyes and death settle in. Her eyes shone as they stared into his. After a few painful breaths, he was dead.

Lacy dipped her finger into the blood pooling around the knife.

"Come bathe in the warm blood of the slaughtered lamb," she crooned.

Megan and Sonny bent down beside her. Lacy kissed each of them on the forehead and then traced with her finger an inverted cross on each of their heads.

"I so baptize you," she said. "In the name of the Devil, and death, and the unholy host. With blood we seal ourselves to our Dark Lord. With blood, we unleash him from his chains and summon him to this hell that is the world."

Chapter Fifty-two

Whitey felt good about finally having his car back. He had picked it up earlier that day, and even though it had all the same old problems—ceiling fabric coming detached and hanging down, stuffing coming out of the splits in the vinyl seats, a dashboard that was spidered with deep cracks—now it ran. And ran pretty well. So all that other stuff wasn't important. He could put up with it as long as the car worked. And besides, he kind of liked that stuff. It made the car feel unique. It made the car *his* car.

He'd called Herman to let him know that he didn't need to swing by and pick him up, that he had wheels again, and Herman had said, "Good, then you can get Heidi as well." He couldn't tell how much anger Herman was harboring toward Heidi. Probably a little still, maybe a lot, but for once Herman was playing his cards pretty close to his chest.

And it was better for Whitey to be the one to get Heidi anyway. For one thing, if she was messed up, he could try to get her together before Herman saw her. For another, well, he just liked Heidi. That was hardly a secret.

He pulled up to the curb. She wasn't on the porch, wasn't visible either, and the light in her bedroom was on, so she was probably still upstairs. He watched the window for a little bit, waiting to see the curtain rustle or if he could catch a glimpse of her face peeking out, but nothing happened.

302

302

He checked his watch. Damn, time was getting tight. Herman would be pissed if they were late. Maybe he should just let her know he was here.

He doused the lights and turned off the engine and then, hands in the back pockets of his jeans, made his way up the front steps. He was looking for her buzzer, getting ready to buzz, when he realized that the front door was open. Since it was cold outside, he just let himself in.

Megan was behind the door to Lacy's apartment, pressing her eye to the peephole. She watched for a moment, then stepped away.

"Looks like our little Heidi has another gentleman caller," she said.

Across the room, Lacy sat in a rocking chair, calmly rocking back and forth.

"How nice," she said.

She was resting her feet on Francis's chest. Every time the chair rocked forward, they made a squishy sound against the blood-sodden fabric of his shirt. The skin of his lifeless face had begun to change, the bones seeming sharper now, the skin lying tighter on the bone as the remaining blood pooled lower in the body and rigor mortis began to settle in. Around him were torn and mangled pages from *The End of the American Witch*, which had been covered with strange symbols painted in Francis's blood. A candle had been set at his head and at his feet, and his mouth had been stuffed full of pages from the book.

Across from her, sitting in an armchair and drinking tea, was Sonny. She took a sip, made a face.

"What kind of tea is this?" she asked.

"Lemon verbena," said Lacy. "It reduces stress. It's very relaxing."

Sonny stared into her cup. "I'm not sure that I like it," she said.

Lacy nodded. "You're used to something a little stronger," she said.

"What do we do about Romeo?" asked Megan from near the door.

Lacy waved her hand dismissively. "Nothing to worry about," she said. "I'm sure that Heidi can manage him. And who are we to get in the way of young love?"

Whitey knocked on the door to Heidi's apartment, but there was no answer. He pressed his ear to the door but couldn't hear anything inside. Or didn't think he could anyway—it was hard to hear anything over the sound of music coming from the end of the hallway.

He turned and looked, saw that the door at the end there was open, with Heidi standing in the doorway. She didn't look like she was doing so well. She was as pale as a ghost, with dark circles around her eyes. He'd heard of Goth chic but this was ridiculous. And he'd never really taken Heidi for the Goth type.

"Hey, what's up?" Whitey asked. "You okay, girl? Whose apartment even is that?"

But Heidi didn't answer. For a moment she stared at him and then she took a step backward, was immediately lost in the darkness of the apartment.

What the fuck? he wondered.

He slowly headed down the hall toward the apartment, the music growing louder as he got closer.

He stopped in the doorway. It took a moment for his eyes to adjust to the dim light. When they did, he saw Heidi moving around the room in a kind of wispy, random fashion, as if she were lost in a psychedelic haze and dancing to her own drummer. Shit, she was definitely on something. Herman was going to be pissed. He had to get her out and dressed and sober, and he had to do it quick.

"Hey," he said. "We should get going. Herman will fucking shit if we're late."

But Heidi didn't answer. It was like she hadn't heard him. She just kept dancing, eyes lidded, head loose and swaying.

"Come on, girl," said Whitey. "Seriously, we should get going."

She still didn't answer. So what was he supposed to do? Physically drag her out of there and force her to get ready? Not exactly his style. Just say fuck it and leave her? Not exactly his style either. Maybe keep trying to reason with her? He stepped into the room and moved toward her. "Heidi," he said. "I really think—"

The door behind him slammed shut with a boom loud enough to make his teeth rattle, making the room a whole lot darker. It was suddenly silent. Confused, he spun around, searching for the door. He felt along the wall, found the edge of the frame, found the door-knob. He tried to turn it, but it wouldn't turn. The door was locked somehow. He felt for a button or a latch of some sort but couldn't find anything. He rattled the knob again, trying to open it, but it wouldn't move.

"Jesus, the door is stuck," he said, turning toward where he thought Heidi must be. "I can't get this open."

He could see her still, though the room was dark enough now that she was more of a vague semihuman shape in the darkness—if he didn't know already that it was Heidi he would have had a hard time identifying her. Again, she didn't answer. She danced, turning slowly, and then suddenly stopped, fell to her knees.

"Heidi?" he said, and took a step forward.

And suddenly she collapsed in a heap on the floor. He moved forward and bent down to try to help her up, but when he grabbed her he realized it was not Heidi at all but just a tangled and twisted sheet.

Astonished, he lifted it up and looked at it. Where had she gone? He'd been sure he'd seen her—otherwise he wouldn't have come in. Where was she?

He looked around the room now. His eyes were beginning to adjust further, the darkness not quite as total as it had been before. Here and there in the shadows, he began to see shapes. He began to think of one of them as human. He stepped forward, squinting, trying to get a better look. Yes, there was someone there, but someone hunched and deformed. He was sure it wasn't Heidi.

"Hello?" he said. "Can you help me?"

He took another step forward, peered closer. Yes, someone was there, just in the corner, head down. Why wouldn't they answer? He stepped again and looked closer. Was there something wrong with their skin? It seemed overly pale in some places, weirdly bruised in others. Mottled. The hair, too, seemed to have come out in clumps.

"Hey," he said, and reached out and touched the person's arm.

The arm was ice-cold, the shock of that so surprising that he yanked his hand back as if he'd been stung. As he did so, the head jerked up and he cried out in horror. The skin of the face had begun to decay, in some places had fallen off to reveal stretches of bone. The lips had fallen off or had been bitten off, revealing a length of jawbone and rotted teeth. The eyes, too, were gone, in their place only two deep black holes.

He stumbled back. *Holy fuck*, he thought. *It's a corpse. I must have knocked it or something to make its head come up like that.*

But then, as he stared at it, he saw the head turn, the empty eyes staring right at him. Its arms stretched toward him and the remnants of its face tightened in a horrific grin.

He made a break for the door, tried to open it again. It wouldn't come. He began to pound on it, shouting and crying out. After a moment, he made the mistake of looking behind him and saw that the creature had made it halfway across the room and toward him, moving slowly but inexorably forward. Not only that, but also there were more of them now, at least three, maybe four. He began to pound harder, shouting himself hoarse.

But the door held firm and nobody came to let him out. He felt something touch his shoulder and he shook it off and then something was on his arm, too. He turned and there were six or seven of them on him, all of them dead, clawing at him, their mouths hanging open. One of them managed to press its mouth against his arm and bite it hard enough to draw blood. He screamed and shook it away and struck out and shoved and kicked and managed somehow to break free and run to the other end of the apartment where there was a window.

He tried to open it but the latch had been painted over and it wouldn't move. The sash had been painted into the frame, too—fuck, there was no way that thing was going to open—and the window was too small. He might be able to squeeze his way out of the opening if he could get the sash raised, but no way he was getting through by just breaking the glass and trying to squeeze through the frame.

Maybe there was a bigger window in the bedroom, he thought, and turned. There were now, he saw, nearly a dozen of them, as if somehow they were able to multiply when he didn't look at them. They were nearly upon him. He tried to skirt his way around the edge of them and make it to the open bedroom door, but one of them got its skeletal hand on his shirt and slowed him down. He wrenched himself free, but got loose too quickly and too suddenly and went skidding down to the floor. He tried to get to his feet quickly but one was already wrapped around him before he was halfway up, and then another came, and another and another. He strained his way forward, groaning under their weight and pressure, feeling them scratch at his flesh, tear his skin away, trying, he knew, to make him one of them. He swayed and slammed into the door frame hard and one of their arms fell off, but even so it kept moving, taking hold of his ankle. He shook himself, and a few of them fell off, but more quickly took its place. There, just a few yards away, was the bedroom window. It was big enough. All he had to do was get to it and then he'd be safe.

One of them sunk its teeth into his neck, making him scream. Another took hold of his ear and tried to pull it off. Others were tearing into his stomach and back with their teeth and claws, gouging and ripping, harder than they had been before, as if they grew stronger as he grew weaker.

He stared down, willing his feet to move. The floor around him was slick with blood. It took him a moment to realize it was his own. *Just a little more*, he told himself.

He took a step forward and collapsed under the weight of them. He tried to push up with his arms and climb to his feet again, but there were too many of them. They sunk their teeth into his arms, and one of them tore his ear off. One of them bit him in the back of the skull, and then worked its fingers into the wound and began to peel his scalp away. He roared with pain and fear, tried again to get up but he was weaker already, all the little wounds adding up. One of them dragged his hand to the side and bit off one of his fingers. Another was slowly running its broken nails up and down his back in the same spot, gradually wearing its way down to bone. All the while they gave moans of pleasure.

He made little motions like he was crawling away, but he didn't move at all. Slowly the pain grew, eventually becoming so great that he prayed for death. Yes, death would come, but it would come very slowly. When one of them tore out one of his eyes and then the other, it felt like a mercy. And a greater mercy still when he finally lapsed into unconsciousness. But even after that, and even long after he was dead, they kept at him, slowly reducing him to a bloody pulp, making him one of them.

Chapter Fifty-three

Herman stood in the alley outside the Salem Palladium. Fucked is what it was. It looked just as deserted as ever, definitely a fire hazard, and nothing had been done to fix the place up. The windows were even boarded over, and so were the entrances, except for one in which they'd pried the boards off and leaned them against the wall next to it. Nobody taking tickets either. He'd gone in, expecting to see some sort of creepy, horror-show setup, something that'd make the most of the deserted space, but there was nothing backstage. There was just a red curtain with nothing behind it. Real amateur hour. A lot of the theater seats were still in place but the inside was also full of piles of trash and rubble, needles scattered around from where junkies had broken in, the whole place stinking of piss. Herman sighed. It was going to be a long night.

For a while he paced back and forth, smoking a cigar. And where was Whitey? Goddamn, if his car had broken down again already, that was fucking it. Plus, no Whitey meant no Heidi, and there was no way in hell he was going to handle this bullshit alone.

He puffed on the cigar a few more times, paced a little. People were coming in, but just a few, not enough to make for much of a show. What was up with that? Plus, they were all chicks. Every fucking one. Probably not a surprise, considering the way that the Smash or Trash had gone with the Lords track, but it was still one more fucked thing about an already fucked scene.

He pulled out his cell, tried to call Heidi's number. The phone rang and just kept on ringing. Maybe that meant she was on her way. He hung up and then dialed again.

"Hello," said a voice. "WXKB. Station manager Chip MacDonald here."

"Chip, what exactly is going on here?" asked Herman.

"What do you mean?" asked Chip. "Is this Herman?"

"What do you mean, what do I mean?" said Herman. "Well, for starters I just looked everywhere and there's nothing. No band. No equipment. Nothing. And for another thing, what little crowd that's in there is one hundred percent girls."

"Are people getting upset?" said Chip. "Are we going to have a problem there?"

"No," admitted Herman. "They're pretty calm so far. But I can only assume that they're going to get mighty restless waiting for a show to happen that I highly doubt is going to go on. Eventually it'll get ugly. There's no way I'm sticking around when it starts to turn bad."

Chip began to natter on, trying to calm Herman down even as he got more and more nervous himself, but Herman didn't want to be calmed down—he just wanted things to be done right. Was that too much to ask?

"And when are you going to get me some reliable help?" Herman finally said. He almost regretted saying it, felt a little guilty about throwing Whitey and Heidi under the bus, but his wife was right: he had to stand up for himself.

Chip was silent for a moment. "Reliable help," he said slowly. "What do you mean?"

"Where's Whitey?" said Herman. "Where's Heidi? Why is it that Herman's the only WXKB employee here?"

"You're fucking kidding me," said Chip. Even over the phone he sounded like he was pulling on his hair. "Hey, look, I wanted to fire Heidi," he said. "I was all set to, and you, buddy, were the one who convinced me, against my own better judgment to…"

But Herman had stopped listening. Someone was coming down the alley and as they got closer and stepped into the light, he realized who it was.

"Yeah, yeah, yeah," he said. "Heidi's here after all. Got to go."

He hung up the telephone with Chip still talking and pocketed it. Then he crossed his arms over his chest and waited for Heidi.

"Where the hell have you been?" asked Herman. "Where's Whitey?"

"Whitey never showed so I walked," said Heidi. She looked a little pale and dazed, maybe was on something, but he'd had it out with her once this week already. No point starting bad blood just before the show.

"Are you serious? Goddamn it, what is with that kid? I thought he said his car was fixed." He looked at his watch. "Fuck, we should get inside. It's almost showtime. Not that it matters since I can't find anyone."

"What are you so uptight about?" Heidi asked.

"I don't know," said Herman. "Something about this whole night is really getting under my skin. Something just isn't right. Feels like a setup."

"A setup for what?" asked Heidi.

Herman shook his head. "I wish I fucking knew."

They made their way through the door and up the aisle, taking a seat toward the back of the venue where some of the chairs were still in pretty good shape. There was still no sign of the Lords. Most of the rest of the audience was up front, huddled together. And yeah, he'd been right. All women. Not a single man in the whole place except for him. If he told the warden that, she'd really give him hell.

He checked his watch again. "Looks like a whole lot of nothing is about to happen," he said. Heidi next to him didn't respond. She looked a little dazed, just stared straight ahead at the stage. "You okay?" he asked.

"Whitey never showed so I walked," she said. She said it in a friendly but semi-pissed-off way, identical to the way she had said it outside, but this time her face remained motionless, expressionless.

"Yeah, you already told me," he said. "I heard you the first time."

"What are you so uptight about?" she replied. Again, same exact intonation as outside. But her face was still as dead and still as that of a corpse. God, she was freaking him out.

"What the fuck's wrong with you?" he asked. He was about to dress her down when the house lights suddenly went off. "Thank God," he said. "I think the show might actually be starting."

Chapter Fifty-four

Slowly, very slowly, the red velvet curtains began to draw apart in a grand and effortless sweeping motion, to reveal a stage empty except for a figure of a man made from sticks, a nearly life-size effigy. A small lantern burned within the figure's belly. The lantern was the only thing lighting the stage.

The sound of a single drum began. A slow, regular pounding. A hush fell over the crowd as a robed figure entered the stage from somewhere out of the darkness behind. A mask covered the figure's face: a rough burlap mask dyed black with a white death's head painted on it. A primitive drum was slung around its neck and was being struck, over and over again, with what looked like a human thighbone.

"What the hell is this bullshit?" Herman whispered to Heidi. "Seems more like some weird religious ritual than a concert."

"Whitey never showed so I walked," mumbled Heidi.

What the fuck? wondered Herman. He grabbed her arm and shook her, but she didn't look away from the stage.

The robed figure began to chant in rhythm with the beating on the drum, in some weird language that for all Herman knew might be nonsense. Lots of hard sounds, like German, but shitloads worse. Made his head ache even to listen to it. But next to him Heidi seemed totally transfixed.

A ring of fire erupted around the figure as the chant continued.

The crowd began moving, swaying back and forth to the repetitive rhythm of the hypnotic drum, a few of them beginning to pick up the sounds of the chant as well, which gave it a weird watery emphasis as it shifted from a single voice to a voice with many other voices layered over it. The ring of fire grew taller, then taller still, until both the effigy and the hooded figure were nearly hidden within it. If you looked at it just right, you could almost believe they were on fire.

Beams of deep red smoke curled along and seeped through the stage as another figure appeared from the darkness behind. This one was similarly dressed, similarly masked, but the mask it wore had had holes burned through it, so bits of a pale white face were visible beneath. As it walked forward, the figure manipulated an instrument made of wood and animal skin. One hand cranked a small lever while the other pumped a rawhide bellows, creating a bizarre cluster of discordant notes. It was the sound, Herman thought, of someone screaming, but worse than that, too. It was much more disturbing than that.

The flames of the ring of fire dipped lower and the figure stepped through them and into the ring, continuing to play. The flames rose again, in one spurt and then another, until Herman couldn't see anything through it. *Shit, must be hot inside there,* he thought. And how had they managed to do that? He would have sworn, when he walked the stage just a moment ago, that there was nothing there.

There was a screeching sound, the scrape of an out-of-tune violin being played deliberately off-key. Another robed figure appeared out of the darkness of the wings, wearing the same burlap mask as the others. Instead of a bow, it played with a bone that looked like a humerus. It made the strings shriek and quiver. The figure didn't wait for the flames to die down, but calmly strode through them and was momentarily aflame.

"Holy shit," said Herman.

The flames fell low enough that everyone could be seen clearly. The robe of the figure playing the violin was smoking but didn't stay lit. The drum was playing louder and faster now, and so was that strange other instrument, whatever it was. With the violin added in, the noise was extremely loud and discordant, enough to make the hall shake and bring little bits of plaster down from the ceiling.

Herman looked up a little nervously, then turned to Heidi. "I have to admit," he said, "this is pretty wild stuff." Yeah, they were getting to him. They were definitely showmen. He had to give them that. But, he thought, looking up at the ceiling again, there was no fucking way this was going to end well.

They played, the music dipping and falling but always staying repetitive and ritualistic and discordant and very intense. They weren't playing songs exactly, or rather it was like they were playing one single song that just kept going and going. It was fucked-up.

In front, down near the stage, several of the audience members began stripping off their clothes and walking toward the stage. They seemed like zombies, moving stiffly and awkwardly. *Must be plants in the audience who work for the band,* thought Herman. *All part of the show.* But then if that was the case, there wasn't much of an audience at all. He watched them ascend a small set of stairs at the base of the stage, gathering around the edge of the ring of fire, bowing before the hooded figures.

Beside him Heidi was mumbling. God, if she repeated again that Whitey never showed so she walked, it'd really freak him out. Anything she said, he told himself, had to be better than that.

Turned out he was wrong. What she said was: "Unholy Father, make your presence known this night. I am but your humble servant in this land of misery."

What the living hell? Was she in on it, too? Was this some kind of elaborate joke that the station was playing on him to fuck with him? Or was Heidi just messing around, playing along to get under his skin? He hoped so, because whatever the alternative was to those possibilities he had the feeling he didn't want to know what it was.

"What was that?" Herman said. "Come again?"

"Help me breed this new world with your blessed spawn of glory."
She stood and left her seat, moving into the aisle.

"Where the hell are you going?" asked Herman. But suddenly she was lost from sight as a powerful gust of wind whipped through the room, sending thick clouds of black smoke spiraling toward the ceiling. Herman coughed and choked, his eyes watering, waving his hands to clear the air in front of his face. When he caught sight of Heidi again, she was nearly to the end of the aisle. She had shed her coat and dropped it on the floor, was taking her sweater off over her head. By the time she was at the bottom of the stairs leading to the stage, she was wearing only her shift: a sheer white dress, see-through and short. On it was emblazoned a symbol that Herman recognized. It was the same as the symbol that had been on the Lords album.

At first, when she first entered the Palladium, her body did not seem to want to go where she wanted it to go. As Heidi tried to maneuver it into a seat near the back, next to where Herman was, something kept trying to turn her feet and steer her forward, down the aisle and toward the front of the stage. It was odd, but not too insistent, something that with a little effort she could control, but strange nonetheless and a little disturbing. Even once seated she still felt the pull, something calling to her to get up, to rise to her feet and walk down to where the other women were, circulating in front of the stage or sitting in the seats near the front. *My sisters*, she thought, and then thought: *That's weird. Why would I call them that?*

And so she had to focus on staying put, on keeping from moving, and that was where other things began to slip. Herman asked her something and her mind thought of something witty to respond, but her voice didn't say it. Her voice said something else, something it had answered to a question that he'd asked her before, when she'd been outside. Even when she'd said it outside it hadn't felt like something she'd been saying but something being said through her. What was wrong with her?

Come to think of it, most of the way over she hadn't felt like she was the one walking. One moment she'd been in her apartment and something strange and troubling had been happening. What was it? She'd been trying to get out, but she couldn't get out. Each time she'd opened the door something had been wrong.

No, she must have dreamed that, right? That sort of thing wasn't real, just simply couldn't happen. She'd been having bad dreams lately. That was simply one of them.

But then again, she couldn't remember leaving the house. She could remember little bits of the walk over, but only bits. Could remember, if she thought hard enough about it, talking to Herman outside, but there, too, it had been as if she was watching her body talk rather than being in the body itself.

And then, inside the theater, Herman said something else, obviously surprised by how she'd answered, and she felt her mind again composing a response but her tongue was already operating, already speaking, giving again a piece of language it had already given, something that was wrong for the situation. She tried to turn toward him and explain that something was wrong, that she couldn't figure out what was happening to her, but her head refused to turn away from the stage. No matter how hard she tried, it remained fixed there, motionless, staring on. All she could do was desperately flick her eyes his way, try to get Herman to see the panic and fear in them. But before he saw it, the music started.

And then things got really strange. The draw of the stage on her body was nearly physical now, as if someone had looped a rope around her waist and was beginning to tug on it, slowly pulling it tighter and tighter. Or, more than that, much more: like someone had cut her belly open and pushed out loop after slick loop of her intestine and was using that as the rope, pulling on her own flesh to drag her forward. She had to hold on to her chair tightly with both hands just to stay put. She felt, too, as if her vision was becoming smaller, as if she had been looking through a mask and as she moved the mask farther away from her eyes the holes she looked through showed her less and less. She could see the stage but it felt distant now, as if she had shriveled up, receded into her own body.

And then her eyelids blinked, and with that blink something else blinked inside her. It was not just that she was receding into her own body, she realized. It was that something else—something that she had never seen, hadn't realized was there—was growing, had switched places with her. So that while before it had been a hard tumor or fistula deep within her, now it filled her whole body and she was the tumor; she was the fistula.

Help me, she tried to say, but nothing came out.

The creature within her laughed. *Something you've never seen?* it said. *Sweetheart, you created me. You brought me to life.* And she saw flashing through her mind a cascade of images, of every way she had lied or cheated or stole, the dark days of using especially, her last time with Griff when she had curled up beside him and slept and then woke up and left, only later hearing he was dead. Did he die from that fix, because of her? No way to know. So that, above all, but also the innocent enough things that she had done that slowly had made her a sort of monster. That had made her into this.

But no, another part of her said, or tried to say. This *wasn't* her. This was all a trick. It was something else trying to take control of her.

As the music started, the beating of a lone drum, she kept hold of the arms of the chair, and the thing inside her let her. No, it was happy to wait, to let her resist until she couldn't stand it anymore. She suddenly realized it believed this holding back would tire her, make her more pliable, and reduce the last of her resistance. But still she couldn't help holding on.

When the creature took charge, it took hold first of her throat and mouth. She was trying to scream *Help me*, but the creature kept the words back. Instead, it offered its own dark chant, a glorification of the Satanic majesty. She saw Herman give a start, confused by what she was saying, and she was confused, too, but she could not stop. And then the creature crept into her extremities, seizing control of her hands, slowly prying her hands away finger by finger from the arms of her seat. Then, tingling, it moved into her legs, tightened the muscles in them, made her stand up, and she was heading stiffly down the aisle, still trying to resist but hardly with any control at all now. She felt her arms groping her body, then slowly pulling pieces of her clothing off, her coat, then her sweater, then her shoes and socks, until all that was left was a sheer see-through shift. She looked down, saw that the Lords symbol was inscribed upon it, written in dark red paint or in blood. When had that happened?

"Heal me, Satan," she heard her voice saying, as inside she screamed for help. "Heal me of these mortal wounds inflicted by the Christian faith. I hold in contempt all of its symbols of the Creator."

She was among the other women now, swaying and dancing with them, her body no longer her own. The figures onstage all at once stripped off their masks, revealing them to be her landlord Lacy and Lacy's two sisters, Megan and Sonny. But no, Lacy wasn't Lacy, she realized, but Margaret Morgan. How could she not have seen it before? And these two other women, her "sisters," were other witches from Salem's past. No, not exactly—they were still Lacy and her sisters, too, but there was something else there now, and that was what she'd seen. Their eyes were crazed, and their smiles seemed painted on. They raised their hands and the flames around them rose. Fires, too, began erupting all around the theater, seeming to burst up spontaneously here and there. The floor began to vibrate, rumbling. The hall began to fill with smoke and she could hardly see. She could feel her eyes tear up and her throat burn, but the creature held her where she was, gripped her throat and prevented her from coughing or choking.

She heard Herman's voice calling her name. *No*, she tried to say. *Run. Save yourself.* But nothing came out.

"Hear me, Lord," said Margaret Morgan from the stage, her voice as clear as a bell. "I am ready to bring your blessed child to this world! It shall burst forth from the body of your enemy, Hawthorne!"

The three sisters kept playing. The volume of the music grew louder. More and more women began shedding their clothes and now they began to caress one another, writhing and moaning with ecstasy and lust. She, too, Heidi realized with a start, was doing the same, caressing the woman next to her, the creature inside of her slavering. She tried to stop but could not.

She felt her body pulled forward, forced to the edge of the stairs, led now not only by the creature within her but by the call of the witches on the stage as well. They brought her body up and held it there, forced her head to look up, look at them.

"Adelheid Elizabeth Hawthorne," Morgan said, gazing down at her contemptuously. "Your forbear John Hawthorne cursed and tortured us in the name of the lamb. But now, through you, we shall have our revenge. We have claimed you. We have made you our own."

Morgan let out a great, cackling laugh. She struck the drum hard enough to shatter the tip of the bone she played with. "In the memory of Satan, I preach punishment and shame to those who would emancipate themselves and repudiate the slavery of the church!" she shouted. "Satan come to me! We are ready!"

All around her the air was black with smoke. The theater itself had changed as well, had begun at first to waver and shake and then to blur around the edges until it was no longer a room at all. The walls fell away or dissolved into black smoke and Heidi found herself feeling she was outside, in a clearing in a forest, the moon blazing overhead. Just behind her, close enough that she could feel its crackling heat, was a bonfire. Around her were the same women she had been standing with before. Many of them now wore animal skins and cloaks, though some of them had stripped these off and had let them fall in heaps on the ground to reveal their naked and grimy bodies painted with strange symbols and daubed in blood. Before her, the three women had lost any resemblance to Lacy or her sisters and had now become, fully and truly, the witches of Salem's past.

"At last thou hast come!" Morgan said. "Hawthorne: I, Margaret Morgan, claim thee for my master the Lord Satan."

Heidi tried to move but couldn't, was barely being allowed to breathe. Margaret passed her hands back and forth, inscribing in the air a symbol that momentarily seemed to glow and flicker.

"Blessed be a thousand times more than the flesh and blood of life," she intoned. "For you have not been harvested by human hands nor did any human creature mill and grind you. Take this noble disciple! Take her, my dark savior! Bring her home!"

Around her the other women, caressing one another and writhing, suddenly began to hiss. They began instead to attack one another, rending and tearing. Some of them groped on the ground for rocks or stones or bits of weapons and when they found them they set about trying to bash one another's skulls in. They shrieked and yelled, and here and there Heidi caught a glimpse not of the hillock and the bonfire but of the inside of a dilapidated theater.

She watched the carnage go on around her. Still she did not—could not—move.

"It was our Lord Satan who took you to the mill of the grave," said Morgan from the top of her hillock, "so that you should thus become the bread and blood of revelation and revulsion."

The two women beside Morgan reached into their robes and removed glittering knives. These they pressed into the hands of two of the struggling women. The noises grew louder and more terrible, as the women became even more violent and the two chosen women began to gash and stab anyone coming close to them. For a moment the creature within her released her and she thought she had control again. She turned her head and tried to move away, but no, it had her again, and now she was watching Herman pushing and fighting his way through the carnage and mob scene, trying to get to her. No, it hadn't released her, she realized, but it was letting her see Herman, letting her watch what was going to happen to him.

He darted closer to her and she saw a woman's knife pass close to his neck, almost cut through it. His jacket had been torn and his face was bloody, but still he kept coming. Tough fucker. He took a knife through the hand, but didn't stop. A moment later he was there, beside her, close enough that he could reach his arms out and grab her. *No, Herman,* she tried to say again. *Save yourself.* But he yanked her to him. Picking her up, shouting, he began to run for his life.

Goddamn, it was some weird shit, and then they'd set fires out in the house, too, likely to burn the place down. And then the whole place shook, and there was a pretty good chance the whole building was going to collapse. He was ready to get the fuck out of there. But he had to get Heidi. He hadn't spent all these years trying to save Heidi to lose her now. He didn't know how much she was in on it or what sort of deprogramming it was going to take, but hell no, he wasn't going to abandon her now. That wasn't how he was built.

So he started up the aisle, coughing and pushing through the smoke. He was going to grab her and pull her away, get her out of there and talk some sense into her. The show could go on for all he cared, as long as he wasn't part of it anymore. All he had to do was grab her.

And then he started seeing what was going on. The women had gone crazy. First they'd been all caresses and lovey-dovey, but now they were bat-shit crazy, trying to scratch out each other's eyes. Some weird shit was going on, he understood, but he didn't realize how weird until he saw one of the women take a knife and plunge it deep into another woman's chest. *Holy shit*, he thought.

The woman was dead, blood at first spurting from the wound and then, as she died, slowing, simply oozing. The woman with the knife had already gone on to someone else, had sliced open another woman's cheek. But the weird thing was the woman being stabbed didn't look upset about it. No, she looked ecstatic.

Fuck me, thought Herman. They'd drugged him. That was what it must be. This couldn't be really happening. Something in the smoke was messing with him and making him see things that weren't there. And indeed, as he continued to look, the old peeling walls of the theater seemed to grow transparent and thinner until he could see through them.

He closed his eyes and when he opened them he was no longer in the theater at all but outside, in a forest, in the open air. In front of him a huge bonfire crackled and on the other side of it raged the carnage: the women struggling with one another, killing one another. Beyond that were the three musicians, seemingly unperturbed. And Heidi: motionless, and so far untouched.

He made a run for it, skirting the edge of the fire and pushing his way through the women still standing, punching and knocking his way through when they tried to grab ahold of him. A knife struck at his side but was knocked away by his leather jacket, which it tore. Another jabbed right into his hand, and it hurt like hell, but he managed to kick the woman in the face and knock her down. And then he had reached Heidi. She was still standing motionless, unmoving. What was wrong with her? He wrapped his arms around her and took off running.

In a moment he was around the fire and had left the clearing. He threaded his way through the trees, fighting still with the dense black smoke that billowed off the bonfire, trying not to get lost, when suddenly one of the crazed women sprang out of the darkness and came at him, trying to claw his face away. He struck her hard in the face with his own forehead, cracking down, and she fell back. He kept running, but a moment later with a hiss she had sprung onto his back and by damn she had bit him, had torn a chunk out of his neck.

He screamed, stumbled. He let Heidi fall and reached behind to grab hold of the crazed, thrashing woman's throat. She flailed ropily, almost like a snake in his hands, scratching and clawing wildly as Herman, blood pumping from his neck, squeezed harder and harder.

There was a snap and she jerked once and went limp. Herman let her fall from his hands. He stumbled forward, attempted to pick up Heidi, and then sank to his knees. He reached up and tried to staunch the wound in his neck but the woman had bitten into the jugular and the blood kept spurting through his fingers.

In front of him, Heidi calmly gathered herself, rose from the ground, and stood. She remained there, motionless, staring down at him.

Herman lifted his head. Her eyes, he saw, were white, without pupils, as if she were blind, or as if there was nobody home. She stared down with a beatific smile on her face. Then she reached slowly out and touched his face.

"Heidi," he said. "Heidi," he repeated. He tried to speak further but blood began to drip from his mouth. Slowly, he fell and lay faceup on the ground, staring at Heidi. His vision grew dim and hazy, and before he knew for certain what was happening he was dead.

For a moment Heidi stared down at the body, and then she turned and faded from sight into the smoke. She walked with a slow and measured tread through the broken bodies and the few woman who still stabbed and tortured the bodies of the dead. But Heidi they ignored. And as she passed, they seemed to recoil a little and offer gestures of obeisance. They stopped their slaughter and followed her.

From deep within her body, Heidi watched it all happen. She could see it all, smell and hear and experience everything around her, but she was powerless to do anything to stop it, and she had no control over the body that now held her. She moved forward toward the leader of the witches, Margaret Morgan. She took her place in the center of the circle, facing the witch.

Around her the remaining women gathered. They bowed and reached out to touch her, kissing her feet and the edge of her robe.

"Take me...take me to hell," Heidi heard her voice say. "I am your godless whore."

Morgan nodded. She took up a knife and grabbed one of the remaining women by the hair, pulling her to her feet. The woman moaned in pleasure as Morgan drew the knife across her throat, spraying Heidi's face and body with blood.

"By the blood of the damned, I do baptize thee and accept thee into hell," the head of the witches said. "Christ, I spit upon you and I cast you down! Satan, we live on the blood of your oppressors!"

And with that the women started up again, howling and stabbing and assaulting one another, kissing each other and then killing each other, not caring if the person they stabbed or embraced was alive or dead. They thrashed and bit and tore, and when there was no corpse or other person close before them, they tore away at their own bodies, stabbing themselves, trying to bite off their own fingers, snarling and growling.

Then suddenly, in an instant, they stopped and fell into silence. As if one individual, they froze and waited in silence.

The flames of the bonfire began to surge upward to a great height and when they fell again, a shadowy figure standing eight feet tall stood within them.

When he stepped out of the fire and onto solid earth, his feet hissed and burned, and he left behind only parched, scorched ground. The few remaining women bowed to him as he came forward, moving across the wasteland of carnage and carnality, stopping here and there over a dismembered corpse or a slick of blood. The world had grown silent, as if all the sound had been sucked from it, as if nothing beyond this forest and its clearing existed. As if it floated in oblivion, surrounded by nothingness. The only sound that could be heard was the deep, monstrous breathing of the shadowy beast and its heavy, leaden footsteps as its cloven hooves struck the ground.

The head witch and the remnant of her coven took hold of Heidi and threw her on the cold ground, spreading her legs wide and holding them there. For a moment she was motionless and vacant, but then something started to change. She seemed to be coming to herself.

And indeed she was. For whatever the creature within her and possessing her had been, it had suddenly, with a little bow and a chuckle, stepped back into the recesses of her subconscious and left her in control of her body again. *Only fair to let you experience this on your own*, it suggested. She struggled, began to try to get away, but the witches held her fast.

And then she felt something twitch inside her. The eyes of the shadowy beast towering over her began to glow with a dim red light, one eye much bigger than the other. It came closer and she saw its barbed, dripping cock curving up into the air before it, and she remembered what it had done to her before, when it had found her before, the way it had sniffed her out in the darkness. It voiced its terrible laugh, and then, slowly and painfully, mounted her, tearing its way into her, whispering in her ear in a strange incomprehensible language as it thrust back and forth, a language that nonetheless filled her mind with images of pain and destruction. But now it just watched her, eager. She felt something twitch again. She screamed but no sound came out, or if it did it was covered over by the beast's terrible breathing. Her belly began to throb and she felt as if she was being torn apart. She convulsed and twisted and the witches struggled to hold her and she could feel something within her beginning to destroy her. She thrashed uncontrollably back and forth and then screamed again. This time the scream was awful, a high, piercing shriek as of someone dying. An explosion of blood spat out between her legs and darkened her robe. She thrashed again, harder this time, and then went silent and still.

The coven released their grip on her. With a smile, Margaret Morgan slit open Heidi's belly and tore open the womb. After a great deal of effort, she pulled forth a bloody deformed mass.

At first it seemed an abortion, an incomplete stillbirth, but as she held it and stroked it, it began to unfurl long curling tentacles that

began to flail and shake. She turned, presenting the deformed creature to the shadowy figure of its father.

Heidi's eyes clouded over, slowly glazing and going dim.

Satan took the child from Margaret Morgan and, cradling it,
stepped slowly backward and away, returning once again to the fire.
The flames again rose around him, and when they died down Satan
and his child had disappeared. With his departure, the landscape,
too, shifted, the trees fading and becoming the walls of the building,
the hillock a stage, the rolling and lumpy grass the seats of a theater.
Where Morgan had stood was now Heidi's landlord, Lacy, her two
sisters beside her.

For a moment they seemed confused. They looked around, scanned
the theater, seeming to take in the corpses of the women and of Herman, and then they smiled.

"We have been avenged, sisters," said Lacy.

The other two did not respond. Megan had found Heidi's body
and was prodding it, pushing her toe into the tear in her belly, and
then letting most of her foot slide in. The others joined her, standing
around the body, staring down at it, smiling.

They reached out and joined hands.

Soon they were dancing.